Jason Stevans & the Mayan Apocalypse

By Matt Goralka

Summary: According to the Mayans, the world was supposed to end in 2012. Why didn't it? Is it possible that the Mayans' predictions were met head on by a band of young adventurers with a vested interest in keeping it quiet? It's not only possible, this is their story.

ISBN-13: 978-0997384604
ISBN-10: 0-997-3846-0-3
LCCN: 2016910804

Published by Larnerghoul Press
Contact: mattgoralka@gmail.com

To my green-eyed beauty

Chapter 1 - Hallucinations?

Jason was conscious of the fact that he was awake well before he opened his eyes. His throbbing head pain intensified with each beat of his heart. He was terrified. His hands and feet were bound. His mouth was gagged. When he finally opened his eyes, it was pitch dark for a hood was over his head.

His body ached the way it did after Frederick had shoved him into the goal post to make him drop a touchdown pass. That was just a game, and a quick trip to the school nurse had convinced him that he would live.

This was not a game. Where could he be? The feel of the ground and the smell of hay made him think that he was in an old barn, but with the hood covering his head, he could only guess. The mumbling in a strange language had ceased.

What could he do?

The awful tasting gag over his mouth prevented him from screaming. Maybe he could cut the ropes using the pocketknife that Uncle Jack had given him. His hands were bound in back, but after a bit of squirming, he slid his right hand into his front jeans pocket. His heart sank. The knife was gone. He fought against the knots a bit more, but all that did was make the ropes burn into his wrists.

"Who uses ropes these days?" he thought. "In all the movies they use duct tape or disposable plastic hand cuffs.

"Boy, am I drifting. I need to get out of here!"

Jason, like everyone in this media age, had heard stories of fourteen-year-old children vanishing into thin air, or worse yet, being found murdered.

As the precariousness of his situation sank in, he focused more intently on listening for signs of his captors' intentions. He heard nothing.

"If these guys were going to kill me, wouldn't they have done it already? Surely they didn't do this to rob me of my pocket knife."

His thoughts shifted.

"Could this be a Halloween prank by Frederick and his buddies? No, they might be mean, but surely they weren't this violent."

Jason's throbbing head interrupted his thoughts once again. He tried to ignore the pain.

"When people are kidnapped, they're usually rich or famous. I'm neither."

Suddenly, the reason for his imprisonment did not seem nearly as important as escaping. He felt around in the wet hay for anything that might help. His bound hands grabbed what resembled the shape of a gardening hoe next to him.

"Maybe if I rub hard enough, I can cut the ropes," he thought.

He decided to give it a try. He had nothing to lose. He rubbed the ropes binding his hands back and forth across the blade. His heart jumped as he felt the ropes shredding. After what seemed like a lifetime, his hands were free. He removed the hood and looked around.

There were no signs of his captors. His instincts were correct. He was inside an old barn.

He removed the gag from his mouth and untied the simple knots binding his feet. He was sore, but all his parts seemed to be working properly.

He quietly crawled over to the door and poked his head out.

"Nobody around," he mumbled to himself.

He slowly crept toward what appeared in the dim moonlight to be a road. He was now in a combat zone. The enemy could jump out at any moment. After a few seconds, he recognized the road from one of the biking trips he had taken last summer. It had been pleasant scenery then. Now it was a dangerous gauntlet.

He quickly started for home. The traffic on the road considerably slowed his progress. Whenever he spied headlights in the distance, he headed for cover, for he had no idea who was after him.

Eventually, battered and tired, he arrived at his front door. The house seemed to welcome him as he walked into the kitchen and drew a large glass of cold water. His thirst quenched, he looked at the clock.

"Four thirty," he mumbled quietly to himself. "I wonder if Jack is home yet."

He walked by Jack's room and peered inside. The bed was empty.

"Doesn't that guy ever sleep?" Jason thought. "Well at least I won't be in trouble."

He then trudged into the bathroom and gazed at himself in the mirror. He looked like he had just participated in the mother of all football games. There was a lump on his head and burn marks around his wrists where the ropes had been. His clothes were loaded with bristles. This seemed to confirm his feeling that he had been at least partially dragged to the barn. His shirt was slightly torn in places, and all of his clothing was filthy.

Jason suddenly felt very tired and dizzy. He barely made it back to his room. His adrenaline rush had ended, and he collapsed on his bed.

Chapter 2 - Family

When he awoke the next morning, he sat up with a jolt. He was pleasantly surprised that he wasn't in the barn. Had it all been just been a dream?

His head began throbbing again. That pain and his dirty clothes confirmed it was no nightmare.

"How could Mom take all that adventure stuff?" popped into his head out of nowhere.

Jason's mother, Della, was constantly trekking off to some far corner of the world on her latest adventure. She climbed mountains, swam with sharks, and parachuted from extreme heights. The more dangerous and exciting it was, the more it suited her. Sometimes she was gone for six months at a time. She supported herself by selling stories of her various exploits.

Like most children, Jason was fond of his mother, but he could tell that she was a little disappointed that he did not follow in her footsteps. He often remembered the frustrated look on her face when, at age five, he froze up climbing the Indian cliff ladders in New Mexico. He was not fond of heights, roller coasters, or any danger. The thought of danger just for danger's sake was foreign to him. He just didn't get it.

Jason's mother had disappeared while surfing off Costa Rica a year ago. Her surfboard was all that was found. The local authorities expressed sympathy and then lectured his father about how American tourists should respect nature a bit more.

"We don't have millions of dollars to spend on Coast Guard helicopters to help protect you idiots from yourselves," the official remarked.

Jason liked to imagine that her disappearance was just another story she was working on to sell to the tabloids, kind of along the lines of attending your own funeral.

He was suddenly brought back to the present by the sound of singing in the kitchen and the enticing smells of coffee brewing and bacon cooking.

"How does he do it?" Jason asked himself again. "That guy never sleeps."

Jason pulled himself out of bed and wandered into the kitchen.

"What happened to you?" Jack laughingly blurted out. "Is the junior NFL starting to beat you up?"

Until he discovered what had actually happened, Jason decided he better keep the events of the previous evening to himself. He didn't want another army of shrinks prying into his brain. They were all too eager to "help" him after his mother disappeared.

"Rough game," he mumbled.

"You don't look good. You could probably use this breakfast more than me. I'll make myself some more."

Jason quickly devoured his breakfast. It seemed to revive him a bit.

With his energy replenished, he opened the door to a gorgeous fall day. The air had that twinge of autumn crispness that anyone who has experienced it, knows.

He decided to go for a walk. With no particular destination in mind, he strolled aimlessly through his neighborhood trying to piece together the nightmare his life was rapidly becoming.

His thoughts turned to his father. For a few months after his mother disappeared, Jason and his father had walked around in a brain fog. They quickly grew tired of talking to well-wishers and started to break off contact with society.

Jason's routine was interrupted when out of the blue his dad came home one evening with a smile and announced, "I've received a six-month contract to be a geologist for GoldXX Mining. They're performing a systematic exploration of some islands near Sumatra. I've already contacted Uncle Jack, and he'll be staying with you. I hate to leave you at this time, but we're rather low on funds. I got them to include options on their stock as part of my compensation--"

"What are options?" interrupted Jason.

"A chance for me to get stinking rich," his father replied.

5

"Another get-rich-quick scheme," Jason sadly thought. John Stevans' schemes never panned out, but Jason enjoyed being around someone who was eternally optimistic.

"One of the things I'm sure I'll miss is the chess games," Mr. Stevans confessed. "In fact, I've got some time now. Let's play."

Jason's father always opened with the Queen's Gambit. "Pawn to queen four," he announced as his opening move.

Jason was getting more adept at defeating his father's strategy. This time was no different, but his father slipped up earlier than usual.

"You let me win!" Jason declared.

"No, you're just getting smarter, Son," he countered with a twinkle in his eye.

He remembered saying goodbye to his father at the airport. They talked frequently on the phone, but less and less as his father became much busier. They played chess on the internet. His dad always made the same opening move.

Jason hadn't heard from his father for about a week and was beginning to worry. He was alone at home watching TV when the doorbell rang. A bit annoyed that his show was interrupted, he answered the door.

It was Dad! Jason couldn't believe it. He opened the door and hugged him.

"How have you been?" Mr. Stevans asked. "Sorry I made you answer the door. I lost my keys somewhere on the job."

"What are you doing here?" Jason asked.

"Remember those options we briefly talked about before I left. Well, we hit the mother lode. I've got my own jet now."

"Those options, whatever they were," Jason thought, "had made Dad a very wealthy man.

"Let's go for a ride," his dad suggested. "The jet is fueled up and ready to go at the airport."

They flew to the city to visit the museums. Jason had always wanted to see the collections there, and going in the jet made the trip way more exciting. He had read many books about ancient civilizations, but the pictures could not compete with the real things. Some of the artifacts almost made him believe he was from another time.

"When everything gets straightened out, we can go to the actual sites," his father blurted out triumphantly.

"Maybe life is starting to get good again," Jason thought.

After the museums, they went to the poorer sections of town, and Jason watched as his father seemed to get amazing enjoyment out of giving stacks of $20 bills to the homeless they met on the streets.

They then flew back to Rockdale and said goodbye for what turned out to be the last time.

His dad returned to the dig, promising to be home shortly. "After all," he exclaimed, "when you're as rich as I am, you can do whatever you want."

Over the next month, the headlines in the papers, on the internet, and all of the news and talk shows were filled with the incredible rags-to-riches stories of GoldXX personnel. Just like any other media story, the excitement gradually died down as interest shifted to the love lives of celebrities and other mindless events.

The interest returned when the scandal hit. The core samples were fraudulent. When the investors went back to confirm the metal concentration, the drillers found no gold. The authorities were looking for Jason's father.

The news only got worse. A helicopter containing Jason's father and two other members of the GoldXX team was seen crashing into one of the active volcanoes near the dig.

"Ruined Fraudsters Kill Themselves," and other similar headlines filled the media. This was the type of story everyone craved.

There was another side to this story, however. Jason was an orphan.

There was a memorial service for Jason's father, but without the body, a conventional wake and funeral could not be held. It seemed like an endless parade of people he barely knew shaking his hand, telling him they were sorry, and wishing him well. It all went by in a blur.

Jason just wanted to escape, especially from the shrinks. He couldn't stand their prying questions.

Jason thought of his father often. He especially remembered him when he came home. To this day, his first thought when he came through the door was to look for his dad. Then he would realize that what he was looking for wasn't going to be there. There was only sadness.

In spite of these feelings, the grief counselors, "And there sure seem to be a lot of them," Jason thought, all recommended that he stay in the area since it would be reassuring to have at least a few familiar things around.

His home was a nice ranch house in the quiet suburb of Rockdale, a typical suburban community where most of the social life centered on kids and the local high school. That is where it was decided he would live with his uncle, Jack.

Jason didn't mind living with Jack. When he was a babysitter in the past, Jack was never there. As soon as Jason's parents left, so would Jack. He would have been his parents' last choice for babysitter. The list of babysitting volunteers was short, however, and the list of people willing to raise a 14-year-old kid was even shorter. Uncle Jack got the job.

Jack, in his late thirties, was habitually off on what he said were "secret missions for the CIA." Jason thought he was probably off at the local bar, but since it meant Jack left him alone, he didn't question him. Jack had rescued Jason from some dubious situations in the past. They seemed to have a mutual understanding not to ask too many questions.

Jack had actually been a Navy SEAL at one time, but from his shape right now you could hardly believe it. He looked like an ex-linebacker ("ex" as in maybe he played in one of his past lifetimes). What was once a mighty warrior now looked more like a lazy walrus. He had great stories about adventures that he supposedly participated in. "Top-secret," of course. He brushed off any specifics with the usual, "If I told you, I'd have to kill you."

Jack and Jason's mother were brother and sister. The adventure gene must have been very strong on that side of the family, at least if you believed all of his stories.

Jason was more of a book-type person. He liked to play computer games. When he was younger, he participated in Judo competitions and actually won a brown belt. He gave it up when the advanced moves could cause some real damage. Books and computer games allowed him to escape into other worlds where he could accomplish some of the daring deeds he knew he would never actually undertake in reality.

As he continued wandering through the neighborhood, Jason's thoughts shifted to the previous evening. He remembered jerking nervously around when he heard a loud sharp noise. He was relieved when he saw it was only a car door closing. He expected disaster as he recalled the time when Frederick and his buddies had bombarded him with water balloons while zooming past on their mountain bikes. He couldn't understand why Frederick and his henchmen kept picking on him. Frederick seemed to resent the fact that Jason would not become a member of his group and bow to his "authority."

More memories of the previous evening were now vividly returning. He recollected that it was dusk when he started into a large field of prairie weeds on a short cut home. The dead weeds were brown and grey in their usual drab autumn colors. The few scattered trees cast dim, odd shadows on the ground below. He remembered thinking that it wouldn't be too hard to convince himself that the tall weeds and small trees were soldiers of some strange army positioning themselves for an attack.

Jason remembered sitting down on a large tree stump to watch the sunset. It was one of the things that he liked to do in autumn. To him, the orange and pink colors of the sky always seemed more vibrant at that time of the year. He sat on the stump until well after the sun went down, not really thinking about anything. It was like he was shutting his brain down to recharge. A quarter moon rose. The air was crisp.

"It's probably time to go home," he remembered thinking as he recalled some homework he needed to finish that weekend.

His left leg twinged as he rose from the stump. It was a little sore from that afternoon's football game. He began walking home. Out of the corner of his eye, one of the darker shadows to his right suddenly appeared to lunge forward. When he looked directly at it, however, it was still. Convinced that he was merely tired, he continued on his way. Then, to his left, the same thing had happened. Then everything went blank.

Chapter 3 - Dylan

Jason's memories of the previous evening were interrupted by a figure heading his way. It was Dylan. Unfortunately, he was now too close to avoid.

Dylan was trouble. He wasn't malicious, but he was adventurous and curious to a degree most people would consider abnormal. This, added to the fact that he was totally unsupervised by his parents, often meant that danger was just around the corner.

He was the Anti-Jason.

When he was young, Dylan was the guy who had to find out if your tongue really stuck to a streetlight pole when it was cold. He was the guy that didn't believe you'd get a nasty jolt from sticking a pen into an electric socket. He was the only guy the school insisted have a chaperone in the chemistry lab.

Jason could remember seeing Dylan over the years with many broken bones. Eventually he became ambidextrous because of this. He never knew which hand he was going to be able to use. Jason also remembered uncountable stitches, burns, and bruises, and a fractured skull.

Rumor had it that Dylan was quite skilled in the martial arts, but nobody had actually seen him in action.

Frederick's gang, oddly enough, seemed wary of Dylan. He was just about the only person they didn't constantly hassle. Dylan was the lone guy allowed to call Frederick by the name of Freddy without a fight. In a way that was mystifying because Dylan always ran from every fight.

There were lots of stories about Dylan in every adventure-type activity imaginable, but nobody could confirm any of them. He was a real life urban legend. The only thing you could say for sure about his endeavors was that he survived.

He even burned his parents' garage down once.

Jason's only peek into Dylan's world occurred when Frederick's crowd hit a small child's ball up on the school roof. Jason and the principal watched Dylan climb straight up the back wall of the three-story building to retrieve it. When Dylan returned to the playground, the principal gave him another in his unending series of detentions.

Jason couldn't understand why Dylan swore him to secrecy on that one.

He was an accident waiting to happen, and he was happening toward Jason.

"Jason!" Dylan yelled. "Wait up!"

Jason ignored him while quickly trying to construct an escape plan.

"Were you wearing a blue shirt or jacket on Halloween?" Dylan asked as he sped up to block Jason's path.

"Why on earth would he want to know that?" thought Jason.

"I think I saw the most bizarre thing ever," continued Dylan, "but you have to swear that you won't repeat what I'm going to say to anybody. I already have a reputation for being, well, sort of odd, and this is way past the bounds of that."

Jason didn't respond.

"Was that you taking the shortcut through the field on Halloween?" Dylan asked again.

"I was there," answered Jason, now a little more intrigued by what Dylan had to say.

"I was too!"

He paused as if he were giving Jason time to think about what he had just said.

Jason's gaze drifted from Dylan as thoughts started racing in his head. "Why is he telling me this? What does he have against me? Do I owe him a good rap on the head?"

"Are you listening to me?" Dylan asked in a slightly raised voice.

Jason snapped back to reality and looked Dylan squarely in the eyes.

"Yes."

"Promise you won't repeat this?"

Jason was getting impatient. "Were you one of the guys that hit me?" he blurted out.

11

"First, promise," Dylan said as if he was teasing his little sister.

Jason was amazed that Dylan didn't seem to be the least bit scared or intimidated since he was now right in his face.

Dylan didn't flinch, but Jason could see that he was watching his hands and had subtly shifted his weight into a more balanced position.

"Promise?" he repeated.

Jason backed off, since he was now very curious about what Dylan had to say.

"I promise," he finally replied.

"Well," Dylan began, "the sun had just gone down, and I was looking for a place away from the city lights to test out my new toy. I bought an old second-hand night-vision scope."

"You mean like the special ops guys use? Where'd you get that?"

"That's not important. Anyway, I saw a person sitting on a stump out in the field who looked like you. When I tried to zoom in on him, I found out why the scope was so cheap. The zoom didn't work. The night vision did work, however, so I kept watching. I was excited by my new toy."

"That was me!" interrupted an impatient Jason.

"I looked around you and saw seven or eight darker shadows lurking off both sides of the path. Initially, I didn't think anything of them. Before I could get my night vision device focused on them, the batteries went dead. I could still kind of see by the moonlight, so I kept watching.

Unexpectedly, one of the shadows moved. I couldn't tell what they were, but they weren't any of the bushes or trees out there. Then a simple explanation crossed my mind. It was Frederick's gang trying to scare you on Halloween."

Jason was now enthralled by Dylan's tale. It was as if Dylan couldn't speak quickly enough.

"Then I heard a shout, and what seemed to be a medieval ambush erupted!"

"What do you mean, medieval ambush?"

"Do you promise not to repeat this?" Dylan asked again, still not sure if he could trust Jason to keep quiet.

"I already did," said Jason raising his voice in irritation.

"Well remember, it was dark, and my night vision wasn't working."

"Go on. Go on."

"It looked like you were attacked by a real horror-film army of sword-wielding skeletons. They knocked you to the ground. When you were there, one of them, he acted like the leader, reached down and grabbed your wrist--"

"Skeletons?" interrupted Jason.

"Yep, right out of a horror movie. Large pieces of rotting flesh covered their bones, but they were basically skeletons. And it was even weirder. Their heads were shaped like cattle skulls with horns on each side."

Jason stared at Dylan with a look of disbelief. "Come on," he uttered.

"Look, I know this sounds bizarre, but what possible motive could I have for making this up?"

"I haven't had time to think about that," a skeptical Jason replied.

"Anyway, from my distance, it looked like one of the skeletons checked your pulse. Then he shouted a few orders in a language that I didn't recognize, and two of his buddies picked you up and carted you off.

"I tried to follow you, but I couldn't keep up. It was kind of embarrassing, actually, with all my training and everything."

"What training? Nobody ever sees you do anything. I saw you climb the school wall once, but nobody's ever seen you train for any sports at all. What could you possibly be training to be?"

Dylan paused for a long time, thinking about whether it was prudent to reveal the truth. He finally reasoned that a candid response might help gain Jason's trust.

"A spy," he reluctantly answered.

"That explains a lot," Jason mumbled sarcastically.

"Anyway, I eventually caught up with you at the old Jenkins' barn and started to look around. A noise startled me, and I turned my flashlight onto a …, don't laugh …, a five foot tall walking, moving skeleton. It had the cattle-skull head, the rotting flesh, the whole deal. It smelled awful. It scared the crud out of me. Fortunately my flashlight scared the crud out of it. It shrieked and ran off. So did I.

"How did you escape?" Dylan continued.

Jason didn't know whether Dylan was telling the truth or whether he was part of some elaborate hoax that was being played on him. He remembered hearing a shriek just before everything went quiet.

"I found an old hoe, cut the ropes, and removed the hood they placed on me. I looked around, and when I discovered my captors had left, I walked home."

"Sorry I didn't rescue you, but those skeletons were disgustingly scary," apologized Dylan.

"I guess, in a way, you did."

It was obvious that Dylan had been there, but Jason still couldn't believe that this was anything but an elaborate prank.

"I'll make it up to you next weekend."

"How's that?" inquired Jason.

"I can't say now, but keep Saturday night open. Bye."

As Dylan turned to walk away, an unfamiliar car pulled menacingly up to the curb. When the driver rolled down his tinted window, Jason recognized Uncle Jack. He motioned Jason over. Dylan, always curious, followed Jason up to the car.

"Jason, this morning you looked like you could use a vacation. I have some business associates that I need to see, so I bought us tickets to Cancun, Mexico. Since I have things I need to do alone, would your friend like to come along? I can get him a ticket, too. You get to miss school."

Dylan blurted out, "Most certainly!" before Jason had time to explain that Dylan was not a friend but barely an acquaintance.

"Good! The plane leaves at 5 o'clock today. Uh …."

"Dylan," Dylan cut in. "The name's Dylan."

"Dylan, go pack your things. We'll pick you up in an hour."

"All right! Pirate gold!"

"What?" questioned Jack.

"I've always dreamt of finding some lost pirate treasure!" exclaimed Dylan.

"Well I don't know about that, but you boys should have a good time and get some much needed relaxation."

Jack stared hard at Jason when he said this.

"Do you need a ride home to pack?" Uncle Jack asked.

"Nope. Got things to do first," Dylan answered. "See you in an hour."

14

Dylan took off running while Jason got into the car.

Chapter 4 - Cancun

The next day Jason found himself sprawled out and half-asleep on a Cancun beach. He felt the warmth of the sand through his towel. He could hear the surf rolling up and the gulls calling out. The sun baked his entire body. An occasional insect buzzed by his ear and was gone. The air had a wonderful salty-ocean smell. That smell and the chance for adventure sent many a young man to his doom in the days of the sailing ships. Pirates, sword fights, treasure, and ….

Jason opened his eyes and sat up. The sand on the beach was close to white in color. The water really was a bright turquoise in Cancun. The beach was surprisingly like the pictures in the travel brochures. The view from the beach was much better than from the tree stump in the field, when he chose to sit up and observe his surroundings. Maybe not better, but definitely different. From this perspective, what had happened to him just a few days ago seemed more and more like a dream. In fact, he still didn't really know what had happened.

He had only the memory of waking up in a hay pile in a barn, blindfolded and tied up. He was missing about two hours. There was Dylan's bizarre story about an ambush by the living dead, but come on! That couldn't possibly have happened, but no one else was lining up with alternative explanations. He really couldn't even ask anyone else without joining Dylan as the town lunatic. Should he call the local police and tell them he was kidnapped by zombies? His star witness, in fact the only witness, wasn't exactly the most believable person in the world. He began wondering whether it was all a dream, and pondering if he was close to being institutionalized.

"Maybe a nice walk would be fun," he thought.

He had heard there were wonderful bargains to be had in the local markets. Perhaps he might even be able to purchase some old Spanish treasure.

"Dylan?"

"Yeah."

"Want to go to the market?"

"Nope. Soaking up the sun is fine by me."

"Some friend you've turned out to be," Jason thought.

He put on his sandals and started hiking toward the market. As he trekked away from the beach on the dusty path, the vegetation by the side of the road became much more jungle-like in nature.

The people at the resort had warned him to watch out for snakes and alligators in the ditches beside the road, but he saw none of these. It was kind of disappointing, actually. The occasional buzzard circling overhead reminded him of just how thirsty he was getting.

After he had covered a good distance, the sound of music from several radios told him that the market was getting nearer. His first stop would be a soda machine because he had been warned about drinking the water and eating the fruits and vegetables. Montezuma's Revenge they had called it. Somebody must have been pretty nasty to Montezuma for him to produce a curse like that. He didn't want to spend his whole vacation sick. Dylan on the other hand would have ….

"Excuse me, senor. Would you like me to be your guide around the market place?" said a voice to Jason's right.

He turned, but no one was there. Was he having another one of his nightmarish hallucinations? He half expected a giant sword-wielding skeleton to appear out of nowhere and attack him.

"Boy, am I getting jumpy," he thought.

Just past where he heard the voice was a booth with the most wonderful woodcarvings he had ever seen. There were eagles on perches, hunters launching spears, dragons that would match anyone's dreams, and all sorts of other animals and imaginary creatures.

"Buy the snake. They have those in all the good restaurants," said the unknown voice again.

"You say something to me?" Jason asked the merchant.

"Huh?" inquired the salesman.

"Are you talking to me?" said Jason in a rather gruff voice. His confusion was starting to make him irritable.

"I'm sorry, sir. I will be with you very shortly. I'm helping another customer."

"Why are these guys messing with me?" thought Jason as he looked around to find the source of the voice. He saw no one.

"Great," thought Jason. "The only person that I know here is on the beach, and I'm hearing voices."

Jason's contemplations were interrupted by the sight of a man roughly shoving people out of the way while chasing after a suspected thief.

"Hey! Come back here!" the exhausted man yelled.

"Jose will never catch him," said the mystery voice.

"Which one is Jose?" asked Jason.

"The guy that owns this business and is keeping me in this cage," responded the voice.

"What?" Jason exclaimed as he glanced around to find the voice's source.

"I'm the animal in the cage just to your right."

"OK! I'm tired of these jokes. If you don't show your face right now, I'm leaving."

"If you don't believe me, tell me to do something, and I'll do it to the best of my ability."

Jason examined the cage. It was a small homemade enclosure made of screen and wood. Inside was a furry animal of some sort.

"Maybe it's a Mexican rat," thought Jason.

The creature stared back at Jason through the screen.

"OK! Stand on your head!" Jason commanded.

The animal did his best but kept falling over.

"My gymnastic skills have deteriorated inside this cage. This is tough to do."

"I wonder if he can count to ten," Jason thought.

"One, two, skip a few…, ten!" came out of the cage.

"He's reading my mind," thought Jason.

"I can communicate with you through telepathy. You are the one."

"I am what?"

"Buy me, and take me home."

"If I did, how would I get you through customs?"

"Just drop me off outside the airport, and I'll be at your place when you get home. I can fit in places you never dreamed of."

"Hey, there you are!" shouted Dylan as he ran over.

A befuddled Jason looked back and forth between Dylan and the cage.

When Dylan got close, he peered into the cage.

"Is that a giant fat rat in that cage? Sure is ugly."

"It's a mongoose," responded a voice from outside the booth.

"Did you hear that?" Jason asked Dylan.

"Of course! What's the matter with you?"

"You like my little mongoose? I'm sure we can make a deal. Let me talk to Jose," said a man who Jason thought was an employee.

Jose presently came around the corner after failing to catch the thief. He looked tired and winded. The sales clerk pulled Jose off to the side so that Jason and Dylan couldn't hear him. They had a heated discussion. The clerk walked back toward the boys.

"Let me handle this," whispered Dylan.

"Jose says you can have it for four hundred pesos," the clerk announced.

Dylan responded, "My friend seems to have had his pocket picked in the marketplace. He has no money …, but I have one hundred pesos that is our lunch money. If he really wants the rodent, I could lend it to him."

"He's actually not a rodent. He's a mongoose. A hundred pesos is really cheap for such a remarkable animal."

"I'm sorry, that's all we have. We'd probably have a hard time getting him through customs anyway."

"Let me talk to Jose."

The clerk left, and Dylan turned to Jason and winked. "Trust me on this one," he said in a hushed tone.

The clerk returned shortly. "He's yours," he announced and set the cage down on the counter.

Jason began to speak, but Dylan interrupted him. "I'm sure he'll have a happy home with you," he added to cut Jason off.

Dylan gave the clerk the money, picked up the cage, and handed it to Jason. He motioned him to leave.

As soon as they were out of hearing range, Jason burst out, "How did you know they would drop the price that much?"

"All good spies know how to read lips. Jose said that that thing was ugly and smelly and that he had had a string of bad luck ever since he acquired it. He probably would have given it to you. By the way, what's the attraction? I kind of agree with Jose."

Jason was about to tell Dylan about his "communication" with the mongoose, but then thought better of it. After all, he didn't really know his new acquaintance all that well.

"It likes me, and I think it's kind of cute," he responded.

Dylan took a good hard look at the mongoose.

"Really?" he questioned. "Well Minsk, your new owner must be going blind."

"Why did you call him that?"

"It's on the wood from his cage."

"That's just one of the destinations of the old packing crate the cage was made from."

"Well I think Minsk is a good name, and that's what I'm going to call this smelly little rat."

Jason looked into the cage. He could have sworn that the mongoose was scowling at Dylan.

Back at the motel they had trouble smuggling Minsk into their room. "No pets allowed" signs were prominently displayed. Dylan seemed to have a million strategies, but the one he finally settled on was, "Just let the little rat out of his cage. If he really likes you, he'll find your room. You're never going to get him through customs anyway."

After saying goodbye, they let the mongoose out in the parking lot and headed for their room. Dylan stopped and bought some candy in the hotel lobby. He always seemed to have money. At school, the rumors were that one of his relatives had won a large lottery, but the more Jason watched him, the more he was starting to believe that Dylan's family may have had a shady past.

They arrived at their room and fumbled with the credit-card-type room key. When they finally got the door open and turned on the lights, they were astonished. There, sleeping on one of the beds, was Minsk.

The next morning, when Jason and Dylan left the hotel, Uncle Jack was already gone.

"Why would Mexico be any different?" Jason asked himself. "The guy stays out all night with his drinking buddies and is gone before we get up. Why would he need to sleep here?"

Jason was becoming a bit jealous of Jack's ability to function on little sleep. He sometimes daydreamed about all the things he could accomplish if he had that talent. He smiled and shook his head in admiration as he and Dylan left the hotel and began wandering the streets of Cancun as young tourists.

The previous evening, Uncle Jack had told Jason and Dylan to meet him at the local bank at noon. He had some "top-secret" business and that sort of thing. They agreed.

They arrived at the bank a bit early. They had purchased a Frisbee on their walk through town and decided to toss it around outside the bank while they were waiting.

While tossing the Frisbee, Jason noticed a young man about his age sitting on a bench watching them.

"Want to join in?" invited Jason.

"Sure! My name is Salah," the young man exclaimed enthusiastically as he rose from the bench.

"Hi! I'm Jason, and this is Dylan."

Dylan waved at Salah, but seemed preoccupied. The game continued with Dylan becoming more and more distracted.

Finally, after almost hitting Dylan in the head with the Frisbee, Jason called him over.

"What's going on?" he asked.

"That car has been parked over there since we arrived," whispered Dylan.

"Now that you mention it, it was there when I got here," added Salah, who also was becoming concerned.

As they talked, four men got out of the car. They wore long, baggy trench coats. Three of the men went into the bank while the fourth remained outside.

Salah suddenly sprang to life.

"My dad works at that bank. Those guys mean no good. I'm going to run toward the guy standing by the door. Throw the Frisbee in that direction, and then help me out."

21

Before Jason could say anything, Salah took off. Jason tossed the Frisbee toward the man by the door. When Salah got close, he jumped in the air and planted both his boots on the man's chest. The unexpectedness of the blow knocked his victim down. Salah reached under the man's overcoat and pulled out what Jason thought was a semiautomatic pistol. He pointed it at the sky and fired a few shots. The men inside were startled by the gunshots and flew out the side entrance of the bank.

Salah, pistol in hand, ran toward Jason and Dylan shouting, "Let's get out of here. There are some places where you don't want the bad guys to know who you are."

Jason and Dylan were temporarily paralyzed with confusion, but after recovering, they took off down the street with Salah. Salah tossed the pistol into a nearby garbage bin. After they were four or five blocks away, Salah motioned to stop and rest.

When they stopped running, between gasps for air, Dylan blurted out, "Where did you learn that stuff?"

"In the Guard. My brother was in the Guard."

"I didn't know the National Guard had such intense training."

"National Guard? I'm from Iraq. I was trained by the Republican Guard. I think I need to stay away from the bank for a while. Mind if I hang out with you guys for a few days?"

Dylan and Jason were, at first, too shocked to reply, but Dylan eventually responded, "Of course you can! Adventure is my middle name!"

Salah was a bit confused by the last part of Dylan's statement, but he was happy Dylan agreed.

Jason, afraid Dylan might think he was a chicken, nodded his agreement.

They spent the rest of the week hanging out with Salah and trying to avoid contact with the human race. Being "on the lam" brought a lot of pressure.

Salah told the boys he was fifteen, but they thought he looked older. He appeared to be much stronger than any of their friends from Rockdale. He had dark hair and an olive complexion.

The adventure at the bank and the new environment made the time pass quickly. It was soon time to return home.

After saying goodbye to Salah, the boys got into a cab with Uncle Jack and headed toward the airport. Jack was in pretty good spirits.

"Did you boys have fun on your vacation?" he asked while looking back and forth between them. "A little adventure never hurt anyone. You were probably correct in avoiding the local news reporters. In this corner of the world, people look after their brothers, and revenge is fairly common .... Er, uh, that's what Salah said anyway."

At times, Jack spoke with an authority which made Jason want to believe his ridiculous stories about the covert operations he had participated in.

"What are you guys going to do with that rat?" he inquired.

Jason had been thinking hard about that for the last few days. For unknown reasons, he was becoming attached to his new little friend even though Minsk hadn't communicated with him since that first day in the marketplace. Perhaps that was just another hallucination like the skeletons. Jason decided he'd let Minsk go outside the airport.

Why not follow through to the end with the story? If he was sane, the mongoose wouldn't show up at home, but if he wasn't ...? Jason didn't even want to think about that. Did he really believe a mongoose could telepathically communicate with him?

They stopped outside the airport gate, and Jason said goodbye to his little friend. He opened the cage, and Minsk jumped out and bolted for a hole under the airport fence.

"That little bugger is gonna get himself killed," Jack remarked.

Jason set the cage down next to the garbage can at the entrance to the airport, a bit sad that he wouldn't see his little friend again. He went back to the cab wondering what sort of nightmare was in store for him next.

The jet encountered some rough weather on the flight home. As one passenger after another became sick, Dylan remarked, "Spies train themselves to be immune from motion sickness."

"Now just how do they do that?" Jason asked himself.

The plane landed safely and without the boys getting sick. Uncle Jack slept for the whole trip, his slumber only briefly interrupted when they got off the plane and hailed a cab.

The turbulence seemed to clear recent events from Jason's mind. Thoughts of all the schoolwork he needed to make up filled his head. When the cab arrived at the front door of Dylan's home, Jason was mentally composing a "What I Did on My Vacation" theme. He knew he was going to be asked to write one, or worse yet, to give a speech.

When they arrived at his house, Dylan jumped out of the cab and declared, "That was a fun date. We'll have to do that again sometime …, but seriously, thanks a lot for taking me."

He went to the trunk and removed his suitcase before walking off to his house.

"Your friend has quite the sense of humor," remarked Jack.

"You have no idea," returned Jason as he rehashed what he had been thinking about recently. Dylan was the only one who had seen the skeletons. He had also arrived in the market shortly after the conversation with Minsk.

"Is Dylan messing with me? Why would he?" Jason asked himself.

Jack dropped Jason off at the house and went off on some "important business." Jason carried his suitcase into the house and turned on the TV. It was almost nine o'clock in the evening, and he was very tired. He fell asleep in front of the TV.

Chapter 5 - Sam

When he awoke the next morning, Jason could once again hear Uncle Jack rumbling around in the kitchen. His shoes were on the floor by the sofa where he had left them. His jacket was on the suitcase next to the door.

"I better clean up my stuff," Jason thought.

He sat up on the sofa, put his shoes on, and walked over to pick up his jacket. When he did, he noticed a large hole in his suitcase. He quickly opened it to make sure nothing had fallen out. All his things were there.

"I guess those baggage handlers aren't as careful as they claim to be," he concluded.

Jason hung his coat in the closet and carried his suitcase back to his room to empty it. He opened the door and flung it on the bed. He was surprised by the shriek it produced.

When he turned on the light, Minsk groggily stared back at him from the bed. A dumfounded Jason gazed at the little friend that he never expected to see again.

After glaring at Jason, Minsk crawled next to the suitcase and fell back asleep.

"Sorry about that," Jason apologized.

He was flabbergasted. The mongoose had somehow managed to get on the plane and accompany him home from Cancun. He must have been in the suitcase and chewed his way out last night.

"This is starting to get beyond weird," Jason thought. "But Minsk hasn't said anything since that day in the market. It's got to be Dylan."

He began to wonder how Dylan got the mongoose into his suitcase.

For the next week, Jason stayed as close as possible to Dylan to see if he had made friends with Frederick's gang. It was tough because the only classes they had together were gym and biology. Most of the time Dylan was his usual stand-offish self, and sometimes, he just seemed to vanish into thin air.

"I guess it's his spy training," Jason would remark laughingly to himself.

Dylan finally approached Jason during Friday's gym class.

"Are you ready to accompany me on an operation tonight? We'll be out late."

"Sure," replied Jason.

"Stay close to your friends, stay closer to your enemies," thought Jason. He had heard somebody famous say that once, but he couldn't remember who.

"What could Dylan be up to? Perhaps this would be the climax of the prank with the skeletons and the mongoose?"

"See you at the park at nine o'clock," yelled Dylan as he walked away.

Jason spent the rest of an otherwise boring day trying to predict the upcoming adventure. He had all sorts of wild ideas, but finally decided to just let it unfold.

As he walked to the park to meet up with Dylan, Jason recalled other nonsense he had been involved in. He remembered TPing his English teacher's house two years ago. It was fun. The goal was to see how high you could get the toilet paper up into the trees. If you spun the roll off your hand correctly, the paper would unwind on the way up and on the way down. You couldn't see the colors at night, but the next day there were beautiful rainbows hanging from the trees.

"The work of a true artist," Jason remarked to himself.

Frederick got blamed for that one which made it especially satisfying.

Jason met up with Dylan at the park. Dylan was dressed in black jeans with a dark sweatshirt. He was wearing a tool belt and carrying a length of rope with a large treble hook on the end.

A simultaneous "Hey!" was their greeting.

Jason examined Dylan's equipment more closely as he approached. The belt looked like it was purchased at "The Cat Burglar Store." It had many different-sized tool-filled pockets. It probably allowed Dylan to do everything except fly. Jason wasn't even too sure about that. The rope looked strong enough for climbing.

"We're going chicken hunting at Professor Sloan's house," explained Dylan in a low voice.

"Excuse me?"

Dylan then explained the "mission."

After listening, Jason actually thought that Professor Sloan would think it was funny, but in any case, he was prepared to anonymously pay him back for the damage.

Professor Sloan was a science teacher at Abraham Lincoln High School. Jason and Dylan were in his biology class. He was average height and in his late fifties. He had long gray hair that he wore in a ponytail. He spoke with a heavy English accent and usually wore an old tweed sport coat. In fact most of the kids joked that the Goodwill truck dropped off at his house while it was picking up elsewhere.

He never attended any of the school activities and didn't hang out with the other teachers. During teaching breaks, he could usually be found in the annex at the front of his classroom soldering circuit boards. When the bell rang at the end of the school day, he was the first teacher out the door.

Jason sort of liked Professor Sloan's class but he couldn't admit that to his fellow students. He really enjoyed it when they dissected a pig. It was gross, but weirdly fascinating.

Professor Sloan lived alone in a fenced-in estate near the south end of the Cherry Hill subdivision. Ever since they were kids, Jason and his friends had the feeling that the place was haunted. There were several buildings on the Sloan land. The main three-story house was something out of an old horror movie. It was built by a rich banker in the early 1900's. From the street, more than half of the rooms appeared unused.

There was a severely weathered large gray barn at the back of the property and a garage off to the side of the house. On top of the garage was a weather vane. It was a metal rooster with an arrow spinning underneath it. That was tonight's object of affection. It was going to be removed and nailed high up the tree in Mrs. Franco's front yard.

"Mrs. Franco has been giving me undeserved attention lately," Dylan explained.

Jason was more interested in seeing Dylan in action than the stupid stunt they were setting out to pull. He was off in the company of James Bond to fulfill a secret mission.

"Once I dreamt this up, I staked out the place for a few days," explained Dylan. "In most cases like this, you can just waltz in through the main gate, but I decided to do this thing right."

Jason was beginning to enjoy hanging around with Dylan more and more. He could feel his heart pounding as Dylan laid out his plans.

"There is a tree overhanging the garage at its south end, so we probably won't need the rope. We'll bring it anyway. No telling when it may come in handy.

"Professor Sloan generally leaves the house around seven o'clock every evening and doesn't return til close to midnight. He probably has dinner and drinks. That should give us plenty of time to accomplish our task.

"If we don't fall off the roof and break our legs, the rest should be easy. I can take apart just about anything with my tool belt, so getting the vane off shouldn't be a problem.

"Normally, in a building like that, it is quite easy to hear someone walking on the roof. However, Professor Sloan won't be there so we won't have to worry. The place is not well lit, so the neighbors won't be able to see us."

"You sure your picture isn't in the Post Office?" interrupted Jason.

Dylan ignored Jason's childish remark and continued, "If the skylight is on, we need to be careful not to pass in front of it before I cover it. Our silhouettes would be visible to anyone passing by. That's about the only thing that could give us away. If there are any nosy neighbors, our dark clothes should blend in well with the roof.

"One thing that's hard to remember when you're on these missions is not to cry out if you slip or need help. It's a natural reaction when you fall, but you need to overcome it."

Jason wondered about Dylan as he listened. He sounded more and more like a professional by the minute. Had he actually been involved on covert operations for somebody? He was only fifteen. That was impossible.

"After I decided on our path of assault, I searched for an alarm system. I have a remote control spy drone I could have used, but for this particular mission, I thought it was better to be on the ground."

"You have a spy drone?"

"Several. They're relatively cheap these days."

Dylan then changed the subject.

"I found something very interesting," he stated.

"What's that?"

"The place is wired like Fort Knox. There are enough motion detectors to get anyone who isn't extremely careful. I found that out when I watched Professor Sloan go to his car. He accidentally set off his alarm and shut it down remotely. I got the code. I tested it out the other night. There is about a five minute window before it turns back on. I think I can keep turning it off until we accomplish our task. There probably won't be any sensors on the roof, but who knows.

"If I screw up, we'll just need to run fast," Dylan stated with a chuckle.

Jason gave him a weird look.

"How could he know all this?" Jason asked himself.

"It looks like it's just about game time," announced Dylan with a wry smile.

As the evening progressed, Dylan seemed to come to life. He normally gave the impression that he was a little slow upstairs. Jason wondered whether it was just a cover.

"When we get there, follow me. I'll disable his alarm so it won't be a problem. And don't get too cocky. All sorts of things can happen to disrupt our plans. A barking dog, a friendly visiting neighbor, more things than you could possibly imagine."

James Bond kept popping into Jason's mind. He was attempting to pull a high school prank in the company of a superspy. Talk about overkill. Well at least they probably wouldn't get caught.

"Do exactly what I do," whispered Dylan.

"Game time," thought Jason.

They both crept out of the bushes across the street where they had been providing nourishment for the local mosquito population for the last fifteen minutes.

Jason wondered whether Dylan could hear his heart pounding.

Dylan produced a small remote control device and turned off the alarms.

Both Dylan and Jason had darkened their faces with charcoal, which together with their dark outfits made them almost impossible to see as they slowly crept closer to their objective.

When they reached the side of the garage, Dylan motioned to Jason in a curious form of sign language which he had invented himself, to stop moving and listen. At least that's what Jason hoped he meant.

Dylan had tried teaching Jason his sign language because he thought that operatives should be able to communicate in absolute silence. Jason still found it confusing.

A lot of things were confusing these days.

Dylan stared at his little remote device again. When the red light came on, he pushed a button on it.

"We should be good for another five minutes," he whispered.

All was quiet.

Dylan motioned for Jason to follow him. He was up the tree and on the roof of the garage like a cat. Jason was much slower, but he was proud of the fact that he moved in absolute silence.

Dylan already had one of the bolts off the weather vane by the time Jason arrived. The second one was much tougher. Then disaster struck.

As Dylan leaned on the skylight to gain leverage to loosen the rusted bolt, the bolts attaching the skylight to the roof gave way. As the skylight slid to the side, Dylan lost his balance and fell through the hole, disappearing into the garage.

All was quiet again.

Jason almost freaked. He didn't know what to do. He felt like his pounding heart had briefly stopped. Hopefully, Dylan didn't fall the two stories onto the garage floor. Jason gained a glimmer of hope from the thought that Dylan's training might be the cause of the silence. Fearing the worst, he slowly peeked through the hole in the roof.

A wave of relief passed over him. Dylan was smiling up at him. He had managed to grab one of the beams cutting across the garage rafters as he fell and was suspended halfway between the roof and the floor. Dylan signaled for Jason to lower the rope. Jason fastened it to a solid piece of the skylight frame and tossed it to Dylan. Dylan then lowered himself to the ground.

"Breaking and entering," Jason thought. "This is going to look really great if we get caught."

Dylan frantically motioned for Jason to come down.

"Why worry? My heart already stopped once tonight," Jason said to himself as he sucked up his courage and descended the rope into Old Sloany's garage. He looked around. The place was fascinating and creepy at the same time. The items, half visible in the darkness, confirmed many of the bizarre tales Dylan had told him about the Professor. How Dylan knew this stuff was beyond anyone's guess.

According to Dylan, Professor Sloan was an admirable, misunderstood man. He claimed to be related to Leonardo da Vinci. He was, by all appearances, quite wealthy. He just missed earning a prominent magazine's Man of the Year Award in his early 20's for pioneering work in the computer field.

"You've probably used many of his inventions on your computer," he told Jason.

After losing a few bitterly contested patent fights, he essentially disappeared off the face of the earth.

About ten years ago, he showed up in Rockdale. He purchased a rundown estate at the edge of town and maintained the buildings in useable, although not perfect condition.

When asked where he had been for the last eighteen years, he initially made some remarks about opening up a new field of science and possibly saving mankind from itself. His first published paper when he returned was entitled, "An Alternative Explanation of the Causes of Strife in the 19th and 20th Centuries." It made some references to a heretofore unknown type of particle that originated from the sun which somehow affected mankind's collective intellect and caused the various wars and other nastiness that humans were capable of inflicting on each other.

His previous reputation got this paper published, but after that he became the butt of jokes by just about every tabloid, talk show host, and comedian. He saw that any more of his ideas on the subject would be relegated to the section of the world that cares about the Loch Ness Monster, flying saucers, and Bigfoot. He again became a recluse.

Professor Sloan thought that being totally isolated would affect his health negatively, so he applied for a teaching position at Rockdale High. The local high school was all too happy to hire an almost Nobel Prize winner as a science instructor. His contact with humanity, as far as the locals knew, was the time he spent as Professor Sloan at Rockdale High.

Jason now stood in the enigmatic professor's research laboratory. There were five or six computers visible in the mess, but it was hard to tell how many, if any, were operable. Electrical devices and circuit boards were scattered everywhere. It looked exactly like Jason imagined a mad scientist's laboratory would look. The only thing missing was a Jacob's ladder.

Everything was quiet.

One of the computer monitors was on. When Dylan moved the mouse, typed words appeared on the screen. It was a paper of some sort. Dylan excitedly motioned to Jason to come over and take a look. The half-finished paper was entitled, "The Reason for the Destruction of Mexico City by Cortez."

"The Aztecs received their power to conquer from an unknown source. In fact, I suspect that their priests were not of this world," the paper began. "These beings had certain telekinetic properties which the common folk would deem to be magic."

"Need any help?"

The boys were startled by a voice which came out of nowhere. They jerked around.

Jason felt his heart stop for a second time.

Confronting them in the poorly lit room was a boy who looked to be about their age.

Dylan did not respond to his question. Jason did.

"This all started as a prank. When we tried to remove the Professor's weather vane, Dylan accidentally fell through the skylight. When he saw all the remarkable things down here, he motioned me to come down. We have no intention of stealing anything …, except of course, the weather vane.

"Who are you, by the way?" Jason asked. "Everyone thought the Professor lived alone."

"My name is Samuel Jones."

"Not *the* Samuel Jones!" Dylan blurted out.

Jason looked puzzled.

"I'm not quite sure what that means," returned Samuel.

"I recognize you from the internet photos. You were quite a celebrity. Let me see if I can sum up your life. Your IQ is beyond measure. At age ten, you wrote a virus using a still unknown anti-encryption algorithm. With it you used deep packet inspection to attack information-gathering databases. All the information that their web crawlers, cookies, beacons, and other little nefarious devices gathered was rendered useless. You made the program freeware so that anyone who wanted to could alter any database and become a six foot two blue-eyed blond with a perfect credit score."

"You assume those are desirable characteristics," the young boy impassively replied.

"You supposedly died with your parents in a car accident two years ago in Oregon. If your parents are dead, I'm truly sorry."

Dylan paused for a moment because the situation was becoming awkward. Then the excitement of the moment took over.

"The rumor was that you messed with some very powerful people, and they silenced you."

"If I'm standing here, then I guess the rumors can't all be true," their new acquaintance smartly answered.

"You were also a huge problem for the government. Even though you broke a myriad of laws with your exceedingly popular program, the government didn't think they could find a jury that would believe a child wrote it, let alone convict him. Also your anti-encryption algorithm was too dangerous for anyone to have except for Our Side. Now I would guess you're working for some super-secret government agency in a witness-protection program. Did I miss any important details?"

"Bravo," Sam heartily responded.

"Now it's my turn. You are two of the Professor's students from high school, aren't you?"

Jason stepped forward. "You are correct. My name is Jason, and your humungous fan over here is Dylan."

"I recognize you from the Professor's classes. He lets me watch from time to time when I get lonely."

Dylan interrupted enthusiastically, "What are you working on now?"

"I really can't talk about most of my government work, but since you guys fell on top of these stone tablets, I guess there's no harm letting you in on this one. By their appearance, we think the stones are from somewhere in Central or South America."

Jason had noticed Dylan frequently glancing at his feet, and now he knew why. The entire floor was covered with giant stone tiles with a form of hieroglyphics etched into them.

"For some reason, the ..., I really shouldn't say the organization's name ..., wants me to try and decipher this language. You can take my word for it; the language is similar to nothing that modern science is aware of. The Professor says the same thing. I think I might have a few words deciphered, but I'm not sure. I need the Rosetta Stone for this language, and I haven't seen any for sale on E-bay lately."

Sam suddenly changed subjects.

"It's almost time for the Professor to come home. I don't know what he'll say about you guys, so you probably better leave the way you came. Please screw the skylight back on. If you really want the weather vane, take it. The Professor doesn't like the way it looks and would be happy if it just disappeared. I'll tell him that it fell off the roof, and I tripped over it in the yard. I was so mad that I threw it out. I'm busy for a while. Can you guys come back in two weeks?"

The boys both nodded.

"If there is a problem on this end, I'll put the flag up on the old mailbox in the junk pile next to the garage."

"Why don't you just call me on the phone?" asked Jason.

"Everything coming in and out of this place is bugged," responded Sam. "We can jam the recordings, but the records of who we talk to are valuable. Who you are talking to and when can be at least as valuable as what was said. Experts can almost reconstruct your life from that information. As of right now, nobody knows that we've met."

"I'm just a novice. What do you think?" Jason asked Dylan.

"It's his party," Dylan responded.

"I'll turn off the alarms for you," Sam announced. He walked over and pushed a button on the wall before lying back down on the couch.

Jason and Dylan climbed up the rope, screwed on the skylight, and returned to the park. It was now getting close to midnight.

Something that Sam had said was bothering Jason.

"Is it easy to access phone records and obtain information from them like Sam said?" Jason asked Dylan. "Can you do it?"

"What brought that up?" Dylan responded quizzically.

"Our conversation inside about the flag on the mailbox."

"Let's just say that the Professor is not the dweeb he pretends to be. He travels to Las Vegas at least every other month, and once a year he travels to the Far East. He always stays at places that have, or are very near to, casinos. I would suspect that he is a card counter of some type. There is usually a lot of banking activity when he returns. It probably involves his gains."

"You have access to all that information? How?"

"Anybody could … with a little bit of effort. Remember, I'm only looking at the pattern of his credit card expenses and phone records."

"How did you get that?"

"I'm afraid that's a trade secret. I might have to compromise some of my sources if I told anyone. It's not really the people. It's just that if the method gets out, I'll need to search for another one because my easy method will be blocked. So …, sorry, I can't help you."

"Have you been investigating me?" inquired Jason.

"Just a preliminary check. Nothing unusual. No red flags."

"Well that's good to know," responded Jason sarcastically.

"Now your Uncle Jack, on the other hand."

"What's wrong with him?" interrupted Jason. "I mean, besides the obvious."

"Well that's just it. He's too big of a loser. I can't put my finger on it, but something's not right."

"Really? Why is that not surprising?" Jason mockingly questioned.

"One more thing before we part," Jason added. "Minsk showed up at my house."

"The rat? Wow!"

Jason watched Dylan's reaction for evidence of his involvement in a prank of some sort, but he seemed genuinely

35

surprised at the news. He appeared to slip into deep thought as he half-heartedly waved goodbye.

Chapter 6 - Meet the Professor

For the next two weeks, Jason spent a considerable amount of time wondering what would happen at their next meeting with Sam. He had so many ideas that he decided to just let the events unfold. His life was turning into quite an adventure.

"Mom would be so proud," he thought.

He busied himself with his schoolwork, and the time went by quickly.

On the day of their meeting with Sam, Jason strolled home from school, deep in thought about the evening's meeting. Dylan had informed Jason that the flag on the mailbox was still down, "so the mission is a go." Jason smirked at how just visiting a new friend had turned into a "mission."

When he grabbed the door handle at his home, he was startled by a face on the other side of the door. It was Jack.

Jason cautiously opened the door.

"Your buddy Salah is quite the interesting character. I don't know how he funds himself, but this postcard here is inviting you and Dylan down to his home town for a little break over the Christmas holidays. The town is way up in the hills. Lots of weird legends and stories come out of that area. Most of the locals are very superstitious and afraid to go there. I think that the stories are circulated by the drug dealers who use the area as a base camp. We have aerial sur .... I mean, when I was at the library I read about it in ..., I think it was National Geographic that had the story about 'The Legends of the Hills.' No, it was Treasure Hunter magazine.

"Anyway, the locals call it 'Los Demonios Juegos.' That roughly translates to 'The Devil's Playground.'"

"Thanks for opening my mail."

"Sorry, but I really didn't open it. It's a post card. Anyone can read it.

"Look at the bright side. I've volunteered to take you guys. I can't hang around because I have other business in Mexico, but I'll make sure you show up at his doorstep. I've taken the liberty to book our flights. Call Salah, and tell him when and where you'll meet him. His phone number is on the card. Here are the computer printouts of the reservations. He says that he's paying, so make sure he gets the correct flight numbers."

Jason's head was spinning.

"Thanks?" he responded in a confused manner.

"Leave it to Uncle Jack to mooch a free vacation," Jason thought.

He put the trip in the back of his mind. Right now his thoughts were on tonight's meeting with Sam.

"Could the FBI, CIA, the SuperHero League, or whoever is technically holding Sam prisoner do anything to us if they found out we were talking to him?" Jason wondered.

Dylan seemed almost certain they wouldn't get caught, but he had also said that missions get disrupted by all sorts of unseen circumstances.

Jason cooked a frozen pizza for dinner. He liked the deep-dish kind with lots of spinach and vegetables. He cooked it long enough to make the crust extra crispy.

"Even *my* life is getting more exciting," Jason thought. "Maybe I'll write a book about it. Briefly son of a billionaire. Kidnapped by zombies. Talks to mongooses, or is it mongeese? Clandestine conversations with, if people knew he was still alive, the most famous person in the government's witness protection program .... Killed in the hills along with Butch Cassidy by a bunch of drug dealers."

"I hope it doesn't end that way," he mumbled out loud, forgetting he wasn't alone.

"What doesn't end?" inquired Jack.

"Oh nothing, I was just daydreaming."

"You've been acting a bit weird since that day you got that big lump on your head. Is something bothering you?" Jack inquired in a way that showed a rarely seen caring side.

Jason glanced over at Jack.

"Just tired," he answered.

38

He was afraid that revealing his version of recent events would bring a new parade of mental health workers upon him.

"I need to go out tonight," said Jack, changing the subject. His normal arrogant tone was back. "Don't wait up, and thanks for the pizza," Jack said as he snatched half the pizza and walked out the door.

"What would I do without him?" thought Jason. "Boy, if he and Dylan are my only friends, my life is really sad."

At dusk, Jason put on his dark clothes and wandered over to the park. As he approached it, he saw Dylan sitting on the swings. He was also dressed darkly and had his cat burglar tools with him.

Jason took a can of bug spray out of his pocket. As he reached to spray the back of his neck, the can was suddenly knocked from his hand.

"Are you nuts?" exclaimed Jason softly.

"You did a pretty good job of not shouting out. You're learning your lessons well," responded Dylan calmly.

Jason was proud that his instinctive reaction would not have given them away.

"Every action an agent takes has a purpose," he remembered Dylan repeating ad nauseum.

"Lack of smell is a part of stealth," Dylan lectured. "How many soldiers do you think were killed in Vietnam because they smelled like cigarettes? We don't want your bug spray giving us away."

They crept silently through the bushes for the last block.

"I'm getting pretty good at this," Jason thought as he followed Dylan through the darkness. Next to a bush near the driveway, Dylan motioned for Jason to stop. They sat there for a while to make sure everything was all right.

Dylan had warned Jason beforehand that this would be the dreariest part of their "mission."

"Everything seems to be as it appears," Dylan had remarked. "But something about this whole affair makes the hair on the back of my neck stand up. Curiosity killed the cat, and it's probably going to get me some day. Let's not make it easy."

Dylan shut down the alarms, and he and Jason crept toward the door. When they arrived, Dylan hooted like an owl a few times. There was no answer to this prearranged sign.

"Should we ring the doorbell or climb in through the skylight again?" Dylan signaled in his commando-style sign language.

Jason just shrugged, for he was more interested in avoiding the mosquitoes that seemed to find him particularly tasty that evening. The fear he felt on his last visit was gone.

Dylan motioned for the roof. Just as he started to climb the tree, the silence was broken.

"Don't you think the side door would be easier?" a voice inquired.

Dylan signaled for quiet.

"Was the voice even talking to them?" he wondered.

"I've a few tricks of my own, gentlemen. It's nice to see you again," Sam quipped.

Dylan gave up and raised both of his hands in the air like a captured prisoner. Sam opened the door and let the boys in.

"This morning I finally deciphered two of these stone tablets," Sam excitedly blurted out as they walked into the room. "I'm not one hundred percent sure, but they seem to tell a story. Sort of a legend or ancient myth."

"Not to interrupt," interrupted Dylan, "But how did you know we were out there?"

"Since I don't really know you that well, I needed to rely a little on my intuition. You seem to appreciate challenges, and this security system is a de facto challenge in your mind.

"You already broke in once, so I figured you'd like to try it again. I installed a pressure sensor on the tree. As soon as you triggered it, I spoke to you on the intercom. Not very impressive, but it does show how effective changing one's security, even minutely, can be."

"I'll be more careful next time," Dylan shot back in an annoyed tone. He didn't like being beaten at his own game.

Jason glanced over at Dylan. He could see that the wheels were turning in his mind. Tension was building between him and Sam, so Jason decided to try to diffuse it.

"So, you solved the puzzle?" inquired a very curious Jason.

"I think I now have a good idea of what's on the stones. Most people thought the Mayans and other ancient tribes devised their calendars to predict eclipses and other astronomical events. If I deciphered the language correctly, these guys were interested in something else. This story says that evil comes into our world at various, but predictable times. The tiles say that this evil comes from hell in the form of horned devils. The next invasion is about a month from now. If it's successful, the stones state, it could be the end of our world. They also mention something about rats being our potential savior."

Dylan spit out the soda he was drinking and almost started choking. He was thinking about Minsk and the skeletons.

"Sorry, it went down the wrong pipe," he explained.

"The evil might already be here," Jason stated.

"What do you mean?" Sam asked.

Jason proceeded to tell Sam his story about his run-ins with Minsk and the skeletons.

When he was finished, a voice boomed from the corner, "The time could be at hand. Sorry to eavesdrop, boys. It's Professor Sloan. Sam moved the sofa into the corner a few weeks ago, and it created a perfect napping spot."

"I didn't want you guys to fall on me if you came back through the skylight," interrupted Sam.

Professor Sloan stood up. His clothes were quite wrinkled from lying on the couch.

"Gentlemen, after what's been happening to you lately, maybe I'll at least get to finish my story before everyone bursts out laughing."

His face turned deadly serious.

"I'm looking for 'Las Puertas del Infierno,' 'The Gates of Hell.'"

"And people call me mad," mumbled Dylan under his breath.

"Somewhere up in the mountains of Mexico lies the source of power for the ancient Aztec civilization. I've narrowed it down to this area here."

The Professor unfolded a map of Mexico and pointed to a location very close to Salah's vacation spot.

"Please sit down while I tell you a story that may seem outside the bounds of your imagination," Professor Sloan continued.

"After what's happened to me in the past month, that's going to be pretty tough," Jason remarked.

41

"Have you ever read anything about the Aztecs?" the Professor questioned.

"You mean the native Mexicans that were conquered by Cortez?" asked Jason.

"That's the empire," confirmed the Professor. "They were pretty much the dominant people of their place and time. Do you know how they got so strong, and why they built those pyramids?"

"In my books, they were for some sort of religious ceremonies. Sun-god worship, maybe?" Dylan answered.

"The religious ceremonies were just a cover. The big ones at Tenochtitlan were built to hide a passageway to Salohcin. The ruling class kept it secret. The Aztec elites got their backing from another world. That's why the Spaniards totally destroyed the city."

"Salohcin?"

"It's the place where those skeletons came from."

"So you're telling me they were real?"

"Yes they were, and for some reason, they find *you* quite interesting."

Jason looked the Professor squarely in the eye. "Any idea why?" he asked.

"None just yet. But let me finish my story. I think beings similar in appearance to a Biblical devil actually live in Salohcin. The horned creatures you saw support my theory. My reasons for thinking so are rather complicated."

For the next half hour, the Professor expounded his bizarre theories.

He concluded with, "Not to be rude, but Sam and I need to get some more work done on a current project, so I'm going to have to ask you to leave.

"Sam says we still have a month on this one, so it's not that urgent."

"How could the end of the world be second in line?" Jason asked himself. "What else could these guys be working on?"

There was an uneasy silence in the room for a few minutes that was interrupted by the Professor.

"I'll turn the alarms off so you can walk out," the Professor continued. "I would like to talk some more with you guys, but we will be busy for a while."

"Nobody knows that we have met here yet," Dylan purported. "Like you, I'd like to keep it that way. Don't call me on the phone. Contact me at school."

The Professor raised a questioning eyebrow.

"He thinks someone will profile him based on his phone records," Jason explained.

"Fair enough," said the Professor. "Let's agree to meet in a month. I'll contact you at school. I will be very interested in whether or not you see any more skeletons."

"I hope my answer is no," Jason emphatically replied.

The Professor did not respond. His mind was already elsewhere.

Dylan and Jason left the Professor's house and wandered back down the middle of the street to the park.

Once they ditched their black "commando" outfits into their backpacks, they looked at each other and almost simultaneously exclaimed, "Can you believe this?"

Dylan regained control of himself. He looked Jason squarely in the eyes. "I don't know what's going on here, but the puzzle is getting many more pieces … and much more exciting."

"I've got another piece for you," Jason added. "When I first saw Minsk in the market, he was communicating with me telepathically. That's why I bought him."

"Yeah right. What did you guys talk about?" Dylan said with a smirk. "The end of the world?"

"He convinced me to buy him. He said I was 'the one.'"

Dylan pondered Jason's response for a minute. Considering everything else that had happened, maybe a telepathic mongoose wasn't so crazy.

He then shifted into "mission mode." When Dylan slipped into "mission mode" he always addressed Jason as if Jason was a student in one of his classes.

"Let's see what we have here. First, you get attacked by a bunch of shadowy figures that from a distance in the dark appear to be rotting skeletons. I had been taking medication for a bad cold at the time, so I left it at that.

"In Cancun, we pick up a talking, or should I say telepathic, mongoose. You had some great conversations with him, but I attributed that to the whack on the head you got from the skeletons. Then, we literally, by accident, fall into a covert government operation run by the Nutty Professor and his teenage wunderkind. They supply us with an ancient legend of horned devils, possibly your buddies, invading our world. Are you the son of Zeus or something?"

He couldn't help laughing as he said this.

Jason stood motionless, staring at the ground, as it all sank in.

"Why am I involved? Is this stuff all related, or just a series of bizarre coincidences? I need to go home and ask Minsk.

"Now I'm really going insane," he thought.

When he looked up, Dylan was already a half-block away. He caught Jason's eye, waved, and shouted, "I want the movie rights!"

Chapter 7 - Into the Jungle

During the next few weeks, Dylan nearly vanished from the face of the earth. Even when he showed up for class, he was "too busy" to talk to Jason. Their trip to Mexico was approaching, and Jason wasn't even sure if Dylan had any interest in going.

Things suddenly changed. On the last day of school before winter break, Dylan approached Jason and asked, "Are we still going down to visit Salah?"

"Uncle Jack is ready to go," Jason answered.

"I'll see you at the appointed time. I have my stuff packed."

"See Yah."

"See Yah."

"Sometimes he sure is hard to read," Jason thought as he walked away.

When they arrived at the airport in Mexico, Uncle Jack immediately left while stating, "I need to get our transportation."

"Why don't we just rent a car?" thought Jason.

Trying to explain Uncle Jack's actions was something Jason had given up on a long time ago.

Jack was gone for about two hours and came back with a military type all-terrain vehicle.

Dylan's eyes lit up when he saw it.

"I've never seen one of these except on the internet. These will go anywhere!" he exclaimed.

Dylan asked Jack a few technical questions about the car, which to Jason's surprise, Jack was able to answer.

When he was finished, he turned abruptly away from Dylan and shouted, "Let's go get Salah."

As Dylan leapt into the car, they all heard a loud shriek and were stunned as Minsk jumped up from the floor.

Jack was totally shocked, but recent events had raised Jason's threshold considerably.

"Why wouldn't he be here?" Jason asked himself. "Like this is the weirdest thing that's happened lately."

Minsk glared at Dylan.

"All right, I'm sorry. How was I supposed to know you were there?" questioned Dylan.

Jason could see by Dylan's expression that he was thoroughly amazed to see Minsk and not too happy about being glared at by a rodent.

Driving to Salah's meeting place would have been quite an adventure in any ordinary car. Twice, they had to cross flooded roads where the water was at least two feet deep. Dylan got out on both occasions and tested the depth of the water by walking into the streams.

Dylan's behavior had ceased to surprise Jason, but Jack's still astonished him. Before Dylan jumped into the water, Jack went around to the rear or the car and pulled out a high powered rifle with a telescopic sight and shouted, "I'll watch out for snakes and alligators."

"Could some of his CIA stories actually be true?" Jason asked himself.

Jason watched Jack as he waded around the front of the car and promptly stepped into a hole and went under.

"So much for the CIA theory," thought Jason as he ran to the rescue and helped Dylan yank Jack's portly body back up onto his feet.

In some spots, there were large humps in the middle of the road, as if huge industrial vehicles had used the roads for a major highway. Jack's vehicle was well off the ground, but at times he still had to drive with one wheel up on the hump to keep from bottoming out.

Twice they saw animals off in the distance that looked like very large cats bolting from the road when their vehicle approached.

"There are cougars and jaguars in this area," announced Dylan with authority.

Jack turned and looked at Dylan with a bizarre expression on his face.

"I wrote a report on it once," Dylan responded to Jack's questioning stare.

The jungle got thicker and thicker until the road suddenly ended in front of a house. Standing just outside the door of the house were Salah and his father. Salah waved to them as they approached. Jack stopped the vehicle, and everyone climbed out.

"Nice to see you guys again. Have any trouble getting here?" Salah teased while looking at Jack's river-soaked clothes.

"No problem at all," responded Jack in his most macho voice.

"Was it raining?" badgered Salah.

"Very funny!" Jack snorted.

After a brief pause, Jack apologized. "Sorry about that snap. I guess it probably was pretty funny if you were watching it."

Jack examined his wet and muddy clothing and kind of smirked himself.

"This isn't exactly the spot I had imagined for a relaxing vacation," he expressed.

"Oh, it's much nicer out in the jungle. There are some amazing pools that for some reason the alligators don't like. That's where we're headed. If you're worried about the animals, I've got this." Salah pulled out a Russian semiautomatic pistol. "And I'm trained to use it."

Salah's father abruptly jumped into the conversation.

"Put that away! That's only a last resort."

He now looked at Jack.

"You may have heard some bad rumors about this area. Unfortunately, many of them are true. However, the people around here owe me some favors, so don't worry about your children. In matters of this nature, they stand by their word. Besides, these boys proved they can take care of themselves at the bank."

Jack didn't seem at all concerned about the danger the boys might be wandering into.

"Well, you guys are big boys now. Salah's armed and Jason's rat can protect you from the snakes. I guess it's time for me to take care of my business. See you in a week," yelled Jack as he hopped into his vehicle and drove off.

Salah's dad, Iraj, led the boys out back. In a giant pile were tents, canoes, backpacks, and other camping equipment.

"I guess you'd better start packing," he suggested.

47

"I didn't want to say anything earlier, but we took the liberty of planning your vacation. Salah knows all of the, how do you say, 'cool spots' to take you to. I can't get away from work this week.

"Who is you're cute little friend?" asked Iraj as he patted Minsk on the head.

In Jason's eyes, Minsk did not appreciate the pat and stared evilly at Iraj.

"I had a smaller one of these as a pet when I was growing up. I hope this one is as friendly as mine was. They can get pretty nasty at times."

Minsk wandered off to the edge of the jungle and sat down.

They first carried two of the canoes down to a river that slowly wound its way through the dense jungle.

"That's the only way in," remarked Salah as if responding to Jason's look of amazement at the jungle surrounding them.

"We call it 'La Entrada al Paraíso,' 'The Entrance to Paradise.'

"If you tried to cut your way through, it would take weeks, and you would most certainly get lost. One of the really neat things about this river is that you can't see it from the air. The jungle has grown over it forming a giant canopy. That's why very few people know about it."

"Let's go get the rest of the stuff," Salah decreed after they dropped their canoes on the bank.

Jason gazed in awe at the river in front of him. Its gentle current flowed opposite the direction they would be heading. They would be paddling upstream. The river was brown in color. Its shores were home to the most amazing collection of butterflies that he had ever seen. The bright iridescent blue, green, and yellow creatures seemed to be enjoying themselves as they flitted from flower to flower. Overhead was the forest canopy. Jason heard what he thought was the jabbering of monkeys, but the jungle was so thick that he couldn't see anything.

"Snap out of your daze," yelled Salah, as he yanked on Jason's arm.

They scrambled back up the trail to the supplies. It took three more trips to carry everything to the canoes. Iraj followed them down the trail on the last trip carrying a long object covered in a felt cloth. He solemnly handed it to Dylan as they arrived at the water's edge.

"It's my good hunting rifle. Please take care of it. Like I said before, you won't have any trouble from the people down here, but sometimes the animals do get a little inquisitive and in some cases even a little hungry."

Salah spoke up.

"I don't want to sound like a power monger, but I've been down these waters many times before. If it's OK with you guys, I'll act as the expedition's captain as long as we are on the river."

"I bow to your authority," agreed Dylan. "What are your orders, sir?"

Jason shrugged a confused OK.

"I can handle a canoe by myself," continued Salah. "Dylan, why don't you start out in the back of the other canoe? I'm guessing you'll be better at steering than Jason. Jason, you sit in the front. I've got my pistol, so you take the rifle. I assume you know how to use it."

Dylan nodded.

"Why wouldn't he know?" Jason thought.

"I'll take Minsk so I have some company," Salah continued. "The supplies are pretty evenly distributed. Can anyone think of anything we might have forgotten?"

"Do we have any matches?" chirped Dylan.

"Are you trying to be funny?" Salah snapped back.

"Sorry …, I got carried away. Everything looks good to me. Let's rock."

"What?" questioned Salah.

"It's just an expression. It means 'Let's go.'"

"Then, let's rock," exclaimed Salah.

The party pushed off from the shore. Salah's canoe went straight-and-true upstream, while Jason's bounced from shoreline to shoreline.

"Guess I was wrong about the steering thing!" laughed Salah. "You'll get the hang of it … eventually."

While he struggled to improve his paddling, Jason intermittently glanced over at Minsk who sat up high on the bundles in Salah's canoe. If a mongoose could laugh, Jason was certain that Minsk was laughing at his canoeing skills.

They paddled upriver, and eventually Dylan and Jason started moving in somewhat of a straight line. When the river forked about two miles out, they went left. Jason's muscles ached more and more as they plowed forward. He never realized canoeing could be so strenuous.

After they paddled for what Jason thought was forever, Salah pulled his canoe up on shore and motioned for Jason and Dylan to follow him. They beached their canoe.

"Are we going to camp here?" inquired Dylan as he looked around and tried to imagine how they were going to find room for their tents without chopping down a few trees. He was tired and had no interest in hacking up the jungle.

"No, I just want you guys to see this cave," responded Salah. "It's not too far in, but the jungle is very thick here. Stay close, so you don't get lost."

"Why don't we eat before we go on? My stomach is sounding like one of those jungle animals," declared Jason.

"Not a bad idea," Salah agreed. "I'll go find some firewood."

He disappeared into the woods.

Dylan threw Jason the rifle and shouted as he was leaving, "I have a few things I need to investigate. Take care of your furry little rat."

Jason had given up trying to explain Dylan's behavior.

He sat down on a large rock and looked over at Minsk. He could have sworn that Minsk winked at him before he curled up and took a nap. Jason was pretty tired himself and dozed off shortly thereafter.

Jason awoke with Dylan's hand over his mouth.

"Listen quick, I don't have that much time. He'll be back soon.

"I thought looking for firewood was a lame excuse, so I followed Salah into the jungle. He searched for markings on the rocks along the way. When I examined the ones he paused near, most displayed curious scratches. Then he met up with and talked to this old man. He had to be at least seventy years old. It was hard to tell because his skin was burnt by many, many years in the sun. The man's clothes were very baggy and ill-fitting. I couldn't really get that close and remain undetected. He gave Salah a map of some type, which they seemed to discuss for a while. I decided that I needed to warn you, so I took off, and here I am."

Jason couldn't believe what he was hearing. This was supposed to be a relaxing vacation, and he was once again in the middle of a gigantic mystery. His eyes lost their focus as he became lost in his own thoughts.

He was snapped out of his daydream by a loud, "Helloooo!" as Dylan shouted and waved a hand in his face.

"Don't mention anything to Salah until we can figure this out a little more, but keep your guard up," he warned.

The boys heard a noise in the brush close by and were surprised to see Salah and the old man approaching them.

"I need to tell you guys something important!" Salah announced. "The truth of the matter is … a vacation is not the only reason I invited you guys here. About a year ago, I rescued Joe from some quicksand in the swamps nearby. We hit it off right away. He's been living off the land here for twenty years. He has a shack back in the bush where I just came from. He has a large garden, and there are enough animals to catch to eat rather well. He came across a map and a story a few years ago. Since I was his only contact with civilization, he decided to share the information with me in case the heavens called him away. I have the map in my pocket."

Joe smiled. "I am 71 years old, you know."

"It looks like it is written in the language of the old Spanish conquistadors," continued Salah. "We think it's a treasure map. We think we know where the treasure is."

"Then what do you need us for?" asked Dylan.

"The people around here are very protective and can be counted on as true friends in any area that does not involve drugs or money. Come to think of it, the money part is probably true of people everywhere. Anyway, we needed someone we could trust to help carry the treasure out. After that incident at the bank, I knew I could count on you guys in a pinch, so we sort of drafted you. Sorry."

"Soldiers of fortune for hire. That's us!" stated Dylan with almost comical pomposity.

"We're not going into battle. But you could look at it that way," explained Joe. "Are you guys up for it? It's equal shares for everyone."

51

Minsk repeatedly jumped into the air and flipped over as if to attract attention. Everyone assumed it meant he was in.

"I'm in," agreed Dylan. "What about you, Jason?"

"Is it going to be dangerous?" he inquired, cautious to the last.

"Come on, man! This is a chance for adventure. Isn't that what life's about?"

"Your life maybe," responded a wary Jason.

He thought for a few moments.

"We go down here looking for the source of all evil in the world, and wind up on a hunt for buried treasure."

"What's that?" questioned Salah.

"It seems we weren't playing all of our cards either," confessed Jason.

He gave a short description of their meetings with Sam and the Professor. He left out his encounter with the skeletons because he didn't want them to think he was totally loony.

"I've heard those rumors too," interrupted Joe. "Is it possible that one of us interpreted our clues incorrectly, and we are both looking for the same thing?"

A stunned silence gripped the party as the possible truth of this statement became apparent.

Joe interrupted the hush.

"Actually, what my map is searching for can be loosely interpreted as the 'source of the Aztecs' power.' What else could it be besides gold? What else?" he questioned while scratching his chin.

They mutely pondered Joe's last question.

Joe broke the quiet once again.

"I'm getting to old to go on an adventure of this sort. If I find a treasure and take it, my life won't be worth much in these jungles. The people tolerate me because I'm harmless, but if they found out I was concealing a fortune from them, I would need to move. I don't want to. I'll probably die here, but I'd like to make it later, not sooner. If you guys take the treasure, you'll be gone, and they really can't get at you."

"We'll have your share waiting," declared Salah, who clearly didn't believe Jason's story about the Professor. "Why don't we make a good dinner and--"

"Let's go to my place," interrupted Joe.

They secured their canoes to a tree, camouflaged everything with pieces of jungle undergrowth, and set off toward Joe's.

After a short trip through the jungle, they arrived at a small metal structure similar to what many people use for a storage shed. It was situated on a bluff that overlooked a small lake. Looking down, Jason could see a large number of fish lazily swimming near the surface.

"Dinner," Joe proudly proclaimed as he pointed toward the fish.

Joe walked down a path to the lake. When he arrived, he reached into a primitive fish trap constructed of bamboo-like sticks. He brought back five fish and plunked them in the sink.

"Why don't you guys go get some vegetables while I clean these?" he asked Salah.

Salah dragged Jason off into the jungle. They came back shortly with an assortment of vividly colored wild peppers.

"Wild ones taste better," Salah declared while referring to Joe's garden.

"You're correct," Joe agreed. "But the cultivated ones are easier for old bones like mine to harvest."

Joe made an excellent dinner, and everyone, including Minsk, stuffed themselves. After dinner, a council of war was held. It was decided that Joe would stay at his place to deflect any suspicion, and the boys would head off and try to follow the map. They quickly fell asleep from exhaustion while contemplating what the morning might bring.

The next morning when Jason opened his eyes, both the canoes were packed and everyone else was upright, looking down on him, and smiling.

"Sleeping Beauty arises!" exclaimed Dylan in an amused fashion. "Commodore Salah says we're leaving in fifteen minutes. Let's get a move on."

Jason jumped up and grabbed a quick breakfast.

Joe wished them well as they launched the canoes into the river. The paddling was easy as the current slowed while they moved further upstream.

The boys were amused as they watched Minsk try to catch the butterflies that passed over the boat. This time he was in the canoe with Jason and Dylan. They were surprised at how high he could jump. Once, when it looked as if he would not land in the boat, Jason tried to swat him back in with his paddle. This temporarily upset the balance of the canoe, and it tipped, dumping the boys and their equipment into the river. Fortunately, the water was only waist deep, so after recovering from the shock, they waded around to pick up their waterlogged belongings.

Salah was laughing so hard that he had to beach his canoe and run into the jungle.

Once or twice, the canoes grounded as the stream rapidly shallowed. Finally, they could go no further. They beached the canoes and readied themselves for the trek into the jungle.

"This map is notoriously inaccurate, so don't be surprised if the cave we're looking for isn't there," explained Salah. If we don't find it, we just come back and try to reinterpret the map. I'm not going to get lost in *this* jungle.

"Everyone have what you need?"

They all nodded.

"Then let's go."

Salah took the lead. Most of the slog was relatively easy, but at times, Salah had to chop thru the jungle with his machete. After a while, he got tired and handed the machete to Dylan.

"Go that way. If you stray too far, I'll let you know," Salah commanded.

Salah stepped in behind Dylan. Stumbling after him was a weary Jason.

"How did I get myself into this?" Jason brooded as he trudged along. "I could be at home in a nice comfortable house inspiring the Packers to victory on my computer."

Minsk scrambled everywhere. First he was lost in the rear. Then he was up in the trees. Finally, he was leading the expedition from about ten yards out in front of Dylan. He was more alert than usual.

As Dylan tired, he began sending nasty comments in the direction of Minsk. "That stupid rat got most of my things wet," he muttered.

"Are they ruined?" asked Jason.

"No, except that now the little pieces of pollen or leaves that explode off whatever I'm chopping thru, stick to me."

"You'll dry out soon," reassured Salah.

"Stupid rat. He smells bad too."

"I don't smell anything," interrupted Jason. "Just take it easy on him. OK?"

Dylan paused for a moment.

"I guess I'm tired from all the chopping. You know …, when you imagine yourself on an adventure, you never get tired. I've been on several 'missions' before, but this jungle really saps your energy."

"I wonder what those 'missions' were," thought Jason.

It was very obvious to Jason that Salah had what the old prospectors called "gold fever." He had seen that look on his father's face many times. He was getting more and more excited as they marched on and was particularly thrilled when they came upon a tree with an enormous circumference. He checked it against his map.

"We won't know, obviously, until we get there, but how's it feel to be rich?" a confident Salah queried.

"Is my dad here?" Jason asked himself. "It's another low probability get-rich-quick scheme." Jason admired both his father's and Salah's optimism. He wished he was more like them, for they seemed always to be having fun.

"At least I picked up my second wind," he thought.

Jason's reflections were interrupted by a break in the jungle. On the other side of a clearing was a set of lush green hills. They were the foothills of the local mountain range.

"The locals really don't like these hills," Salah expounded. "The tribes from the Aztec times hated them more.

"Look up there!" he exclaimed as he pointed toward the hills.

Both boys squinted as they looked into the sun in the direction that Salah pointed. Salah already had his dark glasses on. Dylan and Jason reached for theirs.

Off in the distance, high on one of the hills, they could see a dark spot against the luxuriant jungle background.

Minsk sprinted toward it.

The jungle was much less dense now, so the boys jogged to the cave. Excitement was pumping their adrenalin. Salah decided that he should go in first. They made torches from some dried brush around the cave and headed in.

The ceiling was about ten feet above them. The boys were amazed by the primitive drawings on the walls. Some of the markings matched Salah's map. As they moved deeper into the cave, they became aware of a soft iridescent glow ahead of them.

"The map says this is it!" exclaimed Salah.

He promptly took off toward the glow, ran a few feet, and almost knocked himself unconscious when his head collided with a low hanging stalactite.

"Maybe we should walk," suggested a practical Dylan.

They helped Salah up and ambled toward the glow.

The tunnel opened up into a fairly large cavern. The pinkish glow gave it an otherworldly appearance. In the center were many large boulders and two giant stalagmites with bases that were at least eight feet across. Sitting on one of the boulders was Minsk.

The look on Salah's face was one of extreme disappointment. There was no treasure here.

Jason was familiar with unsuccessful moneymaking schemes, so he just shrugged his shoulders and asked, "Are you sure we read the map correctly?"

"I think so. I'm going to look around a bit," a disappointed Salah answered, refusing to give up hope.

Chapter 8 - The Klinglesprachs

Dylan was busy munching on a granola bar when Minsk jumped up and grabbed it. He scurried around the stalagmites with Dylan in hot pursuit.

"You stupid rat!" Dylan yelled.

Minsk led Dylan in a figure-eight chase around and between the stalagmites. Dylan thought he had him cornered when Minsk stopped for a split second, but Minsk ran right at Dylan, scooted between his legs, and started a figure-eight in the opposite direction.

Suddenly, they weren't in the cave anymore. The stalagmites had turned into a giant forest of palm trees.

Minsk dashed off into the jungle.

Dylan temporarily gawked at the forest surrounding him.

When the shock wore off, his survival instincts kicked in. His first thought was to protect himself from the local animals, whatever they might be. He reached back and was relieved that the machete was still in its sheath.

He listened for any clues to his whereabouts. He heard birds chirping and the drone of a large number of insects. He was definitely in a jungle somewhere.

The melody of nature was interrupted by the sound of Salah and Jason crashing into the brush a few feet away.

"It looks like we found the Nutty Professor's magic kingdom," exclaimed Jason with a smile. "After you guys disappeared, we at first thought it was a joke. When we couldn't find you, Salah suggested that some strange magic might be afoot. We ran around the stalagmites like you did, and here we are."

"The question, more precisely, is, where are we?" asked Salah. "And not to be a party pooper, but how are we going to get back?"

"Maybe it's time to give the Professor a call. We aren't going to do anyone any good if we're dead."

Salah and Dylan both produced their phones and simultaneously exclaimed, "Mine's dead!"

"What next then?" an exasperated Jason inquired.

"I don't see any easy answers to that question," Dylan replied. "I think our first goal should be to find some shelter. We don't know what kind of animals or people live here, but it seems to me that as long as they don't know we're here, we're better off. Salah, don't fire your pistol unless it's absolutely necessary. Let's try to stay out of sight while we look for some food and water."

"It's amazing how fast his mind works," remarked Jason to Salah. "All I was thinking of was 'cool magic.'"

"I think we are both going to be glad he's here before this is all over," returned Salah.

"Perhaps we should look around and try to figure out the lay of the land," Dylan suggested. "We can cover more ground if we split up. Let's meet back here in fifteen minutes.

"That means that in about seven minutes, you turn around and come back," Dylan counseled while staring exclusively at Jason.

Dylan was impressed that Jason thought to bring the bow and quiver of arrows.

"You have your bow for protection," Dylan stated as he shifted into "spy mode." "Take your little rodent with you, and if you get into trouble, let out a yell. Otherwise, try not to disturb anyone or anything."

They set off in different directions to explore the jungle. Salah and Jason accidentally met up and were startled by what they saw next.

They hurried back to tell Dylan.

"We saw a large four legged animal drinking from a stream," Jason excitingly recollected. "When it finished, it lifted its head, gazed around, and slowly strolled away. We got close enough that Salah could have shot it with his pistol. You'll laugh, but it looked like a unicorn."

"A unicorn horn would be very valuable," Salah added.

"But here's the even weirder thing," Jason continued.

"You didn't fire the gun, did you?" interrupted Dylan. "I didn't hear one go off."

"No," returned Jason.

"Did the unicorn start talking to you like Minsk?" questioned Dylan with a sparkle in his eyes.

"The gun didn't work," Salah finally interrupted.

"Did it get wet?" inquired Dylan.

"No! I took it apart, gave it a quick inspection, and tried to get another shot. It just didn't work. I am very familiar with this type of weapon, and it just didn't work."

"Can I take a look?" asked Dylan.

"Sure!" said Salah while handing him the gun.

Dylan took it apart and put it back together.

"It should work," he confidently stated.

Before Dylan could say anything else, Salah grabbed the gun, pointed it in the air, and pulled the trigger.

There was dead silence.

"See!" Salah retorted.

Dylan then changed gears.

"Well, if it doesn't work, we are going to need some other form of defense. We can probably make some crude spears from the materials available to us here. I'll cut some shafts from the trees tomorrow. My machete and your arrows should be fine for the time being. Let's find some food and water, and then build a small shelter. A fire should keep the critters away."

The three companions continued searching the jungle for sources of food and water. When Jason and Salah became weary, they sat down to rest for a moment.

Dylan still bounced with energy, so he decided to gather some dry wood for a fire. He disappeared into the jungle.

While he was gone, Jason and Salah discussed their situation further.

As they talked, Jason spotted Dylan emerging from the jungle dragging a heavy branch. It took considerable effort to move it, so Salah and Jason slowly got up and walked over to help.

"What a moron," Jason muttered to himself, knowing they only needed a branch or two for a fire.

As Salah and Jason got closer, they noticed that it wasn't a branch at all. It was a dead animal. The creature was as big as a goat, and resembled a brown dog without any fur. It had huge teeth, and two even bigger canines. Its eyes were blue. It had small, pointy ears, and a long tail. The head of the beast had a large machete wound. It was bleeding profusely.

"Free food," Dylan boasted, triumphant and feeling good that at last he would have something to eat.

Without warning, a terrifying new beast exploded out of the tall grass and head-butted Salah into a tree. It let out a roar and charged to finish him off. Salah ducked out of the way just as the monster's huge jaws were about to chomp down on his head. Its powerful bite snapped the tree instead. As the severed top of the tree fell, Dylan, Jason, and Minsk barely dove out of its way.

The small tyrannosaur thought it had finished Salah off. Seeing Jason, it bounded after him. Jason weaved in and out of the trees as he frantically tried to escape. The zigzag path didn't help, and the predator quickly narrowed the gap between them. When it was close enough, it sprung at him, attempting to knock him down. As he leapt aside, one of the monster's claws ripped off a small piece of his ear.

Aggravated by missing, the creature jumped again, but Minsk met it in mid-air.

Minsk's antics allowed Jason to escape once again. He climbed up a tree and watched the gigantic beast fight the tiny mongoose.

Minsk ripped at its eyes. As soon as he blinded it, he jumped off of its head and slowly scooted away. He thought he was safe. The creature could smell Minsk though and chased after his scent.

"Shoot, Jason! Shooooooooooooooot!" Minsk frantically yelled as the monster gained ground.

Jason froze. He hadn't heard Minsk speak since the marketplace.

He quickly came back to his senses and remembered he still had the bow with him. He took it off of his back. He grabbed an arrow, drew the bow string, aimed, and let it fly. The arrow soared about fifteen feet, piercing the creature's tail. It just made it madder. It roared again. Jason reached back and grabbed another arrow. He fired, and the arrow struck the behemoth in one of its muscular legs. This limited its mobility and made Jason's next shot easier. He aimed again, and was about to shoot when out of the corner of his eye he saw Dylan running towards the beast. Dylan jumped on its back and hit it on the head with his machete. Blood came gushing out, but this only infuriated the brute more. It tossed Dylan from its back, and he crashed to the ground.

Jason knew that this was his chance. He aimed and fired. The arrow struck the creature in the neck. It let out one last howl and fell to the ground dead.

"And you thought you didn't have your mother's adventure gene," remarked Dylan as he stood up and brushed himself off. "Sounds like a story even Jack would have trouble topping."

Jason smiled as he tried to stem the bleeding from his ear. It hardly hurt, but it was making a mess.

"Are you wounded badly?" Dylan asked.

"It's my ear. I can't see. Could you take a look?"

"You're missing a small piece of your earlobe. Your first battle scar," Dylan proudly announced.

"Does it look like it will be easy to stop the bleeding?"

"I'll give you a piece of cloth," Dylan replied. "Go over to the stream and wash the wound out."

Dylan, always practical, then butchered the recently slain creatures. After he finished, he built a fire to cook the meat.

The other boys constructed a small shelter and covered it with palm leaves. They then all feasted on Dylan's epicurean delight.

"A masterpiece, if I may say so myself," Dylan proclaimed. The other boys nodded in agreement.

After they gorged themselves, Dylan stood up.

"I'll take the first watch," he announced. "Until we know for sure what's around here, we must keep our guard up. I'll wake one of you guys up in four hours. My watch isn't working, so I'll need to borrow someone else's."

"That's odd, mine's not working either," Salah announced.

"Nor mine," Jason added.

"I'll just use the stars then," Dylan declared.

"No need," responded Jason. "Let me take the first watch. I'm too excited to sleep anyway."

"Fine by me," Salah agreed.

Salah and Dylan fell asleep immediately. They were exhausted from fighting for their lives and the mental fatigue caused by trying to figure out exactly what was happening.

Jason sat up pondering their possible options. It seemed to him that if the Professor was right, then finding a way home was going to be difficult. His little encounter with the skeletons meant there must be a way back, but if the journey wasn't near impossible, the creatures from this place would be constantly overrunning our happy planet.

"Maybe they are? Could the Professor's theories be true?" Jason wondered.

Jason looked over at Dylan, Salah, and Minsk who were fast asleep.

"How can they sleep?" Jason asked himself.

"It must be their training," he answered.

Jason could see that Salah had had some formal military training, but Dylan's abilities were becoming more and more unfathomable.

After sleeping for some time, Dylan arose to take his turn at the watch. "Your four hours are up," he announced. "I'll take over now. Any strange noises?"

"Nope," Jason answered. "Now just how do you know it's four hours?"

"All good spies have an internal alarm clock," Dylan responded. "It comes in handy at times …, like now. Good night," Dylan stated dismissing Jason. He turned away and scanned the forest for signs of trouble.

Jason was soon fast asleep. After a few hours (Jason didn't know how long for his watch had stopped.), he was aroused by a faint singing in the distance. He worriedly looked around for his companions. Salah was fast asleep. Minsk was curled up next to him. Dylan was gone, but that was not unusual since "all spies need to train themselves to function on two hours of sleep nightly."

The singing was closing in on their camp. As it got louder, it seemed to surround it. By now, Salah and Minsk were awake. Salah instinctively grabbed for the machete.

When bushes near the camp rustled, Jason and Salah tensed up ready for action. The last thing they expected to see was Dylan tripping through the bushes immediately followed by a host of what appeared to be walking, singing, pine cones. Once the odd little party made it into the clearing, there was dancing to go along with the singing.

"One hundred twenty seven bottles of beer on the wall,
One hundred twenty seven bottles of beer,
If one of those bottles should happen to fall,
One hundred twenty six bottles of beer on the wall," sang the multitudes.

"We started at one thousand!" shouted Dylan, who then immediately guzzled a large drink from an animal skin canteen that he was carrying.

"I need to talk to my friends for a moment," remarked Dylan to one of the pine cones. "Keep up the song. I'll be right back."

The pine cones with arms, legs, and faces continued on with their merriment.

Dylan dragged Jason off to the side.

"These are the Klinglesprachs. I was out in the woods doing a little reconnoitering when I stumbled upon a clearing that was loaded with these creatures. I was mesmerized by their song and dance.

"Every so often, one would wander off into the woods and come back with a wooden keg of drink. I put myself in stealth mode and followed the next individual that left. He walked over to a pile of wooden casks, picked one up, and carried it back to the party.

"Nobody was left guarding the casks, so I decided to investigate. I opened one of the spigots and stuck my mouth under it.

"Do you know what it was?"

"Whiskey?" responded Jason who had seen its effect all too often on his uncle.

"Close, it's some type of ale. Well, I had a few more sips and turned around to find that I had become the hunted instead of the hunter."

"What do you mean?" Jason asked, fascinated by Dylan's story.

"I was surrounded by our little friends here. We awkwardly stared at each other for a few moments until one of them approached me with a mug full of drink. Being the diplomat that

I am, I immediately accepted, and the hooting and hollering started up. After a while, and a few more mugs, silence fell over the crowd, and they all stared at me again. I was temporarily overcome with a feeling of dread.

"I was relieved when one of them requested, 'Sing Master …. I don't believe we know your name. What are you called?'

"'Dylan,' I replied.

"'Sing please, Master Dylan,' requested the crowd.

"The ale was already taking effect, and the only song I could remember was the one you hear now, 'Ninety-Nine Bottles of Beer on the Wall.'"

"Didn't you think it was a risk to bring them back here?" Jason asked.

"As far as I could surmise, their leader is Skork. He was the one that was ordering all of the other ones around. He told me not to worry. They had been shadowing us for a day. He described all of you and especially wanted to congratulate you for your arrow shot into the lonizard."

"That's what they call them?" Jason asked.

"He gave me some food, which you see here, to bring back. He told me that if they meant us harm, it would already have occurred."

Skork strolled over toward Jason.

In the confusion, Jason really hadn't had an opportunity to closely examine their new little friends. They were nearly a foot and a half tall, and without their arms and legs, their dark brown bodies could easily be mistaken for pine cones. They had eyes, a nose, a mouth, and arms and legs just like humans. Each hand had three fingers and a thumb on it. Their feet were covered by animal skins. They were the happiest creatures he had ever seen.

"Greetings, Master Jason! I am Skork!" exclaimed one of the pine cones when he was close enough to be heard over the din.

"Greetings Master Skork! It is a pleasure to make your acquaintance," Jason replied.

"We are the guardians of our kingdom. We were sent out when rumors of your presence filtered back to our home. Once we determined that you meant us no harm, we decided to follow our customs and hold a small festival in your honor. Before we could send a representative to invite you, Master Dylan stumbled upon us. It seems, thankfully, that all has ended well.

"Be careful how much you drink," laughed Skork as he pointed to the body of Dylan sprawled out on the ground.

"He'll be OK in the morning," he roared and walked back to join the revelry.

"Fifty-seven bottles of beer on the wall, fifty-seven bottles of beer," and on went the singing.

Jason and Salah were both determined to stay awake and learn as much as they could about their new friends, but the ale and the excitement of the day proved to be too much for them. By the time the chorus had reached "Ten bottles of beer on the wall," they were both out for the evening.

Too bad.

They probably would have enjoyed watching Minsk dance the night away because none of them had ever seen a mongoose dance before.

Chapter 9 - Really?

Dylan was the first to wake up in the morning. His head pounded as he tried to focus his eyes on the surrounding campsite. His three companions were fast asleep. His singing and dancing buddies were nowhere in sight.

"Was last night just a dream?" he wondered. "Is there some type of poison in my wounds from the lonizard?"

As his blurry eyes surveyed the campsite's fringes, he noticed large piles of what appeared to be pine cones. Pine cones without arms and legs and faces.

"Maybe it was the water from the stream?" he speculated. "Perhaps, in the future, we should test that stuff before we drink it."

He then decided he could put off his early morning reconnoitering, since he vaguely recalled looking around the previous evening and finding "singing pine cones."

"Nasty stuff!" he thought. He rolled over, closed his eyes, and dozed off again.

When Dylan finally woke up for good, the camp was bristling with activity. He wondered why the activity hadn't awakened him earlier.

"A spy shouldn't sleep through this bustle," he chastised.

Jason and Salah were frying up the lonizard steaks. The remaining twenty or so Klinglesprachs were munching on a peculiar looking fruit.

"Apparently it wasn't a bad dream," mumbled an astonished Dylan to himself. "They're real."

His head began banging again from the night before.

"Be quiet!" he thought, but didn't say, to the others.

Skork walked over to Dylan.

"He returns from the dead," he laughingly proclaimed.

Dylan didn't know how to react to this statement, but the look in Skork's eyes told him it was made in jest.

"How about some breakfast, Laddie," continued Skork. "Perhaps some clagos or the dead animals your friends are eating."

"What's a clago?"

"Clagos may become very important to you in your journeys. Here, taste one!"

Skork handed Dylan what appeared to be a small yellow apple with two spines, one on either side.

"You just pull out both spines simultaneously, and a scrumptious dinner or snack is at your disposal. Be careful though, if you don't pull them out together, the clago will just disintegrate."

"You mean like a party favor?" Dylan asked.

"I'm not sure what that is," Skork replied.

"If I eat this, we aren't going to have a repetition of last night, are we?"

Skork didn't respond, but again, the twinkle in his eye told Dylan that mischief might be afoot.

Jason was walking past on his way back to his grilling duties, so Dylan handed him the fruit that Skork had already removed the spines from. He looked at it for a second and took a bite.

"Not bad," Jason exclaimed and walked away.

Skork looked Dylan right in the eye. "I just wanted to see if you'd trust me. After all, you're at least partially to blame for last night. You helped yourself to that jungle juice before we could stop you."

Dylan pulled the spines out of a clago and took a bite.

"These clagos are really good," he exclaimed. "Are they nutritious?"

"They contain everything a young growing Klinglesprach needs," laughed Skork. "But seriously, we eat most of the fruits and vegetables that your kind eats, and all the creatures that look like you enjoy them immensely.

"We don't eat a lot of meat," Skork continued, "but every once in a while, a good lonizard steak hits the spot."

Skork then wandered over to the fire to get in line for some tasty grilled lonizard.

Jason looked up from his cooking chores as Skork approached. "I heard you mention once or twice that clagos could become very important to us. They taste good and apparently don't cause any harm, but what's so important about them?"

"You guys really don't know, do you?"

Jason shook his head.

"If you put a clago in a sack overnight, the next day you have two, and the next day four."

Jason quickly grasped the importance of this.

"It's a replenishing food supply for anyone who can carry at least one," he exclaimed.

"As long as you don't eat the last one," alleged Skork.

"They need total darkness for a little longer than a day to double. That's why our countryside doesn't become one gigantic pile of clagos. They also need a touch of sunlight to start the process. This prevents them from exploding out of the ground if one should happen to roll down a hole."

After they finished a hardy breakfast, the boys and the Klinglesprachs held a council to determine their options. It quickly became apparent that their new friends didn't quite understand what Jason's group was looking for. The boys decided that they would eventually need to search elsewhere for a way home.

The group broke camp and traveled for nearly an hour. Salah and Florak, his new Klinglesprach friend, continually lagged behind. They were enthusiastically comparing their different childhoods. The group intermittently paused to wait for them. Nobody seemed to mind though, because it gave them all time to examine the tropical scenery on a very beautiful day.

Their journey took them to the top of a ridge.

Jason looked down upon a slow moving green river that was meandering through a lush meadow. The river was about forty yards wide and very opaque. He couldn't figure out what the color came from, but "if I fell in, I bet I couldn't see my hand in front of my face."

To the right, the banks became tall grasses as far as one could see. To the left the river flowed through a rock canyon with walls anywhere from ten to fifty feet high. Jason could see black marks along the walls, which he assumed were caves. It was hard to be certain from their present location, however.

"That's our border," Skork volunteered. "It is very difficult to cross."

"What's so daunting about that?" Dylan asked. "All we need is a small raft, and we'd be across in twenty minutes. In fact, I could even swim across if we didn't have all these confounded supplies," Dylan declared emphatically.

Skork didn't say a thing, but walked halfway down the hill to a small tree. With a few swift strokes from the axe he had slung on his back, he cut it down. He motioned the others to come near. When they arrived, Skork ran toward the river and pitched the sapling like a javelin as far as he could.

It floated downstream a ways before it was engulfed by a swarm of snake-like creatures and disappeared.

"Giant squid?" inquired Jason.

"No, much worse. And we better back off from the river a bit. As you probably have observed, there are no animals near it.

"Do you see those caves in the cliffs over there? Each one sleeps at least twenty of those creatures. They are the Skacali. Nasty pack hunters. Most are at least twenty flanks long when fully grown. Their fangs are about 2 snicks long."

As far as Jason could tell, a flank was about a foot in length. Later he would find out that it was the length of the Klingelsprach king's scepter, and that there are six snicks in a flank.

"We don't know how they do it, but they can stun their prey in the water without even touching it. Probably some kind of magic spell," Skork postulated.

"Sounds like an electric eel," Jason thought. Then he remembered that electrical things like their watches and phones didn't work in this world. "Perhaps the eels figured a way around it."

"When a few Skacali act together, prey rarely leaves the river," Skork explained.

"Why don't we just build a rope bridge and get across the river that way?" inquired an impatient Dylan.

As they talked, a brownish bird wandered aimlessly over the river. A snake-like shape shot fifty feet out of the water and snatched it with its jaws.

"Do you still want me to answer that question, Master Dylan?" replied Skork.

"I still don't see what the big deal is," said an exasperated Dylan. "Why don't we just walk down the river until we find somewhere to cross it?"

"Those creatures can read minds to some degree. Once they've determined that crossing is your goal, they will tirelessly follow you in order to get a meal. In fact, there are probably a few following us right now. Once they've hooked onto a potential victim, they can sense its presence at distances close to one thousand flanks."

"How do we get across then?" inquired Jason.

"There is a way. Don't mind taking a sporting risk, do you?" questioned Skork.

"What do you mean?" asked Jason.

"Well, the river encircles us. It is the border of our land. If you are searching for a way home, you will need to cross it. We don't cross it often, but we can when we need to. Actually those nasty creatures offer us some degree of protection. It's hard to get across from the other side, too. We do, however, have a way of accomplishing it. Have you ever been sling-flying?"

"What's that?" asked Dylan, who had taken a keen interest in the plot to cross the river.

"We have a machine with a huge counterweight that will heave you high into the sky. You then float down using a dried Ionizard stomach attached to ropes."

"Like a parachute!" interrupted Dylan. "I'm in! How about the rest of you guys?"

"I've jumped before!" exclaimed Salah. "I'm in!"

"I think I'd like to see it first," said Jason dragging his feet.

"How high can those Skacali jump?" inquired Dylan.

"Oh, you'll easily clear them. The only danger you'll have is when you hit the ground," laughed Skork.

"We'll need supplies. How soon can we get enough food for our journey?" asked Dylan.

"You've already got some clagos. If you manage them correctly and supplement them with things along the way, you should be fine.

"How soon do you want to leave?" asked Skork.

"How soon can you get the trebuchet here?" asked Dylan.

"What's a trebuchet?" inquired Skork.

"It's our name for what I think your sling-flying device is," responded Dylan.

"We must go to it!" Skork countered.

"It's probably a good idea to start an open ended journey such as the one you are attempting in a well-rested state. Why don't we shoot for tomorrow around noon?" advised Skork.

"Sounds good," returned Dylan, already primed for another undertaking.

"It'll give me some time to think this over," answered Salah.

"I guess if you guys are going, I can't very well stay here," threw in Jason, who was really happy that he had at least one more day to live.

Minsk's eyes sparkled, so the boys knew he wanted in.

The whole party proceeded to set up camp in a spot Skork assured them was a safe distance from the river.

The kegs of jungle juice reappeared and the party from the previous evening started up once again. Jason and Salah, who remembered the drink's effect on Dylan, consumed their drinks in moderation.

Dylan conversely stated, "A man's got to determine his limits, and I'm going to find mine."

He danced off to rejoin the party.

"Someone's got to watch over that boy," Skork remarked to Jason.

"That's what they all say about him back home!"

The singing got louder as the night progressed, as was customary with these types of parties.

"Not to pry, 'cause it really isn't any of my business, but where exactly are you guys from again?" Skork asked.

"I live in a country called the United States of America," explained Jason.

He then proceeded to describe their journey up to the present, hoping something would awaken a possible solution to their problem in Skork's brain.

It didn't work.

"I hope you find a way home," Skork wished him, "but I don't think it's around here."

The drink was starting to take effect.

"Why don't we go back to the party?" Skork proposed.

"Sounds good?" Jason responded.

They both rejoined the revelry which lasted well into the night.

Chapter 10 - JJ

The next morning, the company was on the move again. The boys and Minsk were accompanied by about twenty Klinglesprachs. The majority of the revelers from the previous night were nowhere to be found. An advance guard of four well-armored Klinglesprachs walked about thirty yards ahead of the main party. To amuse themselves, they jokingly poked at each other with their spears. Since no one screamed or bled, Jason concluded their armor was very strong.

"The lonizards like to ambush from the trees in these parts," explained Skork. "Our scouts just roll up into an armored ball until help can arrive. We can easily take care of a few lonizards if we don't get hurt in their initial attack.

"We're too close to the river on most of this trail for them to attack. Even beasts like that are afraid of the Skacali. But keep alert when we start moving through the trees.

"Minsk seems to be very wary right now, but I don't think he needs to worry. He's probably too fast for them to catch."

"Who worries about him anyway?" interrupted Dylan.

Minsk was out near the advance guard, so he didn't hear the blasphemy.

The Klinglesprachs continued to maintain a safe distance from the river while moving parallel to it.

It was a warm sunny day. Birds chirped and insects buzzed as they marched along a hilly route through waist high weeds. The forest occasionally invaded the path, and in these areas the Klinglesprachs were especially alert.

The relaxing sounds of the forest creatures were occasionally interrupted by the sound of a monster exploding out of the river to capture an unsuspecting bird or shore creature. When this happened, everyone was glad they kept their distance from the river.

"Over the next hill, you'll see our launchers. You're in for a treat. I always enjoy flying," exclaimed Skork.

"You're coming with us?" inquired a surprised Dylan.

"And Florak too. Like I said, I enjoy flying. I never miss a chance. Since it's your first time, you guys will have enough trouble taking care of yourselves. I'll help by taking Minsk. Once we get to the other side, I'll make sure you have the proper supplies and send you off."

"Thanks," interrupted Jason. "How can we pay you back?"

"Your company and stories are enough. Dylan's song about the beer bottles will be sung forever in our land. When you run into the pirates, just make sure you tell them how formidable our defenses are. Remind them of the Skacali. You haven't really seen our fighting powers, but the pirates have in the past.

"In any case, a little reminder to stay away wouldn't hurt."

They reached the top of the hill and were met with a view that stopped them in their tracks. Three gigantic trebuchets waited to fling the fliers high into the air and across the river.

"No way," Jason mumbled to himself.

At the sight of Skork, what appeared to be an empty field erupted with activity.

"It's amazing how well camouflaged those pine cones are," Jason remarked.

"I counted twenty-five of them before they started moving," added Dylan. "I've been trying to detect a pattern in their hiding so they can't surprise me again. Unfortunately, I only saw twenty-five of them, and there are at least forty. Still not good enough to count on in a pinch," Dylan mumbled as he walked away.

"That guy's crazy," Jason said to himself, "but crazy has a better chance of surviving around here.

"Glad to have you around," Jason whispered to Dylan who didn't hear him. He was too deep in thought about the Klinglesprachs he hadn't seen.

As they got closer, Jason examined the trebuchets just as one fired. Their physics were the same as the ones used in medieval times.

The huge machines had support braces as large as telephone poles.

On the command of "Fire!" a throwing arm launched the contents of a mesh net basket high up and over the river. As their supplies began their descent, a skin parachute opened to carry them softly down to the ground.

Jason then watched as the Klinglesprachs, with the aid of an elaborate pulley system, reloaded.

A Klinglesprach ran up to the approaching party.

"We're ready sir. Your skins have been folded, and the machines are loaded and ready to go," he stated in military fashion. "And the Skacali don't seem to be particularly hungry today," he added with a wink and a smile.

"Thanks," replied Skork.

The messenger returned to the trebuchets.

"It's not that I don't trust them," continued Skork, "but you should always check your own air skin."

"Or you might lose your real skin!" Dylan chimed in.

"Precisely!" exclaimed Skork.

"Florak and I will go first," he continued. "Watch how we pull on the various ropes of our air skins to maneuver. We always wager on who will come closest to a target. In this case, it's the supplies. I'll go against Florak, and you guys go against each other."

"Great!" Dylan and Salah gleefully replied.

Jason's response wasn't quite so enthusiastic. "If you guys are all going, I don't see how I can stay behind."

Skork and Florak attached their rolled up air skins to their backs with thin leather straps. They were very similar to parachutes. The boys attached theirs with the help of the many Klinglesprachs nearby.

"Just pull this rope when you start going down. The skin will open up and you will float to the ground. I have a special pack on the front that Minsk can ride in. I can't say that I've ever been so close to one of his kind …, and I hope it doesn't bring me years of bad luck," moaned Skork.

He glanced over at Minsk. Minsk scurried forward and hopped in.

Florak and Skork each curled up like a ball in a launch net of one of the machines.

"Are you ready?" the Klingelsprach commander shouted.

"Ready to go," they both answered while giving the thumbs up signal.

"Fire!" boomed the ranking Klinglesprach.

Two Klinglesprachs leaned on each firing lever, and Skork and Florak were airborne.

"Yaaaaaaaah!" they both screamed as they rocketed some three hundred feet up and in the direction of the river. A Skacali exploded out of the river after each of them, but they were much too high and out of danger.

When Skork and Florak were well past the opposite bank, they pulled the ropes that released their air skins. They slowly floated down with each one trying to extend his journey. They laughingly collided about a foot over the supply package and crashed to the ground.

"It looks like a tie," Skork shouted to his friend.

"Now it's your turn!" they shouted back together.

They realized that they were much too far away to be heard, so they waved the go-ahead signal to reload the trebuchets. Dylan, Jason, and Salah each climbed into one of the nets.

"Are you ready?" shouted the commander.

"Do we have to scream like they did?" inquired Jason.

"It makes it more fun! Like on a roller coaster," answered a clearly excited Dylan.

"Cut the chatter!" ordered the commander.

"Sorry," all three boys responded.

"Are you ready?" shouted the commander.

"Ready to go!" they replied with a thumbs up signal.

"Fire!"

"Yaaaaaaaah!" the three boys screamed as they followed the same trajectory as Florak and Skork. Jason freaked when the monsters came out of the river, but once again they could not gain the height needed to bring down their prey.

The boys opened their chutes after they crossed the opposite bank. Dylan and Salah gained some control over their devices and actually landed within twenty yards of the target. Jason had absolutely no control over his air skin and "landed" thirty feet up in a tree.

Skork went to the supply pack that they had previously launched and removed a large coil of rope.

He looked over at Salah and Dylan and in a merry voice asked, "Would you gentlemen like to accompany me?"

Skork paused for a moment and then continued, "Actually, we shouldn't be too hard on him. It required quite a degree of bravery for him to launch himself. He was shaking when we attached his air skin."

Minsk was the first to arrive at the tree and scrambled up to Jason.

"I'm all right," Jason exclaimed as Minsk stared into his eyes.

Dylan and Salah were the next to arrive.

"Do you want us to help you build a boat next time?" yelled Dylan.

"No way! That was great. I hope we go back the same way," returned Jason.

Florak and Skork walked over to the tree at a much slower pace. They had removed what looked like machetes from the supply pack and scanned the area for danger.

"You just never know who the brave ones are going to be," Skork remarked to Dylan when he arrived.

"Minsk! Come down here and get this rope so you can put it over the branch I'm pointing to," commanded Skork in his military tone.

Minsk glared back in a manner that showed that he was not in the habit of taking orders.

"Sorry 'bout that," Skork apologized to Minsk. "The flight got my blood flowing. Would you please put the rope over that branch so we can help Jason get down?"

With the help of the rope, Jason made his way down from the tree. He had learned to climb a bit on some of his past adventures with Dylan and was glowing with excitement.

"Did those monsters come after you guys too?" he breathlessly asked.

"Every creature that gets near the river has at least one Skacali tracking it," explained Skork. "Two or three, if they're really hungry.

"It's still pretty close to midday. Let's march for a few hours and then break for dinner," Skork suggested.

"Sounds good," was the general reply.

77

"In these woods," Skork lectured, "the lonizards are pretty active. Being loud seems to make them a little more wary of attacking. Stick together, for they like to pick off stragglers.

"If you go off the trail, you can encounter some pretty large carnivorous plants. We always travel at least in pairs around them. If one person gets caught, the other can hack off the branch and release him. If two get caught, it could be a problem, so try not to get too far from the pack.

"There are a few other nasty creatures in this area that you want to avoid. My rule of thumb is 'if it's moving, leave it alone.'

"One thousand bottles of beer on the wall, one thousand bottles of beer …," Skork led off as Florak and the others chimed in. Dylan, Jason, and Salah were now part of the choir.

They started off in the direction of the sun. The singing gradually died down.

Florak and Salah soon paired off and discussed famous battles that they could remember. Florak seemed to be particularly impressed with the phalanx formation used by the ancient Greeks.

"That might work against the Phosphorata," concluded Florak.

"Who are the Phosphorata?" asked Salah.

"The Phosphorata are the soldiers of evil in this world. They are almost invincible in hand to hand combat. They march in formation, but scatter at the moment of impact."

"I would think that their lack of discipline would cause them to lose many battles," interrupted Salah.

"It makes them harder to fight."

"I can't see how."

Florak halted and gave Salah a bewildered look.

"You don't know, do you?"

"Know what?"

"They can turn themselves temporarily invisible."

"What?"

"The soldiers attend special schools from the time of birth. By the time they're eight years old, they've partially mastered the trick, or they're out of the crack units."

"How do they do it?"

"Nobody knows for sure. Our experts think it's a combination of genetics and training. The training is very tough, but some who survive it still can't pull off the invisibility thing.

"There are a few who think it's magic."

"What do you think?"

"I think I would prefer not to run into any of them. Besides, I'm not in a position to make a good judgment. I've only seen them once, and it was an experience I don't really care to remember."

"How so?"

"Eight hundred and fifty bottles of beer on the wall," Florak sang as he changed the subject. "Eight hundred fifty bottles of beer …."

Salah imagined battling the Phosphorata for the rest of the march. In the war games in his mind, he most often lost.

His thoughts and everyone else's were intermittently interrupted by a strange dance between Minsk and Dylan. Minsk amused himself by running up ahead and leaping out and trying to startle Dylan whenever he could. It worked the first few times until Dylan started to anticipate his moves. It ended when Dylan snuck up behind one of Minsk's ambush spots and gave his tail a hard yank. Minsk screeched, leapt five feet in the air, and landed in a pricker bush. After that, they shared an uneasy truce.

When all the bottles had fallen off the wall, a quiet weariness took over. They marched on.

They were startled when a herd of creatures exploded into view from beside the trail before vanishing into the forest.

Dylan leaned over to Jason and quietly asked him, "Did those horses look like they had horns?"

"I thought I saw unicorns too," answered an astonished Jason. "I wonder if any of these ever escaped into our world."

"Suddenly, the old myths don't seem so foolish, do they?" Dylan preached.

They walked along the trail for a few more miles. They heard noises and saw shadows, but no other creatures showed themselves.

When they reached a crystal clear pool that was filled by several glistening ribbon-like waterfalls, Skork regrettably announced, "This is as far as we go. We want to get back before dark. The sun is already low in the sky."

Skork and Florak solemnly shook everyone's hand.

Skork's last words to the young adventurers were, "When the millionth bottle falls off of the wall, we hope you will come back and visit. If you have survived this long with that ratooi, you are probably golden. Take care and protect yourselves. You are entering a hostile world. Fighting is not always the answer. It is likely you will meet new friends, but be prepared to defend yourselves."

He and Florak then turned and departed.

The boys pondered Skork's statement as they watched their Klinglesprach friends disappear around a bend in the trail amid the sounds of "Ninety-nine bottles of beer on the wall, ninety-nine bottles of beer ...."

Dylan finally brought them back to the present.

"The trees around here look like they could provide us a safe place to sleep if we can find some good branches, but I don't see any right here."

"Me neither," Salah concurred.

"Want to go see what else is out there?" Dylan asked.

"Why not?" Salah answered.

Dylan led them deeper into the trees.

The boys wandered along the trail, not finding a suitable resting place. Darkness was setting in, and it was getting difficult to avoid the many vines, trees, and bushes that encroached on the trail. When their eyes adjusted to the dim light, they thought they could tell the dark shapes of the trees from the many other odd shades of blackness in the jungle. They were sometimes mistaken.

"Ow!" exclaimed Salah as he planted his face into a tree.

Dylan was in full "spy mode."

"Don't cry out if you bump your head or stub your toe. In real life operations, it could be far worse," he lectured.

"How the heck does he know that?" Salah thought.

Dylan moved over toward Salah.

"I thought that I saw an opening in the trees in that direction when we came to the top of a hill earlier," he announced while pointing with his finger. "Let's see how quickly and quietly we can get there. We can then move a little more easily by starlight. If we can't, we'll light some torches."

"I'm in," Jason added.

After a few more painful collisions with the jungle, they broke through to a clearing.

Dylan unexpectedly felt an odd pressure at the base of his neck as claws slowly pinched him. The shock of it caused the superspy to shriek loudly, grab Minsk, and throw him off his neck.

Salah laughed so hard it was difficult for him to hold his match steady and light his torch.

"I'll get you, you little rat," screamed Dylan. "Show yourself!"

"What about stealth?" whispered Salah with as straight a face as he could possibly muster.

"I'll stealth him!" screamed Dylan.

He looked around in a circle for Minsk.

"What's that?" Jason questioned while pointing off into the woods.

"Put out your torch, but bring it with you. No traces!" commanded Dylan as he regained his composure.

The woods had suddenly become lighter in all directions.

Salah glanced around. He could see dim lights approaching from the direction Jason had been pointing. He turned the opposite way and saw the same thing. He looked at Dylan.

Dylan's sharp mind was already formulating a plan.

"Quick! Up the tree! There's lots of moss and vines for us to hide in. If we run, I don't know where to go."

Minsk scurried out of the underbrush and up the tree before the three boys made it to the trunk. The climbing was relatively easy. They stopped about twenty feet up. They settled into three convenient forks that were hidden by large clumps of moss and looked down as they awaited the sources of the light.

"If they were looking for us, they would probably find us up here ..., but why should they be looking for us?" Dylan whispered. "Let's be still and see what happens."

The wait was short. From one side, ten armed men and five slaves or servants approached. They escorted what appeared to be an important prisoner. Their curved cutlasses suggested they were fierce fighters. Their varied hairstyles and assorted clothing gave them the appearance of road bandits.

A few moments later, ten members of an organized military group advanced from the opposite direction carrying two heavy chests. Their torches illuminated the otherwise pitch-black jungle they emerged from. They carried short stabbing swords in sheaths at their sides.

Jason was fascinated by the Roman soldiers.

The soldiers stopped about twenty yards from the bandits. One of them marched out toward the thieves. Two of the bandits approached with their prisoner. The prisoner was clothed in a hooded robe and walked with his head down. The military leader motioned for his troops to bring the chests forward.

An exchange was made, and the military men escorted their newly ransomed captive back into the jungle until the darkness swallowed them up.

The bandits set up camp in the clearing directly beneath the boys. Three small fires in a triangle formed the boundaries of their makeshift camp. They forced the servants to sleep outside the boundaries and posted a guard next to them.

Jason was terrified, yet captivated, as he watched from his perch in the tree.

The camp gradually darkened as the fires burned down.

Salah looked over at Dylan. Dylan shrugged his shoulders. He moved a little to make sure he was secure in his perch and closed his eyes.

Salah couldn't believe what he was seeing.

"Is this guy going to sleep?" he whispered to Jason. "I could never do that. He must have nerves of steel."

Shortly thereafter, however, the cool night air and the excitement of the previous hours took its toll on Salah and Jason. They too drifted off.

It was still dark when the exhausted travelers were shocked out of their slumbers by the most hideous screams. From the sound of it, a major battle was being fought below.

Dylan moved closer to Salah and whispered, "It looks like our two groups of friends don't like each other very much."

Salah nodded in agreement.

"We should wait til daylight to do anything," Dylan suggested. "No use trying to fight unless we know what we are up against. Escaping in the dark is out. I wouldn't know where to go."

They sat wide-eyed in their perches listening to the sounds of the battle. After a few minutes, the noises petered out.

"The quiet makes the situation even less predictable. Nothing to do til morning. See yah," Dylan whispered.

He went back to his fork in the tree and was asleep within minutes.

To Jason, Dylan's reaction to the situation was totally unbelievable. He and Salah both tried to imitate Dylan's carefree manner and go back to sleep, but it was impossible. They sat wired, twenty feet above the invisible battlefield. The tension gradually sapped their energy, but sleep would not come.

It seemed like weeks before the sun produced enough light for a tired Jason to try to piece together what had happened under the cover of darkness below. No one was moving, but he didn't trust his judgement.

"What if they are just asleep?" he asked himself as he looked toward his friends.

Salah surveyed the battlefield for a long time before he signaled to Jason that it looked safe to go down.

Dylan was still snoozing as Salah and Jason quietly climbed down from the tree.

Salah had spotted a cutlass with a jewel-encrusted handle that he badly wanted. No sense having to compete with the others for it. Salah removed the cutlass from the dead bandit's hand and was searching around for more booty when he heard a crash.

He laughed and started walking toward where Dylan had fallen out of the tree.

"Not quite as cool as you think you are," remarked Salah as he walked through the shoulder high vegetation separating him from Dylan's landing site. "You're lucky those weeds were there."

As he cleared the greenery, he was startled to see that it was not Dylan, but the hooded prisoner from the night before. He was lying on his side with his head turned away. Salah reached out to shake the prisoner to see if he was OK.

The prisoner jumped up with a knife in each hand. One was pointed at Salah and the other arm was poised to throw.

Salah jumped back. He was aghast. The face glaring back at him through wild blond hair was angry, crazed, and female.

Jason came laughingly upon them and only managed a "Whoa!" before stopping dead in his tracks.

Unbeknownst to Jason and Salah, Dylan had climbed down immediately after they did. His rummaging for food in the abandoned camp was also interrupted by the crash.

When he went to investigate, he was startled by an edgy girl brandishing knives at his friends. He quickly tried to diffuse the tension.

"Madame, can I take your order?" he calmly asked.

When he smiled at her, she relaxed and pointed her knives at the ground.

"Who are you?" she demanded.

"We could ask you the same thing," countered Dylan. "But how about after breakfast? I'm starved. By the way, if you helped kill all these guys, we're not going to mess with you."

She seemed to relax a bit after that comment, but the spark in her eye at the mention of food made it clear that she, like the boys, was hungry.

Dylan fixed a tasty breakfast from the spoils of war and served it to the group.

As they ate, the boys tried to size up their new companion. She was fairly tall, but no matter how hard they tried, the bagginess of her robe made it impossible to tell what was underneath it. She was tan, and now that she was calm, they could see that the wild blond hair was a bit curly. Minsk walked over and sat down by her leg. She was not the least bit afraid.

She coldly broke the ice. "You don't look like members of any of the groups I know of. Where are you from?"

Salah went through a brief description of some of their adventures, but left out anything which could tie them to any group which could be her enemy. He also omitted the fact that they were from a different world.

"How did you guys end up here?"

Dylan chimed in. "We were out exploring, when suddenly torches were approaching us from each side--"

"In the middle of the night?"

"There's more adventure in the night. You're the excellent-looking proof of that."

Dylan detected a slight blush, although he wasn't sure if it was pleasure, or anger, or both.

"OK. You guys are smart not revealing anything important about yourselves. Since we are going to need each other to get out of here, I'll tell you my story."

Dylan and Salah shrugged their shoulders and said, "OK."

Jason was star struck.

"In my part of the world, kidnapping is a very profitable business. For a few groups, it is their main activity.

"I was a target because my family is quite wealthy. We supply the animals to the armies of this area. We capture and train stagolots for the cavalry."

"What are stagolots?"

"They are bipedal creatures with huge heads and teeth that are the main mounts for our cavalry. They are very carnivorous. We train them to devour our enemies.

"I was kidnapped by a bunch of bandits," their new acquaintance continued while pointing to some of the recently slaughtered combatants. "Someone, I assume it was a friend, hired these soldiers to come out and pay my ransom. The results were disastrous for them. I guess that's why they get paid so much."

"I thought you were rich. Why didn't your family help you?" Dylan questioned.

"They disowned me when I announced my career decision."

"And what was that?" Dylan asked in a tone he hoped wouldn't be interpreted as being too nosy.

"Soldier of fortune!" was her confident response.

JJ removed her robe. She was wearing a belted tunic and a leather battle skirt. Bronze colored greaves protected her shins. Leather forearm guards were laced to her arms. Her upper arms and shoulders were wrapped with strips of gold metal. It was hard to tell whether they were armor or decorative.

The boys' jaws dropped. Not only was her response dumbfounding, she was gorgeous. They stared silently in awe for quite some time.

"Call me JJ," she announced to interrupt the awkward silence. "Using my real name might bring misfortune on people that I still care about."

After the shock wore off, the boys introduced themselves.

"That smelly little rat over there is Minsk," Dylan proclaimed.

85

JJ glanced down at Minsk.

"Nice to meet you," she said with a broad smile and patted him on the head.

"Not to change the subject, but I bet we could find more really nice weapons here," Salah suggested while glancing at the mess around them.

They examined the battlefield to decide what to take.

"The ransom is in the chests over there," JJ revealed. "We should probably take some spending money, but don't load yourselves up. It's not worth getting killed over."

Everyone walked over and removed a few gold coins.

From the appearance and location of the bodies, it was clear the number of casualties was about the same on both sides.

"Who were these guys?" Dylan asked.

JJ's eyes averted Dylan's glance. She had no interest in answering his question. She began collecting weapons. She grabbed one curved cutlass but seemed particularly interested in the daggers.

After she had examined her new weapons, JJ stated in a very authoritative voice, "It looks like we'll need to rely on blind faith for a while. You don't really know who I am, and is it Minsk? He makes you guys very suspicious," continued JJ.

Dylan tensed up a little for he had inadvertently relaxed from his "spy" mode. For some reason, he felt very comfortable around JJ.

"What do you mean?" inquired Salah, who had snapped out of studying JJ's figure.

"Well, he's a--"

JJ was interrupted by Minsk scurrying through the camp at full speed. He looked back as if he wanted everyone to follow him.

Dylan jumped up.

"I let down my guard! I should have suspected that someone would return to see their friends' fates," he squawked while glancing at JJ.

"They're not my friends. They were wiped out in the battle," JJ declared.

"You're more familiar with the terrain than we are. I don't think we want to fight. What's over where Minsk went?" Dylan asked while trying to formulate a plan.

"I'm not exactly sure where we are, but the best place to hide is probably in the mountains and jungles over that way," JJ answered. "Grab some weapons and food. We need to move! Fast!"

Salah grabbed a bow and a quiver of arrows and slung them over his back. He and Dylan each grabbed a spear and wrapped a belt with a scabbard containing a cutlass around his waist. Jason grabbed two cutlasses and a spear. The boys stuffed a few daggers in their backpacks, filled the remaining space with food, and took off.

As Jason ran with the pack, the absurd "How did I get involved in this?" feeling helped to at least mitigate the sheer terror. They sprinted along one of the many animal trails through the jungle. As they ran, Minsk acted as their scout. He disappeared ahead, and then slowed down to wait for the others. After running a few miles along the trail in this manner, they came to a wide clearing.

"Let's cross the clearing and wait on the other side to see if they are still following us," suggested Dylan.

"Good idea," Salah and JJ agreed in unison.

Jason was a bit winded and tried to catch his breath. "I could use a little break. I haven't run that far in a while," he panted. "Why don't we rest behind those bushes over there?"

Dylan gave the thumbs up signal, and they hustled to the bushes. They crouched down and intently watched the other side of the clearing.

Minsk, who had been leading, came back to search for the cause of the delay.

After about ten minutes, two creatures on leashes followed by their masters broke through the bushes at the opposite edge of the clearing.

"Those are skagglehoofs," whispered JJ. "They can sniff us out."

"What do you mean?" inquired Dylan.

"They can follow our scent. We need to find some water, or we will not be able to shake them."

"Do you know where we are yet?" inquired Dylan.

"No, but I suggest we keep moving. They haven't seen us yet, so they don't know how far ahead we are."

As she turned to leave, Salah let out a yelp. His leg was fiercely gripped by of one of their pursuers.

He fell to a dagger from JJ's hand.

She removed the dagger, and they took off again through the jungle. This time, their pursuers had actually seen them and moved more quickly to close the gap.

About a mile down the road, Minsk halted.

Dylan stopped as he approached Minsk and let out a sigh of, "Uh oh."

Everyone else froze. They stared out at the abyss ahead of them. They were standing at the top of a sheer cliff, and it was at least three hundred yards to the bottom.

"Look for a way down!" ordered Dylan.

A quick search made it apparent that they would not be able to climb down.

"What are we going to do now?" inquired Salah.

"I will fight!" said JJ as she drew her cutlass. "I will not be captured again."

Salah took the bow off his back and loaded an arrow.

Jason drew his cutlass, although he was not that sure what to do with it.

Minsk jumped on Salah's back and began yanking something out of his backpack.

"The skins!" exclaimed Dylan. "We can float down just like we did over the river. Good idea Minsk."

"You're going to do what?" questioned JJ, who for the first time had a bit of fear in her eyes.

"We can jump off the cliff and float right down. We've done this before."

"I'll fight!" exclaimed JJ once more.

"You don't stand a chance," answered Dylan. "You're going to have to trust us. Jason, you go first. The rest of us will go in pairs. I'll take JJ. Salah can take Minsk. Let's hurry and get the skins ready."

They could hear the skagglehoofs approaching. The skagglehoofs made a peculiar yelping sound, not unlike hunting dogs, when they were in hot pursuit.

Dylan refused to be hurried as he prepared the skins. Before he finished, the pursuit suddenly quieted down.

"They must know we're stuck on the edge. In their minds, there is no need to hurry," said Dylan with something of the old swagger in his voice.

Salah had climbed up a nearby tree to act as a lookout. They heard the twang of his bow and a scream on the receiving end.

"Get down here!" yelled Dylan.

The boys helped each other attach their skins.

Just as they finished, JJ severed the head of one of their pursuers.

"Let's go!" yelled Dylan.

Jason sprinted toward the abyss and jumped off.

Dylan watched JJ as she stared at Jason while he slowly drifted over the jungle below. He had no idea what she was thinking.

Minsk jumped on Salah's back as he headed for the edge. With a scream, Salah launched himself over the edge. The skin opened perfectly, and Salah and Minsk floated toward the rainforest below.

"You've got to trust me," pleaded Dylan once again.

"No way!" JJ answered.

As she turned to fight again, she saw three foes screaming toward her, all with their blades drawn. She turned, ran toward Dylan, and leapt straight at him. The force of the collision launched Dylan off the edge of the cliff. JJ held on in a bear hug, looked him straight in the eye, and whispered, "Do your stuff."

As they careened over the side of the cliff, Dylan looked calmly into JJ's eyes. "You need to move your arms off the skin in order for me to open it," he calmly requested.

JJ was frozen, staring at the ground below. She had a death grip around Dylan's back.

"If you're trying to scare me, it's starting to work," Dylan whispered in a little more worried tone.

He again received no response from JJ. He needed to do something to snap JJ out of it. Never had he imagined that she would freak.

"If you're messing with me, this is getting kind of scary," Dylan warned as he looked at the ground which was approaching all too quickly.

Dylan then calmly kissed JJ on the lips. She smacked him in the face, but all Dylan could think about was that the chute could open. It released, and they quickly decelerated and slowly floated down over the trees.

Dylan looked around, but the others had already disappeared into the jungle.

Their skin caught in the trees high above the ground.

JJ seemed back to her usual self now that she was almost back on solid ground.

"Are you OK?" Dylan inquired. "You seemed pretty out of it back there."

"I'm fine. I'll explain after we get down."

"Are you sure? How many toes am I holding up?" Dylan asked.

"They're not toes, they're fingers," responded JJ with a less than amused look.

"Just checking," returned Dylan.

Dylan spotted a vine that looked to be the easiest route to the next branch ten feet below.

"Can you climb down a rope?" asked Dylan in his "mission mode" authoritative manor.

"Why do you keep insulting me?"

"I'm not trying to. It's just that after what happened in the air, I need to be sure. We can worry about feelings after we're down."

"Fair enough," said JJ as she grabbed hold of the vine.

JJ was an expert climber and easily made her way down the vine to the branch below. Dylan climbed down and joined her on the branch.

"The rest of the way down should be fairly easy," Dylan declared.

He then gazed into the forest, searching for any potential sources of trouble. When he turned around, JJ was halfway down. Dylan quickly followed, and in no time they were both on the ground.

"Are you afraid of heights?" Dylan asked. "I never would have guessed. It doesn't seem like anything bothers you."

"I didn't freeze up because of the height. I didn't freeze up at all. I was looking for something below. This jungle is the home of Nahula."

"Who or what is Nahula?"

"That's the name we have for the spirit of this part of the jungle. I recognized some of the landmarks on the way down. Many people have entered this place looking for riches. Few have returned."

"How do they die?" inquired Dylan.

"Nobody knows. They just disappear. There are all sorts of stories. Some speak of monsters, some of spirits, and others say the earth has a mind of its own here and just swallows them up.

"When we reach the age of thirteen, our journey to adulthood requires that we make a spiritual journey into this jungle in search of the cara cara plant. Everyone from our city must take an annual dose of an elixir made from the cara cara, or we die.

"No one over the age of sixteen has ever come out of this jungle alive. No one can explain it. It's just the way it is.

"There are rumors of a magical vine where gold nuggets grow wild like grapes," JJ continued.

"Has anyone ever brought back the nuggets?" Dylan asked.

"Occasionally they bring back a few, but no one ever finds a nugget until they are loaded to the hilt with cara cara plants. That's the funny thing. It's almost mystical. People only see the nuggets when they are looking for something else. Expeditions searching exclusively for them never find anything and rarely return."

"Have you made your journey, yet?" inquired Dylan.

"Twice …, but I think we better start looking for our friends now," responded JJ as she started off into the woods.

"Do you have any idea where you are going?"

"I survived the last two times in this jungle by following my instincts. Some of the ideas didn't seem to make sense, but I followed them anyway. I'm here …, so I'm either very lucky, or there's something to it."

"Well I haven't a clue, so lead on," Dylan suggested, even though he was extremely uneasy about wandering around in the jungle following someone he barely knew.

"At least when following her, the view won't be so bad," he happily thought.

"Spy mode" kicked in again.

"Before we start, don't you think we should make some protection against the larger beasts we might encounter?" Dylan suggested.

"What about our cutlasses?" JJ asked.

"The beasts need to get very close for us to use those. Maybe we could fashion a few of your knives into spears by attaching them to some branches. Then we can fight from a greater distance."

"Well, I suppose I can part with a few of them, but as you saw in the past, I'm very good at throwing them."

JJ handed Dylan one of her knives. The expression on her face was that of a mother giving away her first born child.

"I'll be careful with it," Dylan promised as he looked for something to fasten the blade to.

He cut down a sapling with his knife and removed its branches. He then cut grooves in the top to help stabilize the blade and fastened it with vines. When JJ saw the spear, she eagerly gave Dylan another knife. He crafted another spear shaft and attached it.

"Now at least we can sting the critters before they eat us," he arrogantly declared.

The rustle of a beast moving toward them startled Dylan and JJ. They reached for their weapons but were relieved when they saw Jason nonchalantly walking out of the forest.

"Did you all have a pleasant flight?" he asked.

"Nice to see you buddy," Dylan welcomed.

"Have you guys seen Salah and Minsk?" Jason inquired.

"No, but we're looking for them. JJ has a feel for where she thinks we are. It's her world, so I am content to follow her."

With his friends found and some protection in hand, Jason could now freely examine the jungle. The majority of the foliage was purple and blue. The trees were very tall, about the size of full grown oak trees. They were covered with purple vines which made them appear thicker. In the areas where the foliage was the thickest, large luminescent pink mushrooms grew. They were so bright that there was no need for lanterns or torches.

Dylan and Jason followed JJ along a trampled path covered with a variety of large, strange footprints. She periodically raised her hand and motioned them to stop. Within seconds, they frequently heard a large animal crashing through the brush. Close enough for them to hear. Not close enough for them to see.

They had been walking for a while when Dylan asked JJ, "What are your plans for catching up with Minsk and Salah?"

"I just have a feeling that if we keep heading in this direction, we'll find them. I know it's not much to go on, but it's all I've got. If you've got a better idea, I'm all ears."

"I would have picked this way too," Dylan replied, "so I'm content to follow. It's probably going to be tough finding them. Salah is smart enough to know that making loud signals could turn him into a meal for one of the local carnivores. I'd bet on them surviving. Salah's a soldier, and that little rat can survive anywhere."

"It can be a little harder if you don't know what you're up against," counseled JJ.

"Isn't that kind of the definition of adventure," Dylan countered.

"In fact, I feel adventurous right now. I'll take the lead," Dylan announced as his alpha dog qualities began to show again. He sauntered past JJ and marched on.

After hiking awhile, JJ and Jason stopped to look at one of the many multicolored plants allowing Dylan to get a good distance ahead. Their study was interrupted by a yell followed by a litany of bad language.

They ran down the trail toward Dylan's scream to aid their friend. They found him hanging upside down with one leg caught in a primitive snare. Minsk was rolling on the ground underneath him. Jason could have sworn the mongoose was laughing hysterically.

Salah looked up at Dylan with a big smile. He tried his hardest not to laugh as he told JJ and Jason, "I thought we caught dinner, but he's not to my tastes. Minsk appears to approve, however."

There was no question about it now. Minsk was laughing so hard that he could barely catch his breath.

Salah walked over to where the rope for the snare was tied to a tree.

"Help me out," he requested of Jason and JJ.

They held the rope as he untied it and slowly lowered Dylan to the ground.

"Looks like it's clagos tonight," Salah remarked as he removed the snare and gave Dylan a gentle pinch. "This one's a little too skinny."

Dylan saw the humor in the situation and responded half threateningly, half playfully with, "You'll all get your turn."

He immediately changed gears to the problem at hand.

"I'm glad to see we're all back together. I was getting worried. Now we can all relax a little.

"This clearing looks like as good a place as any to have dinner. Any objections?"

They must have been hungrier than they realized. Without a word, they plopped down and rummaged through their backpacks for food. The buried clagos they found tasted delicious.

After eating, they each climbed up one of the nearby trees and found a convenient fork in its branches. It had been an eventful, exciting, terrifying, exhausting day. They drifted quickly off into deep, dreamless slumbers.

Chapter 11 - The Swarm

The sun had already been up for a few hours when the group finally awakened from their exhausted sleep. As they prepared for the day's journey, they each secretly hoped someone else had an idea about which way to go.

While they were mulling around, Minsk wandered back into camp. He had been out exploring.

"What's that on your back?" inquired Dylan. "Are you starting to attract giant size fleas?"

Minsk glared back. He wandered over by JJ as if he was looking for some companionship. He appeared to be very fond of his little friend and wanted to show it off. It looked like a tiny grey monkey with giant eyes and clung to Minsk's back with miniature claws.

JJ had her back to Minsk as he approached. She was adjusting some of her body armor that she didn't wear while sleeping. She turned around with a broad grin when she heard Minsk approach. The smile quickly changed to a look of terror.

Dylan noticed.

"That happens to me too when I see him!" he stated playfully.

"We need to move now!" JJ ordered. "We don't have time to clown around. Get as many of your things as you can travel quickly with. Leave the spears. They will do no good. Take all of your swords. We need to get out of the trees, for they can drop on us from above."

JJ quickly collected her belongings.

Although they weren't sure why, everyone else followed.

"What is after us?" Salah asked as he obeyed JJ's commands and stuffed things into his backpack.

"The Rangali!" shrieked JJ. "They come at you by the thousands. Minsk's little friend is one of their scouts. They are playful and cute enough to distract their victims, but imagine ten thousand of those hungry little buggers with razor sharp teeth. That's what's after us now. We need to get out in the open. We need to get to those plains I saw while floating down here. If we get up on the rocks, we might just have a chance."

"Can't we just bolt down the river?" asked Salah. "Why fight if you can escape without it?"

"These guys hunt strategically. I'm sure they've thought to cut us off from the river. We need to move quickly before they get in the trees above us, or we're finished."

Salah turned his ear toward the river and remarked, "I hear a soft chattering noise."

"That's the sound they make," confirmed JJ. "They move at about the speed of a slow jog. If we sprint, we can make some space and set up our defenses. We can't outrun them because they never tire. We eventually need to rest."

Their pace quickened as they sought the relative advantage of the rock islands in the open field where the terrain was similar to an African savannah.

As the forest thinned, the going got easier. The bushes and trees they needed to avoid grew fewer and smaller but were still thick enough to hide their pursuers.

Dylan started to think out loud.

"How do they know exactly where we are going? We aren't making enough noise or leaving a trail for them to follow. Maybe they can sniff us out."

"Minsk!" JJ screamed. "Get rid of your little buddy, or he's going to be eating us for dinner."

JJ ran toward Minsk, who was jumping around trying to remove the Rangali from his back.

"Stand still!" she ordered.

She reached over her shoulder and drew the cutlass she had sheathed on her back. Minsk spun round and exposed his back to JJ. One swift slice and the only things left on Minsk were a few severed claws.

"Now they won't follow so quickly," she assured the boys.

The boys looked questioningly at her.

"They communicate with sounds that are too high for us to hear. We'll have a little more time now. One other thing to remember; if they get on you, don't try to stab them with your knives, or you will injure yourself.

"It's much easier if you remove them before they latch on with their claws. Grab them by the base of their tail, and fling them at the ground. If you throw them hard enough, it will temporarily stun them. Then you can finish them off. If you don't get rid of them quickly enough, you'll need to cut them off."

"Have you faced this foe before?" asked Salah as they ran along.

JJ said nothing, but lifted the hair off the back her neck to reveal a series of small scars.

"It took me a while to get them off. Those little buggers wished they had left me alone. We went back and cornered that colony on the edge of a cliff. We were too many for them to handle, and we eventually drove the bulk of them into the ocean."

It was obvious to Dylan that JJ had a plan. One of his mantras was that if you were on someone else's turf, unless they were a complete idiot, you let them draw the battle plans.

"When we get to the rocks, what do we do?" asked Dylan, who was in remarkably good shape and barely breathing hard from their run.

"We get to the highest flat rock we can stand on and protect each other's backs. If we kill enough of them, they may decide to hunt an easier target."

"We used to say it ain't over until it's over," Dylan chimed in.

"Amen," Salah added.

They spotted a large flat top rock a good distance out in the field. The odd pillar-shaped rock formation was as tall as a two story house. It was about two car lengths in diameter, and the top was covered with basketball-sized boulders.

"We can throw those down as our first line of defense," said JJ pointing to the boulders. "Then it should be easier to defend the perimeter."

She suddenly stopped talking and looked at the three boys.

"I hope you guys aren't offended by me taking charge here. After all, you helped me escape, not the other way around."

"Spies need to be opportunistic and not let egos get in the way," Dylan answered before taking off to examine the rock.

"Spies?" JJ questioned.

"It's a long story. We don't have time for it now," Jason answered. "We're not spies. He thinks he is."

Fortunately for Jason, Dylan didn't hear him.

"After I see them fight once, I might be able to offer some advice. As for now, you have my vote to be general," Salah agreed.

Jason didn't care who was in charge. His only thought was of getting there quickly.

They hurriedly followed Dylan to the rock pillar. On closer examination, they could see that the sides were very smooth, and there were no footholds.

"If I can get my rope anchored on top, we should be able to climb up," Dylan speculated. "Let me tie it to a stick and heave it up. I'll try to get it lodged in a crevice."

As Dylan uncoiled the rope, he felt a small pebble bounce off his head. He looked up at Minsk who was staring down at him.

"If he got up there, there must be a way on the other side," Dylan guessed.

The chattering of their pursuers was growing louder.

Salah quickly moved to the other side and shouted out, "There seems to be a cave. Maybe it's a tunnel to the top."

He squirmed his way in and shortly thereafter was standing next to Minsk.

"You guys probably should get up here. They haven't broken out of the trees yet, but the chattering is getting louder," Salah yelled down.

Dylan hurried to the tunnel and climbed up. He turned and expected to see JJ and Jason right behind him. He was surprised he only saw Jason. He looked down and saw JJ trotting back to the edge of the forest.

"What are you doing?" he yelled.

"I think those sticks we passed might serve our purposes better. I'll be right back."

She ran toward a scattering of branches near the edge of the forest and began searching among them. She picked out six. After she snapped off the ends, they were about the size and shape of baseball bats.

Dylan was beginning to deduce JJ's strategy, and he liked it. The bats would be excellent for their purposes.

98

"If my guess is right, we should be able to defend this for a long time," Dylan confidently thought, "but eventually we're going to get tired. I wonder if she has a plan for that."

Jason and Salah began readying themselves for battle. They handled each of their collections of cutlasses, swords, and knives to try and figure out which would work best against their current foes.

JJ was soon back at the base of the rock.

"Try not to get hit with these when I toss them up," she yelled.

It took a few tosses for each one, but after bouncing them off the side of the rock, she eventually got the clubs up on top. Then she climbed up.

Once on top, she picked up one of her new-found clubs and confidently stated, "These will work better than swords against these guys."

Dylan and Salah each picked up one of the sticks and swung it.

"Play ball," Dylan said with a smile.

"Or cricket," Salah threw in.

"Play ball or kill crickets?" questioned JJ.

Salah let out a gentle laugh. "Those are just games we play with a stick similar to these where we come from," he explained. "Someday we can teach them to you."

"Sounds great. I would love to see where you come from," she sighed, "but right now we should plug the tunnel with these rocks and make those little buggers climb up the outside."

Jason began filling the tunnel with anything he could find. The rest joined in, and the tunnel was quickly half-filled.

The chattering suddenly got much louder.

One by one, the group turned toward the jungle. The malevolent Rangali hoards burst into view. They looked like a furry rug moving toward the rock tower. The thousands of vile creatures encircled the pillar just out of throwing range. They stopped moving and for what seemed like an eternity, just stood and chattered.

Jason looked around. Everyone else appeared calm, but he could feel a wave of terror creeping over him. The confidence he had in his friends was the only thing that prevented him from completely losing it.

"When we were looking for a way up, it was obvious that there were no easy routes," JJ explained, "so those little devils probably won't be able to swarm upon us from all sides. Once the battle starts, it should be clear which routes they are taking. Our goal should be to stand near the edge at those spots and belt them off. Obviously, we stand a better chance if there are only a few paths up. Let's hope I'm right, and they can't attack from everywhere.

"Hopefully we can tire them, and they'll go looking for something easier," she added.

The boys liked her plan.

"Get ready, it looks like they're starting to move," JJ warned.

They each picked up a bat.

"My training didn't include battling ten thousand ferocious mini monkeys, but--" Salah looked at the monkeys and screamed at the top of his lungs "--bring it on!" His eyes began to sparkle as if the thought of battle was actually fun.

The Rangali scurried toward the rock. Two things were immediately clear. The first was that the tunnel was successfully blocked. The second was that the Rangali were going to have difficulty climbing to the summit. There seemed to be only two paths to the top.

Salah encountered the first invader and sent it flying off into space. He smacked three more before they also started emerging on Dylan's side. The path that Jason had positioned himself above was not accessible, so he watched the battle unfold.

It was a pretty lopsided at first. Salah and Dylan each sent about a hundred monkeys flying to their doom. JJ picked off any stragglers that made it past the boys. Then the Rangali backed off to rethink their strategy.

"We probably should eat something while they are allowing it," suggested Salah. "We need to keep up our strength."

They grabbed some food from their backpacks as they watched the events below unfold.

For a while, the Rangali again did nothing but chatter. Then they began carrying branches toward the base of the rock.

"It looks like they're building siege towers," Salah declared.

They wolfed down their food as they watched the little monkeys carry more and more branches to the base of the rock.

When the towers reached about three quarters up the rock, they stopped.

"Maybe they're getting tired, and they'll just go away," wished Dylan.

He continued to chow as he watched for clues of the monkeys' next tactic. His heart sank when he spied a monkey carrying a torch toward the pile.

"I don't have a good feeling about this," he warned.

"They're going to try and smoke us out," JJ yelled as she realized along with everyone else what was about to happen. "We can hold out for a while if we breathe through wet clothing, but things don't look good right now. Any of you guys have any ideas?"

They all shook their heads.

"Well it looks like we'll meet again in the next world," said JJ rather flippantly given the situation they were in.

As the smoke thickened, they covered their mouths with wet garments to filter the air. It soon became difficult to see each other.

Minsk suddenly attracted their attention as he stood up on his hind legs and looked toward the sun. A second flaming sun was now its partner in the sky. There was a slight rumble in the distance which quickly became much louder.

"I can't believe this," yelled JJ. "Everyone into the tunnel!"

Minsk was already there.

JJ pushed Jason and Dylan into the hole and pulled Salah in on top of her. There was a violent explosion and a burst of light. The ground shook, but nobody could feel it for they were already unconscious from the concussion.

Dylan was the first to awaken. It was difficult to move with both JJ and Salah on top of him and Jason underneath him. He took some water from his flask and rubbed it on JJ's forehead. She turned and moaned slightly. After what to Dylan seemed forever, she opened her eyes and tried to focus on him.

"What the heck was that?" he asked a still groggy JJ.

From her expression, he could tell her vision was a problem.

"I'm sorry," Dylan continued. "How are you feeling?"

"I … I think I'm OK. It's a little hard to tell with Salah on top of me. Salah! Salah! Are you all right?"

Salah began to wiggle, and after a few more shakes by JJ,

he was awake.

"Let me climb out of here and get off you guys," he rather sheepishly stated.

"Just make sure you're OK before you move," ordered JJ, who was by now, pretty much back to normal.

Salah climbed out of the tunnel. He reached down and helped both JJ and Dylan out. Jason made it out on his own.

"I felt like I was tackled on the goal line," Jason remarked.

"The goal line?" JJ asked.

Before anyone could respond, she shoved all three of them to the ground and crawled behind the few remaining rocks along the perimeter of their mini plateau. She motioned for the others to follow.

"I never thought I'd see this with my own eyes. That big rock that's smoldering over there was brought in by the Sky Miners."

"The who?" inquired a puzzled Dylan.

"There is a legend among our people of a mysterious clan living in the jungle that can pull rocks from the sky."

"Do you mean meteors?" inquired Dylan.

"What's a meteor?" asked JJ.

"Never mind. Go on," responded Dylan.

"They harvest the gold from the rocks and survive by trading it with the pirates."

"How do they get the rocks out of the sky?"

"No one seems to know. Actually, as far as I know, we are the closest anyone has come to seeing them harvest a rock," JJ chimed in.

"Then let's be invisible and watch," whispered Salah.

The explosion had extinguished the Rangali's fire. Out in the charred field, they observed a car-sized rock smoldering. Most of the vegetation was destroyed for a good distance around it. What little remained was still smoking. A cloud appeared over the rock and rained on it. The cooling was so quick it produced huge cracks.

"It looks like they can control the weather, too," added Salah.

"This is really cool. I need to learn how to do this," yearned Dylan.

He started to stand up, but was immediately yanked to the

ground by JJ.

"We don't know what they will do if we interrupt their little party. Let's stay out of sight for a while," she suggested.

"Good idea. I guess I lost my head."

As it rained, the group of five Sky Miners meditated a good distance from the rock.

When the rain stopped, the Sky Miners slowly walked toward the pillar. Jason thought the youngest one, who walked in front of the group while talking to another member, was their leader. They all seemed very pleased with their present operation's success.

As the Sky Miners approached the pillar, the curious adventurers crept closer to the edge of their hideaway to keep them in sight.

"We're going to eat like kings for a while," their leader boasted as he picked up a roasted monkey carcass. "Not only was our mission a success, but we get this tasty meal too. I wonder what they were hunting. They don't group up like this unless they are swarming on a victim."

"I don't see any large animals around, except of course, for that group that is spying on us from atop that rock," stated the leader's companion. "Come on, show yourselves," he commanded.

JJ looked at her companions. They all stood up together.

"Where's the other one?"

"There are only four of us," responded JJ.

"Come. Come. We can smell that ratooi even where we are."

Dylan laughed. "Another race that thinks you're a smelly little rodent," he said as Minsk crawled out from beneath a rock and glared at him.

"Why don't you climb down and join us for lunch. If they were hunting you, you must be tired and hungry," said the leader's companion.

Dylan motioned to pause as JJ moved toward the edge of the rock.

"We'd be dead without them," whispered JJ. "They saved us. I'm for trusting them. After all, that's how I fell in with you guys."

Salah didn't add anything but gave JJ the thumbs up sign.

Jason just shrugged his shoulders. Minsk had already tried to make it down the tunnel, but came back because it was blocked.

Dylan couldn't think of a better option.

"OK, then. Let's climb down," he agreed.

"You were a good friend," Salah solemnly said to a club he picked up and tossed aside.

The rest abandoned their clubs with similar feelings. They picked up their other weapons and wandered to the edge.

Salah hooked a rope to one of the few boulders remaining on top and threw the rope over the side. Rappelling down was quite easy. Dylan went first. JJ followed. Next came Jason. Salah was last.

"Why don't you join us for lunch?" the leader graciously requested again. "It isn't often that we get to spend time with such attractive company."

Jason noticed what he thought was a slight blush as JJ looked down and away to avoid eye contact with him.

"These cooked Rangali are very tasty," the leader continued. "Kind of ironic. They were going to eat you, and now they're your meal. Look, the skin pulls off easily."

After Dylan introduced his group, he looked more closely at their new friends. They were about five feet tall and very stout. They all had beards except for the leader who looked like he had never shaved a day in his life. They were dressed in well-tailored animal skins and leather. The group wore fur hats, except for their leader who was completely bald. Large quantities of hair stuck out around the edges of their hats. The Sky Miners carried small knives which appeared to be their only weapons.

Their leader stepped forward.

"My name is Solo, and my friends are Fila, Hewer, Flords, and Visgoth. It is a pleasure to meet your company.

"We generally don't find anyone in this area. That's why we can bring the rocks in here. As you have experienced, this area is very dangerous. What are you doing here …? If you don't mind me asking? "

Fearful that a poor response might show weakness, Dylan hesitated before answering. He couldn't think of anything else, so the truth finally prevailed.

"We're lost," Dylan answered. "On top of that, we are being pursued by those filthy little monkeys."

"Those things are nasty. They'll certainly be back, so why don't you come home with us?"

Solo detected uneasiness in his new acquaintances.

"How much worse off can you be than you just were?" he added.

"You think they'll come after us again?" questioned Salah.

"Oh, they'll be back," Solo confirmed.

The tired adventurers huddled together for a moment. They discussed in soft voices whether they should put themselves in the power of these strange people. Dylan looked at JJ, for he realized that they were on her turf, or at least closer to her turf than his. She just shrugged her shoulders as if to say, "Why not?"

After a few more minutes of discussion, JJ stepped forward.

"We'd be delighted to accompany you," JJ said, accepting the invitation. "I, for one, already assumed I was part of the next world. Can we be of any assistance in whatever your expedition is trying to accomplish?"

"Not right now, but maybe later," responded Solo. "The metallic pieces of these rocks are what we are interested in. They're still too hot for us to do anything with now. We'll need to come back another time. Since it will take a while for what's left of these Rangali to regroup, and we're hungry, why don't we eat something?"

Dylan looked at Solo with questioning eyes.

"We'll be finished and long gone by the time they come back," Solo answered to temporarily relieve Dylan's concern.

"You people all know how much you can eat in a sitting. You want to collect three rations for our trip," instructed Solo.

"Visgoth, why don't you go and get the juice and the fraggles."

After Visgoth departed, they collected their provisions. Picking up the already cooked Rangali was an easy task, and shortly everyone was finished. They made themselves comfy while waiting for Visgoth to return.

"How do you do it?" JJ asked Solo.

"Do what?" Solo eagerly replied.

"Bring those giant rocks in."

"We are sworn to secrecy on that one, unfortunately …. Perhaps I can tell you when I get to know you better," Solo added with a wink.

JJ was pondering the ramifications of that statement when Visgoth returned.

He carried a giant skin filled with juice, some cups to drink out of, and a bag full of purple fruit. When he reached the circle of diners, he asked, "Can some of you guys help me with this stuff? Here, take the cups and steady them on the ground while I fill them with juice.

"The fruit is delicious," he added, "but watch out for the seeds. They are very, very hard. There are only two of them in each piece, so it's easy to let your guard down and break your teeth. They are like biting into rocks."

Dylan grabbed a fraggle. It was a round, baseball-sized piece of purple fruit. He had never seen a piece of food so perfect in shape.

"This is really tasty," he remarked after biting in.

"Wait til you try these," Visgoth remarked while holding up a skinned Rangali. "You just bite around the bones, and out here, toss them on the ground. It will send their cohorts a nice message when they come back."

"You're right. These are delicious!" Salah announced as he bit into one of the little cooked monkeys.

The entire group then gorged themselves on the roasted Rangali and fraggles.

While they were eating, Solo moved closer to JJ.

"Why are you so heavily armed?" he asked her.

"I was a prisoner and was rescued by those three gentlemen over there."

Minsk stood up on his hind legs and beat his chest.

"Excuse me .... These four gentlemen. We've had a few other encounters that proved that we needed our weapons. You just saved us from one. It's better to be prepared in this country. Don't you think?"

"But people might mistake you for invaders or bandits. They are everywhere."

"That's why we need to defend ourselves."

"I understand."

"This is the best meal I've had in a while," exclaimed Dylan enthusiastically.

"Make sure you fill up. We've got a lot of distance to cover before dark. We want to be far enough away from those things when we bed down," instructed Solo as he pointed at the carcasses littering the field.

After everyone was thoroughly stuffed, Salah went back to the rock to get their rope. Jason was amazed that he only needed to tug on it in a certain way for it to release.

The group set off for Solo's home. Solo was convinced they were safe from the Rangali as long as they left quickly. They traveled until dusk.

The Sky Miners said that they needed permission to bring "unknowns" into their land. Solo decided to let his four friends leave early to request that permission. He stayed behind.

Solo was very interested in Dylan's tales of his activities at home. When Dylan detected this, he embellished his stories with all kinds of wild imaginary exploits.

Salah, Jason, and JJ listened nearby. They at first rolled their eyes, but then needed to walk away to keep from laughing.

Solo was very interested in JJ. The boys had noticed that whenever she needed anything, he was always there.

When they finally settled down by the fire to sleep, the boys warned Solo not to get too close to her.

"We don't really know her all that well," Jason remarked to Solo, "but I know she knows how to use those weapons she sleeps with. You wouldn't want to surprise her in the night."

Solo positioned himself on the opposite side of the fire from JJ, but he wondered if Jason was trying to keep him safe or just trying to keep him away from her.

Solo instincts incorrectly told him that there was more going on with this group than they were letting on. He was trying to discover their possible motives and secrets to determine if they were a threat. Their camaraderie and activities were such that he never really believed they were just lost teenagers.

Chapter 12 - Fairy

Dylan wondered which of his senses had caused him to awaken. It was still in the very dark part of the night. The embers of the fire were barely glowing orange, but they provided enough light for him to check on everyone. Salah was asleep, cutlass in hand, hugging it almost like a teddy bear. JJ was sleeping on her back, with Minsk curled up on her stomach. Jason was leaning against a large boulder. Solo was snoring very loudly. Everything seemed peaceful.

Dylan knew that if he was in enemy territory and made a noise, he would try to remain still and quiet for as long as possible, hoping the enemy would attribute the noise to anything but him. After all, most noises are caused by things other than a dangerous adversary. Not commonly, but often enough, this is a fatal mistake. He waited for something else to stimulate his senses.

Just as he started to fall back asleep, he was snapped back to consciousness by a sound. It reminded him of a little girl sobbing. It was very high pitched. He didn't think Salah or Jason could produce it, even if they were talking in their sleep.

Dylan crawled over next to JJ. He heard the noise again. He didn't think it came from her, but he had to be sure. Dylan put his ear next to JJ's mouth. Again he heard the sound. It wasn't coming from JJ.

Suddenly, he was flipped onto the ground and had JJ's knife at his throat. She instantly recognized him and opened her mouth to speak. Dylan placed a finger to his lips to indicate silence. JJ caught on and slowly removed herself from on top of Dylan.

Minsk glared at both of them. He had been thrown when JJ jumped up and did not take it too kindly. The whole thing happened so quietly and quickly that Salah, Solo, and Jason remained soundly asleep throughout the entire incident. Salah did, however, tighten his grip on his cutlass.

Dylan, Minsk, and JJ then heard the whimpering again. It seemed to be coming from behind a large rock that was a few yards from where JJ had been sleeping.

Dylan motioned that they should go on opposite sides of the rock. With swords drawn they crept toward, and then around, the rock.

"Put your sword away. She's a nobbly," JJ commanded.

"A what?" inquired Dylan.

"She's a nobbly. And we could be very lucky. Folklore has it that all nobblies have treasures and will gladly give them up if you set them free."

Dylan couldn't believe his eyes. He was staring at an eight inch tall girl with dragonfly wings. She was glowing slightly. Tears were streaming down her face as she looked back and forth between him and JJ.

"We're not going to hurt you," JJ reassured her.

The nobbly broke down sobbing.

"All is lost," she blurted out. "My dort was stolen. I can't even give you my treasure to set me free. I gave it to the kidnapper to get Misha back. He just took my jewels and left, laughing."

JJ paused and thought for a moment.

"Calm down," she soothed. "I'll ask my friends. Maybe we can help you."

By this time, the commotion had awakened the rest of the group. Their wide open eyes all stared at the amazing creature in front of them.

"A fairy princess," Jason mumbled. "Unbelievable!"

"What's a dort?" interrupted Dylan bluntly.

"It's a small furry animal," JJ responded. "Nobblies keep them as pets. They can become quite attached to them."

"Maybe we should help her. We don't know where we are. We don't know where we are going. How can it hurt?" she asked while looking back and forth between the boys.

"Nobblies are usually very secretive and elusive, but they do know these parts well," she lectured.

"Maybe if we help her, she will volunteer some information to help us get out of here," interrupted Dylan.

"Not a very generous attitude," returned JJ.

"You're right. We should help just because we can," replied

an embarrassed Dylan.

"Anything is better than sitting still," a clearly astonished Salah chimed in.

Dylan looked over at Minsk and asked, "Why don't we leave it up to the rat? He has very good survival instincts …. Well?" he questioned as be stared deep into Minsk's eyes.

Minsk scooted over next to the nobbly. She jumped and flew back out of his reach. He looked a little sad, for he was hoping that the nobbly would be his friend. She unexpectedly fluttered back to him.

"Hi, my name is Butah," she said while extending her hand to Minsk.

He shook it with his front paw.

JJ introduced the rest of the group.

"How are we going to get her dort back?" inquired Dylan. "We don't have any idea who took it or where he went."

"Any ideas, Butah?" asked JJ.

"This may sound ridiculous to you, but I can always sense the direction to my Misha when I can't see him. Unfortunately, I can't tell how far away from me he is."

"It's a he?" asked Dylan.

"To tell you the truth, I don't really know. You don't find out til they fully mature. It won't be for a few years," explained Butah.

"Which direction would we head now?" asked JJ.

Butah pointed in the direction where the jungle was thickening.

"We should probably wait til daylight to start," Dylan proposed. "After all, we are not familiar with this area. Solo, would you like to come along? We could use a guide."

"I would very much like to accompany you," he replied while looking at JJ. "I have just recollected some pressing affairs back at home, however. I think I will head back before the others come looking for me. I will be fine traveling in the night. Don't linger too long, for the Rangali will be searching for you. JJ, please reconsider my offer. Your volunteering to help Butah makes me even more enamored. Until next time."

With a wave, a very disappointed Solo disappeared into the woods.

They all looked quizzically at JJ.

"He asked me to go back with him and be his girl," JJ responded to the unasked question on everyone's faces.

"Well at least the rest of us still have a chance now," Dylan mockingly quipped. "After all, that kiss while we were flying brought stars to my eyes."

"Whatever," JJ mumbled under her breath.

Dylan changed the subject.

"Well then, we start tomorrow," he declared while once again assuming command.

"It's a little different from the spy career that I always envisioned for myself, but hardly less interesting. Before we start off, we should at least have an idea of what we are up against. Any dangers we can't overcome out there in the jungle, JJ?"

"I have never been in precisely this part of the world, but I assume that there isn't anything that's too much different than where I come from. Most of the animals are afraid of us. There are probably one or two types of predators unknown to me, but we've all survived this long, haven't we? I think the most danger will come from our own species."

"I agree," Salah concurred. "In my jungle experiences, you had to be aware of the lions, snakes, and other creatures, but the main threat was from humans. I suggest that we be as quiet as we reasonably can be. Unless someone is specifically looking for us, we should be OK. After all, aren't we looking for a little adventure?

"The other thing we should be trying to do is find a way home," continued Salah. "Staying here surely isn't going to help us do that."

Jason and Dylan nodded in agreement.

With a definite goal in mind, they easily went back to sleep.

Chapter 13 - The Rescue

The next morning they ate and prepared themselves for their quest. When everyone was ready, they stared at each other as if waiting for a signal.

"Lead on," Dylan finally requested of Butah to get the ball rolling.

"I'll try not to go too fast," Butah explained. "Since I am out in front and not armed, I will count on you for protection. Flying will make it much easier for me, so let me know when you start getting tired. And one more thing .... Thank you very much for helping me. I was absolutely devastated when Misha and my treasure were stolen. Now, at least there's some hope."

The group followed Butah down a trail through the jungle. As they walked, the canopy of trees above thickened and hung lower, darkening the jungle. They never actually saw anything, but often the bushes moved as some creature was surprised and fled from their path. Sometimes the noises were quite close, and whoever got startled became the butt of jokes until the next occurrence. Surprisingly, whenever Dylan was startled, Minsk was nowhere in sight.

The trail was fairly narrow, so it was difficult to walk side by side. With no one next to them to converse with, everyone drifted off into their own private thoughts.

Jason thought about how unbelievable all of this was. Here he was, one of three teenagers following a fairy through the jungle with a gorgeous blonde fighting machine and a mongoose. Salah and Dylan were a bit more practical and searched the surrounding area for signs of danger. JJ watched the three boys and tried to figure them out.

"How could they, and especially Jason, have survived this long as naïve as they appear to be?" she wondered.

Minsk disappeared in and out of the jungle for short periods of time.

After walking for a few hours through the dense jungle, they came upon a grassy clearing.

As he looked around, Dylan pontificated, "No need to get too exhausted right away. I've read about the great explorers of the past. The ones who survived always conserved their energy. We may need our strength to fight or run. Let's take a break."

They sat down quietly for some time.

"Perhaps we should figure out where we will rest for the evening," suggested Salah. "I, personally, would feel more comfortable up in the trees than on the ground like last night."

"Two questions," JJ chimed in. "How long is an hour? And, would you guys like me to show you how to rig up a way to sleep safely in the trees? We can do it with vines."

"I'm all for it," Salah agreed. "To answer your other question, an hour is one twenty-fourth of a day."

"That's weird, we divide our days into twenty-four periods also," remarked JJ.

"What can we eat?" asked a perennially hungry Dylan.

"There are many fruits and berries just off the trail back there," Butah contributed.

"Let's go get some," JJ suggested.

They followed Butah into the jungle and soon were gorging themselves on the fresh fruit.

When they finished eating, everyone unexpectedly dozed off.

JJ was the first to awaken. They all slept so lightly that her brief rummaging around woke them. When she could see the others were awake, she announced, "I've got some ill feelings about this particular place. Why don't we move and find somewhere that's a little less foreboding?"

Butah led them across the clearing to a spot where the tunnel through the jungle growth started up once again.

"Misha traveled this path," she proclaimed.

Jason became a bit claustrophobic as the overhanging canopy closed further in on him. At times, the trees were almost close enough to jump and touch. To help block this feeling, he searched the growth above him. He was surprised at how much hullabaloo could be made by the unseen creatures overhead and wondered what they looked like.

"Something's wrong with one of my sandals," announced JJ in an annoyed tone. "You guys go on ahead. I'll catch up to you after I fix it. I can just follow the path. My little buddy Minsk, here, will protect me."

"Why don't we just wait?" suggested Dylan.

"It's getting closer to evening. If you scoot ahead, maybe you can find a place to set up camp. After all, I did take care of myself before I met you guys."

"OK," responded Salah. "Don't dawdle to long."

"Dawdle?"

"Waste time!"

"I'll be there before you even miss me."

"I'm going to rest here, too …, even if I'm not welcome," Jason declared while feigning the face of the unwanted.

"OK, you can stay," JJ consented with a big smile.

Everyone laughed and the group split up.

Dylan and Salah set out after Butah. After traveling about half a mile, Butah slowed down.

"I don't have a good feeling about this place," she remarked to Dylan. "Normally I can escape danger just by going up. In this tunnel, I feel trapped. I've been picking up some strange scents. I feel as if we're being follo--"

Before she could finish, two large doglike animals crashed through the side of the tunnel and bounded toward her. She turned and streaked back, passing Dylan and Salah.

All Salah could see were claws and teeth as the first creature knocked him down and slobbered over him. It bent down and bit him in the side of the neck. Salah had a small knife in his belt which he was able to grab, and he slashed the creature in the throat. Blood gushed from it as it squealed and fell off of him. It writhed and squirmed on the ground for an instant before it quivered for the last time.

Dylan had dashed after Butah and the other attacker. When it heard its partner squeal, the beast turned from Butah and sprinted back toward Dylan to come to its friend's aid. Dylan drew his sword, but the hound from hell bounded by him and galloped toward Salah. Dylan turned to follow, but as he did, something grabbed his arm. He wasn't prepared for an attack from that side and let out a sigh of relief when he realized it was JJ.

"Let's go help Salah," Dylan urged as he tried to pull away.

JJ put her fingers to her lips to indicate silence while she whispered into Dylan's ear.

"That beast is owned by someone. I saw a jewel in its ear. People in these parts are very protective of their pets. We need to be very careful. Let's go slowly."

"But Salah!" Dylan protested.

"Those creatures kill very quickly. I fear there is nothing we can do. I'm sure the fight is over one way or the other by now. You really need to trust me on this one."

At that moment, they heard another loud squeal as Salah sank his sword into the other beast.

Butah flitted back toward JJ and Dylan.

"Butah, you need to conceal yourself. Don't let your glow give us away," ordered Dylan, who had already regained his wits from the surprise attack.

"I'll hide up in the branches," whispered Butah. "Can either of you make any animal calls to alert me when to follow?"

"I can howl like a coyote," Dylan proudly revealed.

"I'm not sure what a coyote is," declared JJ. "Do they live around here?"

"You're right. Let's try something else. Remember those large birds we saw as we floated down with our skin? I can imitate those pretty well."

JJ looked at Butah.

"The golden wronks. When you hear their call, look for us. But be careful and approach stealthily. I'm not quite sure what we are getting into."

Jason had basically frozen in shock at the start of the attack. He now started to come out of it, but was still a bit groggy. JJ and Dylan grabbed his arms and led him off the path toward the voices of Salah's captors.

When they got close enough, they heard Salah explaining, "Those creatures attacked me without provocation. One knocked me down and took a good bite out of my neck."

He removed a cloth that he had placed on his neck to stop the bleeding. Blood oozed from the wound. He placed the cloth back to stem the flow.

"I'm sorry, but there was nothing else I could do."

"Daddy, he killed Ruin and Splendor. Don't let him get away with it."

Salah turned and saw a young teenage girl charge toward him and reach up to slap him in the face. Salah instinctively blocked it. He then looked around at the group of large men that accompanied her with the hope that someone would tell him what to do next.

"Son, we are arresting you for the murder of Ruin and Splendor. They have never hurt anyone before. You obviously don't know how to behave around them," accused the largest of the well-armed party that had surrounded Salah.

"Bind his hands and take him away," he ordered.

Three large men walked up to Salah and tied his hands in front of him. They roughly shoved him forward as they started off through the jungle.

Dylan called to Butah. It was amazing how he could imitate the sound of just about any animal with very little practice.

"Spies need to communicate at times," was all he would say when asked about it.

"Looks like we'll need to stop looking for Misha for a while," Dylan explained to Butah. "You probably know how to remain out of sight better than I can tell you. If it wouldn't be too much trouble, I'd like you to come along with us. You can get into places we can't. We'll continue searching for Misha after we get Salah out."

"OK ..., and thanks again for helping me. I don't know what I would do without you guys. I carry this hooded cape which I wear when I don't want to be seen. It's very lightweight. Folded up, it fits around my waste like a belt. I can't fly while wearing it, though, so I guess I'll be walking along with you."

Butah unraveled the cape and put it on. Her face was all that glowed now. She reached to the ground and picked up some dirt to rub on it. It worked.

"Now I'm just like the rest of you," she confidently stated.

"Not exactly," thought Dylan as he looked at her tiny body.

"Minsk!" commanded Dylan.

Minsk glared back at him. The look hit home.

"Sorry for yelling," Dylan apologized.

Minsk and the others were surprised by Dylan's tone.

"That's OK," interrupted JJ. "Don't feel bad about taking charge. You let me command in the battle with the Rangali. Stealth is your area of expertise. We bow to your authority. What's next?"

The look in Minsk's eyes as he stood up on his hind legs showed that he agreed.

"We should follow close enough, but out of sight. If the chance presents itself, we grab Salah. There were ten men, plus the father and daughter. They were rather heavily armed. Unless we take them by complete surprise, I think we should avoid a fight.

"Who rules this land, JJ?"

Before responding, JJ tinkered with her weapons like she was itching for a fight.

"This land is run by little clans like these people," she explained. "They are settling the wild for a larger civilization. They probably pay some form of tribute to a larger group which allows them to govern themselves. These fortune hunters are generally very independent and fierce fighters."

"If you think they fight well, we better be careful," Dylan warned. "Why don't we ask Minsk to tail them and come back and warn us if anyone stops? We don't want to accidentally rear end them. They can't be eternally vigilant. My guess is we will get a chance to spring Salah. Especially if they don't know we are trying."

Minsk bolted from the group and shadowed Salah and his captors from a safe distance. The rest of the group trailed as quietly as possible. When the jungle abruptly ended, Minsk stopped at the edge of the trees. As everyone caught up, they could see Salah and his captors marching across acres of lush green crops toward a well-protected walled-off compound.

"Any idea what they are growing here?" asked Dylan.

"It looks to me like contleberries," JJ answered.

"Can we eat them?"

"You won't die, but you'll have very weird dreams and hallucinations. They are illegal in most of the places I know of."

"So they have drug dealers here too," Dylan mumbled under his breath. "At least I know what we're dealing with now."

"Why don't we grab a bite to eat and a little sleep before it gets dark? Then we can have a closer look around."

As they ate, Dylan asked JJ, "What were those things that attacked Salah?"

"They are lionogs. They are kept as pets and used for hunting. As you can see in Salah's case, they value them more than people."

"You mean these people aren't just crazy?"

"Call them what you want, but their pets are way more important to them than some person they don't know. We should act accordingly. They will probably leave Salah alone until they figure out that he is not connected with one of the more powerful clans around here. We had better rescue him before then."

Dylan looked at JJ and explained, "I do some of my best planning with my subconscious. I'm going to zonk out for about forty-five minutes, and I'll come up with a plan. You're foot seems to be bothering you a bit, so why don't you fix your sandal while I dream up our night mission.

"Butah, before it gets too dark, and they can see your glow, would you mind flying around the compound and telling me what's on the other side?" asked Dylan. "And be careful, you don't want to get eaten by some large bird."

Butah laughed. "Those things will never catch me. Besides we taste bad to all but a few of them, and the nasty ones aren't around here."

Dylan watched as Butah buzzed off toward the compound. He then sat down against a tree and dozed on and off until she returned. He immediately jumped up, completely refreshed as if he'd slept all night.

"How was your trip?" he asked her.

"Easy and interesting."

As Butah fluttered over a bush, Dylan could see smoke rising in the distance behind her from what were probably cooking fires.

"Anyone see you?"

"One can never tell, but I think not."

Just as she finished speaking, a hand rose out of the bushes and grabbed her leg.

"Gotcha!" its owner exclaimed. "We're going to be rich now!"

He was one of the men that had taken Salah away. He was big and broad shouldered with a beard. He was armed with a cutlass.

Another man walked toward Dylan.

"I think my boss will be very interested in seeing you," he said.

Dylan's sword was leaning against a faraway tree. He debated going for it, but the distance was too great.

The man smiled menacingly for he knew he had the advantage over Dylan. It was his last conscious thought. A knife from JJ struck him in the chest, and another hit his counterpart in the same spot. He let go of Butah and hit the ground.

"I don't know how they got so close," exclaimed an embarrassed and startled JJ. "They're not wearing camouflage or anything."

JJ blankly stared at the ground. She couldn't figure out how she had failed on her watch.

"What do you think this is?" Dylan rhetorically asked as he lifted up a weed covered door just behind the bush Butah had been fluttering over.

"It looks to me like an escape tunnel from the compound," continued Dylan. "If they came out of it, maybe we can go in through it. They probably won't miss these two clowns for a while. They were definitely on their own little get-rich-quick mission. Otherwise there would be more of them. We can probably wait til dark, but we should move tonight."

JJ regained her self-confidence when she realized that the men had come out of a tunnel and not eluded her watch.

"Butah, it's time for a debriefing," stated Dylan. "By the way, are you OK? That guy grabbed you pretty hard."

"It hurt my wings a bit when he yanked me down, but I'll be OK. I've been through worse. What's a debriefing?"

"Just tell me what you saw when you flew over the compound."

"What do you mean? Perhaps you should ask me exactly what you want to know."

"Good idea. What sort of defenses do they have?"

"There's a walkway about five feet below the top of the wall for sentries. There were two men walking around on it while I was there. There are parapets to hide behind and shoot arrows or other missiles."

"How many men did you see?"

"Just men?"

"What do you mean?"

"A couple of carriages arrived while I was watching, and eight women got out. It looked like they were dressed to party. They left the carriages outside. They were each pulled by four horses."

"How many men did you see?" Dylan asked again.

"I can't be sure. They were going in and out of the buildings the whole time."

"Give me your best guess."

"Well, I saw twelve different men while I was there. I didn't see the father and daughter though, so there are probably more."

"How many ways into the compound did you see?"

"We are on the backside. There are two doors leading out on this side and a large main gate on the other side where the guests arrived."

"What else is over there?"

"There is a pretty large river a short distance from the front gate. There is a dock and moored to it is a ferryboat that uses a rope and pulleys to cross the river."

"Are there any boats there besides the ferry?"

"No."

"Does it look like the river has a swift current?"

"Yes."

"Which way does it go?"

"To our left, but then it winds around toward the evening sun."

"Is that the direction of Misha?"

"As a matter of fact, it is."

"Did you see Salah?"

"No."

"How many buildings are inside the compound?"

"There is one large fancy building in the center of the compound."

"That's probably the main residence where the father and daughter live," interrupted Dylan. "I'm sorry. Go on," he said.

"There are two other fairly large buildings. The women went into the one on the left. The men did too. Sometimes they came out alone to have a smoke, and sometimes they came out with one of the giggling women and smoked together. There was music coming out of that building. I think there is a party going on."

Dylan looked at JJ. "Is it possible to smoke contleberries?"

"Yes," she replied.

"I hope that's what they're doing because that could make this a whole lot easier. Are the sentries smoking?"

"Yes! And the girls occasionally bring them something to drink."

"Maybe that will be the edge we need," said Dylan excitedly. He walked away and was completely caught up in his thoughts.

Minsk came over and sat next to JJ. They both looked at Dylan who now appeared to doze off while sitting against a tree.

"I wonder what he has in store for us tonight, little fellah," JJ whispered to Minsk.

After about ten minutes, Dylan jumped up and walked over to the group. "Here's my plan," he announced. "Let me know if you guys have any better ideas.

"We send the rat down the tunnel."

Minsk initially glared back at him, but then relaxed.

"He can come back and let us know if we can enter that way. If he's not back in thirty minutes, I'll have to break in some other way. That could also mean that he's been captured, so things could get pretty dicey.

"Since the family lives in the big house, and the party is going on in the building on the left, I will assume Salah is in the structure on the right. We have incomplete information, but that's how most missions are.

"These guys are too strong for us to confront outright, so we are going to need to rely on stealth and surprise to get Salah out.

"When I get into the compound, I'll find Salah and bust him out. I can pick most simple locks, so I should be OK. If there are guards, I may need to improvise."

He then explained the rest of his plan to the group. They were a bit nervous about the risks, but nobody had any better ideas.

"Sounds dangerous. I'll be there if you need me," added JJ.
Minsk was already down the tunnel.

Butah put on her cloak.

"Good luck, you smelly little rat," said Dylan to himself.

Minsk returned quickly and indicated that they should
follow him. Dylan, Jason, and Butah boldly entered the pitch-
black tunnel.

JJ removed her body armor and crept off into one of the dry
irrigation ditches. She was almost invisible as she inched toward
the compound.

"Should I open my cloak for some light?" Butah asked.

"It's more important that we arrive undetected. Remember,
if you bump into anything, don't cry out. We're operating in
silent mode from now on."

The going in the tunnel was slow at first. They were totally
blind in the darkness. Jason reached out his hand to feel for
Dylan. He felt for his back and placed his hand there.

"Don't freak. It will be over soon," he kept repeating to
himself as he felt his insides ready to explode from the terror of
the blackness.

Another thought almost shoved him over the edge.

"What if this isn't Dylan I'm following?" he asked himself.

"Come on. Get a grip," his almost paralyzed mind finally
commanded.

Dylan could feel Jason's hand and sense Butah behind him.
The ceiling was so low at first that they had to crouch down
while they inched along. It eventually rose to where they could
stand upright. After that, Dylan moved with much more
confidence. As long as he could feel the walls, the support beams
every ten steps gave him some measure of his progress.

Dylan then sensed something unfamiliar. The feel of one
leg, then another, rising and falling from his hand was petrifying.
He stopped moving for a second, but was relieved when he
figured out what it was.

"Minsk is messing with me again."

He took a swipe at where he figured Minsk would be, but
caught nothing but air. Dylan was puzzled, but while he was in
"mission mode," he was very difficult to rattle. He had trained
himself well.

He next felt the same weird sensation on his neck. He felt it on his back. Then all over his body. Dylan was terrified, but remained calm. It couldn't be Minsk, but what was it?

"Butah, are you still back there?" he whispered.

"Yes I am," she returned in a soft voice.

"Can you spare us a little light for a second?" Dylan inquired.

"OK. I'll open my cloak a bit."

In the dim light, Dylan could see six-inch centipede-like creatures crawling all over his body. The entire area was infested with them.

He looked around for his companions. Minsk was relaxing on the ground with two of the creatures sticking out of his mouth. He was thoroughly enjoying his snack. The fact that Minsk was eating them meant that they weren't poisonous, at least to a mongoose.

A few of the vermin were crawling on Jason, who was calmly trying to convince himself that nothing could freak him out as badly as the lionogs had.

Dylan noticed there were no creatures up ahead, so he motioned for the others to follow as he brushed himself off and hurried forward in the tunnel. Jason and Butah happily obliged. Minsk lingered while enjoying his feast.

When Dylan was confident there were no more centipedes, he turned to Butah.

"Those creatures seem to have a nest back there. I think we'll be OK now. You can close up your cloak."

She did, and the tunnel immediately became pitch-dark again. Dylan felt Minsk brush past his leg as he once again assumed the lead. There were no more insects in the tunnel. They crept on past twenty more support beams. Dylan could now see the silhouette of Minsk's legs as he paced back and forth across the sliver of light at the base of a door.

He stealthily approached the door.

"Hopefully there are no booby traps," he thought.

When Dylan reached the door, he placed his ear against it and listened.

"You now owe me 25 crabitzes of gold, Mr. Prisoner," a voice stated with a laugh.

"I guess I'm not very lucky today," Dylan heard Salah's familiar voice respond, "but my luck's about to change."

"Come here," Dylan heard one voice say to the other. Dylan heard footsteps walking closer to the door he was listening at.

"Those two drunken idiots went looking for a nobbly. Like they actually exist. We're going to make our fortune in a much more realistic way ..., with this idiot prince. He already owes us more money than we can make in a lifetime. He's the worst gambler I've ever seen."

"It's kind of sad, but we may end up protecting him to get our money" responded the other voice.

Dylan smiled.

The voices again addressed Salah. It was very difficult to tell them apart.

"Are you ready for another round?"

"Remember, when I win back my money, the bet is money against my freedom," Salah stated.

"Money to be paid within the month."

"Agreed," said Salah. "Prince Waleh never welshes."

"And remember, our agreement is separate from anything you might have with our boss."

"We will find you if you don't deliver," the voices threatened together.

"As I said, my word is good. But remember, when I win you must let me free, or one of my wizards will cast a spell on you."

Dylan was intrigued by the conversation. Salah maintained his wits in a pinch. He was trying to lose as much money as possible so that his captors couldn't afford to kill him.

Apparently, the two men that came looking for Butah were very drunk, so nobody would miss them for a while. A plan began to unfold in Dylan's head. He whispered it to his companions.

"We got the nobbly," Dylan screamed. "Come and help me with the door."

"Stay by the prisoner," one of the voices said to the other.

Footsteps came toward the door. Dylan stood at the door and held Butah in front of his face with one hand. She had her cloak off and was glowing brightly. In his other hand, Dylan held an unlit torch that he had removed from a pile by the door.

The guard opened the door.

"You really did see a nobbly," the guard happily proclaimed.

He immediately began thinking of how he would spend his share of the treasure.

Butah took off.

"Help, it's getting away," exclaimed Dylan.

Both guards' eyes were glued on the fairy.

Minsk ran past the guard by the door and jumped on the other's face. The guard grabbed Minsk to throw him off. Salah immediately grasped the situation. While Dylan clobbered one guard with his torch, Salah picked up his chair. The other guard, who was bewildered by Butah's light and Minsk, did not even sense it coming. It was all over in a matter of seconds.

"Thanks guys," Salah said as he stepped over the two guards to shake Dylan's hand. He gave a salute to Jason and Butah.

"Nice to see you again," said Dylan. "Nice job ..., losing all that money trying to get the guards to protect you."

"I was proud of that one myself."

"These guys lack training. They didn't even blindfold me before they brought me here, so I was able to scout out the place."

"What did you see?"

"We are in the cellar of the storage building. They keep everything in this building. Weapons, harvested contleberries, food, tools .... Everything! There is a main house that the family and their servants live in. The third house is like an army barracks. I counted fifteen different faces coming in and out of there before they put me down here."

"That's too many to take in a fight," declared Dylan, "but that's not what we plan to do."

"How are we getting out?"

Dylan explained his plan to Salah. Salah was pretty sure it would work. He was especially sure after he heard that the guards were partying.

Salah picked up his cutlass and dagger on the way out.

"Maybe I'll take a souvenir," he whispered as he grabbed a gold-handled dagger from one of the unconscious guards.

They crept up the stairs to ground level. The rest of the building was empty. They had already dispatched four of the guards, two in the cellar and two by the bush. That brought the number of guards they were aware of down to around a dozen. Luckily, the party would give them cover until morning.

Butah took off and flew over the wall to where JJ was supposed to be hiding. She looked for her, but couldn't find her.

"I hope she didn't get caught," Butah thought as she landed on a low tree branch.

Butah was startled as she felt a couple of fingers over her mouth. She turned quickly and saw JJ behind her.

"Everything going OK so far?" JJ asked.

Butah nodded.

"JJ's really good," Butah thought. "I was right on top of her, and I couldn't see her."

JJ walked up to the guard near the carriages and smiled.

"Hi, pretty lady," he said, admiring JJ. "I haven't seen you before."

"And you won't again," JJ avowed as she labeled him with a right cross.

JJ quickly unhooked the horses from the carriages.

"Help! Help!" she yelled as she stampeded the horses away from the compound.

The guards in various states of drunkenness ran out of the gate and followed the horses. JJ continued screaming and chased the horses close to the river. When they turned to race along the banks, JJ headed straight for the river and dove in. She swam toward the ferry raft.

The partiers didn't notice that as they ran out of the gate, Dylan, Jason, Salah, and Minsk were right behind them. When the guards pursued the horses, the jail breakers turned the other way and ran toward the raft. They saw JJ rapidly swimming toward them when they arrived.

"Howdy handsome," she said to Salah with her ingratiating smile as he helped her dripping body climb on board.

Salah smiled back and gave her a long hug.

Dylan grabbed the rope and slowly moved the raft across the river. Halfway across, one of the guards spotted the escape. He ran over and began pulling the raft back.

Salah took out his cutlass and hacked at the rope.

"Looks like we're in for a ride," yelled Dylan as the rope began to fray. His eyes sparkled at the thought of another escapade.

"I hope not too soon," yelled Butah.

"Why's that?" asked Dylan.

"That's why!" cried Butah while pointing at the shore.

Dylan turned and saw the girl that had Salah imprisoned running out of the house screaming, "Daddy, daddy, please help me fix it. It's sooo embarrassing."

They all looked back at a bald girl in the distance, crying and whining like a baby.

"Body hair makes flying difficult, so we use a potion to remove it. I guess it works on heads too," Butah said with a big grin. "On the way to get JJ, I put some in the little brat's hats. I guess I'm not one of her friends now."

The rafters all smiled from ear to ear.

Eventually Salah's hacking was rewarded. The ferry rope broke with a jolt, and the raft began speeding toward its unknown destination. They had no way to control its direction. It spun as it glided with the current. When it got close to shore, the swirling waters pushed it back to the center. The current picked up speed as the river narrowed. The shore line rose as they made their way down the river, and pretty soon the raft was rocketing through a canyon. As the speed of the river increased, so did the volume of spray that soaked the riders.

They merrily laughed and shouted, enjoying themselves like they were on a carnival ride.

The moment was interrupted by a roar in the distance.

"I don't like the sound of this," warned Salah as the roar got louder and louder.

As they sped faster and faster through the canyon, a feeling of hopelessness engulfed everyone on the raft.

"The fates must really hate us," yelled Dylan over the roar.

"Somebody likes you," countered JJ. "You're still alive, aren't you?"

JJ collected her thoughts. "I'm getting sick of saying goodbye to you guys," she exclaimed. "Soooo ..., see you at the bottom!"

Jason stared over the edge.

"Oh @#8#!" he yelled as he and everyone else tried to jump clear of the raft.

Butah had it easy. She calmly flitted off the raft as it tumbled over a forty foot waterfall and crashed into the water below.

Chapter 14 - Larnerghouls

For Jason, the water was deep enough for a safe splashdown. He felt the force of the raft smashing into the water close by and was thankful it missed him. He hoped it missed the others as well. As he gasped for air in the moonlight, he saw Dylan and JJ surface and simultaneously yell out, "Salt water, we're near the sea!"

Jason then looked for the others. Salah and Minsk were already swimming for the shore. Satisfied that everyone had survived, Jason swam after them.

When they finally reached the shore, they were too exhausted to move. They woke up the next morning.

Dylan was the first to come back to his usual self.

"Everyone has their weapons. That's a relief, since we once again find ourselves in a strange land. What dangers are lurking here, JJ?"

"We try to avoid these uncharted coastal areas at all costs," she answered. "There are rumors of dragons and sea monsters that inhabit these shores. Many people that stray here don't return. We were extremely lucky to wake up this morning. I suggest we find a place away from the beach and make a secure camp. This place makes the hair on the back of my neck stand up."

"Can I see?" asked Salah with a wry smile.

JJ scowled back and then ignored him.

"I get the creeps here, too," Dylan threw in. "I can't quite put a handle on why."

"Have you ever been here before, Butah?" JJ asked.

"Remember I told you there were a few creatures that eat our kind. They live around here. I am starting to pick up their scent. I am going to stick very close to you guys if you don't mind," she said as she walked over and stood next to Jason.

Jason felt a little pride when he realized that someone was

coming to him for protection. When he realized he might actually need to defend her, a minor wave of panic overcame him.

Salah was fatigued from his captivity. He decided that he would search the surrounding area for a place to set up camp and rest. Minsk walked over by his side, which everyone guessed meant he wanted to stay with him.

Dylan, JJ, and Jason thought the beach would be the best place to find food. They went off for a stroll. Butah wanted no part of the beach and flitted over by Salah.

Warm breezes brushed against their faces, and the smell of the sea enveloped them as they explored the shoreline.

"It's not Cancun, but you wouldn't know it from here," exclaimed Dylan.

The relaxing atmosphere relieved their worries, and they began to frolic down the beach. They threw sand and anything they could find at each other. After the previous few days, it felt good to goof off and act like kids again.

When they tired of throwing things, Jason turned and gazed out toward the sea. The sun was very bright, so he squinted and put his hand to his forehead. As the horizon came into focus, he could see a school of what looked like dolphins playing in the surf.

"That sure looks like fun," he thought.

He continued watching the dolphins as he wandered down the beach daydreaming. Reality intruded when he tripped, stumbled, and barely caught himself to avoid falling. He looked down at his feet. He had tripped in a hole, but it wasn't really a hole. It looked like a large footprint of the mother of all birds.

Dylan came over when he saw Jason staring at the ground.

"I think we better play a little defense here," he counseled. "Who knows if that thing is coming back? Have you ever seen anything capable of making these tracks, JJ?"

"Nope, but I told you there were stories," she answered.

Dylan went over and lifted up JJ's hair from the back of her neck.

"Just checking," he joked as she shoved him away, "to see how much danger we're in."

"I can see I shouldn't use that expression again," she retorted.

"Not to change the subject, but I wonder what it looks like in the flesh," pondered Jason.

"You may not want to see the answer to that question," Dylan answered. "I think we should get out of here and shore up our defenses. We should find somewhere safer to camp than last night. It's not clear that we are in immediate danger. This thing could be an herbivore after all."

"I don't think so," cautioned Jason as they came around a bend in the shoreline.

Suddenly the carefree attitude was sucked out of the moment.

Both boys and JJ stared at the lumps of fresh flesh strewn along the beach. It was evident that some creature had recently been torn apart by another much nastier than itself.

"Let's look for tracks leaving the scene," suggested Dylan.

The tracks leaving the scene were of a different nature than the ones Jason had tripped on. In fact, there were no tracks at all.

A mysterious sense of bewilderment overcame the group.

"Maybe it was a giant crocodile and it swam away," suggested Jason.

"Possible," responded Dylan, "but then we should see its path back to the water."

They were suddenly startled by a loud shriek. They jerked around toward its source.

Coming down the beach about ten feet off the ground were two of the ugliest creatures Jason had ever seen. They looked like giant lizards with wings.

He froze while staring at their gleaming fangs.

"Follow me!" JJ screamed as she sprinted toward the jungle.

Dylan grabbed Jason's arm.

"Follow JJ! Head for the trees! Their wings are too big to fly in there!" he yelled.

They both ran for the trees and managed to arrive about five feet ahead of the harpies.

"I could smell their putrid breath," exclaimed Jason between pants.

"At least you're alive to say that. Our big friend over there wasn't so lucky. I wonder how many of those things tore him apart," JJ threw in between gasps.

"I think if we stay among the trees, we are probably safe

from those monsters," she added.

Jason looked up and could see the beasts circling high above the treetops.

"You creeps just had breakfast," he said even though there was no way they could hear him. "Lunch is going to have to wait a while."

"Let's go back and warn the others," commanded Dylan.

The three former beach combers were in a heightened state of awareness as they wandered through the trees on their way back to camp. Every sound, however slight, had them glancing in its direction and jumping quickly the opposite way.

"Who knows what other monsters might be lurking here?" Jason asked himself.

About half way back, the tension eased a bit. It had been a good fifteen minutes with no assault from anything lurking in the woods. Suddenly, Minsk jumped out from a tree branch and landed on Dylan's head. Dylan screamed and vaulted into the air.

Minsk jumped off and sped into the woods.

Salah, who had been coming up the path looking for Minsk had seen the whole incident and burst out laughing.

"'Brave warrior … dies of heart attack … caused by rat!' the headline … would read," Salah blurted out between his laughing jags.

"I'm going to get that rat!" screamed Dylan in a very loud and irritated voice.

"Calm down, Dylan, I'm sure he was just messing with you," soothed Jason, who was getting comfortable with his role as peacemaker. "After all you have been rather hard on him."

Salah regained his composure and blurted out, "If you could have seen the look on your face …. If a picture is worth a thousand words, then that was worth two thousand. You're generally not so jumpy. What happened to you guys?"

After calming down and resuming his normal "in command of the situation" attitude, Dylan related their story of finding the ripped-apart beast and their narrow escape from the flying devils from hell.

"We should find a cave where we can rest up," Dylan suggested. "We could build a gate of thorn bushes to prevent entry by anyone or anything we don't want."

"I saw some hills when I was looking around this morning,"

Salah volunteered. "Perhaps we can find one there. The jungle goes right up to them, so I don't think we need to worry about your flying friends."

"We really should post a sentinel at night," Dylan declared. "The other thing we should do is figure out how to get out of this stupid place and go home."

"Even too much adventure for you?" Salah said with a laugh.

He knew Dylan was just shaken by his most recent encounter.

"We should keep moving," JJ suggested. "We need to find Misha before the trail grows cold. We can't stay here too long. As soon as we recover our strength, we should resume our quest."

Dylan and Salah led the move toward the hills in search of a secure cave. Even though the flying monsters could not reach them in the forest, the strange new place was filled with a feeling of trepidation.

Who knew what else was around?

When they reached the hills, the supply of caves was abundant. They checked out many, but none was large enough. As they entered and explored the caves, their drawn cutlasses at least partially notched down their feeling of terror.

Just as everyone was about to call it quits after a full day of tromping around, Dylan spotted another dark shadow along the base of the hills. It was almost totally invisible behind the jungle growth.

As he started to chop at the growth with his machete, a voice rang out from the darkness inside.

"Hey! Don't do that!" it commanded.

A startled Dylan jumped back.

"Who's there?" he inquired.

"My name is Jagmire," said the small man emerging from the cave. He wore a tattered tunic and had a long grey beard. He was about four feet tall.

"I've been watching you guys today. This is my land, and I wanted to see if you meant any harm. I am generally a sound judge of character. I think I can trust you people. Perhaps we can help each other."

"How so?" asked Dylan.

As a curious Salah wandered over, Dylan could see that Jagmire was a bit apprehensive.

"Don't mind him, we think he's ugly too," quipped Dylan as he looked at Salah.

"Sorry," apologized Dylan, "it was too easy."

Salah fashioned a phony smile.

"Sorry to interrupt a family quarrel," said Jagmire with a mischievous grin, "but here's what I need. Those dragons that chased you down the beach are called larnerghouls. They live at the top of these mountains. I need one of their eggs to make some medicine that can help me stay alive. I will help you go wherever you want if you get an egg for me."

"How are we supposed to do that?" Dylan inquired.

"If you got your little furry buddy up to their nests at the top of the mountain, I think he could steal an egg. Two would be even better. His kind is very good at that kind of work."

"His kind? What exactly do you think he is?"

"You don't know?"

"Perhaps you can tell me," answered Dylan. "All I know is that he's a smelly little rat."

"Well, let's just say that you better be sure that he is not in a situation where he can benefit from harming you."

"He's too small."

"If he is who I think he is, he's got influence and powers that you won't believe. As long as he needs you though, I wouldn't worry about it. I might not be …."

Jagmire gasped for breath and crumpled to the ground.

"Please get me my medicine!" he pleaded.

"Are you going to be all right?" inquired Dylan as he supported the old man.

"I'll be fine, but please start soon. My time is limited."

"It's getting close to dark. Are those creatures more active at night or in the daytime?" asked Dylan.

"They sleep at night, but the climbing is a lot more difficult then."

"We can handle it," Dylan assured him.

"When you get close to the summit," Jagmire continued, "there is a ledge that encircles the mountain. Getting to the ledge is relatively easy. Then comes the hard part. There is an overhang above the ledge that prevents easy access to the top. It sticks out pretty far. The dragons feel very safe above it. You guys seem pretty active. I think you can overcome that obstacle."

"We'll at least give it a try. Let me go back and get the others, and we'll get started."

"Don't you think we should ask Jason? And JJ?" asked Salah.

"Why? I know JJ will want to come. Jason would rather die with us than perish alone. I've had a few conversations with him along those lines. This is a chance for another adventure. I think we can be up there and back in a couple of hours. The mountain really isn't that high. It only looks that way because it is the tallest thing around."

"Jagmire?" Dylan inquired.

The old man looked up.

"Are there any other creatures we need to worry about?"

"None, other than a few snakes. They can give you a nasty bite, but they aren't poisonous. You saw what happens to other large creatures that wander nearby. In a weird way, the dragons sort of protect me."

"How many of them are there?"

"For unknown reasons, only four seem to live here at once. When the little ones get to a certain age, the numbers over four are chased off."

"Do you ever see them flying at night?"

"I see shadows from time to time, but it's hard to tell what they are."

"Get your medicine recipe and the directions out of here ready. We'll be back shortly with your egg."

"Please take these with you," Jagmire insisted as he stumbled back into his cave. "You may need them."

He emerged slowly dragging a battle axe and a couple of spears. The exertion took a toll on what little strength he had left.

"Remember, I want you back alive, too," Jagmire said as he handed Salah the weapons.

"Thank you," said Salah as he accepted the gifts.

"Hopefully, we won't need to use them," Dylan threw in.

"Hopefully," Jagmire repeated.

When Dylan and Salah returned to their camp, they discussed the situation with JJ, Jason, and Butah. They all agreed that it was risky trusting their new acquaintance so soon, and they really wanted to get after Misha. In the end, though, they couldn't refuse someone who needed their help.

Butah revealed that although she would like to come along, the only thing she saw herself doing was becoming a meal for the larnerghouls. Unless anyone knew how she could specifically help, she preferred to hide in the jungle.

The group agreed.

"Do you understand what they want of you?" Jason asked Minsk.

Minsk responded with a big twinkle in his eye.

"Everyone come here," commanded Dylan. "Sorry to sound so bossy again, but I have a plan. There's a ledge that encircles the mountain about eight feet from the top. The problem is an overhang above it that protects the creatures from assault from below. I obviously haven't seen it first hand, but from Jagmire's description, it should afford us with some protection if the beasts start getting nasty. When we get to the top, we'll have to improvise, but I think Minsk should be able to climb up there and get us an egg."

Salah and JJ nodded their approval as they finished preparing their tools. They then ate the food that Jagmire had given them and set off on their quest.

The shape of the rock formation that the larnerghouls lived atop was unique and easy to find. When they arrived at its base, they paused for a moment. The jagged rocks at the bottom conjured up a primitive feeling of fear. Jason could sense uneasiness in his fellow adventurers as they prepared to start their journey to the summit.

The feeling disappeared when they started moving. Most of the way could be climbed without a rope. Even so, Dylan insisted they use a safety rope in case anyone slipped in the darkness.

The climbing was for the most part easy. When they neared the ledge, Dylan scaled the last tricky section of the mountain alone.

"He did that quicker than the wall at school," Jason remarked to himself.

When he reached the ledge, Dylan attached a rope which let the others climb up more easily. JJ went next, followed by Salah who had insisted on bringing the battle axe and two spears that he was given by Jagmire along with his cutlass and knives.

"Although the main plan is stealth, we might need to fight our way out," Salah argued.

Dylan thought Salah was bringing along the extra weapons just because he thought they made him look macho. Quick and light was Dylan's philosophy for this mission, but in the end he really couldn't dispute Salah's reasoning.

Jason came last.

"It's a good thing it's too dark to see down," Jason thought as he struggled up to the ledge.

As the other boy's yanked Jason up onto the ledge, he accidentally shoved off one of the many large rocks resting there. The rock crashed down the mountain and vanished into the night. Jason was relieved that he didn't follow the same path.

JJ wandered out of sight of the boys as she searched along the ledge for a gap in the overhang.

Without warning, a huge shadow approached the ledge. The boys dove behind some of the enormous rocks there as a blast of flames headed their way.

"Stay apart. Maybe it will confuse him, and he won't know what to aim for!" commanded Dylan. "Make sure you stay close enough to dive behind one of the rock piles."

After a few near misses Dylan yelled out. "It seems to take about thirty seconds between blasts. Geez …! Nobody told me we'd be facing this kind of firepower. At least the overhang isn't letting him get too close."

The boys scrambled back and forth across the ledge. This larnerghoul was much bigger than the ones on the beach. He seemed to be working his way closer with each blast. Occasionally, his wings scraped against the overhang, and he tumbled toward the ground. Unfortunately, he always recovered in plenty of time.

"It looks like he's gliding in for the kill," yelled Salah. "He knows he can't burn us while we're behind the rocks. His wings aren't going to hit the overhang this time. Time for a little hand to hand combat."

The dragon let out a blast of fire when it was within range of the ledge. As the smoke dissipated, the beast continued forward and landed on the ledge, apparently surprised that its prey wasn't charred to a crisp. When it roared to try and unnerve the boys, Salah jammed a spear into its mouth. It hit home. A warm liquid sprayed out of the dragon's mouth. Its head collapsed onto the ledge. Its eyes stared malevolently at Salah as it slid back into the darkness.

The dragon shrieked as Minsk jumped on its neck and bit in.

Jason's stomach tied in a knot as he saw Minsk go over the ledge riding the dragon. As it fluttered in the black night sky, he could barely make out its dodging and weaving maneuvers as it tried to rid itself of Minsk.

"Now's our chance," whispered Dylan, still under control. "Keep quiet. We don't need to attract anymore unwanted attention. We don't know what his buddies are up to."

Dylan found a spot where the dragon's wings had broken through the overhang and climbed up. He signaled for Jason to join him, and to bring Salah's battle axe.

"Good gosh," Jason said to himself.

Then he realized that his blood was barely pumping. He had calmly weathered the storm. He realized he was now more afraid that the others would call him a chicken than he was of the dragon. He was becoming a warrior. He climbed up.

JJ, who was still busy searching for another way up, had missed the entire fight with the larnerghoul.

Salah was very tired from his ordeal in captivity, not to mention their recent encounter with the dragon. He stayed put at just about the spot where he had rammed his spear into the dragon's mouth.

"This is better than old Sloany's barn, eh?" Dylan remarked in a low whisper.

"If you say so," Jason said while trying to hide his terror. It was the unknown waiting that was stressful, not the battle. He had to fight off the panic that was creeping back into his soul when he realized that a future encounter with the larnerghouls was forthcoming.

They crept toward the larnerghouls' nest. It was about a hundred paces from the edge. As Dylan and Jason stealthily inched forward, Jason was overwhelmed by the smell of rotting flesh. He was surprised he hadn't perceived it until now. The odor was so strong that he could barely tolerate it.

When they reached a spot where they could see into the nest, they spotted two fast asleep dragons.

"They must be sound sleepers to snooze through all that commotion," Jason thought.

He immediately became a little braver.

The dragons nest was shaped like a bowl with waist-high sides. It was about twenty feet across. The two dragons occupying it were sleeping head to tail on either side of the eggs with their wings folded up. Their loud snoring was another thing Jason's terror had not allowed his senses to pick up.

"I'm sure Dylan noticed it," he said ashamedly to himself.

Dylan grabbed Jason's arm and pulled him over to the side of the nest where the space between the two dragons was largest. They paused every few seconds to listen for changes in the dragons' breathing that would indicate they were waking up.

Dylan quietly lowered himself down the wall to the bottom of the nest. Jason handed him the axe and proceeded down the wall as well. He made a slight noise when he hit the bottom. Both boys froze to see if there were any changes in the dragons' breathing. There weren't. Dylan handed Jason back the axe.

As they snuck past the nearer dragon's head, they were so close they could feel his hot breath as he exhaled. It was almost more than Jason could take. He felt like he was going to explode.

Then something happened that almost ruined the expedition. One of the dragons passed gas. It made a very loud rumbling sound and produced a ghastly smell.

Dylan turned to Jason with an outrageously disgusted look on his face and did all he could to prevent himself from bursting out laughing.

Jason remembered Dylan's lecture about missions being compromised by the most unexpected things. "But a dragon fart?" Even he was having trouble containing himself.

Dylan raised his hand, and they both stopped moving for a good five minutes to regain self-control. They could not look at each other.

The dragons continued their rhythmic breathing, indicating they were still asleep.

As the joke wore off, the boys quickly returned to "mission mode." They crept over to the eggs. There were four eggs about the size and shape of footballs with rounded ends. They were light in color, but the exact color was difficult to discern in the darkness. The eggs were covered with glowing red spots that looked like small LED lights. Dylan motioned for Jason to guard against the closer dragon waking up. Jason, armed with the axe, positioned himself near its neck. He turned to watch as Dylan carefully removed two eggs from the nest. As he picked up each egg, the red spots glowed brighter and eerily illuminated the sleeping dragons until the lights disappeared into Dylan's backpack.

As Dylan finished closing his backpack, all hell broke loose. Jason turned as he heard a hideously painful wailing sound behind him. A third larnerghoul had sneaked up behind him and was thrashing around with a knife stuck in one of its eyes. Its wings threw up clouds of dust as it fluttered across the ground.

Jason heard JJ's now familiar voice shrieking, "Strike! Strike! Strike!"

He raised his axe and severed the head of the now stirring larnerghoul in front of him. Blood splattered over the nest when he connected. The axe was sharp, and the deceased dragon barely moved as its head rolled away from its neck. After struggling for a while, the dragon with the knife in its eye finally managed to take off. The other previously sleeping dragon followed it into the night sky.

"They will probably be back. Let's move," commanded Dylan.

"We need to get his teeth," JJ argued before grabbing the axe and quickly hacking out a few. "These things have very special properties."

Dylan, JJ, and Jason scrambled out of the nest. They hurried back to Salah, their strength renewed by the adrenaline rush of the battle.

JJ handed the bloody axe down to Salah who remarked, "It looks like it did its job. Did you get the eggs?"

"Two of them," Dylan answered.

Then he went into lecture mode.

"We have almost completed a very dangerous mission. It is no time to relax. We are not finished until we get back to Jagmire alive. Try to remain focused on the way down ..., so we all make it."

Jason took a few deep breaths as did JJ.

"Where did you meet this guy?" she remarked under her

breath as she walked past Jason.

"And by the way, thanks, JJ," Dylan remarked. "We never heard that third dragon show up. We owe you one."

"Let's not go there. We're all on the same team," she countered. "Now let's move before they come back."

The climb down through the now familiar terrain was far easier because the ropes were already attached. They kept looking uneasily over their shoulders, but none of their new adversaries reappeared. They quickly made it to the bottom. Unbelievably, Minsk was waiting for them. Apparently he got the better of the larnerghoul, but nobody knew for sure.

Jagmire was ecstatic to see them.

"Did you get the eggs?" he inquired eagerly.

Dylan didn't say anything, but took his backpack off and set it on the ground. The eggs produced a slight glow as he opened it.

Jagmire's face lit up as he took the eggs out.

"You don't know how much this means to me," he thankfully declared. "I will show you where my boat is. It is all yours. You can have any of my other possessions you want."

"Your happiness is reward enough," Jason said graciously. "Apparently our journey takes us inland, so we won't need your boat, but thanks for the offer just the same."

Everyone stared at Jason, stunned by the leadership tone in his voice.

"We may have created a monster," Dylan remarked to Salah. Both he and JJ agreed.

Jason didn't see their smiles for he was preoccupied. He had spotted a version of a fiddle among Jagmire's possessions. He picked it up and asked Jagmire if he would play it.

"Most certainly," Jagmire responded.

He played a few lively tunes, but gradually the music shifted toward the softer sounds of a violin. The tired warriors drifted off into a well-deserved sleep.

When they awoke the next morning, a strong, handsome young man was tending the fire. Jagmire was nowhere to be seen, but his clothes were on the ground next to the young man.

JJ jumped up and drew her cutlass. She threateningly approached the young man.

"What have you done with Jagmire?" she demanded.

"Nothing," he calmly replied.

"Then where is he?" she badgered while pointing at his scattered clothes.

The noise of their encounter had awakened everyone, and they all stared at JJ and the young man.

"He is right here."

"Where?"

"Here! I am Jagmire!"

"How can this be?" JJ asked incredulously. "Prove it!"

"I don't know how I can, other than by recounting what has happened between us over the last day," he responded. The young man then described their adventures in detail, convincing everyone that he was indeed Jagmire, and that the eggs had done their special job.

"Wow," was all anyone could say when Jagmire had finished convincing them the eggs had rejuvenated him.

They then invited Jagmire to come along on their quest for Misha. He thanked them for asking, but politely refused. He explained that the "magic" that allowed him to keep rejuvenating only worked near the mountain that the dragons lived on.

"I am very tired from the renewal process," Jagmire continued. "I thank you all for your monumental efforts. Good luck on your journey. You may keep the axe. I must rest."

With that statement, Jagmire disappeared back into his cave.

"Well, I guess other matters are calling," Dylan proclaimed. "Everyone looks well rested, so why don't we eat and then pack up and resume our quest."

Chapter 15 - A New Friend

They spent the next few days trekking through uncivilized territory. Butah was relieved that she was no longer picking up the scent of the dragons and flitted happily along as they walked. She was euphoric that they were again moving toward her Misha. The terrain varied between forests and plains. Fortunately, the forests had trails, and there was no need to hack their way through them.

Jason was a bit disappointed that nothing so far pointed in the direction of home.

"At least we're moving," he thought. "Something's eventually bound to come up."

As the sun moved directly overhead on the fourth day, the search for Misha took them toward a small village. They stopped at its outskirts.

"If I get a chance, I'm going to pick up some new body armor," JJ announced. "I lost mine when we rescued Salah."

"We might as well get a good meal, too," suggested Salah.

"Look at the sign," JJ exclaimed. "They have fratoglob fights here. I always wanted to see one."

"The fights or the fighters," Butah chimed in.

"They generally are quite cute," a blushing JJ admitted, "but the sport is good too. It's the brave warrior versus the evil fratoglob. All of the fratoglobs in the ring have killed people or livestock. They are evil."

"I'll pass," declared Jason. "Even though we were defending ourselves, or hungry, I've seen enough creatures killed recently."

"I'm in for the fights," announced Dylan. "Spies need to expand their cultural background, you know."

"Being a warrior, I'm always interested in new techniques," Salah added.

"Why don't we meet on the other side of town in about four hours," suggested Jason.

"I'll see you over there," Butah responded. "I can't go into town anyway. Everyone will try to capture me for my treasure."

"Sounds good to me," Dylan agreed. "Four hours should be more than enough time to watch the fights."

"Minsk, do you want to come with me?" Jason offered.

Minsk walked over to Jason. They split off and went to the marketplace. The others went to the fights.

Jason could hear relaxing music as they approached the market. It was as if they had been transported back to medieval times. People were hawking every type of food imaginable with some of it being in the not-quite-dead-yet category. Magicians performed tricks, clowns juggled, and musicians played weird double flute shaped instruments that produced a wonderfully tranquil sound.

"If it wasn't for the smell, this would be a delightful place," Jason thought.

He walked along trying to figure out what to eat. He didn't mind being separated from the others. He was starting to gain confidence in his ability to take care of himself. After all, he had slain a larnerghoul.

In his mind, the fratoglob fights were similar to bullfights. He had no interest in watching animals get killed, even nasty fratoglobs.

His private thoughts were disturbed by a noisy crowd that encircled something to his left. He heard a voice plead, "Gentlemen, please leave me alone. I mean you no harm."

"You are an evil wizard from Blarkorov. Your kind can only come here with your master," an angry voice shouted.

"We should stone you right here," threatened another.

"I just needed some medicine. I am an old man."

"Take your curses, and get out of here," said one of the larger members of the crowd while knocking down the old man. The others joined in and started kicking him.

What could he do? He felt sorry for the man. There were so many in the crowd, and the old man was alone. It was just he and Minsk.

He remembered Dylan telling him, "In a mob situation, you never confront the crowd head on. Always try to deflect their force. Agree with them, and try to do an end run around them."

"What's going on?" Jason asked the closest mob member.

"He knows we can kill him if he comes to town without his master," the man angrily replied.

Jason hatched a risky plan. "Hopefully, it's my lucky day," he said to himself as he wandered over to the old man.

"Casper," he said. "Casper, there you are." He grabbed the man's hand and pulled him off the ground. "You must stay closer in the market. You know the rules. These people have a reason to be afraid of you."

The ruse was successful, and the crowd backed off, seemingly upset that they didn't have someone to stone that day.

Jason then led him away from the hostile mob.

As soon as they were far enough from the crowd, the rescued man asked Jason in a low voice, "Why did you save me?"

"We all need a little help at times. For instance, I don't know where to eat. Perhaps you could help me there?" Jason said with a smile.

"I don't have enough money for food."

"I'm buying. My name is Jason."

"I'm Blantor," returned the grateful old man.

"Lead on, Blantor."

Blantor lead Jason through the marketplace. They weaved in and out of the various booths and shops. Minsk, who had disappeared when the crowd became rowdy, returned.

At last, they entered a small pub. As they breached the door, Jason pointed at Minsk and asked, "Is he OK?"

The bartender motioned them in.

A few of the patrons recognized Blantor and said hello. Jason and Blantor found a table in the corner. A waiter approached. Jason motioned to allow Blantor to order for both of them. After Blantor ordered something Jason had never heard of, they settled back in their chairs and looked each other over.

Jason thought Blantor was at least in his fifties. His face showed signs of too much sun. He had a few days growth of a beard. Jason could not tell what shape he was in under his cloak, but he had moved quickly and surely after Jason had rescued him.

"I must thank you again for saving me," he said to Jason.

"These people will kill us if we don't obey their rules. And actually, they are sort of justified. A few of my associates went a little crazy a couple years back and nearly wiped out the town. The few of us that survived are indentured servants to the ranking families for the rest of our lives. Our children are free, so we are not slaves. We cannot, however, go out in public without our masters, or their designated person."

"It's none of my business, but if you don't mind, what were you doing in town by yourself?" asked Jason.

"The person who is my master treats me fairly. He essentially lets me do whatever I want as long as we are not around the townsfolk. Then we must put on this charade. He is ill, so I came to town looking for some medicine. I got caught. I'd hate to think what would have happened if it wasn't for you.

"By the way, I've never seen you before. You must be a stranger in these parts if you weren't aware of my situation. Not to pry, but what's yours?"

"My situation is almost indescribable. Let's just say I'm looking for something, and then I want to go home."

Their food came, and they both enjoyed a delicious meal.

"That was fantastic," declared Jason. "What was it?"

"You don't want to know. Take my word for it ..., but it sure tastes good."

They sat back and looked around. Minsk had wandered over to a table of young girls. He was the center of attention as he did flips and other assorted acrobatic tricks for them. Jason had all sorts of conflicting thoughts about Minsk. Some groups were very afraid of him. Others, like these girls, had no past opinion of him and thought he was cute. Dylan thought he smelled. He was obviously more than just a mongoose, but what was he?

"Excuse me, sir," said Blantor. "You seem to be drifting off."

"Sorry," returned Jason. "I was thinking about Minsk, my little friend over there. Do you know anything about his kind?"

"I've heard rumors, but nothing I'd like to spread."

"Not to change the subject, but why exactly did your kind get into trouble ...? If you don't mind?"

"In certain cases, we can bring back the dead."

"So I could see my parents again?" Jason excitedly asked.

"That's the weird thing. We can only bring back people you

have never met. And that's the problem. You really don't know people from history. Sometimes the greatest heroes from the history books turn out to be total scoundrels in their personal lives. One other thing, if the person we bring back comes into contact with someone they have actually met while living, the living dead just vanish. So I can't help with your parents. Sorry."

"Is this bring-back-the-dead thing what got you guys in trouble?"

"Our city was involved in a petty border dispute with one of our neighbors about a rocky region of land that no one went to anyway. When skirmishes started, we thought if we brought back Gardley, he could save the day."

"Who is Gardley?"

"He was our first president about three hundred years ago. He was thought to be a great mediator. We hoped he could resolve the issue without bloodshed."

"What happened?"

"He turned out to be a cannibal."

"A what?"

"People started disappearing. After about a month, they found quite a few body parts in his secret quarters. A posse caught him while he was asleep and slaughtered him again."

"Again?"

"Remember, he already died once."

"Right."

"We were all convicted because they had to blame someone. The village wise men thought that the sentence they gave us would keep us apart and not allow us the opportunity to create any more mischief."

"Can you still bring people back from the dead?"

"Yes, but it takes me a few years to store up the energy. I'm currently fully charged. Think carefully about who could help you in your journeys. I'd like to pay you back for your kindness."

Blantor then left the table for a moment to talk to some old friends.

Jason looked around the bar and spotted Dylan, Salah, and JJ walking in. His friends had obviously enjoyed themselves at the fratoglob fights. They were poking each other and laughing hysterically.

The man at the door pointed over to Jason's table. They

made eye contact, and Jason waved them over.

"How'd you find me," Jason asked.

"Just chance," Dylan replied. "We've been asking in all the establishments we pass."

"Who's your new friend?" JJ inquired.

"His name is Blantor."

Jason then told Blantor's story. Everyone sat in disbelief as Jason revealed Blantor's strange claims. As Jason finished, Dylan accidentally knocked a fork onto the floor and bent to pick it up. As he crawled under the table, he mumbled mockingly to Jason, "I'd like to see Odysseus."

"What did he say?" asked JJ, who didn't hear Dylan's muffled voice.

"I'd like to see Odysseus," answered Jason.

"Very well," said Blantor as he returned to the table.

"Very well what?" asked Jason.

"Odysseus will be here shortly. Now I've got to run. My master needs his medicine. I'll be more careful on the way back. Thanks for your help once again."

Blantor vanished out the back door.

Dylan resurfaced holding his fork. "What was his problem?" he said, still irritated by his trivial quest.

"He says we are going to meet Odysseus, and Odysseus will help us in our journeys," Jason answered.

"Whose idiotic idea was that?" Dylan quipped.

"Yours!" they all responded together as they stared at Dylan.

"I'm hungry," Dylan said as if he was totally oblivious to what had just occurred. "A meal is a fair price to pay for a good story ..., and that was a good story. I'll even chip in. What about the rest of you guys?"

"I'm hungry too," agreed JJ.

"What did you guys have?" asked Salah.

"I'm not sure, but I'm sure they can bring us three more plates. It was very tasty."

Jason motioned for the waiter. When he came to the table, Jason told him to bring three more plates of what Blantor ordered.

While they were waiting for the food, Dylan described the fratoglob fights to Jason and Minsk. They were particularly gory, and Jason was glad that he didn't go.

When dinner arrived, the talking pretty much ceased while everyone dug in.

"What was that?" asked Salah after he finished.

"Blantor said that I didn't want to know. I'm going to take his word for it," declared Jason. "I'm quite content with my meal and don't need to spoil it with tales of octopus eyes or some other nonsense."

"Same here," agreed Salah. "What next?"

"Well, I guess we should go meet Butah at the other side of town," suggested Dylan. "No rest for the weary."

"Weary?" impugned JJ. "We've been goofing off all afternoon. It's time to help our friend again. Let's get out of here."

Jason settled up with the waiter. They left the bar and wandered down the street toward the other side of town. Everyone was pretty much caught up in their own thoughts until Dylan came over to JJ.

"Don't turn around," he said. "There is a man back there who has been tailing us since we left the bar. It seems to me that he is watching you. When you and Minsk went into that store a few minutes ago, he lingered outside. He had no interest in us."

JJ glanced behind her as she bent down and pretended to fix her sandal. When she stood up, she turned to Dylan.

"I've never seen him before in my life. What do you want to do about it? Remember, this isn't our turf, so we don't want to cause too many problems here."

"We should find out who he is before we meet Butah. We need to talk to the others."

Dylan walked into another saloon and everyone followed. Minsk was stopped at the door.

"He can't come in here," yelled the bartender while pointing at Minsk.

Minsk glowered at him and jumped up on a bench to wait outside.

Once inside, they sat down at a table to discuss the issue.

"Why don't I just go ask him who he is?" questioned JJ.

"He might flee if we walk toward him," Dylan replied. "He could later come back and harm us. I get nervous when I'm being shadowed."

"Why don't you guys go out the front door and walk for a few blocks and circle back?" JJ suggested. "If he's looking for me, he'll think I'm alone and come in here where we can talk. If he means harm, I can take care of myself. If he has friends, that's what you guys are for. I'll delay them until you get back."

"Maybe he just thinks you're cute," interrupted Salah. "You have been turning a few heads since we got to town, you know."

"Yeah, right," said a flustered JJ.

After pausing for a moment, Dylan started the ball rolling by loudly proclaiming, "Very well! We're off!"

"Take care of yourself," Salah warned JJ in a hushed voice.

The boys sauntered out the front door and lingered in the street so their shadow could not possibly miss them. They were joined by Minsk as they rambled away.

JJ purchased a drink and sat down at a table near an exit. She hoped she wouldn't need to use it. She then took off one of her newly acquired greaves and pretended to adjust it.

In a few moments, the stranger was standing at her table. JJ looked up at a handsome man she guessed was in his late thirties. He stared down at her with questioning eyes.

"Athena, can you help me again, for I am lost?" he began. "At least give me a clue, so I can find my way home. You helped me at Troy, and on parts of my journey. I do so want to see Penelope again."

"Why do you call me Athena?" questioned JJ.

"Please don't toy with me," implored the man. "I am tired from my journeys. I would so like to see my son and wife again."

As he spoke, four drunken patrons of the bar stumbled over to the table.

"We saw her first pal, get lost," one of them belligerently stated.

Not even looking at the men, the stranger said in a strong voice, "I mean you no harm. Please go away. I have business to conduct with this lady."

"We have business too," replied the biggest of the bunch as he shoved the stranger off to the side.

The stranger knocked the drunk down. He had two short swords on his back which he drew very quickly. As he straddled the drunk's body, he put one sword on the man's throat.

"I think you should apologize to the lady and leave," he said in a calm voice.

When the stranger got off the drunk's chest, the man slowly got up and walked toward the door. He turned and shouted, "You haven't seen the last of us. Come on guys. Let's get out of here."

The irate man and his three companions slowly walked out of the bar.

The stranger then turned to JJ. "I've dealt with more jerks like him than you can imagine …, but you already know this, Athena. Can you not help me in this strange new land?"

JJ stood up slowly. The stranger looked over her arsenal of weapons. He sort of smiled which JJ took as a fellow warrior's sign of respect.

"Why do you keep calling me Athena?"

"Are you not Athena, daughter of the gods?"

"My friends call me JJ. Who I am is not important, but I can tell you what I am definitely not, and that is a daughter of the gods."

"You so strongly resemble Athena, my friend and protector. My name is Odysseus. I am King of Ithaca. I am lost on my way home."

"We are lost, too. Listen, why don't we get something to drink? I'm still thirsty. I'm traveling with a group of three other people. I don't think we should go outside until they return. Those toughs look like they mean trouble. I'm pretty sure I could handle them alone, but fighting doesn't always turn out the way you expect. The strongest and best doesn't always win, especially in a no rules street fight."

"You are blessed with wisdom. We also don't know how many friends they have outside," said the stranger.

They ordered a few glasses of a particularly refreshing fruit drink and waited for the boys to return. Shortly thereafter, the boys walked through the door. When they arrived at the table, the stranger stood up. He reached to pull his swords.

"Please sit down, Odysseus. These are my friends. This is Salah, Dylan, and Jason."

"Odysseus?" thought Dylan.

Odysseus looked at Jason. "Did you see any groups forming outside the bar? Your friend JJ seems to have attracted some unwanted attention."

Jason thought he detected another awkward smile and shrug from JJ.

"There was a group of about fifteen people forming across the street and looking at this establishment," interrupted Dylan, who was now in total "spy mode." "I detected a certain aura of no good in their behavior. Did you guys offend them in some way?"

JJ quickly recounted the last few minutes. While she was talking, their new friend appeared to be distracted. When his mind came back to the present, he proposed, "Here's my plan. While I'm talking, pretend like you are getting more and more agitated by me. When I finish, Salah, take a poke at me. Nobody here knows we're friends. I'll block it because I know it's coming. Then all three of you go storming out of the bar."

As Odysseus explained the rest of his strategy, Dylan, Salah, and Jason got more and more demonstrative in their apparent disagreement with him. When Odysseus was finished, Salah took a swing at him. Odysseus blocked it and drew his swords.

"I don't think you want to mess with me, boy!" he threatened.

Jason grabbed Salah and pulled him away.

"Enough of this," he shouted. "We can find women elsewhere. We'll fight at the time and place of *our* choosing. Keep an eye over your shoulder, buddy. The world is full of surprises."

Jason motioned to Salah and Dylan, and the three of them stormed out of the bar.

When they were about half a block away, Salah turned to Jason and taunted, "You're such a weenie. We could have taken them. There are three of us, and one of them was a girl."

"You take that back," Jason replied.

"Weenie!"

"Take it back!"

"Weenie! Weenie!"

A crowd gathered around them as they made a louder and louder commotion. The men who were waiting for JJ and Odysseus also wandered over.

"Last chance. Take it back!" shouted Jason.

"Weenie! Weenie! Weenie!" retorted Salah.

Jason and Salah both drew their swords. They circled around preparing to fight.

"I've always wanted to know who was tougher," declared Salah.

"You'll find out in the last few seconds of your life," Jason sneered.

As their swords met, Odysseus led JJ out the side door and away from the bar. They were very quickly a safe distance from the crowd.

Dylan jumped in between the two boys when they broke apart.

"Whoever wins is going to have to answer to me ..., and I don't think either of you want that," he shouted while glancing back and forth between the two boys.

Salah and Jason calmed down now that Dylan was between them.

"Drop your swords and shake hands," ordered Dylan.

They both dropped their swords and reluctantly moved toward each other with their empty hands extended. They shook hands as Dylan lectured, "Remember all the times you saved each other's lives. It would be a pity to have it end this way. Now pick up your swords, and let's get out of here."

The crowd that expected bloodshed drifted off. The men interested in confronting JJ and Odysseus went back in front of the bar to wait for them.

Odysseus and JJ were long gone.

They arrived at the prearranged spot well before the boys.

Butah was in a tree close by but stayed hidden because she didn't know Odysseus.

Odysseus and JJ sat on a couple of logs. JJ found it odd that she could feel so relaxed with Odysseus, since she barely knew him. For some reason, she trusted him. She couldn't figure out why, but it was the same feeling she had when she first met the boys.

They showed up laughing and talking loudly as they crashed through the bushes.

"An Academy Award for the both of you," announced Dylan with mock seriousness.

"I accept on behalf of my mongoose and nobbly," returned Salah as the group broke out laughing.

The revelry was interrupted by JJ.

"Where's Minsk?" she asked.

There was a stunned silence.

Then Dylan offered an explanation.

"That little rat is preparing to attack me from somewhere."

"Come out! Come out! Wherever you are," coaxed Dylan.

Minsk appeared not five feet from Dylan with a disappointed look on his face.

"Maybe next time," said Dylan with a laugh to the mongoose.

Dylan, Jason, and Salah each shook Odysseus' hand to welcome the newbie.

"Did you say your name was Odysseus?" inquired Dylan with a look of disbelief on his face. "If you don't mind saying, where are you from?"

"Ithaca"

"Have you blinded the Cyclops yet?"

"Yes."

"Have you sacked Troy?"

"Yes."

"Have you slain the dreaded fratoglob?"

"What's that?"

"Just testing," returned Dylan.

"How did you know these things?" questioned the stranger. "Are you gods?"

Dylan tried to explain how he knew about Odysseus' adventures, but it just got more and more twisted and complicated. Eventually, he gave up.

"Why don't we just accept we don't understand everything, and help each other with our immediate problems?" suggested Odysseus. "The gods act in strange ways, and so far this is the strangest I've seen."

Chapter 16 - Hunting Dragons

After camping at the edge of town that evening, they followed Butah along Misha's trail for three more days. The forest gradually turned into plains and the going was rather easy.

On the morning of the fourth day, Jason and Odysseus left camp early searching for food. They were gone much longer than expected.

Although no one spoke of the matter, the remaining group members were becoming increasingly anxious, for they barely knew the man who claimed to be Odysseus. They were relieved when Jason excitedly burst into camp followed by his very calm companion.

"It was a battle for the ages," proclaimed Jason as everyone gathered around.

He backtracked a bit while continuing, "While we were out looking for food, we unexpectedly smelled the sea and headed toward it. As we gathered clams in the shallow water, five sailing ships appeared on the horizon. Four of them had one mast with a giant sail. They had a shallow draft like Viking ships. The wind was weak and a line of oars on each side propelled them. There was one large ship that looked like an eighteenth century British man-o-war. It had three large masts and two cannon decks. One of the port covers was open, and it looked like a giant ballista arrow was pointing out of it. Since we didn't know if they were friend or foe, we backed off from the beach and watched. The ships drew closer to the shore but didn't drop anchor.

"After sitting for a short time, the ships were attacked by giant winged creatures. They looked like huge pteranodons."

"What do pteranodons look like?" JJ interrupted.

"They resemble giant bats in some ways," Jason continued.

"Pteranodons' heads are shaped much differently, though. They have a large pointy beak and a symmetrical spike on the back of their heads. Pteranodons have a wingspan of around twenty feet. Some of the smaller attackers were that size."

"We would tell make-believe stories about creatures such as these," Odysseus added.

"The dragons seemed intent on carrying off any sailor they could capture," Jason continued. "The screams were horrible. They flew down to the ships and tried to snatch off sailors with their talons. Sometimes they would impale them on their pointy beaks. The sailors, on the other hand, appeared to be hunting the flying creatures."

"How do you know they were hunting them?" asked Dylan.

"They would occasionally down one of the creatures with either a massive volley of arrows or a giant ballista arrow. A longboat was then launched to retrieve the dragon. The sailors in these were particularly vulnerable and used their cutlasses and swords to fend off the beasts. With considerable effort, the sailors would then harpoon the downed monster and haul the impaled creature back to the larger ship. If it wasn't dead, the hunters fired another volley of arrows into it or hacked at it with their swords. After the battle was over, they towed the carcasses to shore with their longboats and butchered them."

"Each side was feeding the other?" interrupted Salah.

"That appears to be what was taking place. Sort of a mutual hunting expedition," Odysseus added.

"Did you hunt anything?" inquired Dylan. "I'm hungry for a good steak."

"Not exactly," replied Jason.

"Not exactly?"

"We brought back something else. I insisted," explained Jason. "Odysseus was a little more wary, and hungry. He said it would only be trouble. I maintained that everyone should make up their own minds. It's so cute. It's in the brush just outside of camp. It was getting hard to carry, so we left it there. We needed to drop the clams we found to bring it back."

"What is it?" asked Salah, whose hunger and curiosity were now starting to get the best of him.

"Not another girl," quipped Dylan as he winked at JJ.

"You couldn't be that lucky," she playfully responded.

156

"And especially *you* couldn't be that lucky."

Salah laughed and punched Dylan lightly in the shoulder.

"Well, let's go see it," declared Salah.

A short trek left them situated in front of a clump of bushes.

"Come here Jack," coaxed Jason. "It's me. These are my friends. They won't hurt you."

"Jack?" questioned Dylan.

"I named him after Uncle Jack. For some reason he reminds me of him."

Out from the bushes crawled a smaller version of one of the creatures they had seen attacking the ships. It appeared to understand Jason, but could not talk. Jason went over and patted it on top of the head.

"Those things are very dangerous and highly carnivorous," remarked JJ, although she did not appear to be afraid. "I've lost more than one friend to them."

"It was wallowing on the ground with five arrows sticking in it," explained Jason. "I convinced Odysseus to allow me to administer a little first aid. After all, look at his eyes. He's so cute. We just couldn't let him die."

The creature eyed the group and snorted at Minsk who jumped back and concealed himself behind a bush.

Dylan just about laughed himself senseless.

When he recovered, he stated in as solemn a voice as he could muster, "It appears that the creature can be of immense help to our expedition. I vote for keeping him."

"If we can trust him, I vote yes," said Salah.

It was obvious what Minsk thought.

"He's your pet," JJ chimed in. "If you trust him, I guess I do too. Hopefully, we won't turn into his late night snack."

"Well, it's obvious we are not going to eat him," Odysseus remarked. "Look, he is regaining his strength already. He should be well enough to fly again by tomorrow. Why not chalk this up as a good deed for the gods and move on? We have other things to do."

"Such as?" questioned JJ.

Odysseus pointed in the direction of the ships.

"Well, Butah says Misha is that way, for one, and we haven't eaten for a while, for another. It seems to me that this is an ideal opportunity to commandeer a ship, steal some food, and release some galley slaves in the process. The crews are getting drunk on the beach. It must be a party for the successful hunt. I'm pretty sure those ships were propelled by slaves at the oars. Perhaps we can sneak aboard and convince them to join our side. After all, Misha *is* in that direction."

Dylan smiled.

"Odysseus, you have once again earned your reputation," he declared.

"It's very confusing when you talk like you know me," remarked Odysseus. "After all, we have just recently become acquainted. But thanks for the compliment."

"How do you suggest we do it?" Dylan inquired.

"I know I can swim out to the ships. The problem is that I will probably be too tired to fight if needed. I think I'm more fit than the rest of you, so that option is out."

JJ was about to protest, but on further consideration decided that this was neither the time nor place.

"There is no moon after midnight," he continued, "so I suggest we wait until then and steal one of their longboats. We should then try to take the large ship. It will be the best in the open sea. If we are silent, I think we will catch them by surprise.

"I doubt if they have too many guards on the ships because they are not expecting anything. If anyone has any ideas about how to disable the smaller ships, I'm all ears."

Nobody responded.

"Sounds like a plan," Salah proclaimed, interrupting the momentary silence. "I can't think of anything better."

"Me neither," Dylan chimed in. "What if we steal the oars from the other longboats? With no oars, the pursuit would be delayed even more."

"Excellent idea," Odysseus agreed. "We will take as many as we can. When you grow up and stop fighting with your furry friend over there, you will be a fantastic general," he remarked with a twinkle in his eye.

"I'll take the first watch," he continued. "Everyone else can get themselves ready. I'll keep an eye on Jack. We'll leave him tonight, but we don't want to turn into hors d'oeuvres before then."

They spent the next few hours eating what little food they had left, getting their weapons ready, and napping. There were a few strange noises as darkness set in, but the watch was basically uneventful.

When he had finished preparing himself, Jason looked around at his collection of new friends.

Dylan was sound asleep.

"That guy could sleep through a war," Jason said to himself. "I wonder if he ever gets nervous about anything."

He looked over at Salah. He'd only known him for a few months, but already Salah was a trusted friend who one could count on in a pinch. If Odysseus really was who he said he was, as unbelievable as this comic book adventure had become, it was more unbelievable still. Minsk was like something out of a Saturday morning cartoon show. JJ was a battle goddess from who knows where.

"How could she have learned to fight like that and be that good-looking?" he had asked himself on more than one occasion.

Butah was something from a fairy tale. In fact, she was by anyone's reckoning, a fairy.

As the darkness deepened, Odysseus walked over to JJ. "Are you any good with that blow pipe on your belt?" he asked her.

"I haven't had much practice lately. I have ten darts left."

"Poison darts?" questioned Dylan who was awakened by the conversation.

"Actually, they're not poison in a sense that they will kill you ..., but they will knock you out instantly and make you wake up with a terrible hangover," JJ explained.

"Why haven't you used them already?"

"I don't have that many darts. I was saving them until I really needed them. I know how to make the potion, but I haven't seen any of the bushes with the correct berries. You also need to get a portion of a particular jellyfish and --"

"Ten darts should be enough," interrupted Odysseus. "If any of the guards aren't asleep, we might need you to do your stuff on them."

JJ nodded affirmatively.

"Are we ready?" Odysseus asked

Everyone gave the thumbs up sign.

"Then let's move," he commanded.

Jason walked over to the sleeping creature he had saved and

patted him on the head.

"Goodbye, Jack," he said softly. "I hope you have a nice life. Go back to your kind. We may never get to do that."

Everyone walked slowly out of camp. They were becoming professional warriors. They were conserving their energy for the fight.

As they left, Dylan ordered in a low voice, "Let's start operating in silent mode. We don't know if they've posted sentries. If they're drunk and passed out in the woods, we don't want to literally stumble upon them. Secrecy is our friend. Until they know we are here, we are at a distinct advantage."

"Yes sir, General," said Odysseus who had decided that title suited Dylan.

It was a dark, moonless night, and if it wasn't for Butah's light, the going would have been very slow. She gradually covered up as their eyes slowly became adjusted to the dark. When the trees thinned out as they neared the beach, they were able to see enough by starlight to move a little more quickly.

Jason spotted the silhouette of a hill ahead of them. He smelled the fresh breeze from the ocean as he climbed the dune. Before he reached the top, he could hear the surf breaking on the shore. It was very relaxing. He felt like sitting down and enjoying the atmosphere. He had almost forgotten their objective.

When they reached the apex of the dune, they observed the activities on the beach for a while. There were only two visible guards at the longboats. The eight small boats were too many to disable by taking their oars. They were beached next to the mouth of a small stream that flowed into the ocean.

There were five fairly large fires on the beach. With the exception of two sentries at the top of the dune to prevent a land attack and two at the boats, everyone else was sprawled out asleep. The two sentries at the top of the dune were smoking and laughing. Nobody saw anyone else.

Odysseus motioned to JJ to take out the sentries at the top of the dune. She crept over and quietly removed the threat of those sentries with her blow gun. She stayed near them, keeping motionless until she was confident that there were no other guards posted there. When she came back to the group, they moved around the perimeter of the camp toward the longboats.

The guards at the longboats were drawing sketches in the sand with sticks. They weren't paying too much attention to their guard duties because they had no reason to expect an attack. They were thoroughly enjoying themselves. The duo broke out laughing when one of them drew a caricature of their leader. The sound of the surf made it easy to sneak up undetected. They also fell to two darts from JJ.

Under Dylan's direction, the raiders grabbed as many oars as they could fit in the boat that was furthest from the sleeping revelers. They quietly pushed it out through the surf and were on their way. The surf had quieted down, but it was still loud enough to drown out any noise they were making. The rowing was easy.

They bypassed the smaller ships and stealthily crept up on the man-o-war. The infiltrators found that it was fairly easy to row quietly if one put forth a reasonable degree of effort. Jason, the self-proclaimed chicken, was actually enjoying himself. When they were close enough, they scanned the ship for signs of movement.

There were no lookouts on the mast, and with the exception of a loud symphony of snoring, the large ship seemed deserted.

The wind had shifted the ships on their moorings so that the starboard side faced the shore. They rowed around to the port side. Odysseus tied the longboat to the ship with a rope. He thought they might need it later.

On Odysseus' signal everyone climbed out of the rowboat and onto the side of the ship. Before they climbed up onto the deck, they paused for a moment to listen. They still only heard snoring.

Odysseus then crawled up and peered over the railing at the ship's deck.

The larger ship's deck was deserted.

Odysseus waved his arm and everyone scrambled over the railing and cautiously looked around.

Jason saw seven ballistae on each side of the deck. Their giant arrows lay immediately next to the machines. They were not loaded to be fired. The invaders scattered and searched for an entry to the next lower deck. Dylan found a hatch which was partly open, and they climbed through it. When everyone was down, they paused to look around. This deck was also filled with ballistae. Only one of the ports was open, but it was obvious that all of the weapons could be fired from their present positions.

There were still no signs of occupants other than the loud snoring. A metal gate blocked the entrance to the next level. It was unlocked, however, and the invaders entered through it and tiptoed down the stairs. The snoring grew louder and louder until they came upon its source.

Jason saw about thirty oarsmen chained to the oars on this level. There were only two visible guards, one near the bow and one near the stern. They were both asleep.

Odysseus motioned to Salah to come over and whispered very softly to him, "We might need the guards to help us sail the ship. If they wake up with a knife pressed against their throats, perhaps they can be persuaded to join us."

Odysseus and Salah both snuck off toward their respective targets. JJ inched over to the person she perceived to be the leader of the slaves and gently nudged him. He awoke with a startled expression on his face.

"Have I died and gone to heaven?" he exclaimed while gaping at JJ. He was quick to grasp the situation and remained silent and still after his initial remark. Odysseus gave Salah a sign, and they both poked their respective guards.

"Don't kill me," Odysseus' prisoner pleaded. "I was press ganged into joining. I have no loyalty to these people. My companion is the same. We only did what we needed to do to survive."

"I have a test to prove your loyalty," Odysseus declared. "I want you to pick one of the oarsmen and throw him overboard."

"I'm sorry sir, but if you don't mind, I'll go myself. These people have done nothing to me. I will not harm them for sport."

"Good answer," said Odysseus as he lowered his knife. "Will you vouch for your friend over there?" he asked while pointing to Salah's captive.

"I'm sure he thinks the same way I do."

"May I have the keys?" Odysseus asked his prisoner.

The man gave the keys to Odysseus who promptly tossed them to JJ.

The other slaves were starting to stir. Their leader, who was now free, gave them the signal to be quiet as he walked around with JJ and unlocked their chains. When he finished, he walked up to Odysseus and asked him what he would have him do now.

"It seems as if we have been quiet enough not to awaken anyone. If we up-anchor, the tides will take us away. Perhaps we can escape before we are found out. That would make it so much easier. Give your men the signal not to row. We will drift silently out to sea. We might be able to get out of this without a fight."

"You are so kind, my rescuer," said Ogarth, the head of the slaves, "but we have friends aboard those other ships. If we take them the same way we took this one, we will eliminate the pursuit altogether."

"An interesting idea," agreed Odysseus as he motioned his group together.

"You could command a whole fleet," Ogarth added while pressing his request. "It might make you a little more persuasive in whatever your endeavors are."

"Let me discuss it with my friends," Odysseus stated as he turned to them.

"Here's the situation as I see it," he explained. "We have two choices while sailing away. They are stealth or power. With one ship, it will be easier to pass places undetected, but if we get into a fight, the other ships will definitely help. I assume these waters are frequented by pirates, so the extra ships will help if we run into them."

Odysseus looked around. "Does anyone else have any thoughts on the matter? What about you, General?" he asked Dylan.

"It's hard to predict the future," Dylan responded. "I can't see how one solution is inherently better than the other. I guess I lean toward eliminating our pursuers by taking all the ships. If we steal one, why not take them all? We might get into a fight, but it could be as easy as this one."

Jason spoke up next.

"We are already on one mission of mercy, looking for Misha. Why not another? It can't hurt to have more friends in the world. After all, who knows how long we will be here? I think we should help free Ogarth's friends."

Salah and JJ both nodded in agreement.

"Then it's settled," said Odysseus. "We go for the ships by your mutual consent. May Athena help us," he prayed while glancing at JJ.

Odysseus led the commandos as they slipped over the side and silently swam toward their destinations.

Jason was astounded that he wasn't even nervous as he swam through the warm salty water toward his target. He was very proud of himself.

The four other ships were easily taken. The guards instantly aligned themselves with their liberators, so they would not need to leave any of their new conquests behind. The anchors were lifted, and the five ships drifted away from the beach. Each new captain let the tide take his ship out as he worked at making his vessel seaworthy.

Soon, the silhouettes of the ships that were once visible in the starlight vanished over the horizon. Jason, JJ, Salah, Dylan, Minsk, and Odysseus made their way back to the flagship in the longboat. The boat then made several more trips between the ships to place the crews in precisely the right place.

Butah had stayed on the main ship. She was a little anxious because most of the crew had never seen a nobbly before and were constantly staring at her. She relaxed when her friends reappeared.

The newly freed crew spent the rest of the night telling stories until one by one they passed off into dreamland.

When they awoke the next morning the sun was blazing at the start of a beautiful day. The ships were well supplied, so they all devoured a tasty breakfast. The former prisoners were thoroughly enjoying their new found freedom. Everyone was a bit exhausted from the previous day's events, so with the exception of the on-duty crews, the energy level was very low.

"Maybe we should name ourselves 'The Slugs,'" Dylan suggested.

Nobody disagreed.

They sailed in the direction of Butah's dort. For two days they ate well and lounged around the ships in the sun. They drank and sang well into the evenings. The moods became increasingly jovial and childish except for Odysseus'. He became more and more withdrawn as the journey progressed.

On the morning of the third day, he called a group meeting. Everyone figured he was about to come out of his funk and entertain his shipmates with one of his childish dances or stories. When the crew had assembled on deck, Odysseus put up his hands for quiet. Minsk was still bouncing around showing off his dancing skills, and JJ had to grab him to make him stop.

When all was finally quiet, Odysseus addressed the group.

"I know that some of you are on a quest for Butah's dort, Misha. But you know deep in your hearts that when you are finished, you will look to go home. I have been away much longer, and that yearning is presently overwhelming me. I strongly feel that if I head toward the morning sun, I shall succeed in my quest.

"I am sure that I am leaving our present mission in capable hands.

"I am sorry to make this announcement. I have never been with a more loyal or brave crew. Unfortunately, my longing for Ithaca strengthens daily. If it is OK with their captains and crews, I would like to take the four smaller ships on that undertaking."

There was a stunned silence among all who listened.

"Ogarth, I would ask you to inquire among your men who would risk joining me. If it is anything like my journey so far, it will be a difficult and dangerous task."

"I will go with you. You freed us from slavery. I am sure that I can convince a crew to come along. Let us pull alongside the other ships, and I will discuss it with them. I will have an answer this evening."

"Thank you for the offer, but stay with this ship. They need you," Odysseus insisted.

Ogarth walked to the side of the ship and signaled with his hands for the nearest ship to approach. When it was close enough, he explained the situation to the crew.

It was agreed that since both missions were equally dangerous, participation would be determined by chance. One by one, the other ships pulled alongside to receive the same news.

That evening, among drink and song, a lottery determined the fates of the crews. If anyone had a strong preference, it was respected. Otherwise the names were put into a small pot. A comical ceremony was made of the drawing with Minsk doing his best to poke fun at the person whose name was drawn. The results were relayed to the other ships. When everyone knew their future destination, the eating and drinking of their last night together began in earnest.

The next morning, the ships halted, and the longboat transferred everyone to their proper locations. When it at last arrived to take Odysseus, he solemnly shook everyone's hand and climbed down.

As he left, he yelled out to JJ, "Thanks Athena. Please protect me in the future."

She smiled and waved back.

Chapter 17 - Waterbats

As Odysseus' four ships vanished in the distance, Jason couldn't help but think that the strangest of his recent bizarre adventures was over. He stared off at the horizon and wondered what was in store next as they sailed in the direction of Butah's dort on an eighteenth-century man-o-war. The sun was bright. The air was fresh. The food was good.

Jason had always wanted to go on a cruise, and he was now enjoying one with his new friends. It was relaxing, although a bit more bizarre than anything he had previously imagined. Danger was further and further from his mind.

The thought was not totally absent, however. The former galley slaves had an almost psychotic fear of a creature they called a waterbat.

Rohm, one of the crewmembers, gave a complete description of this cross between a manta ray and gigantic bat.

"Their wingspan is the length of four men," he stated. "They have two horns projecting out of the front of their heads. Waterbats spend most of their time in the water, but can fly short distances when attacking their prey or defending their turf. They have huge jaws filled with razor-sharp teeth and are the most feared thing on the high seas. They crave the taste of wood, and attack any ship they come across. The sailors are just the hors d'oeuvres.

"Waterbats generally attack in schools of about a hundred. They apply various methods in their swarming onslaughts. Some burst out of the water and crash onto the deck. Once there, they try to eat anything in site, including and especially, the ship. Waterbats are a bit clumsy out of water, but they can get around a bit by flapping their wings and using the tiny claws they have on the front of them. If they can't get their teeth into the hull, they crash into it with their two horns and use their weight to rip out pieces. Once they get a spot where they can start eating, the game is generally over.

"Their main weakness is that they are cannibalistic. If you can bloody up a good number of them, they will start to eat their own wounded instead of the ship. That appears to be the only way to defend against them. That's what the ballistae are for."

"You've seen them?" Dylan asked.

"I am one of the few survivors," Rohm somberly responded.

When they came into possession of the ship, the first thing the former slaves did was to crank the bowstrings back on the ballistae. From past experience, they stated that if they were ever needed, it would be too late to load them.

The members of the crew constantly scanned the horizon for the beasts which apparently attacked in this part of the sea. Jason couldn't help but think they were just an old sailors' superstition, but the ballistae were very real. After what he had seen so far in this world, anything was possible.

The former prisoners also had a primordial fear of Minsk. "It is a bad omen to have a ratooi on the ship," they said to a man. Even Ogarth was a little afraid. They were thankful for their rescue, however, and never said anything to Minsk's face.

It was decided that since Jason, Dylan, Salah, and JJ had never sailed before, they would be better off observing for a while before they participated. The ship was overstaffed as it was.

The ship sailed along for a few days with nary an incident. Then one morning as Jason and his friends were beginning to stir, he heard the loud sound of a man blowing into a conch shell followed by the warning, "Battle stations! Battle stations! Waterbats approaching!"

Jason jumped out of his hammock and ran up the stairs to the deck. JJ, Dylan, and Salah followed. The crew members were running helter-skelter across the deck.

Jason looked for Ogarth.

"How can we help?" he yelled.

"There's always something to be done with the ballistae," Ogarth bellowed. "Get down on deck two and lend a hand. If things get tough, you need to get mad dog mean. You cannot waver, even for an instant."

Glancing out to sea, Jason could see what appeared to be a school of dolphins with wings rapidly approaching the ship.

168

They were in and out of the water about every twenty yards.

As the boys and JJ ran for the stairs, they were knocked off their feet by the blow of the first wave of waterbats hitting the side of the ship.

"Thank god we got the covers off in time!" Ogarth shouted. "Fire at will!"

As they reached the second deck, they could see that some of the port holes were covered by waterbats that latched on to the side of the ship. When this happened, a giant arrow was immediately released into the beast. At times, the giant arrows skewered the creatures and stuck out the opposite side. A fair number of arrows had met their mark in this manner. The arrows were fired at such short range that the ship was covered with blood. The stench was awful.

The boys and JJ joined in when they saw how strenuous it was to turn the two winches to ratchet a ballista bowstring back to firing position.

Right next to Salah, a monster broke through the hull. It gnawed at his crew's ballista before it could be reloaded. Salah grabbed a jagged splinter of wood and rammed it into the beast's eye. Blood shot out. As the creature slid back through the opening in the ship's hull, it sprayed blood everywhere. A second bat was upon the wounded beast in an instant. Soon ten bats were devouring their comrade.

When the creature slid off the port hole, Jason stuck his head out. The attackers everywhere now seemed more interested in their wounded companions than in the ship. It was a horrible but welcome sight. The carnage was similar to hyenas ripping apart a carcass.

Jason heard a loud cheer from the main deck. The rest of the portholes suddenly showed daylight. The crew on deck two responded with a similar cheer. They had killed enough of their attackers that the bats were now exclusively feeding on each other. The current battle was over. Jason felt a sense of relief come over him. He looked at Dylan and smiled.

"Victory!" yelled the man in charge of Jason's crew.

He then looked over at Jason's group.

"Thanks for the help. You can never reload these things fast enough. You may go now."

Jason looked at him questioningly.

"We can't stand down until we get the order," the sailor continued. "You aren't officially part of the crew, yet. Why don't you go up on deck and slice off a few good pieces for us? We're going to feast tonight!" he exclaimed.

JJ smiled at the boys.

"Not too many people are victorious over these guys," she reminded anyone who was listening.

An amazed JJ then turned to Jason.

"Let's see now. You killed a lonizard, rescued Salah from drug dealers, stole a few eggs from and killed a larnerghoul, helped destroy a school of waterbats, survived the Rangali, and captured a fleet of ships and freed their galley slaves. I'd say our naïve little boy has become quite a warrior. Even if it's just dumb luck, which I doubt, I want you on my side."

"I'd say that it's instinct and talent," Dylan threw in. "Most of the best spies have an abundance of both. A little luck never hurt either."

"I'm not a spook," Jason insisted, thankful that the blush brought on by JJ's compliment was fading.

"Maybe not, but you're the closest thing to a special ops guy that I know. If I read your current resume, I'd be hard pressed to find one that's better," Dylan quipped.

Jason was temporarily overwhelmed. Until this very moment, he had never thought of himself in those terms. He had just been worried sick about his next move. He had always thought of himself as the inexperienced guy in the group. In his mind, he was just surviving. Now, he felt a glow of pride as he thought of his life in JJ's terms.

"Anyone home?" Salah asked while waving his hands directly in Jason's face.

Jason snapped back to reality. "Sorry, what's up?"

"Let's go up on deck," Salah suggested.

They climbed the stairs into the sunshine on the main deck to join the revelry.

As Jason looked around and surveyed the crew, the order was given to stand down. If a sight could be the definition of the word "joy," he was looking at it. The crew assembled in small groups and happily reviewed the events of the battle. One group even started butchering one of the dead waterbats to cut out the tasty sections. The party went on all day.

Toward evening, Jason and Salah were both on deck enjoying the revelry. Suddenly things quieted down. One by one, the crew members turned their heads toward the sun setting on the horizon.

After just about everyone else had turned, Jason finally spun that way. He squinted into the bright light and saw what looked like a large swarm of insects approaching the ship. The sun was blinding, so Jason turned and watched the crew members. On each face, one after another, a look of panic and fear appeared.

Jason finally focused on the horizon again. The swarm of insects was now close enough to identify. It was a giant school of waterbats.

"How can we possibly defend ourselves against that?" he asked himself.

Dylan and JJ discussed their options as they came over to Jason and Salah.

"Any thoughts?" JJ threw out as casually as she possibly could.

"It looks like we are in for one heck of a fight," Salah answered.

The swarm closed in on the ship as the crew scurried to their battle stations.

"Please keep your people on the main deck this time," Ogarth barked as he looked at Dylan. "The men manning the ballistae had them under control last time. Things were a little more dicey up here."

"Aye! Aye! Captain," Dylan screamed back.

"See you on the other side," JJ yelled as the first wave of waterbats slammed into the side of their vessel.

The crew felt the ship recoil as the wave hit. Some of the giant arrows found their targets near the side of the ship and sprayed blood everywhere. Many of the attackers now turned on their own kind, but the force attacking the ship was still overwhelming.

Bats landed all over the deck. They snapped at anything they could with their razor sharp teeth. Crew members who were unlucky enough to be bitten screamed in pain as their compatriots lashed out with anything that they could at the bats flopping around on the deck. In some places, there were so many bats that they were even stacking up.

Salah had just finished destroying one of the bats with his cutlass when the main mast collapsed onto the deck. He did not see it coming, was unable to get out of the way, and was knocked unconscious by one of its pieces.

JJ saw the mast fall and ran over to Salah.

"Jason! Dylan! Help me get Salah into the longboat over there."

The boys ran over on JJ's cry for help. They lifted Salah and struggled to carry him to the longboat which was hanging three feet above the port side of the deck. The trip was treacherous. JJ attempted to clear the way of their hungry attackers with her cutlass. If she couldn't move them, she just chopped at the nasty beasts. They were hard to kill, so for most of the trip they had to lug Salah across slimy half-dead creatures. If they slipped, they risked becoming victims themselves.

After dropping Salah a few times onto their disgusting foes, they finally lifted their unconscious comrade into the longboat and covered it with its tarp.

Without warning, the bat-weakened port side of the ship collapsed, throwing all of them into the sea along with the longboat. The boat flipped over, and JJ dove down to rescue Salah. She grabbed his belt and pulled him to the surface. As she struggled in her wet clothing to keep Salah's head above water, Dylan swam over to help. Jason righted the longboat and tried to install the oars so he could row over, but by the time he succeeded, Dylan and JJ had pulled Salah to the boat's side. Minsk, who no one had seen for a while, popped up next to the boat and climbed in.

As they hauled Salah into the boat, a waterbat crashed into its side and almost flipped it. Jason saw it coming, drew his cutlass, and slashed off a small piece of its head. As it fell back into the water, it was immediately swarmed upon by its fellows who had sensed an injury.

Nothing was now attacking. During the temporary lull, Dylan, Jason and JJ looked back at the ship. It was gradually disappearing. There was still spirited fighting on the deck, but the ship was slowly sinking and simultaneously being devoured by the waterbats. They felt helpless as their friends gradually met their doom. They knew that it would soon be their turn.

Everything suddenly got fuzzy for the riders in the boat.

In their next conscious moment they were lying on a beach.

Jason raised his head and stared into eyes of Jack, the dragon he had rescued a few days earlier. The dragon looked him over. When it was satisfied that Jason was OK, it launched itself into the sky and was joined by its five companions. They disappeared into the distance.

At least that's what Jason thought he saw. He was still groggy from the waterbat slime and passed out again.

JJ was the next to awaken. "Whoa! I guess the rumors I've heard about that waterbat slime are true! What a trip!"

She looked around to make sure everyone was OK. When her eyes intermittently focused, she could see that they were all breathing.

"Anyone know how we got to wherever we are?" she asked, hoping for an answer.

She really didn't expect one from her semiconscious companions. She patiently waited as one by one they started to come around. Getting up and walking, however, was quite a different story. Salah was the first to try, and he fell flat on his face in the sand. Dylan laughed, stood up, and did a similar face plant. It was so pathetic that even Minsk could not laugh.

They decided that maybe they should wait a little longer for the effects of the waterbat slime to wear off.

When Jason finally fully awakened, they tried to goad him into standing up. He saw the others' footprints on the beach that suggested something was amiss. He started to try standing up but didn't even come close.

"I think I'm going to wait a while," he announced.

While they were lying on the beach laughing at each other, Butah flitted up. "You just had the escape of your lives," she explained. "I followed from a distance because those dragons will eat me for a snack."

"What dragons?" Dylan asked.

"The beasts that those kind gentlemen that gave us that ship were hunting," Butah explained. "I thought for sure you guys were goners. The dragons had you firmly in their talons. I followed, but there was nothing I could do. Then they gently deposited you on the beach and flew away. I couldn't tell for sure, but their leader looked a lot like Jack, that little monster that Jason and Odysseus rescued."

"It looks like we were repaid for a little kindness," Jason proposed. "I wonder what Odysseus would say about that?"

Everyone shrugged and looked at each other with a "How can this be true?" expression.

They decided that Jack and his friends had probably left them somewhere safe. In their current states, the best they could do was to crawl off the beach and wait until the effects of the slime wore off. When they reached the trees they all became lost in their own thoughts regarding Odysseus and their recently deceased friends.

Exhausted sleep finally rescued them.

When they awoke the next morning, the effects of the waterbat slime had ceased. They were relieved when Butah indicated that Misha was in a direction away from the sea and toward the jungle-covered hills in the distance.

"Butah, can you fly a little ahead and tell us if we just need to cross a few hills or an entire mountain range?" Dylan asked.

"I'll be back in a bit," she replied and zoomed away.

Chapter 18 - Klaterites

When Butah returned, she explained that it was no mountain range, but only four large hills, and beyond that, a forest. They needed to find food, so it was decided that Jason, Butah, and JJ would search on one side of the hills. Dylan, Salah, and Minsk would look on the other. They would meet in two days at the base of the last hill.

The boys all thought that Butah seemed depressed, so they asked JJ to try and find out why. Butah was trailing behind, so JJ walked back to her.

"Something is bothering you," JJ maintained. "What is it?"

"I think I've lost Misha. I keep getting the feeling that the direction we need to go is up. I hope he has not died and gone to the great beyond."

"We will keep going in the last direction you sensed. Perhaps we can pick up the trail again. Don't mention this to the others," JJ instructed. "We'll at least get a few more days out of them. Then we'll need to come clean."

"Thank you," Butah responded.

JJ went back and told the boys that everything was OK. The search was just draining her energy.

The group split the remaining food and started their trek around the hills. Butah flew directly to their meeting place to rest.

After half a day's journey, Jason and JJ found themselves peering over the top of a small hill. Down in the valley below were ten of the strangest creatures Jason had ever laid eyes on, and he had seen some pretty strange creatures lately. These were large feathered birds, at least twice as big as a horse, with two long necks, each topped with its own head. Each head had a large mouth that contained two rows of very large teeth. They had long sharp talons on each of their two legs. They were a dirty white or light grey in color.

Jason tried to stand up, but JJ pulled him back down. She put her finger to her lips to indicate silence and motioned him to follow her back a little out of sight of the creatures.

"What are those things?" whispered Jason.

"We call them natmaroos, which loosely translated means moonbirds. Few people from my land have actually seen them. They are the stuff of legends."

"They sure have a lot of legends where you come from," replied Jason. "Why do they call them moonbirds?"

"Folklore says that they can take you to the moon."

"The actual moon? The thing that floats in the sky at night?"

"I thought it was only a story, but now things are starting to make sense."

"How so?"

"Well, remember how sad Butah has been the last few days. She told me she thought she lost the direction to her dort. She had the feeling that he was above her, yet when she looked up, she didn't see anything. What if Misha is on the moon?"

"I suppose that is no more ridiculous than the rest of the stuff that's been happening to us lately," Jason concluded after considering it for a while.

His mind began racing in another direction. "Is it possible for us to commandeer a few of those creatures?" he asked.

"Supposedly they are the possessions of the Klaterites, a tribe of traders that allegedly travel between the earth and the moon."

"Is that who was tending to them?"

"You noticed someone with them?"

"I thought I saw a young woman or girl sitting on a rock brushing the beasts' feathers."

"Maybe the Klaterites are here now," JJ postulated.

"A few years ago, a girl from my clan claimed she was abducted and carried off to the moon by men flying on natmaroos. That's where I heard about them. She claimed that as long as she ate the berry of a certain plant, she could survive on the moon. The men who took her to the moon thought she looked like a missing relative. As soon as they discovered their mistake, they brought her back."

"They even have alien abduction stories here," Jason

thought.

"Do you believe the story? Did you know her personally?"

"I met her once. I kind of liked her. She sounded like she believed the story herself ..., but it all seemed so ridiculous at the time. Now, I don't know."

"Do you think it would be unwise to try to get a closer look?" whispered Jason.

"Why not? If they fly away, we're no worse off than we were to begin with."

As Jason and JJ stood up, a half dozen armed men popped out of the surrounding bushes and threatened them with arrows.

"State your purpose!" demanded the largest of them.

"We mean you no harm," answered JJ. "We are in pursuit of the companion of one of our friends. It's a furry creature about as big as your thumb. We call it a dort."

The leader motioned to the others to lower their weapons.

"Does the creature resemble a small hairy fox with a faint glow?"

"Yes it does," responded JJ.

"I have seen such a creature. It was brought back to our city a few days ago. They intend to auction it off to the highest bidder. Rumor has it that it is one of the ingredients of an immortality potion."

"Are you Klaterites?" asked JJ.

"Yes we are. We have come here to trade with the people of this world."

"Where is your homeland?" asked Jason.

"You cannot generally see it during the daytime, but I believe you people refer to it as the moon."

"How do you get there and back?" asked an astonished Jason.

"If we eat vagelberries, we can fly on the natmaroos."

"What's a vagelberry?"

One of the Klaterites reached into his pocket and pulled out a handful of red pea-sized berries to show Jason.

"We can last for about one week on a ration of vagelberries. After that time, if we stay here, we need another ration, or we slowly weaken and die."

"Would it be possible for us to go to the moon with you if we ate them?" asked an excited JJ. "We think the dort that you saw is the one that belongs to our friend."

"We need your help first. Then we will talk."

"What would you like us to do? By the way, my name is JJ, and this is Jason."

"My name is Wilthor. My assistant here is Slag."

Wilthor turned to the rest of his men. "You can go back to Maura now. Slag and I will entertain our new friends."

Wilthor turned back to JJ.

"Maura was bitten in the leg by a large snake. The poison is starting to take hold. There are rumors of a magic plant to heal such things. Do you know of such a plant?"

"It depends what kind of snake it was. Did it have any distinguishing markings?"

"The head had a red triangle on it …, but that was not its most distinguishing characteristic."

"What was?" asked JJ.

"The snake slithered through the air."

"Are you sure it didn't just fall out of tree and bite her?"

"I saw it slither away. It was near waist high off the ground. I'm absolutely sure of it."

"That's not good. That sounds like a jaysnake. I know of the plant that is part of the cure for such a bite. I do not know, however, where it grows in this area," JJ declared.

"We can search large areas on our natmaroos. What does this plant look like? Perhaps we have already seen it."

"The plant has an enormous red flower. Its diameter is the size of a man's foot. Each petal has a large blue dot on it. If the petals are mixed in with spangle juice, the mixture can heal that snake's bite."

"I have seen the flower," announced Slag. "What is spangle juice?"

"The spangle is a round fruit. It is very common and used to make intoxicating beverages. I can easily find some. It grows in the wild all around here."

"Slag, take two men and go get the flower petals," Wilthor ordered.

"Bring the whole plant. They keep their freshness longer that way," JJ added.

"JJ, we would like to invite you and Jason to be our guests for dinner. We'll introduce you to Maura, and perhaps you can make a friend or two among the natmaroos."

Jason looked at JJ. He could tell that she was a bit nervous about being at such a disadvantage if their new found friends turned hostile. He also knew they didn't have much choice if they wanted to go to the moon after Misha.

"We will gladly accept," Jason quickly responded, fearing that a pause would arouse suspicion.

They walked down the hill toward the natmaroos. Maura was sitting on a large boulder and looked them over as they approached. She appeared to be Asian, with long dark hair and dark eyebrows.

"This is JJ," introduced Wilthor. "And this is Jason."

"Very pleased to meet you. My name is Maura."

"We hear you have a little problem," Jason asserted. "JJ may be of help with your leg."

As JJ walked over to look at the leg, a natmaroo blocked her path.

"That's OK, Wallah. Let her past," Maura requested in a calm but firm voice.

The natmaroo moved aside, and JJ approached. She saw the three puncture marks in Maura's leg which were the unmistakable sign of the jaysnake.

"Does it hurt much?" JJ inquired.

"It is very painful to walk, and I seem to be getting weaker by the hour."

"Don't worry! Your friends are looking for the antidote. We should have you fixed up quickly," JJ counseled optimistically.

"You're not just saying that to comfort me?" Maura questioned.

"No. I was bitten by a jaysnake when I was five years old. They fixed me right up. It's very dangerous if you don't get the antidote, but Slag said he knows where one ingredient grows. I'm going to go look for the other ingredients. Jason can help keep you company. Perhaps you can tell each other about your homelands to pass the time. He is also from a distant place."

"Good idea. It will take my mind off the bite."

"Wilthor said that you come from the moon," Jason blurted out.

"That's true. My friends and I are Klaterites. We trade with the people of this world. The vagelberries allow us to survive here."

"Vagelberries seem to help one survive in a foreign environment. Is that right?" asked Jason.

"I never thought of it that way, but I guess it's true. There was a girl from this world that we mistakenly brought to the moon a while back. She became more and more ill until she ate some vagelberries. The girl needed them to survive in our environment, and some of us need them to survive here."

Jason had an inkling that Maura was looking past him as she talked. She did her best to hide this fact, but eventually she just gave up.

Jason turned and scanned the sky. In the distance, he saw three far off specks. As they grew larger, it became obvious that they were Slag and his companions urgently approaching on their natmaroos.

When Slag's landed, he jumped off and hurriedly carried a sack to them.

"There are many plants with petals in here," he proclaimed. "Hopefully they are the right ones."

JJ approached from the other side.

"I found some spangles," she declared. "If you let me have the petals, we can start to mix the antidote."

JJ peered into the bag.

"You found the right ones," she confirmed.

Wilthor brought a glass container, and JJ squeezed the watery orange spangle juice into it. Next, she added the flower petals. Purple smoke spewed from the container while any juice spilled on its surface boiled away.

"Wilthor, will you come over here?" JJ asked. "I need to show you something."

Wilthor walked over. When they moved out of hearing range of Maura, JJ pointed to the ground.

Wilthor looked puzzled as he scanned the earth.

"Keep looking down. I am going to draw an irrelevant picture in the dirt. Pretend you are looking at it. I didn't tell you the difficult part of making this antidote yet. I don't want to sink Maura's hopes."

"What's the difficult part?"

"We need something else for the antidote."

"What?"

180

"We need a spine from a jaysnake's tail."

"Jaysnakes are wretched critters," she continued. "They bite each other frequently. The leader must then brush the bitten snake with the spines on its tail to neutralize the poison. That's how they keep the underlings in line."

"Are you telling me that we need spines from a snake's tail?"

"I'm afraid so. It's a big nasty snake too. It'll be risky, but we should be able to pull this off. I didn't want to tell Maura yet. Her spirits seem to be improving, and we don't want to dash them."

"How do we find this snake and cut off its tail without being bitten ourselves?" inquired Wilthor.

Jason wandered over, heard the last part of the conversation, and asked, "Do you think that Minsk can find that snake in time?"

"That's one way, but I don't think it's the best. I'll explain when we catch up with the others."

JJ turned to Wilthor and confessed, "I need to be honest with you. There are a few more members of our party that we will need to pull this off. They are brave and cunning warriors."

"I'm glad Dylan isn't hearing this," she thought.

"Can your men carry us on the natmaroos to get our friends? It's the easiest way I know of to get the snake."

"We will go at once. Where can we find them?"

"It's not that far. We split up to look for food. We should be able to locate them quickly on the natmaroos. We will need to bring back two adults and a small creature about this high," JJ stated while motioning with her hands to show Minsk's height.

Wilthor strode off to ready the natmaroos.

JJ and Jason walked back to Maura.

"This will stay unnaturally hot for a day," JJ stated as she pointed to the container with the antidote. "When it cools down, we pour the juice thru a cloth to filter out the solid material, and we have an antidote. You'll be good as new in no time."

The tension that was obvious on Maura's face was showing some signs of melting.

"Where are you guys from again?" she asked.

"We're just lost adventurers," answered Jason. "We are in search of a friend's pet dort. It's a small furry animal about as big as your thumb. It was kidnapped, and we are trying to get it back. Wilthor said that he thinks the dort will be auctioned near your home town. It is thought to be the rarest ingredient in an immortality potion."

"There are a lot of wretched people who do nasty things to get the treasures they sell there. If you try to stop one of them, we won't stand in your way. In fact, we will help you."

"We have a few friends that we need to bring along," Jason continued. "We've been through a few scrapes together, and they will be invaluable in solving our little problem."

"Let me discuss it with my people."

"Can I ride one of the natmaroos?" Jason impulsively inquired while switching gears. He didn't know what was coming over him, but since he was launched by the Klinglesprachs, he was starting to crave flying.

"They are very suspicious of new people, but they make friends easily. It should be fine. We'll get a rider, and you can get on back. JJ, would you like to go too?"

"I'd love it."

"Give us a few moments to get ready, and you'll get the ride of your lives. Oh, if you really want an experience, eat some vagelberries before you go, and they'll take you to the stars."

"Great!" exclaimed JJ and Jason together.

"The natmaroos won't let you wear your weapons because they don't know you. You'll need to take them off," Maura explained.

JJ acted a little peeved, but Jason didn't seem to care. He trusted his new friends.

While JJ removed her weapons, Jason was captured by his own thoughts.

"Here is Mr. Chicken volunteering to go on a mission as a mercenary. And better yet, on the wings of some strange creature with people he only met hours ago. His trusted companion is a warrior princess from who knows where. Hopefully, he will live to tell his adventures. The odd thing is that he doesn't seem to care, and he's starting to crave the adventures for their own sake."

Wilthor returned.

"The natmaroos are ready!" he proclaimed.

There were five natmaroos, each with its own rider.

"Give them some vagelberries," Maura commanded. "They take effect almost immediately. Have fun!"

Maura paused for a moment before adding with a slight chuckle, "The natmaroos are generally pretty good at keeping their passengers alive."

JJ and Jason each hopped on the back of a natmaroo and wrapped their arms around the rider's waist. A Klaterite came over and gave them each a handful of vagelberries.

"Chow these before you take off," he commanded.

Jason grabbed his vagelberries, hoping that they doubled as motion sickness medicine. He feared losing his lunch on the back of the rider seated in front of him. Jason and JJ both hurriedly devoured the berries.

"They would like a short trip into space first," Maura requested.

The natmaroo riders nodded. JJ's rider looked over at Jason's and shouted with a laugh, "I think I got a better deal than you did."

Jason's companion just smiled and kicked the natmaroo slightly with the back of both heels. Jason's natmaroo unfolded its gigantic wings and launched itself into the air. The others followed. They shot up at an incredible speed. Both JJ and Jason applied a death grip to their riders to keep from falling off. Higher and higher they went. Jason finally opened his eyes when he felt the acceleration slowing down. He was awestruck by the dazzling stars around him. He looked over at JJ and could tell she was experiencing the same feelings.

The natmaroos soared endlessly in circles. Jason repeatedly switched views between the cloud covered earth and the stars. Both were exhilarating. Finally, on Wilthor's signal, they headed back down into the clouds.

They flew in a tight V-formation to reduce wind drag on the natmaroos. They occasionally shifted leaders so as not to tire out any of their mounts.

On Wilthor's command, they slowed down and smoothly landed.

JJ casually jumped off the back of her natmaroo.

"You seem to have taken it well," Wilthor remarked to her, "but your buddy seems to have developed a camouflage face," he pointed out with a laugh.

JJ tried not to giggle at the pale green color of Jason's face.

"My lunch is still with me," Jason proudly proclaimed.

"What did you think?" shouted Maura.

Before JJ could answer, she continued, "You seem to have found a new friend."

JJ turned around. A natmaroo was following her.

"She trusts you now," exclaimed Maura. "You can rearm yourself."

JJ turned around and patted the natmaroo on each of its two heads.

Maura turned to Jason.

"Put your sword back on, grab your other weapons, and go stand over by your natmaroo."

Jason followed the request, and the natmaroo did nothing.

"You have a new friend also. That will make things easier," said a relieved Maura.

"It's probably time to go look for their friends," interjected Wilthor.

"Yes it is," replied Maura. "Good luck."

The group walked back to the five natmaroos. They hopped on, and Wilthor gave the signal to take off. They rocketed up at amazing speed, came back for one final wave at Maura, and then headed off to the horizon.

Maura watched as they became smaller and smaller and finally disappeared into a cloud bank. She then whistled for her favorite natmaroo to come over.

"I hope we can trust them," she whispered in its ear.

Chapter 19 - Jaysnakes

"Get me out of here!" Dylan demanded.

Salah was mildly amused at the whole situation. Minsk thought it was hilarious.

"I don't even know where the walls are. I keep bumping into them."

"Until the others show up, maybe you should draw a line in the dirt at the base of the walls. Then you will know how far you can stray without bumping your nose. I've already asked your little gambling buddies to release you, but they said they want their money. Can't blame them for cheating better than you," said Salah with a smirk. "I figure you'll be in your little invisible cage until sometime tomorrow when the others come looking for us. Perhaps you can persuade JJ to part with one of her gold bracelets to get you out. In the meantime, it's me and Minsk against the hordes here. I think I would rather party with them than fight them. When in Rome, act like--"

"I know, I know," an agitated Dylan cut in, "but at least you could quit laughing. And since I am currently not talking to him, you can tell your little furry friend that he's toast when I get out of here."

"Do you hear that Minsk? Tonight we party, tomorrow we fight. Let's go make the most of it. I think we can be friends with you guys for at least another day," Salah declared to one of the little people. "Let's go get some food."

Gort, the leader of the group that had imprisoned Dylan, looked up at Salah. "It is customary for both parties to bring something to the table."

"Well we could go foraging or hunting, but I just thought of something else. Have you guys ever had clagos? They are very tasty."

"What's a clago?" asked Gort.

"I have some here in my backpack," said Dylan as he

reached in and pulled out a clago.

He then explained to Gort all of the clago's wonderful properties besides taste.

"If you give me one of those, I think we might be persuaded to let your friend out," Gort proposed.

All three of them looked over at Dylan, who was now sitting in what appeared to be deep thought on the ground.

"You can have one, but let him stew awhile. I happen to agree with Minsk. This is kind of funny, and we can't continue our search until the others show up."

"What are you searching for?" Gort asked.

"We're trying to rescue a dort. It's a companion of one of our friends," replied Salah.

"We'll split the gold with you," volunteered Gort.

"What gold?" questioned Salah.

"We know who hangs around with dorts. If we help you, will you split the treasure with us?"

"Our friend, Butah, lost her treasure."

"Did you say her name was Butah? What does she look like?"

Salah described Butah to Gort.

"She rescued me from certain death a while back. She is my friend. Please continue with your story."

"She gave her treasure as ransom to a thief who stole her dort, but he did not give it back. We are on a quest to recover it. We are lost, but we thought it would be better to help someone than to sit around feeling sorry for ourselves."

"Very noble," interrupted Gort. "I believe you. Anybody that doesn't know our reputation for trick playing is not from these parts. Let's have dinner, and I will ask my friends if they have any ideas on how we can help you. Any friend of Butah's is a friend of ours."

Except for height, Salah's new foot-tall friends were in all aspects human. They moved very quickly with purpose and reminded him of ants scurrying around as they went about their various tasks.

The appetizing scents of the cooking food soon filled the air.

While he waited for dinner, Salah relaxed in the grass. The violin music added life to the clouds that drifted by.

"Your friend Dylan is a poor gambler," Gort declared while interrupting Salah's daydreams.

"He's a good gambler; he's just a poor cheater. You guys outsmarted him at his own game. You have to know that he was going to give you your money back. He engages in these little contests as battles of wit."

"I have to admit that he's the best we've seen at that game, but it's hard to beat someone at the shell game when they can make the marble appear wherever they want it to."

"Can you let him out after dinner?"

"Better yet, I'll remove the cage now and see how long it takes him to figure it out," replied Gort mischievously.

"I love it," Salah replied. "This should knock him down a peg or so."

Gort focused his eyesight in the general direction of Dylan and concentrated.

"There. It is done."

"Can you teach me that invisible cage trick?" asked Salah. "I can think of a few instances where it would have come in handy."

"Come back when you have more time. All of these 'mind over the matter' tricks require serious training. It takes the members of our group at least two years to learn that one."

"Messing up people on the shell game would really be fun, too. Is it a trick, or can you actually transport the marble with your minds?"

"We tricksters will never tell," Gort replied with a smile. "Actually, that's such an old trick around these parts that I can show you. It only takes a short time to strengthen your mind to do that one. Come with me. Since you are on a volunteer charity mission, I will teach you. It may come in handy before your undertaking is complete."

Gort motioned for Salah to follow him into the woods.

"We are going looking for some food," Gort announced to the gathering to disguise their true intentions.

Minsk was entertaining a group with his gymnastic abilities. They were in awe of his flipping and twisting ability. The Blonks, the name their friends called themselves by, were tossing him up in the air from a makeshift trampoline, and he showed off to their great admiration. The crowd grew larger as he continued. First he did a flip. Then he accomplished a double with ease. Next, he did a laid out back flip. He had an incredible selection of moves, so the show went on for a long time. In fact, it was still going on when Salah and Gort walked back out of the woods.

Salah strolled over to the invisible cage that imprisoned Dylan.

"Everything OK?" he inquired.

"Yeah, I guess I learned my lesson. I should have scouted the opposition a little better. Fortunately, this time the mistake wasn't fatal."

Dylan paced back and forth like a caged animal as he spoke. Every time he turned to avoid a collision with a nonexistent invisible wall, Salah couldn't help but smile.

"What are you laughing at?" asked Dylan rather rudely.

"Oh nothing," Salah replied while looking away to avoid laughing in Dylan's face.

"Did your new friends say when they were going to let me out?" Dylan asked.

"They said that your debt will be repaid as of tomorrow morning. Butah helped them in the past, so they will not harm us. Anything you see cooking suit your fancy? They said you could have what you wanted for dinner."

"I'll just take the same as you. I trust your judgment."

"OK. Then I'm going to return to our guests."

"Darn," Dylan mumbled quietly. "How'd I get this rock in my shoe?"

Salah smiled at Gort.

"Mission accomplished," he said.

Gort nodded and smiled with satisfaction. He had taught his protégé well.

The gathering of Blonks suddenly scattered. Being small, they were constantly on the lookout for predators from above. As long as they had warning, Gort explained, the Blonks were just too quick. They always posted a lookout when they gathered in the open. He was blowing furiously on his horn.

Salah looked up in the direction the Blonks were pointing. He saw five large creatures flying toward him at a rapid pace. As they got closer, Salah could see that they each had two heads, a large set of wings, and something on their backs. When they

188

were directly above Dylan, they began circling.

Gort stood by Salah even though the rest of the Blonks had run off into the woods. Salah inched toward Dylan.

"He thinks he's safely inside the box," he said.

Gort yanked on Salah's leg to get his attention.

"Even though it's not there, he's safe," Gort explained.

"What are those things?" asked Salah.

"We can relax," Gort answered. "They are not carnivorous. They are natmaroos. The Harvesters ride on them when they are collecting their berries. In fact, someone is on them right now."

As the natmaroos flew closer to Dylan, it was clear that people were indeed riding on the beasts, but the creatures' wings blocked their identities.

"Is that laughter I hear?" thought Salah. "In fact I know that laugh."

"Having a bad day?" a female voice asked Dylan.

"Show yourself, and perhaps I will make yours worse," countered Dylan.

"You already have. It sure as heck just got a lot uglier," returned the voice.

Minsk recognized the voice and ran toward its owner. As JJ jumped off the back of her natmaroo, Minsk leapt up into her arms and almost knocked her over. While she gave Salah a hug, he whispered something in her ear which made her laugh. She strolled over toward Dylan. She pretended to tap on one of the invisible walls while making a tapping noise with her other hand on one of her swords.

"Now what would cause a person to sit in the middle of a field? Let's see. Minsk is here, so you're not heartbroken. I don't think you're working on your tan. Could you deservedly be in jail?"

Salah sauntered over.

"You don't need to pretend that he is your enemy. They were just about to let him out."

"Oh, really," she said as she looked back at Dylan.

"Aren't you having a little too much fun?" questioned Dylan.

"You seem to be in trouble with the Blonks. What did you do?"

"He tried to hustle them at the shell game. He lost,"

189

explained Salah. "He is here until he can pay off his debts."

Gort picked up on the joke and could hardly contain himself.

"Tisk! Tisk! Tisk! Will any of my jewels help?" asked JJ as she walked up and put her arm around Dylan.

"They already agreed to let him out for a clago," explained Salah.

Suddenly Dylan's face lit up. Everyone else burst out laughing.

"How long has this cage been gone?" Dylan demanded.

"At least forty-five minutes," replied Salah when he could finally contain himself.

Salah walked over to Dylan.

"Welcome back," he stated. "Gotcha."

Dylan kind of smiled. He looked toward the group. Everyone was laughing.

"I guess the expression 'my turn in the box' has new meaning now. Be warned. You will all get your turn."

"Woooooo!" the group answered with a grin.

"Not to change the subject," Dylan said to JJ. "But who are your new friends, and what's the game plan now? I'm sure you didn't get those creatures at the rent-a-dragon store."

JJ explained Maura's situation, how Misha was on the moon, and how they had really cool transportation to get there.

"Up for another adventure?" she asked.

"That's my middle name. I love it," Dylan enthusiastically replied.

Wilthor looked at JJ with a "who is this guy expression" on his face, but refrained from commenting.

"It looks like we need to save Maura first. Anyone know anything about jaysnakes?" Dylan asked while resuming command.

JJ explained, "Jaysnakes are nasty creatures. They generally hunt in packs of about forty. Their usual strategy is to send about ten members at you through the air to distract you."

"They can fly?" asked Dylan incredulously.

"They don't really fly, but they have the ability to slither through the air up to about waist high."

"My curiosity is piqued. Sounds like going after them is going to be risky," declared Dylan.

"It's very dangerous," warned JJ. "Their venom won't kill you for about a week, so most people ignore the fact that they are bitten until it's too late.

"They have a very effective method of attack. While the air snakes come directly at you to keep your attention, the remaining members of the clan surround you. They blitz along the ground from the other three sides. Jaysnakes generally hunt in areas where the ground snakes have cover. Their prey generally doesn't see them until it's too late. If they can rip you apart with their bites or constrict you, they will. Otherwise, the snakes follow their prey at their own leisure, and about a week later, dinner is served."

JJ then explained about the head snake and its tail.

"How does the head snake fit into the battle plan?" asked Dylan.

"The head snake follows from a distance and will only emerge after the kill has been made."

"So we need to lure it out?" questioned Dylan.

"Yes. I think we can circle around behind the attackers and find the leader, but we are going to be in for a war until we get the boss snake."

"Won't they just keep fighting even after we get the head snake?"

"Once the leader is slain, they tend to wander off, looking for another pack to join. They draw their energy from their chief. Without a leader, they only have about a week to join another clan. Otherwise they will die from the little bites they received from their buddies."

"Don't we already have some bait?" asked Dylan.

"That's not exactly a nice way to say it, but since Maura has been bitten, they will be hanging around waiting for her to die. The jaysnakes are probably fairly close to Maura right now," concluded JJ.

As she said this, she instinctively looked around even though the snakes were very far away.

"Minsk, can you sniff them out?" blurted out Jason who had so far contributed nothing to the discussion. He was very proud of his idea.

Minsk jumped up and headed for the woods.

"No, not yet! We need to fly back by Maura," exclaimed JJ.

"Why don't we eat and then make a plan? I'm starving."

The natmaroo pilots and their passengers could not easily sit at the small tables of the Blonks. Everyone wanted to learn the other's story, so it was agreed that there would be at least one large person at each table. The food was delicious.

Once again Minsk turned into the main entertainment. Anyone who wanted could put a pebble on the table with their hands spread about shoulder length apart. Minsk would stand with one of his front paws about a foot away. A referee would say "go" and the pebble was gone before the person could close his hands around it.

Dylan thought about betting on Minsk, but he had learned his lesson last time. Who knew what other magical powers these miniature people possessed?

When dinner was finished, they planned their attack. Gort said that he wished there was something that he could do, but he didn't see how the Blonks could help. The snakes were just too big. It was agreed that everyone would get a good night's sleep and carry out their plans in the morning.

"That means no spy business tonight," JJ insisted while looking over at Dylan. "You may not need any sleep, but we cannot afford any time to go bailing you out of trouble."

"Agreed," returned Dylan. "I'm kind of tired tonight anyway."

The adventurers settled down by a fire. Minsk crawled up next to JJ, and soon they were all fast asleep. Wilthor and his natmaroo riders settled next to their own fire. The natmaroos were tethered to the trees close by. The Blonks went off into the woods.

"Everyone appears to be friends," thought Jason before turning in, "yet, we don't seem to totally trust each other. We've all survived this long, so I guess that's how it should be. Everyone is relying on their instincts."

The next morning, just before the sun peeked over the horizon, Jason awoke to the sounds of the riders feeding their natmaroos. The natmaroos made loud crunching noises as they devoured the tree branches they were given. They seemed totally content to let the riders bring them their food.

"Why don't you let them forage for themselves?" asked Jason while propping himself up on one elbow to watch the feeding.

"They will eat just about any plant. There are a few they are allergic to. It doesn't cause great harm, but we can't afford for them to be sick today," Wilthor responded.

Gort and his little friends were all over the camp talking to whoever was awake. They seemed to enjoy the strangers' company. They also cooked a large breakfast for anyone interested.

The goal was to eat early and then carry out the rest of the plans they made the previous evening. After eating, they said goodbye to Gort and his friends and took off to save Maura.

Dylan and Salah had never ridden a natmaroo before. They were a little bit apprehensive, at first, of the abilities of the natmaroos to maneuver safely at the speeds they were attaining.

Minsk had a different problem. He was much too bold. He climbed halfway out on the neck of Wilthor's natmaroo. He was thoroughly enjoying himself and appeared unaffected by the danger. When the natmaroo changed direction suddenly, he fell off and cartwheeled downward. Wilthor's natmaroo calmly circled back and retrieved him before he was anywhere near the ground.

Jason and JJ were getting more and more comfortable riding on the beasts. Jason even had his eyes open the whole time. He motioned his rider to move over closer to JJ.

When he got closer he yelled out, "Minsk looks like a dog sticking his head out of the window of a moving car. Look at him!"

"What's a car?" JJ yelled back.

Jason didn't know how to respond.

Their natmaroos separated again. The view was fantastic, but the ride didn't last long. Maura's camp wasn't far away, and Salah, JJ, and Dylan weren't going back to camp anyway. They split off to a different destination. Wilthor and Jason flew back to the camp. Dylan thought Jason should go along with Wilthor because the jaysnakes had already seen him, and he also appeared to be the least capable of defending himself.

"Thanks a lot," Jason responded to Dylan's suggestion.

"Appearing defenseless is a great quality to have in the spy business," countered Dylan. "You can get into many places that a potential threat could not. I'm a bit jealous."

"Don't patronize me," Jason indignantly replied.

"You know I don't pander to people's feelings when I'm on a mission," Dylan shot back. "It's for the good of the mission," he reemphasized.

Jason's feelings were soothed when he realized that he had never thought Dylan looked very threatening either.

When the others didn't show up at their meeting place, Butah flew back to find them. She was searching Maura's camp when Wilthor and Jason landed.

Wilthor charged to the fire around which the other Klaterites were sleeping. Minsk had hidden himself in one of the saddlebags and stealthily crept off after Wilthor and Jason dismounted.

The sleeping Klaterites were rudely awakened by Wilthor yelling, "You guys are all asleep. Where are your sentries? Someone is going to pay for this."

The men did not know what to think because everyone in camp knew that natmaroos are the best sentries possible. They scurried around looking for their weapons.

Jason felt sorry for Wilthor's men, but there was no way to pull this off without temporarily deceiving them.

Wilthor next went over to Maura's tent to see how she was feeling. He came out sobbing.

"You clowns let her die, too! I didn't even get to say goodbye," he sobbed.

Wilthor broke down and put his head on Yogla's shoulder. He pretended to sob hysterically while explaining the plan.

"Maura is gone!" Yogla announced. "We need to build a funeral pyre. Let's get to work."

Yogla and the others constructed a chest-high funeral pyre out of dead branches from the nearby jungle. It was built in the middle of the large clearing they used for their campsite. As they collected the branches and built the pyre, nearby sounds made them suspect that the jaysnakes were close.

The Klaterites next went into Maura's tent and carried her out and laid her on the pyre. While they were moving Maura, the other three natmaroos came back to the camp with their riders. They were minus JJ, Salah, and Dylan who were now positioning themselves behind the jaysnakes.

While plotting their strategy, Dylan had previously

explained, "The jaysnakes have been following Maura for a while now, so they will surely know our numbers. They have not seen Dylan and Salah. If some of us are missing, they will suspect an ambush. JJ is a girl, so they probably won't think she is much of a threat."

"Thanks a lot," JJ interrupted.

"Remember what I told Jason. Keep your pride out of this." Dylan shot back. "They will probably attack soon after the others come back," Dylan warned.

The other natmaroo riders played their parts to perfection when they returned and were told that Maura had passed. They joined the line of mourners with their backs to the jungle as the funeral ceremony proceeded.

The natmaroo riders were dressed in the best clothes they could find in the field. The shine of their weapons was the only element of pageantry present. There were thirteen men in a line, plus Jason, mourning over Maura's body. Jason was in the middle of the line because he was the shortest one. Yogla thought it would be more symmetrical.

Wilthor began anointing Maura's head with ceremonial oils to start the ritual.

Out of the corner of his eye, he detected movement at the edge of the jungle. About three feet off the ground, a number of giant snakes slithered in behind the line of mourners. Time stood still as the snakes slowly crept toward their intended victims. Wilthor was having trouble maintaining his forward gaze. The men could see the strain on his face. Their arms tensed up as they expected the order to attack. On the ground, on each side, there were a dozen more snakes slithering silently toward the group. The air snakes paused within striking distance of the backs of their victims, one for each man, as if waiting for a signal.

It was getting tougher and tougher for the mourners to maintain their poise.

When the head snake emerged from the edge of the jungle, it let out a loud hiss. At the signal to attack, the well positioned snakes lifted their heads and extended their hoods like evil giant cobras preparing to strike.

Dylan saw that the time was right and let out his best Comanche yell. The assembled Klaterites each drew their swords, raised them above their heads, twirled, and with a two-handed baseball swing lopped off a jaysnake head. The snakes that were spared the first pass were so startled that they stood motionless as they were also beheaded.

The ground snakes that came from either side generally relied on surprise. They were befuddled when JJ, Dylan, and Salah burst out of the woods behind them. As the pursuers slaughtered the ground snakes, Jason was inadvertently left alone. Sensing an opportunity, the head snake slithered toward him at eye level.

Jason was hypnotized by its large yellow eyes. He was paralyzed. As the giant snake opened its mouth, Jason could see three sharp fangs being readied to sink themselves into his hide.

"What a way to die!" he thought.

His brain was still working although nothing else was.

Suddenly, in a blur, Minsk was on the back of the giant snake's neck. The snake raised his head and shook it violently to try to remove him. Minsk bit hard and would not let go. When the snake's eyes left Jason, Jason snapped out of its spell. He took two steps forward and sliced through the snake's neck with a swing so violent that he fell over. After a roll on the ground, he returned to his fighting stance, but saw there was no need for it. He stared at the headless snake body writhing on the ground. Minsk sat proudly on its head, and Jason was suddenly very thankful that his aim with the sword was true.

All that was left was the mop up. The remaining snakes were either slain or chased off into the jungle.

After making sure the job was done, JJ walked over to Jason.

"I don't know of anyone who has slain a jaysnake in battle," she began.

"How did they cure you then?" Jason asked, again fearful that he was being patronized.

"I was lucky to survive the bite with only half the antidote. The other people that are cured use the spines that the jaysnakes shed throughout their lifetimes. We find the spines in the jungle and save them for when they are needed."

"What?" squawked Jason. "Are you telling me that we could have used shed spines and avoided this whole battle?"

"We needed the spines immediately, and I wasn't sure

where to look. If we searched in the jungle, we could have turned into victims ourselves. Besides, wasn't this more fun?" she haughtily proposed.

"There is something seriously wrong with you," Dylan asserted while butting into the conversation. "And you guys think I'm crazy."

"But life's more fun my way. Don't you think?" JJ quipped. "Cut out his fangs," she continued as if she hadn't even heard Dylan's comments. "Some say they have magical properties. What have you got to lose?"

As she looked at Jason, JJ noticed he was in a trance, staring at the snake. She snapped her fingers in front of his face.

"Wha ... what?" Jason responded as he came to.

"The rest of us at least had the element of surprise. You took out the chief snake in a one-on-one battle! You're a warrior!" JJ declared.

Dylan sauntered over. "Sometimes war produces the most unlikely heroes. Good job buddy," he professed as he reached out to shake Jason's hand.

"Go ahead. Cut out the fangs."

Chapter 20 - Zambusti

Even though the sun was not yet up, the camp already buzzed with activity. Dylan was out on a secret reconnoitering "mission." Butah, who had been introduced to the Klaterites the previous evening, flitted from person to person, asking if they had seen Misha on the moon. Salah cleaned his weapons.

Maura strolled closer to where Jason and JJ were eating breakfast. The antidote had taken effect, and she felt much better.

"I think he'll probably try to sell it at the market in Zambusti," Maura uttered as she looked over at Butah.

"Sell what?" asked Jason who was still half asleep and not quite sure of what was said.

"The dort," responded Maura who suddenly realized she was thinking out loud.

"What kind of market is that?" asked JJ.

"You won't believe what is for sale there. It's best that I not ruin it for you. Dorts are one of the ingredients in a mythical immortality potion. No one has recently tested it out, but I'm sure all the rich old folks would like to give it a try."

"And possibly some rich young ones, too," Salah quipped while joining in.

"When are you going back?" asked Dylan. "If they are going to kill Misha, time is of the essence."

"We need to trade for a few more things with the pirates--"

"Aren't you afraid of them," interrupted Dylan.

"They can be dangerous, but we have things they cannot get elsewhere. Harming us is not in their interests."

"You are so few," Dylan countered. "What if they just decide to take whatever they want?"

"Then we wouldn't come back, now, would we? Look, we had a temporary setback when I was bitten by the jaysnake, but we are not as incapable of taking care of ourselves as it may seem. There is a designated spot where the pirates drop off their payment. We are paid in small jewel type stones. They are much in demand in Zambusti.

"Metallurgists in Zambusti know the secret of making very very strong sword and dagger blades. Our swords can slice right through a common sword produced by the Phosphorata. They are invaluable to the pirates. The pirates get us a few other things, and they get the weapons. We send one of our members back with the location of their goods after we receive ours."

"The Klinglesprachs also briefly mentioned the Phosphorata," Dylan remarked. "Who are they?"

"They are another group you need to see to believe. Most of the time our only contact with them is during their small border raids, but those are more of a nuisance than anything. Folklore states, however, that once in a great while, they swarm out of their land and completely overrun the countryside, destroying everything and everyone in their path. They are very similar to locusts in that respect. Then, after holding the land for a short period of time, they retreat back to their own turf. Nobody knows why. It's almost as if it's biological. Few that are alive today have ever seen it. According to our records, the last time they marched was centuries ago. Once they start moving, it is nearly impossible to stop them."

"JJ, do your people have these stories too?" Dylan asked.

"Yes, but they originated a long time ago. Who knows if they are true?

"They are true," Maura decreed. "I have seen them."

"Then you are centuries old?" questioned a skeptical Dylan.

"I was attacked by a Ratalap when I was very young. You sleep for hundreds of years from their bite. My people were very good to me and kept me alive. I woke up about five years ago, and here I am. I have seen the Phosphorata in action and have a score to settle with them."

"Amazing," Jason and Dylan said together.

"The pirates have been very anxious for our weapons lately which might indicate they believe the Phosphorata are preparing to march again soon," continued Maura.

"In small numbers, the Phosphorata are constantly skirmishing with the pirates at the borders of their lands. As long as they don't come en masse, the pirates generally win. I think if

I take you to one of these spots, it will help answer your questions. The natmaroos are getting more comfortable with you. Since we need most of them to conduct our normal business, you guys will need to double up without the help of our pilots. Salah, why don't you pilot Yowza. She seems to be growing fond of you. You can take Dylan along. I will take Minsk."

"I'll give it a try," Salah confidently answered while feeding Yowza.

"And JJ, why don't you ride with our timid Slayer of the Jaysnake? He still seems a little uncomfortable up in the air."

"I had my eyes open last time," Jason proudly proclaimed.

"One fine point about riding natmaroos. They are fun loving and high spirited creatures. They love to do loops and fly upside down. Sometimes it can be difficult to hang on if they catch you by surprise. They won't intentionally throw you, and they will come back and retrieve you if you're thrown. Occasionally their timing is a little off, and they don't arrive before you hit the ground. Obviously, the results of that are not good. Natmaroos will only do this if they forget they have a rider, so keep pressure on the reins to remind them that you are there.

"Wilthor, I am going to take our new friends to see the Phosphorata in action. Perhaps, you could finish up our business and meet me back here later today."

"Sounds like a plan. Let's go troops," commanded Wilthor. The remaining men joined Wilthor and took off to fulfill their missions.

"Are you guys ready to expand your vision of the possible?" Maura shouted as she hopped onto her natmaroo.

The other natmaroos sped after her as she rocketed into the sky.

Both Dylan and JJ had grown quite proficient on their natmaroos. They had a real talent for flying. Dylan was much bolder, however, and seemed to go out of his way to ignore Wilthor's last words of advice.

"There are old flyers, and there are bold flyers, but there are no old bold flyers," he preached.

"They're going to need some bold flyers," Dylan thought, "if what they say is true and this ever comes to a battle."

Jason's eyes were now open as he clung to JJ's waist. He even thought of asking for the reins on the way back. As he held on, he was starting to understand why the other men were attracted to JJ. The scent of her long, blond hair was enticingly sweet as it blew back and encircled him.

After flying a short time, the natmaroos deposited them on the highest branches of some very tall trees. The sun had not yet peeked above the horizon, but light was already starting to filter across the plain in front of them. The stars were gone. The moon was still faintly visible in the sky. They were twenty miles into enemy territory and watching for any signs of the impending invasion that Maura had hinted of.

Dylan's acute vision picked up the first signs of movement. He spied what appeared to be a Greek or Roman battle formation in the distance. Groups ten across and ten deep were marching toward them. It was as if giant squares were moving across the field.

Each soldier was armed with a giant pike. His shield was attached to his back, and a scabbard with a sword hung from his belt. They were close to a thousand strong. These were the Phosporata, the soldiers feared most by the inhabitants of this world.

Dylan watched as the soldiers moved in and out of a fog. Then with a jolt, he realized that they weren't moving in and out of a fog. The Phosphorata had the unnatural ability to turn themselves invisible for short periods of time. They were like walking fireflies, but instead of temporarily blinking light, they blinked invisible. Dylan guessed some genetic mutation in the distant past along with intense training allowed them to do this.

"Making themselves invisible is easy," Maura explained. "Making weapons and armor invisible takes a lot more work and concentration. That discipline in their elite troops makes them deadly in hand to hand combat."

Dylan thought that if the Phosphorata were to march out of their homeland, it was imperative that the opposing army knew they were coming. Then it might be possible to drop dye, powder, or some other substance on the enemy to make them visible. If surprise was part of the attack, he had no idea how to defeat them in their invisible state.

About midway through the field, the soldiers halted. They stood motionless for a moment and then scattered about as if reacting to orders. They were making camp. Tents were pitched, and it looked like they were settling down for a few days.

Dylan was very curious about the Phosphorata. He was already trying to determine their potential weaknesses if it came to battle.

While they worked on the encampment, they never seemed to "blink" as Dylan soon came to describe their peculiar ability.

Dylan wondered if he could teach himself to become invisible. After all, he had learned many of his other "spy" skills in a very short period of time.

"This is amazing," Dylan remarked to Jason. "I couldn't even imagine that this was possible. Any ideas on how we could beat up on them?"

Jason did not respond. While everyone else was gawking in amazement at the soldiers' ability to turn invisible, Jason never lost sight of them. They did not turn invisible in his eyes. He was staring at their cattle-skull shaped heads and wondering if he had met any of them before.

He remembered Dylan mumbling something in the past along the lines of, "If the enemy doesn't know you speak their language, they may talk in front of you. Sometimes you want to keep your talents to yourself."

He decided to keep his mouth shut for now.

After observing the Phosphorata for about an hour, Maura suggested that they head back and rest up for their journey to Zambusti. "It looks like the Phosphorata might be on the march again," she added, "but we need to get Misha before we attempt to solve this problem ..., if we even want to."

"We may not have a choice," JJ warned. "If the stories are true, once they get started, they pretty much wipe out everything in their path. I do have friends here, and I suspect that all of the people that helped us so far will be in danger."

Maura's comment about the upcoming battle disrupted Jason's thoughts. He was mulling over his many problems. How would they get back to Rockdale? Would they ever even get back? If they got back, would they be wiped out by these cattle-skulled monsters anyway?

What exactly was Minsk? He screamed when the Ionizard was chasing him, but other than that, Minsk had not communicated with him since that time in the market. Maybe he was hallucinating, but Minsk definitely was an extraordinary character.

Would they actually be able to get to the moon and back while rescuing Misha?

Would he die in some mindless skirmish with his adventure-loving friends? Worse yet, was he becoming one of them?

The other thing that was nagging at him was the question of who all his new found friends really were, and could they be trusted? In their recent battles for self-preservation, they had all come through like champs. Did they have any ulterior motives for this journey, or were they just trapped in the adventure like he was?

These deep thoughts were interrupted by his present realization, "I'm turning into a mercenary."

A breeze shifted the branch that Jason was perched on. Reality suddenly crept back and brought with it a change in Jason's contemplations.

"I'd like to try it for myself. I want to be the pilot," Jason said to JJ.

"I guess I can't have all the fun," JJ answered.

"Let him fly with me," Maura suggested. I can help if he gets into trouble."

She had once or twice seen a novice flyer freak out and had successfully negotiated a safe landing.

Making their way to their natmaroos was a little tricky in the treetops.

"The trees are more scary than dangerous," Jason thought, "because even if I slip the branches are so thick that I can't fall far."

Once everyone was aboard, the natmaroos spread their wings and launched themselves from the treetops. JJ rode with Minsk. Dylan was now the pilot with Salah on the back. Jason grabbed the reins and commanded Maura's natmaroo. Maura whispered to go slowly at first. Gradually, Jason took a little pressure off the reigns and the speed increased. Since Maura was with him, they took the lead while the others followed along.

Soaring freely in the air removed all of Jason's cares and worries. The rush was unbelievable. He even let Welker go into a barrel roll a few times, and the others followed. He felt very comfortable as he became more and more, one with the creature.

In Jason's mind, they arrived back in camp way too soon.

Wilthor had already returned and was preparing for the trip to the moon. Wilthor's men continued to secure goods to the natmaroos until they were so loaded that Jason wondered if they could even fly.

One of the objectives of Maura's group was to bring back whole plants to increase the availability of vagelberries on the moon. The plants could grow on the moon, but earth was much more fertile. They were one of their major cargoes and were attached in every possible way to the natmaroos.

There were a few items hidden under tarps that Maura's group was extremely secretive and protective of and would not allow the young adventurers near. Dylan, as usual, was extremely curious. He didn't press the issue, though, because he feared jeopardizing their passage.

"We will be ready to leave shortly. You newbies to space travel should consume your vagelberries now just to make sure that they take effect," Wilthor proclaimed as he passed a handful to each of them.

Butah was very apprehensive about accepting hers.

"I've never been in space before. I'm a little scared," she admitted.

"Remember, we need to go there to get Misha," JJ added in a comforting but firm manner. "You've done far riskier things."

"Poor little Misha," Butah mumbled to herself. "I guess you're right."

Butah quickly consumed her portion of vagelberries.

"Down the hatch," Dylan said as he shoved his into his mouth. Everyone else followed his lead.

"I feel a little buzz this time," Dylan reported.

"You live life in a buzz," JJ jeered.

Minsk thought that JJ's comment was hilarious, and he went off on one of his laughing jags. He made such weird noises that everyone nearby stopped what they were doing, fearing he was dying. He had a pretty large audience before he finally stopped. He calmly looked around, winked, and went about his business.

Nobody else had any reaction to the berries.

All of the fourteen natmaroos were now loaded and ready to go. Some of the merchants had to double up with the new travelers. Maura thought that each of the newbies should ride on the back with a seasoned flier on their first long trip into space.

"You may slip into a condition we call 'space trance' from the length and beauty of the trip," Maura explained. "You eventually become immune to it, but we don't want to take any chances now."

"JJ and Jason have already been in space for a while and nothing happened to them," Dylan asserted.

"It generally occurs when you pull away from the earth," Maura warned. "They really haven't done that yet."

"I'll bow to your authority," said Dylan, agreeing to her precautions.

Although it was Maura's group, Wilthor was in charge of operations. He gave the order, and everyone followed him into the sky.

The flight was nothing short of spectacular. The stars, nebulae, and other interstellar objects were incredibly beautiful from space. It was unbelievable how bright and clear everything was from outside the atmosphere. Once, they needed to scramble quickly out of the path of a silently approaching asteroid, but for the most part, the journey was straightforward.

Surprisingly, the only person that went into a partial trance was Dylan, and he was out of it by the time their journey was three-quarters over.

Everyone in the group was astonished to see how green and alive the moon was. The topography was very similar to earth. There were mountains and rivers, oceans and forests, deserts and prairies. Wilthor lead the natmaroos to just outside of a small village. They circled once before landing there.

"Congratulations," Wilthor announced. "You have just survived your first trip to Zlagall, or as you call it, the moon."

They dismounted from their natmaroos, which seemed happy to graze on the nearby vegetation.

JJ came over to Jason.

"I bet you never had a ride like that before," she said, her eyes glowing with excitement.

Minsk followed along behind her, seemingly uninterested in plotting another attack on Dylan. The flight had overwhelmed him. Salah's eyes again sparkled with excitement.

"Welcome to Zambusti," Maura announced.

Chapter 21 - Life in Zambusti

When the Maura's caravan arrived at the edge of Zambusti, the locals were very happy to see them. Many of them had invested heavily in the trip and were now set to reap the financial rewards.

Maura and Wilthor joyfully greeted their business associates. They explained to the locals that the newbies were to be trusted and had saved Maura's life. The natives were more interested in the cargo. Another set of strangers from a different land did not seem to pique their curiosity.

"We don't want to jinx them by showing them to you," was the only response Dylan and Salah had previously received when they asked what was under the tarps.

They now watched with interest as the special cargo was unloaded.

"Pumpkins?" Dylan questioned as the ropes around the tarps were untied, and the tarps slid off. "Why would pumpkins be such a big deal?" he said to himself and the others.

Dylan couldn't take it anymore. He just couldn't figure out what the pumpkins were for. He walked over to where Maura was talking to her companions and pulled her aside.

"I have seen many strange things since I've been here, but this pumpkin thing takes the cake. You risked your life and almost lost it on a dangerous journey for pumpkins?" Dylan inquired.

"Strange is in the eye of the beholder," Maura responded. "But at the soonest possible time, I will show you what they are used for. I need to check the schedule. I will leave you with your friends. I have some personal business to attend to. I am also going to discretely inquire as to the whereabouts of your dort. I will meet you back here at sunset.

"Oh, and by the way, you and your friends have been voted shares in the profits. You are now quite rich people. You might want to think about what you are going to do with your fortunes."

She placed a handful of small multicolored stones into Dylan's hand and closed it. "These are very valuable. Don't lose them. You will get more when we settle up."

"Fortunes?" Dylan questioned as he looked at the stones in his hand.

"I've got to go. See you later," Maura called back over her shoulder as she walked away.

Dylan walked over to the others. Maura's riders had all wandered off to share their adventures, leaving the group unaccompanied in the crowded marketplace. It was, to Dylan, absolutely amazing that four strangely dressed people and a mongoose did not attract any unwanted attention.

Salah looked at his friends.

"Why don't we try and find something to eat?" he asked. "I'm starving."

It was a soldier's constant lament, especially a teenage soldier.

"We don't have any of the local currency," JJ responded.

"I beg to differ with you," Dylan interrupted in his know-it-all manner. "Everyone huddle up."

"Huddle up?" questioned JJ.

"It means gather closely so I can explain something to you quietly. Follow me," Dylan ordered as he led them away from the crowd.

When they were alone, Dylan began, "There are some things you don't want to advertise around strangers. Especially ones whose intentions and motives you are unaware of." He then explained what Maura had just told him and ended with, "I have twenty-one stones. Each of us will get five, and we'll try to use one for dinner."

Minsk made a nasty growling noise.

"Each of us, including Minsk, will get four stones," said Dylan as he laid them out on the ground.

"What are you going to do, bury them like a squirrel?" Dylan gibed.

Minsk scowled nastily back.

207

JJ's eyes lit up. "These stones with the red spot in the middle are extremely valuable where I come from. I am not an expert, but I will do my best to divide them up fairly. My thoughts are that we should each carry a few and use them as necessary. Don't get greedy. Use them if need be. When everything is settled, we will divide what's left in a fair manner. What does everyone say about that?"

"Being suddenly wealthy requires much more thought than we can possibly give right now," Salah contributed. "I must admit that becoming wealthy was my goal when I left for this place. Now, other things seem more important."

Jason suddenly perked up. "Why don't we give the stones to Butah? It seems like part of her identity was lost with her treasure. It would make her feel much better. After all, rescuing Butah's dort is the reason we've had all of these adventures in the first place. We should keep what we need to survive and give her the rest."

"I'll go along with that," JJ agreed.

"Me too," Salah concurred, "Although I've always dreamt of being rich."

"I guess if you are all in, then I can hardly be the lone holdout," Dylan resolved. "After all, you can't buy more adventures than we're having. All the spies that have ever lived would change places with me right now. No use dulling my senses by getting fat and comfortable."

Minsk was gone, so no one knew what he thought.

"By the way, where's Butah?" Dylan asked.

"She has never seen the people here before," JJ answered. "'She mentioned that as soon as she was sure she wouldn't be captured, she would show herself."

"Seems logical," Salah threw in.

They wandered into town to search for a meal. By following their noses, they quickly came to a suitable establishment. Dylan walked over to the man he thought was the owner and asked what he could get for one of the stones.

"A meal a day for you and your friends for eternity," was the response.

"Are you kidding?"

"No sir!" the man responded. "The only people that come into contact with stones of that nature are the ruling class and the natmaroo Sky Traders."

"The Sky Traders?"

"They are a group of a few hundred people that live away from the villages. The Sky Traders are in possession of natmaroos. Possession is not quite the right word, for these creatures have minds of their own at times, but the traders are the only ones who can ride them. Others have tried with disastrous results. They fly off to undisclosed locations and come back with the most wonderful things. Nobody knows where they go, since it is impossible to follow them if you can't fly. Rumor has it that they have something on the ruling class because the king pretty much leaves them alone. The rest of us are highly taxed.

"One of the only things we do have is the orange battles that go on once a month."

"The orange battles?" Dylan asked.

"Yes. We don't know where the combatants come from, but they look like round orange balls with faces .... Giant heads. Twenty of them are placed in an arena at once, and at a given signal, they try to demolish each other. Their means of movement are a mystery. They have no arms and legs, and seem to float on a cushion of air. They have a metal spike on top and large teeth which they use as weapons. The creatures come to life on call, and the winners return to a dormant state after the contest is over. They scrape up the remains of the losers. Betting on the competitions is huge. It is about the only entertainment we have."

"Pumpkin fights?" Jason inquired.

Dylan changed the topic of conversation.

"Take the stone," Dylan insisted. "How about bringing us the house special?"

"You are so generous. I am Trent. I will start preparing your meals."

"I am Dylan."

Dylan introduced the others to Trent.

"You're not going to come back later and accuse me of stealing this stone, are you? It's happened before around here. A lot of the really wealthy around here cannot be trusted. In fact, I don't know how I am going to turn this into something I can spend without visiting the Hole."

"What's the Hole?" inquired Dylan.

"It's a section of town where all the sordid elements hang out. I mentioned that the orange fights were all that we have, but if you risk going to the Hole, there's a lot more. I'll probably get only a small percentage of the stone's full value, but what else am I to do?"

Trent left to prepare the meals. The hungry and exhausted adventurers sat back and relaxed at the table. Each drifted off into personal thoughts. They were interrupted when Maura unexpectedly pulled up a chair.

"I see you had no trouble finding the best place in town to eat," she declared.

"Huh?" was the combined response as everyone came back to reality.

"Trent's Tap is a hidden gem around these parts. Good food. Good company. Good spirits. You guys haven't built up a tolerance, so I would stay light on the spirits."

"I gave Trent one of the stones, and he said we would have meals for life," Dylan disclosed to Maura. "Was he joking?"

"It was probably a good trade for both sides. Trent hears a lot of things. He may be able to help us find Misha. I'm pretty sure he is going to be auctioned off somewhere in the Hole fairly soon. Trent may give us a reason to be there that will help us avoid scrutiny. The Hole is where all the area's shady transactions take place. Fencing the stone would be good cover. They prey on naïve outsiders like you in the Hole."

They were interrupted as Wilthor sauntered up to the table.

"Mind if I join you?" he asked.

Jason got up and brought over another chair. Wilthor looked very tired. He breathed a sigh as he plopped down into his chair.

Trent reappeared with four waiters bringing an enormous quantity of food.

"You didn't tell me there would be others," he said with surprise. "I will go get some more food."

"This will be fine," Dylan responded. "We will not finish this, even with our new friends."

"Let me get the drink," exclaimed Trent.

"Let me help you," Dylan insisted.

He followed Trent away. When they were into the next room, Dylan cornered Trent.

"I noticed a brief look of terror on your face when you saw

our new guests. Why?"

"It's none of my business, but those Sky Traders you are with are not to be trusted. They would trade their mother for a coin. I know it's not my place to say this, but as of right now, you are my best customers, and I would hate to lose you. If you have any more of those gems, they will con them out of you."

"They actually gave them to us," explained Dylan.

"What?" exclaimed a disbelieving Trent.

Dylan then gave Trent a brief summary of their adventures with Maura and her gang.

Trent looked at Dylan with shock on his face.

"They really gave you those stones voluntarily?"

"They brought it up. We didn't even know the stones existed."

"Wow ...! Wow!" was all Trent could muster.

Dylan changed subject. "We are essentially on a rescue mission. We are trying to liberate a dort. It is a small creature that is a pet of one of our friends. Folklore says it is used to make an immortality potion. The rumor is that it is going to be auctioned off shortly near here, possibly in the Hole. Have you heard anything about that? You must hear a lot of things at this tavern."

"I will make discreet inquiries for my best customer. Perhaps I can accompany you if you visit the Hole? I can try and sell my stone there."

"That's precisely what I had in mind," said Dylan who was already constructing a plot to rescue Misha.

It was agreed that everyone would rent a room upstairs at Trent's while they searched for Misha. The boys roomed together, but on this particular occasion JJ insisted on being alone. Everyone wanted her to at least have some protection, so after protesting strongly, she agreed to room with Minsk.

She became very private and for the next few days went about her business alone.

During that time, the boys wandered through the town observing many strange things that were for sale. One of the items Salah found particularly interesting were fish in glass bowls that could be trained to jump in the air and recite a phrase. Salah desperately wanted to purchase the one that jumped into the air and shouted, "Hello gorgeous!"

"It will help me with the ladies back home," he revealed.

"How are you going to get a fish back home?" Dylan questioned.

"Good point," returned Salah after giving it some further thought.

"The ladies would probably have other issues, anyway."

"Such as?"

"Have you looked in the mirror recently?" Dylan inquired with a smirk.

"I don't see the ladies fawning over you either," Salah replied. "Perhaps if you weren't around, I would have more success …. Actually, they probably feel sorry for me because I need to take care of my somewhat limited friend. Thanks for hanging with me."

They both laughed and looked around for Jason.

Jason was over by a booth selling a variety of small furry animals. The owner was taking them out of their tiny cages and showing them to him.

As soon as Dylan realized what was happening, he rushed over to Jason and blurted out, "No more furry rodents! One is too many!"

"Relax. You yourself once told me that sometimes the best place to hide things is in plain sight. I was looking for Misha."

"The student becomes the master. Great idea!"

The man who was showing Jason the animals looked around and then quietly whispered, "I couldn't help overhearing your conversation. Are you looking to acquire the mythical creature known as the dort?"

"Actually, I am not, but I represent someone who is," Jason embellished.

"Perhaps, if you buy something, I can help you."

"I don't have any currency with me, but I can get it."

"Can I help you for a percentage of the deal?" asked the merchant.

"There are too many people involved for me to agree to something like that. I will get some money to pay you if you come up with some good information. How much time do you need?'

"The man I need to talk to will be back in three days. Come back in four days, and I should have something for you. Bring something to trade for it."

"I'll do that. Who should I look for?"

"My name is unimportant. Be at this location at this time in four days. I should have some information."

"Good luck," Jason said as he offered his hand for the man to shake. The man took it with a firm grasp before he turned to another potential customer.

"Good job," said Dylan to Jason. "It shows that good things can happen if you are out and about. Spies don't acquire information by sitting still."

Salah, by this time, had joined them. Dylan explained to him what had just occurred.

"Three days is a long time. We should probably keep looking. What else have we to do?"

They spent next few days wandering through the market seeing strange things and hearing of even stranger things that were rumored to occur in the Hole. They saw a man that could juggle with his feet. He had a prehensile big toe and could keep four balls in the air at a time. They saw large rat-like creatures trained to play musical instruments. A merchant was using them to attract customers to his food stand.

"Did I just die and go to hell?" Dylan inquired as he disgustedly turned away from the rats. He was sure that somewhere Minsk was laughing at him.

After their third day of prowling the streets, they headed for Trent's. When they arrived for dinner, JJ and Minsk were already there. JJ looked tired. She had a few scratches on her face and a large bump on her forehead.

"I was looking at a cute guy and walked into a tree," JJ explained.

Jason thought he detected a slight hesitation in her voice, but attributed it to the long day and the injuries.

Minsk was snoozing on a chair.

"Why don't we eat? I'm starving," JJ suggested.

They looked around for Trent. When they saw him, they motioned him over to the table.

"Any word on the dort?" Dylan asked.

"Nothing yet. I will continue to keep my ears open. Would you like dinner now?"

"Yes, please," they all answered together.

While Trent went off to the kitchen, the boys told JJ what had happened during their day. Nobody had seen Maura or Wilthor.

After stuffing themselves, they all agreed that it was another Trent masterpiece.

When asked what she did all day, JJ brushed it off with a comment about keeping an eye on Minsk, who was surely a danger to himself and others.

Everyone laughed in agreement. Surprisingly, Minsk did not scowl back as was his usual custom when insulted.

After dinner, JJ excused herself. She said she was very tired but would love to go with everyone the next day. She left the table and went upstairs to her room. Minsk got up and followed. The three boys were left to themselves.

"What shall we do for the rest of the evening?" Salah asked as he pushed his chair back from the table.

"Why don't we try to get in that game of darts with the locals?" suggested Dylan.

Jason walked over to the three men playing and asked if they could join in.

"We play for small stakes."

"I don't think that will be a problem."

He turned and searched the room for Trent. When he spotted him, Jason walked over.

"Can you cover our wager with these gentlemen?" he asked. "We don't have any small currency. Could we maybe trade the meals for the second half of our lives for some small change? After all, we are going to lose, so they'll keep playing and drinking, and you'll get your money right back."

"Since you're brimming with overconfidence, I don't know how I can refuse," Trent laughed. He gave the boys more than enough to play.

"You may need it later," he indicated.

The boys joined into the darts game and shortly became the locals' favorites because they were so bad. When they finished, they covered their bet with a small portion of the currency Trent had given them.

As the victors were leaving, one of them whispered to Jason with a glint in his eye, "You seem like men of good judgment ..., although your athletic skills seem to be wanting. Would you like to go where you can use your judgment instead of your skills to win some real money?"

"I don't know," responded Jason. He was thinking that maybe his new friends were looking for an opportunity to take more than his money.

The man could sense his hesitation. "Trent will vouch for us. We have never lost one of his customers yet. You don't need to tell us now. If you're interested, meet us here tomorrow shortly after dinner."

"Sounds fair," Jason answered.

Jason watched his new friends leave and was shocked by who he thought was JJ going out the door ahead of them. Dylan and Salah didn't see her, so he let it pass.

"I'm getting tired," Salah proclaimed with a yawn. He walked toward their room. The others followed, too tired to disagree.

The next morning, they waited downstairs for JJ and Minsk. When they didn't show up, Jason went up and knocked on her door. JJ opened it after a long wait.

"Are you going with us today?" asked Jason.

"I'm a little tired," said a frazzled looking JJ. She had, in Jason's opinion, a few more bruises on her face, but it was hard to tell whether or not they were just the old ones under a different light.

"Were you out last night? Not that it's any of my business," continued Jason.

"I had a couple of errands to run, so I think I'll pass on this morning's activities."

Minsk was genuinely annoyed at being awakened. He gave Jason a nasty look and then curled up and went back to sleep.

JJ looked so tired that Jason decided not to press her on the issue and left while asking, "Will we see you for dinner tonight?"

"Yes, I'll be there."

She carelessly slammed the door, and Jason assumed she went back to sleep.

Jason walked away not knowing what to think. She had not denied being out last night, but what could she be doing out on the town by herself? He tried to come up with a theory as he walked back to the others. He decided that if JJ wanted her privacy, then so be it.

The boys spent a quiet morning and afternoon walking through the town and listening for any signs of the location of the dort auction. Their chats with the locals led nowhere. When they casually brought up the subject, most people told them that dorts don't really exist.

Shortly before dinner, they ran into Maura, who was carrying a few swords from the local blacksmith.

"Good afternoon," she greeted enthusiastically. "Any news on your dort?"

"No, but we have a few people discreetly inquiring for us," replied Jason.

"Same in our camp," Maura countered.

"You're one of the people we know we can trust here," Jason revealed.

"Why thank you."

"I need to ask you a question," Jason continued. "A couple of the locals we met at Trent's last night want to take us out gambling tonight. What sort of events do people bet on in the Hole? Do you think we should refuse because it is too dangerous?"

"Actually, it's probably a good idea. Most people at those events drink heavily. At times they are indiscreet. You may hear a thing or two. Just make sure you are armed, but try not to fight anyone. The weapons will make people think twice about annoying you, but it's tough to tell how many friends someone has in the crowd until you really provoke them. You are on their turf.

"As to the events, the most popular event is Gronko. It is a type of gladiator fight where each contestant has a wooden sword and a shield. Their faces can be covered with light armor, so a fighter can fight anonymously, but that is rarely done since most of the fighters crave the fame. The goal is to knock out your opponent. Since the swords are wood, they cannot pierce their intended targets. They are wielded like clubs until one opponent is disarmed or the swords break. Most of the contests turn into hand to hand combat after that. It is very violent. My guess is that's where they will be taking you."

"It doesn't sound all that interesting," Jason responded.

"What do you mean?" cried Salah. "It's a chance to possibly

216

learn a few new fighting techniques."

"Or get your skull crushed."

"Spies must sometimes work under disagreeable conditions, buddy," Dylan threw in.

"Just the same ...."

"My guess is that if you spend some time at the fights, you will hear something tonight that will give you a clue to the dort's location," Maura interrupted.

"I've got to run. Here, take these swords. They are the strong type we spoke of previously. These are the ones the pirates crave. Consider them a gift for saving my life. Good luck this evening. If I come across anything, I will look for you at Trent's. Bye."

Maura then vanished into the crowd.

"Well I think I'm up for an expedition this evening," Dylan declared. "How about you guys?"

"The smell of adventure is in the air," Salah proclaimed.

"Well, we're not going to find anything sitting on our butts. I'm in!" Jason exclaimed.

The tone of his own voice shocked him. It was flippant and careless as if the dangers were irrelevant. After thinking about it for a while, he was rather proud of himself.

They waited for JJ to show up at dinner, but she never came. Jason went up to her room, but there was no answer when he knocked on the door. He had already suspected that she would not be there. There was no sign of Minsk, either.

When he came back downstairs to the table, two of their three dart-playing friends from the previous night were sitting at a table.

"Hey Jason," Bart let out. "Where's your girlfriend?"

"She's not my girlfriend," Jason responded. He was confused by the man's belligerent tone.

"Don't let him bother you," Bart's friend Ethan said apologetically. "He's been drinking all day. He gets a little ornery when he's drinking, but he won't harm his friends. Franco couldn't even make it here tonight for the same reason. He won't wake up until tomorrow."

"Now that we're all here, why don't we fill our bellies and then disappear into the night," suggested Dylan. "Since you are going to show us around this evening, dinner is on us."

Dylan motioned Trent over.

"We'll have the house special this evening. I'm not sure where we stand with you financially ...."

"You're fine for quite a while," responded Trent.

"Then include Bart and Ethan here as our guests," Dylan declared magnanimously.

"I will be back shortly," Trent declared and vanished into the kitchen.

"I think you will have more fun if we don't tell you about our destination beforehand," Ethan suggested. "The initial shock is part of the experience. Just don't pick a fight with anyone. Back down if someone wants to fight with you. There are a lot of beer muscles in the crowd, especially after things get going. The people who say nasty things don't hate you. They will be your friend in the morning, so try to avoid mixing it up with them tonight. They just drink too much."

"Well it seems like we have our marching orders, so why don't we eat," suggested Salah as Trent brought the food to the table.

Everyone dug in. When they all had their fill, Bart stood up and in as solemn a voice as he could muster, recited,

"Into the night we adventurers go,
Hoping to witness a remarkable show.
The enemy may try to inflict some pain,
But possibly we will be rewarded with gain."

Bart then sat down and looked around at the faces of the others.

"He gets that way when he's nervous," Ethan threw in. "Actually, his poems aren't bad. They generally sum up the situation quite well."

"We're impressed," said Jason. "Hopefully the pain part can be avoided tonight."

"Amen," said Salah and Dylan together. "Let's go!"

With that, everyone stood up, thanked Trent, and walked out the door on the way to another adventure.

Chapter 22 - The Hole

Ethan led the boys down a maze of narrow roads and alleys. It was partially illuminated by torches, but occasionally it was pitch-black. At times they passed groups of three or four individuals that did not make eye contact. Those groups were essentially minding their own business. At other times Jason got the feeling that folks were sizing his group up. They gave him the creeps with their hostile and prying eyes. He would slowly squeeze his sword, but he never had to draw it.

Jason tried to apply Dylan's spy theories to the problem of remembering how to get back to Trent's. He suspected that Ethan and Bart would be of little use on the return. Jason tried to remember every little detail of their journey. The sweet smell of the bakery might help if he got lost. The sound of the blacksmith banging on horseshoes could point him in the right direction. He knew a little about astronomy. The stars in this world appeared brighter, but in the same location as at home. He found the North Star. They were heading straight north.

When they reached a walled-off four story building, Ethan stopped. Jason could hear wild cheering from inside. Ethan led them along the wall until they came to a spot with a door. He pounded on the small closed wooden window. It eventually opened.

"Who goes there?" inquired a voice from inside.

"It is Ethan of Zambusti come to reclaim some of his lost fortune."

The window opened, and a small set of eyes examined Ethan and the others.

"I see Bart is with you. Who are the others?"

"They are travelers from foreign lands with money to spend on your entertainment."

The eyes looked the boys over one more time.

"Enter and enjoy yourselves," the voice commanded as the

door opened.

Ethan and Bart lead the others through the door.

A crowd of people milled around the grounds that separated the building from the wall. Torch-lit booths sold food and drink. The crowd appeared intent on having a good time. Judging by their clothing, they appeared to be from all different classes and occupations. The craftsmen and farmers mingled with the aristocrats. All seemed eager to get back into the building to watch whatever entertainment was going on inside.

"Last chance to bet on the Cat! Last chance to bet on the Cat! Odds are thirty to one against her. A chance to win big money. The King of Disaster is not as tough as he thinks he is," Jason heard a man hawking.

He turned toward the source of the voice. There was a booth where a small line of people were placing wagers. Jason wandered over to the booth.

"Who is the Cat?" Jason asked the man who was last in line.

"She's a new fighter. She destroyed the favorite last night before his fight. It had to be cancelled. Everyone who saw it said she was extremely lucky. I saw it, and I disagree. I'm betting on her. We don't get too many women fighters here, and they rarely win, so I'm getting long odds. Who are you betting on?"

"I think I'll just watch for a while. This is my first time here, and I would like to make an educated bet."

"Generally a wise decision, but after tonight she's going to be the favorite. I've seen a lot of fighters, but I've never seen anything like last night. It wasn't even in the pit. She was sparring with a fellow fighter. The King of Disaster made some comment about her appearance, and she challenged him right there. He was out in ten seconds. People think he was surprised, and that's why she won. I've never seen anyone so quick. We are going to have a new champ tonight. He's angry, but in this business you can't afford to be."

"You said he commented on her appearance?"

"That's the rumor ..., but I heard it from a good source. I was too far away to hear what he actually said."

"What did she look like?" asked Jason, his suspicions aroused.

"Tall and thin. You wouldn't think someone built like that would pack that kind of power. She wore a mask, so you couldn't see her face. Her hair was golden. She was accompanied by a small rodent-like creature that she appeared to be very fond of. He took off right after the fight, and she went hauling after him. That's why they call her the Cat. Nobody really knows who she is, but they do know she's good business."

"That explains a lot," Jason thought.

"The King of Disaster is going to be just that," he mumbled under his breath.

"What's that?"

"I changed my mind. I think I'll bet on the Cat."

The stranger motioned Jason to join him in the betting line. When he reached the front, he took out what currency he had left from Trent and placed it on the Cat at thirty to one.

"Thanks for the tip," Jason said to his new friend. "My name is Jason. Perhaps we will meet again."

"Perhaps," said the stranger with a wink. He then placed his bet on the Cat and disappeared into the crowd.

Jason walked back to his friends.

"Where have you been?" asked Dylan. "Find out anything about the dort auction?"

"No, but I think you'll find the next fight very interesting. I got thirty to one on the Cat."

"When did you become a betting man?"

"This is a sure thing," Jason replied confidently.

"Many broke gamblers have repeated the same phrase," Dylan countered.

"It is my money, and I can do what I want with it. Where are Salah and the others? We should go inside. We don't want to miss this fight."

They looked around and quickly spotted Salah, Ethan, and Bart who were engaged in a conversation with four of the local girls. They were old acquaintances of Ethan and Bart.

Dylan led the way to them and introduced himself. The girls were polite but didn't seem to be interested in anyone as young as Jason and Dylan. They apparently thought Salah was older. The girls excused themselves, and the original group was reunited.

"Thanks a lot," Bart remarked sarcastically.

"I told you it was you driving the ladies away from me," Salah commented.

Dylan sensed his gaff and quickly responded, "I'm sure a person of your charm can do much better than that, Bart. There are lots of other ladies around. That bunch obviously had bad taste."

Bart laughed and looked over at Ethan who also thought it was amusing.

"Our buddy bet on the Cat at thirty to one," Dylan proclaimed. "I'm sure when you present yourself as a rich man, your opportunities will increase dramatically."

"You bet on the Cat?" Bart questioned. "Why? Did you hear something?"

"Let's just say I have a hunch," Jason responded. "And besides, I think betting allows me to more fully experience the flavor of this event. Isn't that the idea? Let's get inside before we miss the action."

They wandered along with the crowd which was flowing toward the entrance.

Once inside, they made their way to an empty spot on the benches. They were about twenty rows back from a circular pit. It was about the size of a boxing ring and surrounded by chest-high wooden walls. The place seated a few thousand people, and it was filling up quickly. The ground sloped upwards from the pit, so everyone had a good view. The walls appeared to be originally white in color, but they were so full of nicks and stains that it was impossible to determine for sure. Most of the crowd had already settled down, and a portion of them had started meowing like a cat. The meowing got louder and louder until practically everyone in the building had joined in.

When the crowd had worked itself into a frenzy, a small man in silk clothing appeared from an entrance at the pit's far side. He raised his arms for silence. The crowd hushed.

"Ladies and Gentlemen! Tonight we have a fight you only dream of. The King of Disaster, undefeated in the ring, will look to avenge the beat down he took yesterday outside the ring in what he claims was an unfair fight.

"I would first like to introduce to you his conqueror, a mystery fighter of unknown origins, the charming and graceful Cat!"

The crowd roared when the Cat stepped into the pit followed by Minsk. She wore her tunic and battle skirt, but none of her armor. The shock of her appearance caused Salah to spit out the food he was eating. He had to apologize to the man in front of him. Dylan also stared into the ring with a stunned expression on his face.

"I see you also think we know the Cat," Salah opined to Dylan.

Dylan had recovered his composure and was trying to figure out how they could help JJ if the need arose. He was coming up empty.

"And now the current champion of Gronko, the King of Disaster!" hawked the little man in the silk outfit.

The King of Disaster walked cockily into the pit. He wore no mask and smiled arrogantly at the crowd as he strolled around the pit. He was quickly throwing up his hands to try to incite the crowd into cheering more loudly. When he reached the area where JJ was standing, he gave her a condescending smile and feigned a movement toward her with his wooden sword.

That was a mistake.

JJ, with lightning speed, swung her sword. It came down on the King's sword hand with such force that his sword flew violently into his foot. As he hopped up and down to try to ease the pain, a baseball swing connected with his head and left him sprawled out in the pit.

JJ walked over next to him and marked off four down strokes with her finger and crossed the imaginary lines to indicate five. She repeated this process one more time completing the required ten count. She then bent down over the King and removed his championship belt. She flung the belt up on her shoulder, blew a kiss to the crowd, and strolled out of the ring. Minsk followed.

The crowd sat in a stunned silence. Most could not believe what they had just witnessed.

As Jason looked around at their astounded expressions, he saw his friend from the betting line smiling contently. When he made eye contact, the man waved and started making his way over to Jason. At times he was swimming upstream against the mob, but eventually he made it over to the boys.

"Nice tip, eh?" he asserted.

"Thank you," Jason replied. "I would never have bet if it wasn't for you."

"And she's a looker, too," the man added in a tone indicating he was suddenly lost in his own thoughts. "It's not often you get such a combination. Those features and that lightning speed and power. I wonder what's under the mask."

He then seemed to come back to the present. "Perhaps we should go collect our winnings before they decide not to pay us."

"Is that possible? This is my first time here?" Jason returned.

"Winning bets is sometimes the easy part. Collecting the money can be more difficult," Jason's benefactor alluded as he motioned for Jason to follow him out of the arena.

Jason was perplexed, so he turned to Dylan. Dylan shrugged his shoulders and began to follow the man. Salah and Jason joined him. As they trailed along, they walked past Ethan and Bart.

Bart pulled Jason aside and whispered in his ear, "We are going to hang around our lady friends. We will probably be out for the night, so you will need to find your own way back. Sorry, but that's life," he said with a smile. "You guys are big boys. You'll be all right."

"Good luck," Jason replied. "Hope to see you again at Trent's sometime."

Bart turned and walked back to his companions.

Jason's new friend had stopped and was now patiently waiting for him. When he saw that everyone was again following him, he continued toward the door and out to the betting booth.

Since the number of people who had bet on the King was considerably larger, the line to collect for bets on the Cat was short.

Jason and his new companion presented their tickets to the clerk in the booth. The man remembered them because there were not too many wagers on the Cat, and none were as large as Jason's friend's.

"Pretty good judgment for a first time bettor," the man in the booth remarked as he handed Jason his winnings.

"I had a good mentor," Jason quipped with a smile.

Jason's friend, whose bet was considerably larger, then presented his ticket.

"I need to go to the safe and get your winnings. I'll need a few minutes," he said and disappeared into the crowd.

Jason's new betting partner looked over the boys, sizing them up.

"I don't do business with strangers," he finally stated while interrupting the awkward silence, "so I will introduce myself. My name is Sean Crankslab. I have sort of a reputation as a successful ..., er ..., businessman in these parts. More than a few people do not like me. I will probably need an escort to prevent being robbed on the way out. I mentioned earlier that it is sometimes difficult to collect your winnings. It is often harder to keep them. I could use some help. Would you guys like to get hired as my escort?"

Salah moved quickly toward Sean. It caught him by surprise, and he inched back slightly.

"My name is Salah, and I will gladly accept," Salah stated as he reached forward to shake the man's hand. "I should be able to convince my two friends here, who have been getting a little too soft ...," he reached out and slapped Dylan in the belly as he said this, "while sitting around Trent's and eating his food."

Jason laughed hysterically at the look on Dylan's face when Salah slapped him.

"I'm in, and how about our master spy?" Jason blurted out.

"Well, I can't hang out here by myself. You guys will probably need saving anyway, so I'm in," Dylan said without too much thought. "It's another adventure.

"Jason, did you ever think you'd get hired as a bodyguard?" Dylan said with a laugh.

Jason looked over at Sean.

"Where do you want us to escort you?"

"Originally, I just wanted help getting out of here," he said as he eyed several members of the crowd suspiciously. "However, since you mentioned Trent's, I wouldn't mind going there myself. I owe him some money that I'm sure he would gladly receive."

"There are two more members of our group at Trent's. We need to take them with us if we are going to leave this area as bodyguards," Salah threw in.

"Are they trustworthy?"

"I think you will be pleasantly surprised when you meet them," Jason responded.

The man in the booth soon returned with Sean's winnings.

They were five of the stones like the boys had received from Maura.

"You need protection for that?" Dylan asked.

"You are obviously not from these parts. I had already come to that conclusion by your dress and mannerisms. I will not pry. You can tell me if you so desire, but part of the reason I trust you is that I know you aren't aligned with any of the thugs from around here."

"I am growing more suspicious of the crowd myself," Dylan interjected. "Perhaps we should be on our way. Lead on," he suggested to Sean.

Salah walked alongside Sean as they headed toward the exit. Dylan and Jason dawdled along looking at the people and eventually fell a little behind.

"You don't know how to get back either," Jason accused. "That's why you accepted so quickly."

"A spy needs to be opportunistic," Dylan professed.

A short time after they exited the Hole, Jason noticed at least one person trailing them at a distance. He wore a hood, and in the shadows, his face wasn't visible. Jason figured that if he had seen him, the others had, too. He decided to trust their judgment. If they weren't apprehensive, then he wouldn't be either.

His thoughts drifted through a list of their current problems. It was kind of odd that how they were going to get back from the moon was not even high on the list. Every journey begins with the first step, so right now they needed to get back to Trent's successfully. They still hadn't located Butah's dort, although he had a feeling they were getting closer. What was JJ up to? Did she really want a career as a gladiator? When they returned from the moon, how were they any closer to home? Jason tried to sort out all of these issues as they wandered down the streets and alleys on the way back to Trent's.

Dylan woke Jason out of his thoughts with a slight nudge.

"Don't turn around," he whispered. "We are being followed by at least one hooded individual. I can't tell for sure how many there are. I suspect they won't attack us unless they figure a way to ambush us.

"Salah, can I have a little of the food you brought with," Dylan yelled out as if he wanted any bystanders to hear him. He

226

then jogged up to Salah and Sean and whispered to them to be prepared. Afterwards, he came back to Jason.

"I don't see our shadows anymore. If there is a time to worry, it's now," Dylan whispered to Jason. As the minutes ticked by, Jason could sense an unusual tenseness in Dylan. Dylan was in total "spy mode."

Then it happened. Something flew out of the darkness and landed on Dylan's face. He jumped off the ground and screamed for help. He couldn't use his knives for fear of stabbing himself. He rolled on the ground, kicking, yelling, and clawing at the assailant. With great effort, he finally removed Minsk from his head. Minsk moved just outside of striking distance from Dylan and sat down quite contently with a "gotcha" expression on his face.

The first thing Dylan saw after removing Minsk was JJ's smiling face cooing, "How's it going master spy?"

Jason and Salah were doubled over with laughter. Sean just stared at the Cat.

Sean looked over at Jason. "You knew her all along. Why did you lead me on?"

"To tell you the truth, I sort of suspected that it was her from your description. I did not know for sure until I actually saw her in the ring. She has been sneaking away the last few nights. Until now, nobody knew where she went. In fact, I think I was the only one that knew she was leaving."

"Why didn't you tell us?" asked Salah and Dylan.

"I wasn't one hundred percent sure, and quite frankly, I didn't think it was any of my business. Dylan, you go on lone 'spy missions' from time to time. I think we would all agree that she is at least your equal at taking care of herself."

Dylan had by now recovered from the shock of Minsk's little surprise. "I guess you're right," he admitted.

"Not to interrupt the surprise," JJ interjected, "but no one has introduced me to your new friend."

"Allow me to introduce myself," Sean said graciously as he stepped forward. "My name is Sean Crankslab. I am a grateful investor and fan of the fight game."

"Investor?" questioned JJ

"He bet on you," Salah threw in. "He got long odds."

"That is correct," Sean continued. "I would like to manage

your career as a fighter. I have seen none better in both fighting skills and crowd appeal. We could grow rich together, Cat."

Jason thought he detected a slight blush from JJ, who was still a bit distressed by the attention she was getting from many of the men they met.

"My name is JJ. I'm not in this for the money. Now that I am the champ, I don't really see the need to continue. We have other activities which are much more fulfilling."

"More fulfilling than fame and fortune?" Sean inquired.

"I already have as much of both as I need. We are currently on a quest to help a friend. I thought the fight game might put me in contact with some information we are looking for. That is much more important to me. We are looking for .... Can I speak?" she said while looking over to Dylan and Salah.

"Maybe he can help us," Dylan answered. "He seems to be enamored by you."

Jason could sense that JJ was more than a little uncomfortable with the situation. He also sensed that Dylan was going to push it for all it was worth.

JJ continued. "We are looking for a dort. It is a small furry animal that resembles Minsk, but much smaller, no bigger than your thumb. We have been following it for quite some time. It is the pet of one of our friends. It was kidnapped from her. We believe that the kidnapper is going to try to sell it in this area. We are on a quest to return it. We have been told by the locals in this area that it is thought to be one of the ingredients of an immortality potion. Supposedly, the kidnapper is going to auction it off somewhere in the Hole in the near future. You seem to be well connected. Can you help us?"

"It is refreshing to talk to people that have motivations other than fame and fortune. It is so rare these days. I know of the auction you are speaking about. It is going to occur in a few days in the swampy area at the other end of the Hole."

Sean continued looking at JJ as he mused, "Come to think about it, I, myself, have been so busy making money lately that I have lost my sense of adventure. Perhaps if we put our heads together, we can come up with a plan," he added with a wry smile as if he already was constructing one.

"It would be an honor to work alongside the Cat ..., I mean JJ," Sean continued with a tone of admiration. "I am beginning to hatch a plan. I will meet you at Trent's tomorrow night, and you can tell me if you approve."

Sean's thoughts then moved in another direction. He looked at the boys and stated, "Even though you guys won't admit it, I could tell you had no idea how to get back to Trent's and were essentially following me."

Dylan was embarrassed and didn't know how to respond. He was searching for an appropriate reply when JJ interrupted.

"I know how to get back," she said, reluctantly saving Dylan from embarrassment.

"I sort of figured that," Sean replied.

"It's settled then," he continued. "Tell Trent I will see him tomorrow. I have a few things I need to take care of before we pull this off. I think it's going to be too hot around here for me after that. I have a few scores to settle, and this seems like the ideal opportunity. Take care of yourselves until tomorrow."

He took one last look at JJ, smiled, and vanished into the night.

Chapter 23 - Stealing the Dort

It was very late when they returned to Trent's. In fact, it was almost morning. The place was dark except for a few oil lamps that lit the way to their rooms. No one else was about. They were all so tired they went straight to their rooms. JJ was coming down from an adrenaline rush from the fight, and the boys also had had enough excitement for the night. The little energy they had left was split between thinking about their rescue mission and trying to figure out what to do after their quest was successfully completed. They closed their respective doors and quickly fell into an exhausted sleep.

Jason was awakened too early the next morning. Salah was gently shaking him and didn't stop until his eyes opened.

"Hate to spoil your dreams, buddy, but Sean came back early this morning," Salah softly revealed to the still drowsy Jason. "He says that the auction is tonight, and that we need to move quickly. You've got about twenty minutes to get ready. He says to eat well because he doesn't know when we will get a chance again. Maura and Wilthor are waiting. They are going with us."

Jason stared back at Salah with a blank half-asleep look on his face.

"Come on, man. Wake up," said Salah as he shook Jason's arm again.

Jason snapped out of his stupor.

"I'll be ready," he declared.

"Good! Sean will explain the rest of the plan when we meet in twenty minutes. I don't know anything either. When I woke up, he was in a somewhat heated exchange with Dylan. I think they were discussing battle plans. I came to get you. I hope they have everything settled when we get there."

Jason quickly dressed and prepared himself for the upcoming day. When he went to the common area, he could see that Trent had already prepared a tasty breakfast. The others were busy gorging themselves.

"Better get down here," exclaimed Salah, "or there won't be anything left."

"When did Maura get back?" Jason thought as he hustled down the stairs and grabbed a plate of food.

While Jason was eating, Sean went over and consulted with Dylan again. At times their discussion became quite passionate. When they were finished, Dylan and Sean sat back in their chairs with a look of supreme confidence on their faces. Sean motioned for everyone to gather round.

"First I would like to give credit where it is due," Sean began. "The bulk of the plan is not mine. It's hard for me to imagine how someone can dream up this kind of stuff on such short notice. Where did you get this guy?" Sean said while beaming at Dylan. "I don't think I'd like to be his enemy."

He then explained the plan. When he finished he added, "Remember, though, no one gets killed unless absolutely necessary. The world has become a little too violent. We don't need to add to it."

He looked especially hard at JJ when he said this.

"Do you really think we can pull this off?" Salah questioned.

"We'll see," Sean answered. "I think it'll work, but we need to hurry since I don't think Misha will be alive too much longer than tonight. I think we have just the crew to accomplish this. If anyone has a better plan, let's hear it."

They looked around at each other. No one said anything.

The area of the Hole where the auction was to be held was built on a swamp. There were a handful of streets that were raised above the water, but they were few and far between. Most of the travel was done by long, thin boats that were polled along in the shallow water. It was a primitive Venice. The main part of town had very stylish gas-lit buildings. The part of town where the operation was to start was almost inhabitable. The water drained through this part of town, so at times the stench was just awful.

The guards lived in this sector. For the most part, they were like soldiers everywhere. They were loyal to their commanders the majority of the time. Currently, conditions were becoming more and more unbearable for the soldiers as the elites routinely cut their compensation. Grumblings were starting to be heard, and rules were beginning to get stretched.

Into this quandary the two boats cautiously entered. They appeared to be filled with rich stupid tourists. Dylan, Salah, and Maura were in one, and Jason and Wilthor were in the other. They noisily poled and paddled their way down the canals.

Their goal was to make themselves familiar to the guards so the guards would not perceive them as potential threats.

As they got deeper into this territory, a boat pulled alongside theirs. In it were four heavily armed men along with a larger man that appeared to be their leader.

He introduced himself as Captain Gerard.

"You are strangers in this area?" the leader inquired brusquely. "May I ask what you are doing here?"

"No problem at all," said Salah as he introduced the members of his party. "Right now we are looking for swamp flowers for this lovely lady and her friends back at the hotel."

Maura giggled loud enough for the soldiers to look at her. She smiled back.

"Would you like a drink?" she said as she offered them a bottle.

"Thanks, but we are on duty now."

"Well, in the interest of security, could you show us where the swamp flowers grow?" Dylan inquired as he offered his hand to the leader. It was full of coins.

"They are very pretty," Maura threw in with a dumb voice and another giggle.

"Another rich air-head tourist," the guard remarked to himself. He briefly added up the value of the coins he was given.

"In the interest of ..., eh ..., security, we can escort you into the swamp. We will protect you. Our leaders would not have it any other way. Follow us."

The boat of soldiers led the way into the swamp. Jason poled his boat next. He was followed by Salah. The awful smell faded as they glided further into the swamp. It was balanced and finally overwhelmed by the fragrance of luxurious flowers.

"Take your pick," decreed Captain Gerard as they gazed up

at the living bouquet. "Maybe we'll pick a few for our ladies as well," he added.

They beached their boats and disembarked.

Dylan noticed a particularly brilliant group of flowers high up in a tree. He pointed them out to Gerard.

"If you could boost me up to that first branch, I'm pretty sure I can climb up there and get them," Dylan stated.

"It's your neck," Gerard responded as he looked at the height of the flowers.

He boosted Dylan up toward the first branch. Dylan scrambled to get his legs up on it, but after that, it was easy climbing. He soon reached the flowers and dropped them down to Gerard. When he was finished, he climbed back down to the first branch. Gerard positioned himself to help him.

"I think it would probably be better if I just jumped," suggested Dylan.

"Like I said, it's your neck," responded Gerard as he moved out of the way.

Dylan jumped down. He looked around at the beautiful collection of flowers.

"I think we're ready to head back now," he announced.

They were alone with heavily armed strangers in an isolated location. Dylan could sense the possibility of something ill brewing, so he moved ahead with the plan.

"Do you guys know of any entertainment we can partake in this evening? We would so like to get the flavor of the local customs."

Jason pulled Gerard aside. "We would like to impress our lady friends," he said quietly with a wink. "We will make it worth your while."

Gerard walked over to his four friends. The five soldiers huddled and conversed for a while. It was apparent that they all welcomed the opportunity to make a little cash on the side.

"We have just the event for you. We are going to be security at the auction tonight."

"The auction?" inquired Jason.

"About once a month, objects of say, questionable ownership, are auctioned off at the giant hall in town. As long as the politicians get their cut, we provide security and look the other way. All of the local society will be there. We can get you in for a price. Rumor is that tonight's auction is going to be one of the best."

"Why is that?"

"It's rumored that tonight a dort is being auctioned off. They never tell us anything definite. Supposedly, the creature was stolen from a nobbly and is used in an immortality potion."

"Nobblies really exist?" inquired Jason incredulously.

"We might find out for sure tonight," Gerard declared.

"I want to go. I want to go," exclaimed Maura in her drunken airhead voice.

"It looks like we're going," Jason remarked. "Not exactly the best way to negotiate a price. What would that price be, by the way?"

"We could get disciplined for doing this, but ... since you've already provided us with these beautiful flowers, how about double what you've already given us?"

"Done!" Jason returned. "We don't have the money with us. Can we bring it to the auction?"

"Yes, but we'll need to make the transaction away from the building. We really aren't supposed to be doing this."

Gerard then described the location where his soldiers would meet them and escort them in.

"I will not be there," Gerard declared. "I have other duties."

"How about if we use a recognition phrase?" interrupted Dylan.

"Sounds good," Gerard agreed.

"Why don't you make up something that won't arouse suspicion?" Dylan suggested.

"My man will say, 'Pardon me, did you lose your wallet?' You will respond, 'Yes I did and it's very valuable to me.' My man will respond, 'Why is that?' You will say, 'It has a picture of my mother.'"

"Very professional," concurred Jason. "Then we will meet you an hour before the auction."

"We'll take you back to where we met you now, if that's OK," Gerard suggested.

"That's fine," Jason responded.

They walked back to the boats and looked at Maura who had pretended to pass out.

"I hope she wakes up by tonight," remarked Jason.

They boarded their boats and headed back.

When they parted ways with the soldiers, Maura waited until they were out of sight to "wake up."

"How'd I do?" she asked Jason.

"An Academy Award performance!" he exclaimed.

"What's an Academy Award?" Maura inquired.

"It's an acting award where we come from. You were brilliant."

They poled their boats back to the finer side of town to get some dinner. They met up with Sean and JJ, who were in the middle of a heated argument.

"I'm not going to wear that," they heard JJ loudly declare.

"But that's what the fashionable society people wear here," Sean countered.

"I am not a fashionable person. I am a fighter. If this thing blows up, there is a good chance we will need to fight our way out."

"You are a celebrity and part of our diversion."

"What's going on?" Jason questioned when he was close enough for JJ and Sean to hear him without shouting.

"He wants me to wear one of those gowns. I've never worn one, and I don't intend to start now. If he wants me to do my hair like the society people, I guess I can do that," argued JJ who was starting to get agitated.

"She is the champ around here," Jason warned Sean. "She's not your usual date. I'm not going to be the one to tell her to do something she doesn't want to do."

Sean looked at the rest of the group. They were all smirking at him.

"All right, if that's the way you want it. You might not look good in one anyway," Sean challenged.

"Nice try," JJ responded.

"Sorry to involve you with our little domestic squabbles," Sean apologized as he turned back to the group.

JJ made a nasty gesture at him and sat down.

"We are in," Dylan declared. "The guards think they are taking advantage of some stupid tourists. Maura played a great drunk .... You sure it was an act?"

"We should probably rest up for a few hours because we will be leaving quickly. Are we settled up at Trent's?" Dylan asked Sean.

"Yes, we are," Sean declared. "Trent said he still owes you guys, so you are welcome back anytime. I settled my account separately. I also got a room for myself at the stylish hotel in town to clean up. I booked one for the Cat also. I don't think the rest of you guys should be seen with us. If you are playing the part of rich tourists, you probably should go clean up too. If you need money, I've got some."

"We're OK," Dylan answered. "Jason bet on the Cat too."

They parted ways to prepare for the evening.

When Sean appeared at the auction with the Cat on his arm, he commanded quite a bit of attention. She had won the gown argument, but her hair was done nicely. He was well known around these parts, and it was suspected that he could even be the owner of the dort. He quickly countered those suspicions by proclaiming that if the price was right, he might even buy it.

"To impress my lady friend, here," he said with a wink.

JJ hated to admit it, but she was a little taken aback by all the attention she and Sean were getting from the aristocrats. People wanted to get a good look at the person that had done in the previous champ. She received many compliments about her appearance, which she was starting to enjoy. It was the few people that remarked that she didn't look so tough that were the problem. It was at these times that Sean had to squeeze JJ's arm very hard to remind her to remain calm and play her part.

The rest of the group wandered to their meeting place and waited for the guards. A few groups of soldiers passed with only a nod. Finally they were approached by two lightly-armed men who had been observing them from a distance for quite some time.

The smaller one asked, "Pardon me, did you lose your wallet?"

Jason responded, "Yes I did, and it's very valuable to me."

"Why is that?" the other soldier asked.

"It has a picture of my mother," Jason returned.

For a short time, they awkwardly stared at each other. Finally one of the soldiers mumbled, "There is the matter of ..., eh."

Jason didn't say anything, but handed the soldier the entry fee.

"Thanks," the soldier said while handing the money to his associate to count.

"It's all here," the man said.

"Come along," the smaller soldier ordered.

Wilthor, Maura, Jason, Salah, and Dylan followed the man through a side door into the auction hall. The two men escorted them to their seats in the back.

"It's the best we could do on such short notice," the smaller man said. "I hope you enjoy the show. If you need anything in the future, everyone knows Gerard. Be discreet, and we will try to help you."

With that, the soldiers turned and walked away.

Jason looked around the hall. By his guess, it could accommodate four or five thousand people. There was a raised stage on which Jason assumed the auction would be held. The room was quickly filling. The crowd appeared to be very excited about today's auction. By the dress of the crowd and the way they carried themselves, they appeared to be very wealthy and important.

Jason looked over toward the front rows and saw a throng of people congregating around Sean and JJ. In fact, it was more crowded by them than by the small wooden box in front of the stage on the other side. In it was the mythical dort that everyone had come to see auctioned. Through the holes in the box, a faint yellow glow similar to Butah's was visible. People walked up and peered through the holes. Most reactions were very similar to the two people that sat down next to Jason after gazing into the box.

"It looked like a little glowing fox to me," the first one said.

"The glowing part looked magical, but an immortality potion? Come on. I think whoever buys it is wasting their money."

"Me too. By the way, did you get a look at the Cat when we were up there? I can't believe she got the best of the champ twice."

"Me neither."

Jason looked over at Maura who was pretending to drink hard alcohol from the bottle she was carrying. Wilthor was smoking a nasty cigar. Everything was set.

There was a commotion at the main entrance. A small group

of people had forced their way into the hall. It consisted of a large fat man, a girl, and eight heavily armed bodyguards.

"Daddy, I have never been treated so rudely," Jason heard a familiar voice say.

It emanated from the young female member of the group that was now moving toward the stage.

"We would like those seats," the fat man demanded while pointing to a few seats very close to where JJ and Sean were sitting.

The menacing bodyguards convinced the already seated spectators to move. The auctioneers didn't care because the man was rumored to be very wealthy.

Salah recognized the group that had held him prisoner after he was attacked by the pet lionogs. He watched as the rude new entrants shoved their way down into the front seats.

He then whispered to Jason, "I have a score to settle with those guys. This could get very enjoyable."

"Did you guys bring them here?" Jason whispered to Maura. "Is there another way besides natmaroos to get here?"

"As far as I know, natmaroos are the only creatures capable of the journey," Maura whispered back. "There are other groups of traders, however, who would have gladly flown them here for a price."

The crowd gradually quieted down when the auctioneer walked onto the stage and raised his hands.

"We normally start with a few of the lesser objects, but since our friend down here in the front seats seems to be in a hurry, we will go straight to the main event. Payment will be made immediately in wealthstones on receipt of the object."

"Wealthstones?" Dylan whispered to Maura.

"The stones we gave you," she replied.

The auctioneer sensed that the man who had shoved his way in would pay just about any price and decided to start the bidding high.

"We have, in the box over to my left, an until now, mythical creature. A creature said to contain the seeds of immortality. But enough of this. Everyone is familiar with the legend of the dort."

He walked over to a small wooden box, opened the lock, and reached in and removed a small, furry creature. The crowd leaned forward in their seats while straining to see it. It had a glow similar to Butah's, but not nearly as bright. He put it back in the box.

"The bidding starts at ten wealthstones," the auctioneer announced.

The audience hushed for no auction had ever started that high.

"Done," said Salah's captor.

"And with whom do I have the honor of doing business?" questioned the auctioneer.

"My name is unimportant, but my money is good," the fat man responded tersely.

"It's so cute, Daddy," Salah heard a familiar voice squeal. He looked at her and smiled when he noticed her hair had only partially grown back.

The man showed the auctioneer his stones.

"I guess we'll take it," he stated.

Sean stood up and stared at the man. The man glared back.

"My lady would like it. I'll bid eleven. I have my stones on deposit at the bank."

The auctioneer looked over at the head of the local bank. He had never missed an auction and was involved in most of the transactions. He nodded affirmatively.

JJ, playing her part, smiled warmly and snuggled up to Sean.

"Do you think you can outbid me?" the man boasted as if Sean's bid was a challenge to his pride.

"Twelve," he countered. "Before you bid thirteen, you need to search your soul and ask yourself if any woman is worth thirteen."

Sean looked at JJ. He looked at his opponent and then back at the auctioneer. "The Cat is! Thirteen."

Sean's opponent was furious. The little game went back and forth until the man finally bid twenty-two. At that number, Sean backed off.

"Enjoy your prize," Sean stated and sat down.

"Sold to our new guest at a price of twenty-two wealthstones," announced the auctioneer. "Please bring up your payment, and the dort is yours."

"Oh Daddy, this is so cool," a spoiled female voice blurted out.

The man painfully counted out twenty-two wealthstones and put them in a small pouch. He handed the pouch to the auctioneer and grabbed the small box containing the dort.

Maura stood up and yelled, "Look it's a nobbly!"

As she pointed at Butah, she dropped the bottle of alcohol she pretended to drink. The glass shattered on the ground, and its contents were immediately ignited by Wilthor's cigar ashes.

"Drat!" he exclaimed and futilely tried to stomp out the flames.

The crowd stared up at the ceiling as Butah flew back and forth over the stage.

"Fire!" Maura yelled.

Smoke filled the room as a curtain caught fire. Half the spectators panicked and ran for the doors while the other half stared in awe at Butah and tried to figure out how to catch her for her treasure. It was complete chaos in the room since both groups were moving in opposite directions.

Salah's job was to use Gort's trick to remove the wealthstones from the pouch. He concentrated hard and suddenly felt a slight bulge in his pocket. Jason, who had become adept at moving larger objects, moved Misha to Butah. Suddenly the pouch hanging from her belt was full, and she headed out a vent in the ceiling. The crowd did not see her leave the smoke-filled room and continued searching for her.

A few of the guards ripped the burning curtains down and stomped them out. Order gradually returned as the smoke cleared the room. Sean and JJ joined the others near the door and turned to watch the unfolding events.

"There are only pebbles in this purse," the auctioneer shouted. "Give us back the dort!" he demanded.

The large man looked into the box.

"There is no dort in here! You stole it. I want my money back," he shouted. "Go get my money," he commanded his bodyguards. They drew their swords and approached the auctioneer.

The auctioneer's guards moved to protect him.

As the two groups clanged swords, Sean looked at his companions and stated, "I think it's time to leave. I don't want to see the rest of this."

Everyone agreed except for JJ, who they dragged away.

Chapter 24 - Back to Earth

Misha was now reunited with Butah. This quest was over.

Before he disappointingly said goodbye to JJ and departed, Sean warned them that even though they had escaped, word of their identity would soon leak out. They should be long gone by then. The people running the auctions were not to be crossed.

They had already prepared to leave quickly.

Maura brought the natmaroos. Wilthor came along to complete a few more transactions with the pirates. The travelers consumed their vagelberries and took off. They were all anxious to get back to earth. The goal that had sent them on many adventures was now accomplished.

Although they didn't want to admit it publicly, the boys were beginning to wonder how or whether they would get back to the twenty-first century. Even Dylan had had enough adventures for the present. He figured they'd be a little closer to Rockdale when they got back to earth, but even he had no idea where to go from there.

The flight back was spectacular. The apprehension that accompanied their first trip into space was gone. Jason was the lead rider on his natmaroo. He was accompanied by Minsk and Misha. Butah rode in one of the saddlebags. In a lot of ways, especially in appearance, Misha was a mini-Minsk. Minsk was way out on one neck near the left head, and Misha was way out on the other. They both seemed to anticipate all of the violent course corrections that the natmaroo made, and neither fell off during the entire trip. Their natmaroo seemed to enjoy their presence.

Jason had his eyes opened the whole time. It was remarkable, but in this short time span, flying had become second nature to him. He commanded the natmaroo to roll or accelerate at his leisure with no thought of mishap anywhere in his mind. He frequently looked over at the others, since he was now to the point where riding a natmaroo did not require his full attention.

JJ rode with Salah. At times she had a little bit of control freak in her, so she had to lead. Salah seemed content to ride with his arms around JJ's waist. They looked like such a cute couple, even though Jason had not seen any signs that would lead him to believe they were an item.

Maura accompanied Dylan. She wasn't feeling well and was content to hold onto Dylan as they zoomed through the heavens. Wilthor led his men in a tight formation and made sure the newbies were safe.

They arrived back to a surreal scene. The sky around them was filled with buzzing glowing objects. The flyers looked in awe as the illuminations approached in many different formations before scattering in total chaos. When the yellow lights finally slowed down, Jason and his friends realized what they were. The objects were Butah's kin welcoming her home.

Butah wiggled out of her saddlebag and soared out to meet her friends. She joyfully zoomed through the sky with them.

When she started to tire, she returned.

"I don't know how I can ever thank you," she stated as she looked at the group.

"There is no need," returned Jason. "Hopefully a stranger will help us someday when we are in need."

"And you gave me a treasure, too. You are the most wonderful people."

"You provided us with many unique experiences, and we made a lot of friends that we never would have met. We thank *you*," Jason explained. "As a spokesman for our party, we wish you well and leave you with the punch line of many of the jokes from our land."

"Don't get caught," they all said in unison while smiling at her.

She smiled back. It was a deep contented smile that they had not yet seen on her face.

"I will do my best to stay away from strangers in the future," she stated, "although hanging out with you guys proves I am a bad judge of character."

"With that statement, you have become a permanent member of our group," Salah proclaimed.

242

Everyone, including Butah, had a good laugh.

"Thanks again," Butah repeated.

And with that, Butah grabbed Misha and soared off with her kin to destinations unknown.

Wilthor explained that he and his group now had a few business transactions to conduct. When they were about to leave, Maura came forward.

"In my journeys, I seem to be more at ease and healthy here than on Zlagall. Even though I have been living there for most of my recent memory, I've never felt truly comfortable. You will remember that I am at least five hundred years old. I heard Dylan mention a few times the name of an unknown city which constantly appears in my dreams. The name of the city is Beijing. I suspect, although I cannot explain how, that I am originally from that city. If you don't mind, I would like to try and find my way back there with your help."

Jason, Dylan, JJ, and Salah didn't say anything, but shook their heads in agreement.

Wilthor was stunned. "Where will we find another leader as trustworthy as you?" he asked in shock.

"He was just speaking," Maura responded.

Wilthor looked around and suddenly realized that she was speaking of him.

"Thank you," he said with a bow.

"The natmaroos are yours until I return. I suspect it may never happen," she said solemnly. "Good luck in your future journeys!"

"I have an inkling your travels will be far more interesting. Good luck to you," Wilthor responded.

He walked up to Maura, and they hugged. Tears were starting to build in their eyes.

He turned and walked back to the natmaroos. He mounted his natmaroo and looked back at the adventurers. "It is doubtful that our paths will cross again. In any case, we are forever your friends."

With that, he jerked on the reins and took off. His riders followed.

Everyone watched as the natmaroos quickly disappeared into the sky.

Chapter 25 - The Pirates

"Now that Butah is gone, which way are we going to go now?" Dylan asked with a confused look on his face. "Any thoughts, JJ?"

"I think I'm going to borrow one of your ideas and sleep on it tonight. Perhaps I can come up with something."

"Maybe we should all do that?" Dylan suggested.

As they searched for a campsite, they were startled by an unfamiliar voice.

"Drop your weapons!" commanded a tall, well-armored man as he leapt from the brush at the side of the trail.

Dylan just laughed. "There are five of us and only one of you. We might surrender if you ask us nicely and say please."

As he said this twenty more men stepped from the bushes.

"That's nice enough for me," said Dylan as he dropped his sword.

Jason, Salah, and Maura followed.

Minsk was quick enough to get out of sight before he was seen. He observed from the nearby cover.

JJ refused to surrender and stood ready to fight with a sword in each hand.

"I should hate to mark such a pretty face," the man remarked.

"You might die trying," JJ countered.

"That's true, but there are many more behind me."

"I can't think of a better day to die," JJ casually announced as she surveyed the opposition.

Jason looked over at JJ. "Remember what our old friend Odysseus said, 'Fight at the time of your choosing,'" he reminded her.

As the surprise of the encounter wore off, JJ had a better chance to evaluate their situation.

"I guess you're right," she remarked as she looked at Jason,

244

sighed, and threw down her weapons.

"This wise person that you speak of, Odysseus, what does he look like?" the leader asked.

Jason stepped forward and described him completely down to the scar on his left forearm.

"We are a scout party searching for spies in the advanced guard of our enemies," the leader announced. "Our enemy is referred to in this area as the Phosphorata. We mean you no harm if you are on our side, but we must know for certain. I must request that you come with us," the leader demanded.

"And if we refuse?" JJ inquired.

"Then unfortunately we will be required to use force. I hope that that unpleasant situation does not occur."

"Since we are surrounded and badly outnumbered, we will heed to your demands," Jason responded with an authority that surprised even him. "We would like our weapons brought along. I'm sure we will need them in the future."

"We will be obliged," the leader said as he gave the order for his men to collect the weapons. "We will take your knives too. You can see that if you were in our position, you would do the same."

Everyone removed their collection of armaments and dropped them on the ground. Jason was surprised at the number of knives that JJ had in her possession. He counted at least six.

They set off in single file down the trail through the jungle. Each of the prisoners was separated by four or five of their captors. The march was long, but relatively uneventful.

As the trail became more trampled, Jason felt that they were getting closer to their destination. He hoped that whoever was in charge would view them kindly. He had no idea what to do if the opposite occurred.

The procession suddenly halted, and the leader turned back to the group. "We have heard rumors of a great warrior that is in our land. We suspect that the slayer of the jaysnake and the larnerghoul is among you. Our leader would like to speak to him ... or her," he announced while gazing at JJ.

"I am the slayer of the jaysnake," Jason declared as he stepped forward.

"You hardly look like a great warrior. You appear so weak. Have you proof?"

Jason thought he heard Dylan snicker in the background.

"I wear the necklace of jaysnake fangs," he responded. "If you will permit me, I can show you the teeth of the larnerghoul."

"Produce them." the man said anxiously.

Jason reached into a purse that was hanging from his belt and pulled out a few of the teeth.

"Come with me," their captor commanded. "I would hope that the rest of you would refrain from causing any trouble until we get back. If what you say is true, we're all on the same side."

He motioned for Jason to come forward.

"We must blindfold you for the remainder of the journey. I'm sure you will understand."

The leader's bodyguard came forward and placed a blindfold on Jason. When the blindfold was secure, the leader, his bodyguard, and Jason set off down the trail accompanied by five more soldiers.

Jason was led by the bodyguard. The walk was fairly easy. Jason stumbled once or twice on partially buried rocks, but the bodyguard prevented him from falling.

When Jason's group reached their destination, they halted. He heard the leader mention that he would be right back. Jason stood alone, wondering about his fate, as every prisoner since the dawn of man surely has.

His anxiety increased when he finally heard a group of people walking toward him. While he nervously waited for the hammer to fall, a familiar voice rang out in a sarcastic tone, "Is the General still with you?

"Take off his blindfold," the voice commanded.

When Jason's blindfold was removed, he was staring at Odysseus.

"Nice to see you again," he said as he came forward to shake Jason's hand.

"I see you've had a successful hunt since we parted," he stated while looking at Jason's necklace. "I've heard rumors of those jaysnake colonies, and quite frankly, they are just about the only thing I'm afraid of around here. Not to change the subject, but is Athena ..., I mean JJ, still in your company?"

"She's still here. She hasn't gotten herself killed yet, although she's tried very hard a few times."

"I like her attitude," Odysseus declared.

246

"Her attitude?" questioned Jason.

Odysseus raised one eyebrow as he looked back at Jason.

"I need to talk to the General. Is he with you now? Events are unfolding, and we need to piece together a strategy."

"He's back with the others."

"Gunther," Odysseus said to the leader of the band that had brought Jason. "These people are my friends. You did the right thing. You did not know whether they were spies. Please go get them. We have fought battles together. We can trust them in a pinch. Give them back their weapons. If that ratooi is with them, bring him too. This one can be trusted."

"I haven't seen a ratooi," a worried Gunther answered.

"Oh, he's around," Odysseus warned. "If you don't want to get startled into a heart attack, heed my warning."

"I am off," Gunther announced as he left to bring back the others.

"So what else have you been up to since we parted ways?" Odysseus asked Jason.

Jason described all of their adventures. Jason could tell that Odysseus was weighing the truth of his stories. He was particularly mesmerized by his battle with the jaysnake.

"Those creatures are lightning fast. How did you kill it?"

He described his fear-paralyzed swing that severed the snake's neck.

"You know, when I am in real danger, time sometimes seems to slow down. Maybe you are much quicker than you think."

"I suppose that's possible," Jason admitted as he thought it over.

"Anyway, rumor travels fast. You are a hero around these parts. What did you do next?"

Jason then told Odysseus about their trip to the moon and the breathtaking journey back. Odysseus sat in awe during the entire story. When Jason finished, Odysseus remained silent for a while, processing the many tales.

"How about you? What have you been up to?" Jason finally inquired.

"Well, you know I'm a pretty good story teller myself, but I'd be hard pressed to top that one. Did you guys really fly to the moon?"

"Scouts honor." Jason responded.

"What?"

"It's an expression that means absolutely true."

"Oh."

Odysseus then proceeded to tell his story.

"After we parted ways, our four ships were approached by twelve fighting ships. Their leader, who might be related to JJ, requested rather strongly that we join their company and prey on the ships of the Phosphorata. I only saw her once from a distance. I negotiated with her underlings. It being my best chance to survive, I became a privateer. I'm not exactly sure whose side I am on, but I'm still alive. You can't do anything if you are dead. I've been searching all along for a way back to Ithaca, but haven't found anything yet."

"Whose side do you think those people hunting the dragons are on?" Jason asked.

"It turns out that they align with the Phosphorata. The pirates normally attack ships of that design, but they gave us a chance to surrender since we were so badly outnumbered. When they realized we weren't the enemy, they offered me a commission. I accepted, and here I am.

"I've made it very profitable for the both of us, but I think the main reason they keep me around is that they expect something big coming from the Phosphorata and are trying to increase the size of their fighting force.

"Since the pirates mainly prey on the trade of the Phosphorata, the other groups tend to ignore their activities."

An armed man approached Odysseus and Jason. "The Captain sent word and would like to speak with our guest now," he relayed.

"Well, it looks like we can finish our stories later," Odysseus remarked.

"I'd certainly like that."

Jason was escorted off to visit the Captain, wondering if any of JJ's relatives were in the pirate business.

The man directed Jason through the woods. They did not speak until they reached a clearing which was occupied by about fifty nasty looking two-legged creatures. They were mini tyrannosaurs about the size of a horse.

"Have you ever ridden a stagolot before?" Jason's escort

248

asked him.

"No," he replied as he remembered that JJ's family was in the business of selling the beasts.

"I'm going to give you a crash course. These particular specimens are very well trained. They will respond immediately to your commands. They will go left or right depending on the direction you pull on the reins. Don't be too soft. Most new riders think they will hurt the creatures if they pull too hard. The stagolots are strong. They can take it. If you want to stop, pull back on the reins. Give them a kick if you want them to speed up. They like to go fast, so it doesn't take much prodding to get them moving."

Jason looked at the creatures and took particular notice of the saddles and stirrups. They were very similar to those on the horses he had disliked riding in the past. He only rode at his mother's insistence.

He was a different person now.

"If all these guys can ride, why can't I? After all, I've been to the moon on a natmaroo," Jason remarked to himself.

"Here is your beast," Jason's escort said as he handed the reins to him. "His name is Silver."

"You've got to be kidding," Jason said to himself as he remembered one of the old westerns he had seen on TV.

"Now watch how I mount my stagolot, and try to do the same," the man commanded. The man grabbed the reins, put one foot in the stirrup, and swung himself up onto his beast. His stagolot remained motionless.

Jason tried to imitate the man's movement. He put one foot in the stirrup and launched himself up onto his beast. He was a little too strong and nearly fell off the other side, but recovered and caught himself in time.

"We'll start out slowly," the commander said.

"Mount up!" he ordered.

All of his associates mounted their stagolots and formed a long line of two across. The leader moved next to Jason.

"We are just going to follow the trail. It leads to our destination. I will be right next to you if you get into trouble."

"I'm ready," Jason managed to say confidently, even though he had severe misgivings about his ability to ride these creatures.

"Yah," yelled the leader and lightly kicked his mount.

Jason kicked his beast with his heels, and they started down the trail. Their pace quickly increased. Given his past unpleasant experiences with horses, Jason was amazed that he was enjoying himself.

The jungle gradually thinned out. They were soon riding across a plain similar to the one where they had made their last stand against the Rangali. Jason looked ahead. They were headed toward a large cliff off in the distance.

As they approached the cliff, Jason could see that it was impossible to scale.

Moving up the wall were platforms that were attached to ropes and pulleys. They looked to be elevators carrying men and objects up and down from the top of the cliff. On either side of the cliff was the ocean. The cliff appeared to block the entrance to a peninsula, but Jason had no way of knowing from his position how large the peninsula was.

Jason and his companion soon broke away from the rest of the group. They approached a tent with two sentries posted outside. Jason's companion halted his stagolot and dismounted, motioning for Jason to do the same. He dismounted.

Jason's companion removed the saddles and other equipment from the stagolots and slapped both of them. They sprinted for the plains.

"We won't need them for a while," he declared.

Jason looked puzzled at this action.

"Don't worry," his companion responded. "They'll come back when we need them. There is someone very important in that tent who would like to see you."

"Who is it?"

"It is our leader. There is no formal bowing or anything. She doesn't need formalities to gain respect."

Jason screwed up his courage and walked toward the tent.

"What could their leader possibly want with me?" he asked himself.

He walked past the two sentries and into the tent. The Captain was seated with her back to the entrance. Next to her was a creature that resembled Minsk.

"We've heard rumors of a great warrior amongst us," she began with her back still toward Jason. She was fiddling with one of her weapons. "We need to increase the size of our forces for an upcoming battle. We don't exactly know what or how many we are up against. We are told that you align with the righteous. This is a fight for the survival of everyone in this world. If our enemies win, they will surely kill us all."

She continued speaking as she turned toward Jason. "We were wondering if ...."

She dropped her weapon and gaped at the newcomer. "Jason?"

Jason couldn't believe his eyes.

"Mom?"

Shock was not quite an adequate description of how they both felt as they stared into each other's eyes. They stood motionless for some time while gazing silently at the impossibility looking back at them.

Finally Della broke the silence. "I've heard rumors we had a great warrior amongst us. Have you really been to the moon on a natmaroo? I see by your necklace that you've had a positive encounter with a jaysnake clan. I've been told of many other exploits by a great champion that we should enlist into our army. Never in my wildest dreams would I have expected him to be you."

All Jason could say was, "Mom? Is that really you?"

"Yes, it's really me, dear," she responded in a reassuring voice. "Sit down and I will try to explain, to the best of my ability, what's going on here. Are you hungry?"

"I could use a little something."

His mother walked to the entrance to the tent and asked one of the sentries to bring them something to eat and drink. Then she came back to Jason.

"How's your father?"

Jason summed up the last few months of his father's life.

"Too bad. I'm really sorry," she said after hearing about the helicopter crash.

"It's been tough!" Jason admitted.

Jason paused for a moment to regain his composure and then continued with, "What are you doing here, and how did you get here?"

"Let me answer the second question first. You will remember that when I disappeared, I was surfing off of Costa Rica. The place that had the best waves ran you into a cliff of solid rock if you didn't ditch early and move off to the side. Well, the game of course became a version of who could get the closest to the wall. We lost a few surfers, but that didn't matter. We kept pushing the limit. A couple of TV stations contracted to come down and film our activities. Things were looking up."

"Then one day, the surf was really high. No one had previously ridden waves of that height at this location, so the game was afoot. I was the first to go. I caught a very powerful wave and headed for the cliff. I was showing off and waving to my friends when I realized I was too close to the wall. By dumb luck I avoided disaster by diving off my board into one of the many caves that the ocean had carved out of the cliff. I assumed my board was smashed by the waves."

"They found it and asked us if we wanted it," Jason interrupted.

"I hope you took it. It was a darn good board."

"You know me, mom. I just wasn't interested at that time."

"Your loss, but I bet after all the adventures you've had in this place, you might be regretting that decision."

"You know, I never thought I would say this, but I'm starting to crave excitement."

"Wait til you've been here a little longer. If you live through what's next, every adventurer that ever lived will be jealous of you."

"What's next?"

"I'm leading up to that. Let me continue."

"Please do," Jason returned as the food arrived.

They sat down and began eating a tasty lunch. Jason was very hungry and had his mind on the food for a while. His mother was content to watch him devour it. He eventually looked up and requested, "Please continue your story."

"When I surfaced, I swam ashore and figured the current had moved me down to the beach. I was surprised by five men who ran toward me on the sand screaming, 'The Phosphorata are coming! Run!'

"One of them threw me his sword and said, 'If you know how, use this.'

"They took off. Three men then approached me. They were wearing what I thought at first were weird looking helmets. They were armed with cutlasses and moving quickly in pursuit of, I

252

assumed, those men. When they got close, I realized that they were not wearing helmets, but that their heads were shaped like cattle skulls. I did a double take on the horns.

"The closest one threatened, 'Your money or your life.'

"As I started to respond that I didn't have any money, he took a swipe at me with his cutlass. I easily dodged it and landed a lethal blow. The other two came at me and attacked in the same manner. They raised their cutlasses high on their right side, and then switched to a two handed swing coming from the left. It was a crude move, and I easily defeated both of them.

"I decided that I might need the slain creatures' weapons to protect myself. I didn't know if they had any friends around. I picked up their cutlasses and carried the weapons down the beach.

"As I strolled along in the sand, another armed party approached from the opposite direction.

"'We heard you might be in trouble,' their leader stated. After briefly surveying the beach, he added, 'It looks like we were wrong.'

"He asked me what happened. I told him that one of these creatures had drawn a sword on me. I explained that my fencing training had taken over, and I got the best of him. When the other two approached me in the same manner, they met a similar fate. He then asked me if they turned invisible while I was fighting them. When I answered no, they all remarked how odd that was.

"That's when I discovered a power that I have, and I bet you do to."

"What power is that?" Jason asked.

"I can see the Phosphorata at all times."

"I can too," Jason answered.

"You have no idea how valuable that talent is. Be careful who you tell.

"I quickly moved up the ranks, and now I am their leader. We are fighting a constant guerilla war with the Phosphorata and can quickly retreat into our fortress. We make our living preying on their commerce. Occasionally, we attack the wrong ship, but everyone puts up with us because we keep the Phosphorata at bay. The Phosphorata have unsuccessfully tried many times to remove us from our fortress. A frontal assault is darn near impossible. If they approach from the sea, we can see their ships, so their big advantage disappears.

"We control the seas near the islands around this fortress," Jason's mom proudly proclaimed.

"Have you ever thought of coming home?" Jason asked.

"In the beginning, I constantly searched for a way back. I found nothing. The rumor is that there is a gateway somewhere near here. I could not find it. As I became more and more successful as the leader of this band of buccaneers, I realized that everything I wanted in life was here. If I go back, I could be the best women's whatever. There would still be ten thousand guys who could take me at just about anything physical that required lung capacity or upper body strength. Here, I am the best in an absolute sense. You have no idea how good that makes me feel."

"What about dad and me?" Jason asked.

"Like I said, I tried to get back. I just don't know how."

"How did Minsk get to me then?"

"Who is Minsk?"

"He's a friend of mine that looks just like your buddy over there."

"You mean Zega?" she said while looking at Minsk's twin.

"Just like him," Jason confirmed.

"I met him in an odd way for which I don't have a complete explanation. We were out on a raid, and we had just captured a ship heading to Slaphor, one of the leading cities in the land that the Phosphorata control. When we were unloading the cargo, I suddenly found myself sucked into a telepathic conversation with my friend. He was locked in a cage. He told me his name was Zega."

"That's exactly how it happened to me," Jason interrupted excitedly. "Poor guys must have a weakness there. I found Minsk in a cage, too. I bought him down in Cancun. Do you know any of the details about where they come from, or what they are?"

"I've just heard rumors. Many of my compatriots think that Zega and his kind are cursed. They don't want them around. On my command, we let them live on some of the outer islands. I'm not sure we could do anything about it anyway.

"There are a few things that have happened since he's been here that would lead one to believe the stories of curses, but I attribute them to chance. There are also some beneficial things that have happened."

"Like what?"

"Remember that ponytailer you and your dad gave me on my thirtieth birthday? The one you said was full of fake jewels. You guys got it from some antique dealer who said it came from a lost tribe, blah, blah, blah, blah, blah."

"Yes, I remember finding it when we were looking through your things after you disappeared."

She turned her head and flipped her pony tail. Jason could see a similar ponytailer.

"Maybe it did come from a lost tribe if there are more of them. Maybe it came from this world, and the dealer wasn't lying," Jason postulated.

"There might be more of them, but this one is mine."

"What?" Jason cried in disbelief. "How could it be?"

"It has a few scratches in the exact same places that mine did. No one else would know about them."

"So you think Zega went and got it?"

"I remember having some conversations with him before he clammed up."

"Minsk did that to me too."

After a brief pause, she continued her story. "In my conversations with Zega, I remember mentioning that I missed my family. I told him the story of my birthday and the ponytailer you gave me. About a week later, I found it under my pillow. He is the only one here that knows about it."

"That means he knows how to get back and forth between our worlds."

"Exactly!"

"What do you think Minsk was up to when I found him?"

"I don't have the faintest idea."

Jason thought for a moment. "Could he have been looking for me?"

"It's possible. If the Phosphorata somehow knew of you, they would probably try to use you to get to me."

She turned to Zega. "Are you involved in this?" she asked.

He turned his head away and would not look at her.

"Can the Phosphorata get back and forth?" Jason asked excitedly.

"I suspect that a few of their kind can, but I don't know for sure. If they all could, why wouldn't they overrun our world?"

"What else do you know about them?"

"You know, Jason, we don't have the internet here. There are no TV's or libraries. It's kind of hard to learn things about an opponent that last marched five hundred years ago. We really have no idea how many of them will be coming at us. We don't know the fighting style of their large groups. We don't know what they are after. The legends say they will come in infinite numbers, but obviously that can't be true. I guess this is what is called the 'fog of war.'

"What we are going to try to do is to shore up our defenses so that nobody can get in. Our positions on the peninsula are capable of being defended against very large armies. We have a few escape tunnels in case they are needed, but we don't want to lose our homes. Like I said before, we don't really know what they are after. They may not even come this way. If they do come in our direction, we can make life very miserable for them.

"Legend says that periodically, the Phosphorata increase dramatically in numbers. They are kind of like locusts in that sense. They overrun this world and blast their way into ours. I'm sure other creatures and diseases follow. It's kind of like when the Bering Strait froze over and let creatures from Asia into North America. That's what the Mayan calendars were predicting.

"When the Phosphorata explode in numbers, the legends say everyone here just hunkers down and tries to survive. Obviously I'm not old enough to have seen it myself."

"That's what the Professor was talking about."

"Who is the Professor?"

"Do you remember Professor Sloan from Rockdale High?"

"I vaguely remember that he was highly controversial. How does he fit into all this?"

"He has this theory that the major gaps in evolution were caused by an influx of genes from somewhere else."

"Like here?"

"This place would fit the bill."

"I never thought about that possibility. I live a little more in the present. I am not out to save the world, this one or ours. My sources have told me that the Phosphorata think one of the ports is located somewhere on our peninsula. I don't know where it is or where it comes out on the other side. Rumor has it they can find the gateway by instinct."

"Do you think they will try?" Jason interrupted.

"I don't see why not, if the port is what they are looking for."

Della then resumed her story.

"Zega has contacts. Maybe Zega suspected that they were going to try to kidnap you and use you to get to me, so he sent out some of his buddies to find you. Maybe that's where Minsk came from."

Zega was sitting next to Della, and if a mongoose could smile, he was smiling.

Jason looked away from his toothy grin when a soldier appeared at the entrance to Della's tent. She walked over to him and then returned to Jason.

"I need to leave for an important discussion." she said. "Don't let on that you are my son. I have reasons for this. Refer to me as Captain Stevans. I will be back in about twenty minutes. Get some rest and have some more food. When I get back, you can tell me the full story of how Minsk found you."

With that, she left the tent.

Jason went back to the food. After filling himself, he looked around the tent and finally over at Zega. Zega looked back at him with a worried expression on his face.

"Don't worry buddy," he said, sensing the mongoose's discomfort. "I won't tell anyone that you guys can't get out of a cage."

"Thanks." he responded with a look of relief.

"So you guys can converse with me after all. I wasn't going crazy. Why did Minsk stop?"

"I'm not sure who he is for we don't refer to anyone by that name. I'm sure he had his reasons, which were his reasons," Zega answered tersely.

"Sorry to pry," said Jason, "but it did make me feel a little crazy for a while,"

Zega turned away and gorged himself on the remaining food.

Jason ate a bit more and awaited his mother's return.

Chapter 26 - Preparing for Battle

When Jason's mother returned, both Jason and Zega had dozed off. She came quietly back into the tent and sat down on a chair and studied Jason as he slept. She could see by the scars and scratches on his face that he had recently been in some skirmishes. He looked much stronger and broader than she last remembered. Now her former nerd son was going to accompany her into battle.

"Funny, the way life twists and turns sometimes," she quietly remarked to herself.

Jason began to stir.

"Did you have a nice nap, dear?" she asked.

"How long was I asleep?"

"I've been gone for two hours …. Your friends should be here shortly. I am told that a few of them have very fertile minds. Perhaps we can figure out how to defend our land. Who are these people anyway?"

Jason gave a brief description of how he met each of his companions and what their personalities and strengths were. His mom seemed particularly interested in meeting JJ.

When he was finished, she asked, "There is a man in his thirties that has fought with your group. He is presently aligned with us. Who is he really? He goes by the name of Odysseus. I have been told that he is of remarkable appearance and guile."

"You are not going to believe this one."

She raised one eyebrow which conveyed the idea to Jason that she believed she had seen it all.

He went on to tell her the story of the strange man, Blantor.

She was riveted by the tale of bringing people back from the dead.

"Who did you bring back?" she asked.

"Well, it kind of happened accidentally, but we brought back Odysseus."

"From the Trojan horse?" she asked incredulously.

"One and the same."

"I've got to meet him."

"When my group shows up, he will be with them. He told me that he is loosely allied with you. He captains a fleet of four ships that we commandeered from a group hunting dragons a while back."

"Those were the Gorks. They are aligned with the Phosphorata."

Jason went on to describe their adventures with Odysseus. His mother's eyes glowed with excitement.

"Do you really think that it's Odysseus?" his mother asked.

"From his behavior, I have no reason to doubt it. From our recent conversations, I believe he is still searching for Ithaca. I'm pretty sure he is convinced JJ is Athena."

They then went on to discuss old times as they awaited the arrival of Jason's companions. It was a very pleasant conversation, but Jason was embarrassed by his lack of courage in his younger days. Whenever those events were brought up, he hastily changed the topic.

The time passed quickly.

Della Stevans couldn't remember Dylan, though she remembered some stories about a strangely curious kid that lived a few blocks away. They talked about Professor Sloan and his theory of evolution. Della particularly agreed with his thoughts on the Mayan calendar. The conversation then turned to college.

"Funny how we still have the same thought processes," Jason mused. "Here we sit talking about college when we could all be dead in less than a week."

The tent flap suddenly opened and a sentry announced, "Your guests have arrived."

Della looked up and watched as Dylan, JJ, Maura, Salah, and Odysseus walked into the tent. Everyone introduced themselves to Della, who stared embarrassingly long at Odysseus. They sat down in a big circle. They were joined by two of Della's lieutenants, Jantoul and Ragnog.

Della stood up.

"We all know why we are here. Our spies tell us that the

259

Phosphorata are days from marching. They have huge numbers, many more than we have ever fought before. In the distant past, they have invaded our land. We shall try to prevent it this time.

"We think they are looking for some sort of portal into another world. They need to get there to reproduce. Our experts think they have a few different reproductive cycles, so if we stop them this time, it will only be temporary. They apparently think that the gateway is located on our land somewhere, so we will bear the brunt of their attack.

"One strategy we could employ is just to leave until this blows over. I don't think we have sufficient numbers to recover our land in our lifetimes. You all know that it is impregnable. The cliffs are near impossible to breach. That leaves the harbor entrance which is very narrow and also surrounded by well-fortified cliffs. I'm not sure anybody could get through the massive number of boulders and arrows thrown at them.

"But the Phosphorata could be the exception. They may have enough soldiers. Folklore says they come in such massive numbers that they could physically tire out our defenses. The good news is that, at least at sea, we can see their ships. Our goal should be to destroy them in the water. They probably know that weakness and will send the bulk of their army on land."

"Do you know where the portal they're looking for is located?" Odysseus asked.

"Currently, we don't. The last attack killed everyone on the peninsula. It was so long ago that we only have stories about what actually occurred. When the current civilization came back to the peninsula many generations ago, they found the place abandoned but for a few scouts. They were easily slaughtered, and the land was returned to its rightful owners. A large number of us are descendants of these people. We accept any immigrants, however, so a good number of us, including myself, come from other places.

"It appears that the Phosphorata's strength and numbers increase dramatically right before an invasion and then decline rather quickly after they have accomplished their goals. They're kind of like cicadas or locusts in that respect."

"What do you think their goals are?" Odysseus asked.

"They appear to need to get to your world in order to breed. They could need to breathe the air or eat something. We don't know what they want there. There is a record of five previous invasions carved into the walls of the caves up in the hills. The carvings are very ancient. We have no idea how long this was going on before being recorded for the first time. There also could be other creatures involved."

Dylan stood up. "Perhaps we can get them to lead us to the portal."

"What?" a surprised Della questioned.

"Why don't we let a small number of their troops break through and see where they go. If they instinctively know the portal's location, we can just follow along?"

"I like this boy," Odysseus remarked to Salah. "No wonder you guys have survived for so long."

"That's a very interesting idea," Della agreed. "Let me talk with my generals privately and see what they think about it. Odysseus, you are battle tested. You may join us if you wish."

They smiled at each other as she looked him up and down.

"Certainly, Your Highness," Odysseus responded. "May the gods be with us."

"Jason, I'll get one of my men to show you around our land. Take your friends with. I don't mean to eliminate you from the planning, but I think it would be a good idea if you know what you are trying to defend.

"Ragnog, go find someone to show these people around. You can show them everything. They are our allies. Later we will go up the elevators and show them our fortress."

"Yes, sir," he responded.

"That term is generic around here," Della threw in as Dylan and Salah looked at her. "We have other things to think about other than who gets offended by terms and titles."

Ragnog came back with another of his men. "This is Montooth. He will show you around."

As they started to leave, Odysseus suggested, "Perhaps I should go with them and see the terrain. It's tough to devise a strategy if you don't know the ground."

A disappointed Della nodded in agreement. She watched longingly until Odysseus disappeared out the door of the tent.

"Seems like you have an admirer," JJ gibed.

"I do seem to make friends easily," Odysseus responded with a confident smile. "It has always helped me. Jealous?"

261

"She's not my type," JJ answered sarcastically. "I hope it doesn't gum up the works," she added.

"It never has yet," said a grinning Odysseus.

He then turned to Jason. "You know, she really does look like you."

"Huh?" Jason responded as his deep thoughts were interrupted.

"She looks like you," Odysseus said point blank while staring into Jason's eyes.

"What can I say, I'm good looking," was the only quip Jason could come up with.

Apparently, no one suspected that Della was his mother. He didn't know why she wanted to keep it a secret, but this was her world, so he trusted her judgment.

Montooth came back with the stagolots. They mounted them and rode away from the base of the cliffs. They crossed many large fields of crops, but nothing that could be easily fortified. The inhabitants all waved while they harvested what crops they could before the battle.

"It looks like you will probably be forced to give up this land," Dylan remarked to Montooth.

We sort of figured that," Montooth responded. "I will show you our fortress later. It will not receive the same fate."

"Let's hope not," Dylan answered. "Is there room for all of these people?"

"We are starting to move them already."

After riding past countless farms, they returned to Captain Stevans' tent to discuss how to defend her fortress. Dylan had no idea how to defend the area they had just traversed. It had no natural borders.

Chapter 27 - The Battle Plan

A soldier approached and asked Captain Stevans, "May I see you for a moment?"

"You may speak freely. These people are our allies and need to know what they're up against," she replied.

"We have reports that the Phosphorata are a day's march from here. Their numbers are said to be uncountable."

"Thank you. Go back and delay them as much as possible, but try not to risk any lives. You soldiers are also my friends and are too valuable to risk if the Phosphorata's numbers are that great."

"Yes, sir," the soldier replied and left.

Della turned to her companions.

"We need to evacuate the low lands and bring our people back on top of the cliffs. And we need to start immediately.

"Jason, why don't you take your friends to see our fortifications? Take one of the elevators up. I have things to do to prepare for the battle. I will send word that you should be given what you need."

As they walked out of the tent, Jason spied a Phosphorata soldier escorted by ten of Della's men approaching with a white flag. He was one of the creatures with a cattle-skull head. His weapons had been removed by his escort.

"I guess they use the same symbol in this world," Salah remarked of the flag.

When the messenger was close enough to speak to Della, his escort stopped him from approaching any further. His odor was terrible even from a distance of ten feet.

"That will be all," Captain Stevans said to the escort. The escort backed off and allowed the visitor to approach.

He spoke.

"I bring you greetings from Clamrit, our leader. He sends his regards along with the following message. 'If you do not allow us freedom of movement inside your territories, we will be forced to crush you.'"

"How many of you are there? We need to know so that we can bring you food," Captain Stevans responded.

"That is none of your business," the horned creature replied. "I don't know if I made myself clear. This is not a negotiation. We demand that you let us in. We will not harm you if you comply. Otherwise we will crush your worthless civilization as we have done to all others that have stood in our way."

"What proof do we have that you will be true to your word? There are many stories that you have broken your word before."

"None."

"Go back and tell Clamrit that this is our home, and we have no reason, in light of your nation's past behavior, to believe your word. If you tell us exactly what you want, perhaps we can come to an understanding. As of right now, we have no desire to agree to your demands."

"Very well," he said tersely. After staring at Captain Stevans for a long time, he looked away.

While turning, he reached inside his clothing and removed a hidden knife. As he started to throw it, Captain Stevans dove away and rolled on the ground. When she bounced back up, she saw one of JJ's knives sticking between the two horns in his forehead. His eyes went blank, and he crashed to the ground."

"Sorry, but I didn't have time to ask for your permission," JJ said calmly as she walked over to remove the knife from the nearly dead carcass. She twisted it a few times just to make sure. The creature shuddered one more time before it lay still.

JJ cut off the horns for a trophy souvenir. "These things are animals," she said disgustedly. "I would not desecrate the body of a fallen foe. This is a devil, and I have no such misgivings."

It was now apparent to everyone that the Phosphorata were coming to the plateau and wanted something on the pirates' land.

"We now know for sure that their word cannot be trusted. We need to prepare our defenses against such creatures," Captain Stevans declared. "Let's get started. Odysseus, can you please stay here? I need your help. You've already seen our ships. Will you command my navy?"

He nodded and walked over by her side.

The discussion broke up. Jason, Dylan, Maura, Salah, and JJ went to the elevators. Minsk reappeared on the way. Jason wondered if he had been talking to Zega and the rest of his clan.

The elevators to the top of the cliff were rope and pulley contraptions that allowed the riders to scale the cliff. Supplies were also being brought up, so there was only room for one extra rider at a time. Jason had overcome his fear of heights and enjoyed the entire ride.

When they all reached the top, the group turned and surveyed the land above the cliff. It rose as they looked away from the edge. There was a large castle, and behind it hills with many dark spots which appeared to be caves. A road headed off in both directions along the perimeter. One also wound toward the castle. There were huge piles of rocks and boulders stacked along the edges. Trebuchets and other missile-throwing devices guarded the rim. It was hard for Jason to believe that the pirates could have built such massive numbers of defensive tools alone.

A man rode up with five stagolots in tow.

"Captain Stevans said you would be interested in a tour of our plateau. I am here to escort you. If you have any questions, feel free to ask. If you have never ridden a stagolot before, let me know so I can give you some tips."

"We've all ridden them," Jason responded. He hoped he was right about the rest of his crew.

"That's a relief," the man said. "Sometimes the first time can be a bit tricky. Let's go."

They mounted their stagolots and rode along the perimeter of the pirates' land. The land looked absolutely unapproachable from the sea. A sheer two hundred foot cliff blocked any efforts. Just in case scaling was attempted, there were lookout towers at distances of about a quarter mile all along the peninsula to detect marine invaders. The lookouts had large conch type shells that they could blow to warn of troops climbing the cliffs. There were three lookouts in each tower in case backups were needed for some unforeseen reason.

Eventually, they reached a gap of about thirty yards in the cliff which was the entrance to a natural harbor where the pirates moored most of their ships. There was a gradual slope in the land down to sea level where the cargoes could be unloaded and carried to their final destinations. They rode down to the docks and then back up on the other side. They were again over two hundred feet of sheer cliff above sea level.

"Who would have thought this place was possible?" Dylan asked rhetorically. "It's a natural fortress against attacks from the sea. All of those boulders up at the top of the cliffs could sink any ship trying to enter the harbor. That would block the entrance. No wonder no one has been able to oust these pirates. They are not getting in this way."

It was apparent as they continued their trip that the large number of missile throwing engines and stacks of boulders at the edges made the pirates' land virtually unassailable. Jason started to feel that his group was most likely on the winning side of this fight.

They stopped halfway for a meal and then completed their journey.

JJ had been very quiet for the entire tour. When Dylan asked her what she thought of the defenses, all she said was, "Interesting."

They rode up to the castle and dismounted from their stagolots.

"Who would have believed this place existed?" Dylan declared to Salah. "A sheer cliff all around except for an easily defendable harbor. Nature has done a better job than man possibly could. No one is getting in here."

"Just remember, it's not over until it's over," Salah reminded him. "The Phosphorata would not be attacking if they didn't think they could win. If the rumors of their numbers are true, anything is possible."

The group then went over to the elevators and helped bring supplies and villagers up to the plateau. It was hard work. Each trip up was not overly strenuous, but the number took its toll. Finally, when they were completely exhausted, they retired.

The group slept soundly after their very busy day.

They awakened to the sound of bustling soldiers. The activity was centered near the elevators. Since they had no duties at the moment, they ate a good breakfast and leisurely strolled in that direction. It was noon by the time they reached the vicinity of the hectic soldiers.

Jason walked toward the edge of the cliff and peered over

the side. His fearless friends sat down there to observe the activities below. Jason backed away.

The pirates had withdrawn from the spot where Captain Stevans' tent had been. It was now too dangerous to venture off the top of their fortress. Marauding enemy patrols were intermittently seen below.

Pieces of metal, bells, and noisemakers of any kind were strung along the edge of the cliff in case any of the Phosphorata managed to gain the summit in their invisible state. It was unlikely they could remain invisible for that long, but as Captain Stevans had said, they didn't know their opponents' true capabilities. If the Phosphorata had ladders capable of breaching the cliff, that's when the trouble would begin.

Jason then joined the others who were captivated by their view from the top of the cliff. A marching mass of enemy soldiers extended as far as the eye could see and beyond. The glint of the sun off their shiny metal armor was visible at a much greater distance than their shapes and increased the feeling of hopelessness that was creeping into Jason's head.

"How can we possibly survive against that?" he thought.

He turned and looked at his companions' faces for support.

Salah's eyes twinkled again like they did when the Rangali attacked. Dylan, calm as ever, dozed off as if this was just another boring moment in his life. JJ fiddled with one of her knives. She counted how many times she could get it to spin before it stuck in the ground. If the knife did not stick, she started over. First one. Then two. Miss. Start over. The game was mesmerizing in a way. Jason counted four as the maximum number of spins JJ had produced.

Maura just scrutinized the enemy. Jason wondered if she wished she had her natmaroos back to escape on. There was no fear in her eyes. Jason hoped he came across the same way.

From the other side of the fortress, there was word that a sea battle had started. The Phosphorata were easily defeated by Odysseus, but the sea battle had engaged some of the pirates' forces. Now, those troops were unavailable to fight on land. There were no sounds from the conch shells indicating that the sea battles had progressed to the cliffs.

The lead Phosphorata troops stopped well beyond missile distance from the cliffs. The troops behind them proceeded to set up camp. They carried large quantities of wood and other building materials besides their normal supplies.

Jason and his friends then joined Captain Stevans in a watchtower. They observed the activities below.

"They're going to need some pretty large siege towers to get up here," Captain Stevans announced confidently.

Dylan was not so optimistic. "If you look closely, they aren't building towers or ladders."

"Then what could they possibly be building?" Captain Stevans inquired.

"I don't know if Jason had time to tell you of our little adventure with the Klinglesprachs," Dylan stated in a half questioning manner.

"No, he hasn't, but I've heard rumors of them. Supposedly, they are harmless outside of their own territory. They don't engage in commerce, so we have no reason to come in contact with them. What could they possibly have to do with our predicament?"

"Well, we had an encounter with them. Their land is surrounded by a river that contains nasty snake-like creatures called Skacali."

"How could that affect us?"

"One of the ways to cross the river is to get launched into the air by a huge catapult and float down on the other side of the river using an animal skin as a parachute."

The color drained from Captain Stevans' face. "They are going to fly in," she mumbled to herself. "I need to address my troops."

She turned and walked back to where a good many of her troops were lounging around waiting for orders. She gave the signal to assemble and listen up.

"Fellow citizens, we think our enemy has invented a new tactic to breach the cliffs. They are currently building a large number of machines to shoot their soldiers high in the sky and allow them to float down onto our land using animal skins. Fortunately, the area we need to defend will only be the first few hundred yards from the edge.

"The strategy we will use is to appoint a team of lookouts. We will divide the rest up into pairs. Each pair will be assigned a target by the lookouts watching the enemy troops floating down.

Try to fire your arrows outward, so if you miss, you don't hit our troops. If you are positioned so you can't use arrows, destroy them immediately after they hit the ground. We can't have them running amongst us.

"The attack will probably come early tomorrow morning when their machines are fully assembled. They hope to drain our strength a bit with the tension of waiting. Don't let them. Get some rest. Tomorrow will be a pivotal day in all of our lives."

Jason had followed his mother to the spot where she addressed the troops. Della turned and spoke to him now.

"It looks like we are going to get to try out Dylan's plan after all, for they are going to breach the cliff. We will hold out as long as we can. Hopefully we can defeat them. If not, it is up to you to close the portal. Take care of yourself. It really was nice seeing you again."

"You sure you don't want to try and come back with us?" Jason inquired.

"My home is here now," she flatly stated. "Who knows what the future will bring, but if the past is any indication, we will meet again. Go back to your friends, and get them rested and ready. These battles are very physical, and you don't want to get killed because you're tired. I have my job to do."

Jason hugged his mother for what he was sure was the last time and went back to his friends. She stood waving, but he did not turn around. He was too disappointed to lose her again, and knew he would break down if he turned.

When he met up with his friends, he was very distraught. Maura sensed that he needed someone to be with and walked over to him.

"Are you OK?" she asked him.

"My mom doesn't want to come home," he blurted out inadvertently.

"What does that have to do with ...? That was your mother?" Maura questioned.

"Shhhhh!" Jason whispered, but the cat was out of the bag.

Dylan heard Jason's comment, and his quick mind deduced, "That's why those skeletons were after you."

"I guess so."

"Wow!"

"Skeletons?" everyone else questioned at once.

"It's what started this remarkable adventure," Dylan answered.

Dylan then proceeded to tell the entire story of their adventure including their meetings with the Professor and Sam. He had some trouble explaining what computers and all the other electrical devices were to JJ and Maura. He finally had to conclude with, "In a few days, you might see for yourselves."

The long story was interrupted by dinner. The combination of full stomachs, the events of the day, and the mind-boggling story had the effect of relaxing everyone and stretching a few listeners' versions of what was truly possible. By the time the tale was over, they were all ready for sleep. They scattered around the warm, comforting fire and drifted off.

Chapter 28 - The Battle Begins

They awoke the next morning to the eerie drum beat of the Phosphorata trying to unnerve their foes. The whole area around them was crisscrossed with soldiers running to their battle stations. The enemy was calibrating its machines. The now-finished trebuchets below were launching human-sized boulders at the plateau. Most of them crashed into the cliffs and slid to the ground. A few landed on the peninsula, but they were only rocks.

The young warriors ran to the edge of the cliffs to observe. They watched the newly constructed trebuchets fire and reload.

Captain Stevans' body armor glistened as she confidently walked up to the group.

"It has started," she announced. "They are now testing their machines. They are outside of our range. Some of the next few rounds will be live. Head for the hills and remember your goal. Good luck! It really was a pleasure meeting all of you."

Everyone stared at Della, now that they knew she was Jason's mother.

"Go! Go quickly! We need to see where the first ones go," Captain Stevens ordered.

After everyone else left, JJ addressed Captain Stevans.

"You have a wonderful son," she said.

"I now realize that. Take care of him," she said as she turned and went back to her command.

JJ, dressed in the body armor she obtained from Della the night before, quickly caught up with the rest of the group. They mounted their stagolots and headed for the hills at the back of the peninsula.

The first wave of forty or fifty flyers was wiped out immediately. Most were hit with arrows before they even made it to the ground. The remaining invaders were destroyed immediately after they landed. The strategy of assigning a stagolot rider and his partner a particular flyer was working to perfection so far. The question became, how long could they keep this up? There appeared to be an unlimited supply of flyers. Captain Stevans had wisely kept half her force in the rear to rest for the afternoon's fighting.

The battle was going well for the pirates. Each wave of flyers was slaughtered before it hit the ground. The Phosphorata then changed tactics. They began sending some of their forces in on devices that opened up to resemble hang gliders. A few of the enemy using those devices hit the ground behind the defenders and made it into the hills.

Jason caught sight of the first one and followed it. His companions joined him. The horned creature did not know it was being pursued through the sparse forest and made no attempt to turn itself invisible. It checked the mouth of one cave after another. Finally, after checking about ten, it stopped at the entrance to a cave near the top of the tallest hill and lit off a primitive flare. The creature then fell to an arrow from Jason.

He and his companions immediately put out the flare and investigated the foreboding cave. It went deep into the hill with many twisting forks. They followed one of the many tunnels, but found no door home.

"We need to go back before our torches burn out," Dylan announced.

They were disappointed as they headed back to the cave's mouth, but hoped to find something with a more thorough search.

"We need to set up our defenses," Dylan commanded. "Much more evil will be coming to this cave, and we don't want to be trapped inside."

By now, the others suspected that Jason could see their enemies even when they were invisible, so it only seemed natural that he assume command.

"I'll take the front position since I can always see them coming," Jason revealed to allay any possible doubts. "They will not catch me by surprise. Load your arrows. Concentrate your fire on them when I flush them out."

Jason stationed himself down the hill a bit behind a boulder.

As the Phosphorata fired more machines, the number of

enemies dropping down from above increased. The reserve troops were called in, but even they were having trouble stemming the tide. A growing number of the enemy escaped into the hills. Captain Stevans was slicing up her very visible foes, but the rest of her army was now in jeopardy. There were now too many invisible invaders to deal with. Captain Stevans gave the order to retreat into the castle. The conch shells blew the tune of retreat, and her army headed for the stronghold.

While the army retreated, more and more of the enemy were meeting their doom at the hands of Jason and his friends. Jason was starting to admire his own skills when a sight from below brought him back to reality. An army of about seventy of the horned creatures that had been assembling below began marching up the hill toward him. They were led by a creature that was similar in appearance, but at least a foot and a half taller than the others.

Jason realized that he could not hold his position. He retreated up the hill toward his friends.

As he fell back, he perceived that their situation was becoming increasingly hopeless. They were severely outnumbered with more and more enemy reinforcements on the way.

"Any ideas?" he asked JJ and Dylan when he was close enough for them to hear.

Dylan shook his head.

"None here," JJ remarked.

As she said this, Jason noticed a look of astonishment growing in Salah's eyes. The group turned to follow his gaze. A second sun had emerged in the sky.

"It's another meteor!" yelled Jason. "Into the cave!"

The noise that it made as it shrieked through the sky just before it hit the earth was so loud it rattled their brains and consumed all of their senses. They entered the cave seconds before the meteor hit. The ground shook as it smashed right into the middle of the enemy trebuchets.

Far off in the distance, Solo turned to Visgoth.

"That was the biggest one I've brought in so far. Do you think I have a chance with JJ now?" he asked his friend.

"So that's what this is about," his fellow Sky Miner said with a sigh. He hoped his friend's heart was not too badly broken.

Unlike the last time, the cave had protected them from the concussion from the blast. After checking on each other, they stuck their heads out of the cave entrance. A dusty mist was settling over the peninsula that became thicker as one looked in the direction of the Phosphorata.

"I wonder how many are left?" Dylan asked. "It looks like it hit somewhere near the base of the cliff. This could end a lot better than I expected. It probably wiped out most of the Phosphorata's forces.

"Look, our friends are no longer there," he continued as he looked down the hill. "They've been vaporized."

"Look out!" screamed Jason as he ran toward Dylan with his sword drawn. He impaled an enemy soldier that was raising his weapon to clobber Dylan.

Dylan was temporarily stunned as the dead enemy soldier suddenly became visible beside him.

Jason grabbed him.

"It looks like these guys are the shock troops," Jason yelled. "They can turn their weapons invisible too. They weren't vaporized. They are coming after us. Let's get into the cave. It will take them a while to figure out which fork we took."

Everyone moved into the cave. Jason remained by the entrance and destroyed the enemy one by one as they came in. After he took out about ten of the horned creatures, the invaders guessed what was happening. They now suspected that Jason could see them. They grouped for a mass attack on the cave entrance. Jason anticipated it and chased after the others down one of the cave's many branches.

Dylan carried a torch while leading the group deeper into the cave. He had decided that they needed to keep retreating and hopefully find some terrain that was more to their liking. He had no idea what it would be.

The Phosphorata again guessed their strategy and moved quickly to try to attack them before they set up their defenses. Fortunately they were slowed a bit by the forking tunnels. Their lit torches and primitive flares showed they no longer cared if they were invisible.

When Jason caught up to the group, he advised them of the situation.

"Hopefully, we can find another way out," Jason wished.

"Let's stand and fight!" JJ suggested.

"If we perceive we have an advantage, we will," Dylan countered. "I remember a wise general saying something about the object of war being to get the other guy to die for his country."

"That guy was pretty smart," JJ agreed.

As they retreated further down one of the branches, they entered a gigantic cavern. The ground was smooth, so they ran across it. When they reached the other side, they encountered a colossal wall of stone. They frantically searched, but there was nowhere else to go.

"This looks like it could be the spot," JJ stated. "We are trapped. There is no way out."

They all stood still for a moment. The realization that their adventure might permanently be over was starting to sink in.

Dylan, a fighter to the last, suggested, "If we get behind those boulders, we can at least take a few of them down with arrows before it's over. Jason, you can tell us where to shoot and try to get the ones we miss."

As everyone positioned themselves for their last stand, the Phosphorata burst into the cavern. They were at least a hundred strong and in various states of visibility.

The feeling of hopelessness was growing stronger. Jason was sure that the meteor had wiped out most of the enemy. Della would be victorious, but it didn't matter to them. They would die in the last battle of the war.

Jason wondered what his obituary would say. Then he realized he wouldn't have one. No one would have any idea of the warrior he had become. He and his friends would just be a few more missing kids that went out one night and never came back.

As Jason searched for a forward position to defend, Dylan noticed a red dot of light on his chest.

"Laser sights! Hit the deck," he yelled.

Salah and Jason tackled JJ and Maura. Dylan hit the ground alone.

Almost before he hit the ground, Dylan exclaimed, "These guys don't have lasers. Are we ...? We must be back!"

He looked up and saw one very large special ops soldier

275

with night vision. The red dot from his gun sight was still on his chest.

"Welcome back, boys," the holder of the gun stated mischievously.

Jason recognized the voice.

"It can't be," he mumbled to himself, but it was.

Standing right in front of him was Uncle Jack.

"How did you find us?" asked Dylan in disbelief.

Jack started to explain to Dylan how Professor Sloan had used a statistical model based on the unusual events of the past few months in this area to pinpoint the spot he thought the door was located. He had tried two other caves before this one.

"Obviously, I hit the jackpot here," he exclaimed.

Jason, ignoring Jack, moved out as the point man in the cavern. He positioned himself behind a large rock twenty feet closer to their foes. The enemy was approaching cautiously even though they figured they had Jason and his group cornered. Jason launched arrows at anything within range. As the overwhelming number of enemy fighters moved forward, the thought occurred to Jason that he should be using Jack's automatic weapon.

While Jason was occupied, Jack decided to introduce himself to JJ and Maura. He was trying to make small talk with JJ when he was abruptly interrupted.

"Jack! Quit messing around!" Jason screamed as he sprinted back to the group. "The enemy is coming at us from over there. Fire in that direction!" Jason yelled as he pointed at their invisible attackers.

Jack was shocked at Jason's tone of voice. He had never heard him issue commands like that before. Something must really be wrong. Jack turned and gazed into the cavern.

"I don't see anyone," Jack yelled back.

"Just fire! You can't see them!"

"What the heck," Jack thought. "It's just an empty cave."

He let fly a burst in the direction that Jason was pointing. A large pile of dead and wounded Phosphorata suddenly appeared less than ten feet in front of Jack. He was stunned.

Maura was terrified. She had never seen a gun before.

JJ's reaction was startling. She walked over to Jack and offered to buy his gun from him.

"Not now, little darling," he returned.

Salah caught her arm as her fist was heading for Jack's head.

"Now is not the time," he whispered in her ear.

She squirmed to get her arm free and backed off.

"How am I supposed to fight these guys if I can't see them?" Jack screamed at Jason.

"Listen to me! I can see them," Jason yelled back. "No one is coming now. They have probably never seen guns before. Most likely they are regrouping for a final rush to overtake us. How far is it to where you came in?"

"It's about two hundred yards in that direction," Jack answered as he pointed at an opening that was created where he had moved a boulder to get into the cavern.

"You can see them?" Jack asked Jason in disbelief.

"Yes I can, and so can Mom. It must be a family trait."

"Then how come I can't see them?"

"How the heck am I supposed to know that?"

Jack thought for a moment. Something else didn't make sense.

"How do you know that Della could see them?" Jack finally asked.

Jason searched for more of the invaders as he explained, "She's not dead. She's leading our forces at the other side of the cave."

"What?" Jack blurted out with an incredulous look on his face. "Have you boys been smoking anything weird?"

"We don't have time to discuss this now," Jason lectured sternly. "We need to get out. I can see hundreds more of our enemies piling into the other end of the cavern. I don't think you have that much ammunition."

"I've got about a hundred rounds left," Jack answered.

"That's not going to be enough. They are starting to move this way," Jason warned.

Jason started issuing commands. He was now their leader.

"Dylan, lead Maura out through the tunnel. Salah, you and JJ go next. Jack and I will try to hold them off as long as we can before we run. Maybe we can all escape and collapse the tunnel once we get out on the other side. If they get Jack and me, you must find a way to block the entrance."

"Gotcha," Dylan responded.

He then took off, leading Maura, Salah, and JJ down the tunnel.

Jason turned to his uncle and said with a bit of astonished admiration, "So you really are a special ops guy."

"Had you fooled, didn't I?"

"Me and everyone else," Jason responded emphatically.

Jason could see that the Phosphorata were creeping slowly toward them.

He looked at Jack and stated, "I've got an idea. If we back into the tunnel and wipe out our first few pursuers, they will temporarily block the entrance. Then, we can escape."

"Let's take out a lot of them first, so we won't have so many to deal with in the tunnel," Jack countered. "Tell me when and where to fire. I'll save about twenty rounds."

"Good thinking. Get ready. They are starting to move this way. They are coming in a wide line, so you can fire just about anywhere. When they get about thirty yards away, I'll give the signal."

Jason was amazed at how calm Jack was. Jack absolutely could not believe he was standing next to Jason.

"Fire!" Jason ordered.

Jack unloaded his first clip. He reloaded and fired again. He was still shocked when the wounded and dead Phosphorata suddenly appeared in front of him.

"I'm down to about twenty rounds."

"Let's go!"

They moved inside the tunnel and backed off about twenty feet from the cavern. The first of the enemy into the tunnel were easy targets. As they piled up, Jack announced, "I'm out."

"Let's hustle then," Jason ordered.

They took off down the tunnel. Jack was not very fast, and Jason was starting to fear that they would get caught. He kept glancing over his shoulder but saw nothing.

As Jack came out of the tunnel, he yelled to his associates who were peering out of the hatches of an armored military vehicle, "Is the tunnel set?"

"Yes, sir!" they answered.

"Throw me your gun," he shouted to one of his troops.

An automatic weapon came flying his way.

"Blow it when you see the first one coming out of the cave!" he continued.

"They can't see them," Jason yelled.

"Then blow it on his command," Jack yelled pointing at Jason.

They all stared at the cave entrance. They saw motion and readied themselves for the command to blast. They were temporarily confused when Minsk poked his head out of the tunnel.

"Hold off! He's on our side!" Jason yelled.

They waited for another few minutes which in their present states seemed like days.

When Jason finally saw the first Phosphorata heads popping into the daylight, he gave the order. Nothing happened.

"Blow the #@% thing," Jack yelled.

Jason jumped over, grabbed Jack's gun, and fired at the enemy. The shock of seeing the wounded suddenly turn visible stunned the men who were desperately trying to figure out what was wrong with their explosives in the tunnel.

After about twenty of the Phosphorata had made it out of the tunnel, an explosion finally collapsed it. No more attackers would be coming. The enemy that was already out of the cave regrouped behind a large boulder. They were trying to figure out what to do against these new weapons.

"I'm out of bullets," Jason yelled. He immediately realized he had made a mistake in revealing that. The Phosphorata soldiers charged from around the rock straight at Jason and Jack. Everyone else was behind the armored car which contained three of Jack's buddies.

"Plan B! Plan B!" Jack yelled. The men in the vehicle closed the hatches. There was an explosion, and everyone except the people in the armored car was out cold.

Chapter 29 - Home

Jason woke up to the comfortable feeling of his own bed. He refused to open his eyes. He was so at ease. Gradually more of his senses turned on. He could smell the familiar odor of bacon cooking in the kitchen as he recounted with pride his many adventures.

"How could those things have happened?" he asked himself. "Maybe it was all a dream."

When he moved a bit, he hurt everywhere.

"Dreams don't hurt," his brain countered.

He reached up. The small piece of his earlobe that he lost in his battle with the Ionizard was still gone. He opened his eyes and looked down at his right forearm. It was wrapped in gauze and burned when he moved it.

"I wonder how that happened," he asked himself.

The last thing he remembered was entering the cavern with the Phosphorata in hot pursuit. He didn't remember anything after that. He couldn't remember how his arm was injured.

"Jack must be up already," he said to himself while focusing on the smell again. "I hope he made some for me."

Jason slowly extracted himself from his bed. He groaned like an old man. There was pain in places he didn't even know existed.

He looked around his room. It was exactly as he remembered it. The sun coming through the blinds made shadows on the wall. His clock calendar said that it was exactly ten days after he and Dylan had left to visit Salah. His adventures surely took longer than that.

Gradually, the full memory of his exploits came back.

"It had to be a dream," he said to himself. "Those journeys took at least a month, and the calendar says it's only ten days from when we left."

As he stumbled to the kitchen, he occasionally braced

himself with the wall. When he arrived for breakfast, he was face to face with Jack's energetic face.

"Nice to see you," Jack stated cheerily.

"What happened to me?"

"Car accident. You're lucky you made it. Your friend Dylan is OK, too. We think that your little furry friend was not so lucky. No one has seen a trace of him. I'm sorry."

"Minsk was real?"

Jason was having a hard time getting a grasp on what actually had occurred.

"Of course he was!" Jack answered.

"I wonder what really happened," Jason mumbled to himself.

"What's that?"

"Where have I been for the last ten days?"

"We took a trip down to visit Salah. On the way to his dad's house, a large cat, probably a jaguar ran across the road right in front of the vehicle we were in. I swerved to miss it. The vehicle flipped and caught fire. We pulled you out. That's where you got the burns on your arms. A sharp piece of metal from the wreck sliced off a small piece of your ear. You were unconscious for a long time."

"If I was unconscious, how did I get here? Wouldn't I be in a hospital?"

"You were for a while. You came to, and the hospital cleared you for travel. We brought you back here, and you blacked out three days ago. It's nice to see you awake."

Jason was still a bit groggy. It had all seemed so real.

"Tomorrow is your first day back in school after break. Why don't you rest up for another day and go back with the rest of the kids?"

Jason felt an itch and went to scratch his neck. He fondled the necklace of jaysnake fangs that JJ had made for him. With an expression of hope he asked, "Then where did this come from?"

"Salah's father gave it to you. He said the spines are from the golden albino porcupine. They are very good luck where he comes from."

"Salah actually exists?"

"He wasn't a dream," Jack answered.

"Then what was?" Jason asked in frustration.

"Concussions are strange things. You'll eventually sort this out."

Jason finished eating and went back to his room. He was thinking about everything he thought he remembered. It all seemed so real.

He was still tired, but he went over to his computer and flipped the switch on the power strip that turned it on.

"Let's see what the Packers can do today," he said to himself as it booted. The game turned into another pathetic defensive performance.

"Well, some things never change," he said to himself.

He spent the rest of the day thinking through his adventures. They had all seemed so real. His mind twisted and turned until late in the evening he was mercifully saved by the Sandman.

The next morning, after a good night's sleep, he was still confused. As he walked to school, he felt a bit less sore, but his memories were just as vivid.

All of the other students were happy to be reunited with their classmates after winter break. Jason's only real friend, Dylan, didn't show up for school that day. That wasn't unusual.

Since he was alone with nothing to do, he wandered into Professor Sloan's class about ten minutes early. Professor Sloan was at his desk.

"Jason," he said. "There are some people in my laboratory I would like you to meet. They are new to this school and country and need someone to show them around. Here, have a Coke. They already have one."

"Great! Another person attempting to find friends for me," Jason thought. "Oh well, the Professor is trying to help. Put on your happy face."

He grabbed the soda and walked into Professor Sloan's lab. He saw two giggling girls watching TV. They turned to greet him.

"Your friend Odysseus was quite a fellow," JJ said with a warm smile while holding and petting Minsk. "I watched a movie about his story called 'The Odyssey.'"

Jason's jaw dropped.

"Hello, gorgeous," she continued. "It's really great to see the familiar face of a battle-tested friend. Everyone here has been so kind, but it's not the same."

"Hi," Maura added. "We are living in Professor Sloan's house. We have been told we are his relatives from Latvia."

She changed the subject. "I watched some movies too. The ones about Beijing were particularly fascinating. You live in an unbelievably wonderful world."

"I'm going to get that Jack," Jason mumbled to himself.

"What's that?" JJ asked.

"Oh nothing."

He looked around the room and saw Dylan smiling in the corner.

"It's so nice to see all you guys. Anybody know about Salah?" Jason asked.

They all shrugged their shoulders.

Jason sighed.

"Did any of the Phosphorata get through?" he continued.

"We don't think so, but we got knocked out, too," Maura answered.

Jason looked over at JJ.

"Try not to get into any skirmishes until you understand the customs around here. They frown upon killing people," he warned.

"She's already been advised of that," Maura added.

Professor Sloan then walked into the room. He shut the door behind him. They all turned their attention his way.

"We are finally all together with the exception of Salah," the Professor began. "Since you were all rendered unconscious at the end, and he is the only one missing, you are probably worried about him. He is OK and is working on a project for us right now. He has already been made aware of what I'm going to tell you."

Jason, along with everyone else tried to guess what it could possibly be. He came up empty. After what he had recently been through, he doubted if anything could surprise him.

"As you probably have ascertained, Jack and I work for an agency of the government. Very few people are aware of our existence. We work in anonymous independent cells. Each cell doesn't know what the other cells are doing. Information is made available on a need to know basis. That is why I won't even tell you our name."

The group glanced back and forth at each other.

"For the time being, I have been instructed that we need to keep the existence of this alternate world quiet. I don't know the reasons. I am only a soldier following orders. From my past experiences though, talking about this will only make people think you are crazy.

"Does everyone agree?"

They all nodded affirmatively.

The Professor ended his talk with, "I need to get back to my class now. I'm sure you'll all find something to do."

He turned and walked out of the room.

The instant the Professor left, Minsk took off with a sense of urgency.

After Dylan was sure Minsk was gone, he pointed at Minsk's travel cage in the corner.

"I guess that little rat will be back where he belongs now," he stated rather smugly.

Shortly thereafter, Minsk reappeared and unexpectedly gave Dylan a great big candy bar.

"Thanks buddy," the two-faced Dylan said as he took it from Minsk. He broke the candy in two and gave half of it to Minsk.

"It must be the concussion," Jason stated.

Everyone nodded in agreement for it was difficult to believe the odd friendship.

When Dylan took a bite of the candy bar, his face turned beet red. He guzzled his soda while Minsk headed for the door.

"You smelly rat! Get back here," Dylan yelled as he took off after him.

Jason picked up a small bottle that was lying where Minsk had been sitting. He read the label and burst out laughing. "It's hot sauce," he revealed.

The group could hardly contain themselves. They weren't worried, for they knew that Dylan would never catch up with Minsk.

"Oh! By the way," Maura mentioned to Jason, "a member of our group, Blarath, received a nonsense message to give to you from a wandering vagabond on our last trading voyage. I didn't think it was all that important, and in the excitement, I kind of forgot to tell you."

"A message for me?" a shocked Jason questioned.

"We were attending a small party. We were sitting around a fire with some of our trading partners and their friends. There were many people we didn't know. We were telling stories. Blarath couldn't think of a better one than the previous guy, so he used your true story, as far as he knew it. Who could top that? When one of the strangers heard it, he asked Blarath if he really knew you. When he replied that he did, the man insisted you be given the following message."

"Me? Are you sure?"

"He said you would understand its full ramifications."

"Well, I don't know about that, but fire away."

"The message was, 'Pawn to queen four.'"

Jason dropped his soda.

www.ingramcontent.com/pod-product-compliance
Lightning Source LLC
Chambersburg PA
CBHW021949170626
46808CB00001B/86